WHITE BUFFALO GOLD

Dedication

To my father, Thomas R. Fleming.

For your years of compassionate service in long-term and hospice care,

For teaching me "Tom and I," not "mean Tom."

And also to my mother, Margaret Kay Fleming.

For your love of prairie grasses, wildflowers

And the creatures both timid and fierce among them.

"Let the Deed Shaw"

Nebraska's Annual Gold Rush

Amy, Emily, and Melissa

Harmony, Nebraska, 1985

Every year around the middle of October, for about a week, little trios from the sixth-grade class at Harmony Elementary could be seen in rubber chore boots, or if it was warmer than usual, in their old sneakers, stomping up and down the South Loup River. They were looking for gold.

"Hey, look!" Amy picked up something from the river bed.

"What is it?" Her friends Emily and Melissa crowded her, and Amy slipped.

"Ow!" Amy sat down in the shallow, muddy water, but she gripped the item tightly in her fist.

"Is it gold?" Melissa wondered.

"I think so. I hope so. Probably not. I'll *never* be rich! Look, my jeans are all muddy," complained Amy. She stood up again, and slowly, her fingers opened. Melissa was jumping up and down.

Emily reached out, took the thing from Amy and inspected it. Melissa kept bouncing about. "What are you so excited about, Melissa? That's not gold; in fact, it isn't even pyrite. This is just some stupid rock some stupid teenager spray-painted gold to fool kids like us." Emily wound up to throw the rock back into the middle of the river where it was deep, but Amy grabbed her arm and pulled the rock from her fingers.

"Just because it isn't gold doesn't mean I can't take it home as a souvenir, or we could use it for Exhibit A in our project, right?

Besides, this little rock is so *cute* ..." But the others cut her off with a look. Clearly, they weren't interested in cuteness when it came to pebbles. With that, Amy shoved the worthless, spray-painted stone in her pocket.

"We're going to have the best project because we're going to find some *real* gold—" Emily declared, then paused. "What are you jumping around for, Melissa?"

"Because I'm cold," Melissa said. (Emily knew that, for a moment there, Melissa thought Amy had found something ... but didn't want to admit it.) "It's nearly dark. It was nice out here right after school, but it's getting chilly. Besides, nobody ever finds gold out here. The gold was all found a hundred years ago. It's 1985, duh. You won't find gold, Emily; nobody ever does."

"There was gold here once," replied Emily, "so there's got to be at least a little tiny bit more, and I'm going to find it. And anyway, if there never was any gold here, I'm going to prove it."

"We're going to be rich!" Amy shouted, throwing her arms skyward.

"I don't care about being rich, I want to be warm," said Melissa.

"I don't care about being rich either," Emily agreed, "but I'm going to stay down here until I find some gold."

"But there's no gold left," Melissa said, "The miners found it all."

"They can't have found it *all*," Emily insisted.

"They did too," Amy said. "People in my family found it, it was my great-great, um, maybe great, great, great, no, wait, um. My *an*cestors found it. I know it."

"Then how's come *you* aren't rich?" Melissa said.

Amy started to cry. Melissa looked surprised, then said she was sorry.

"You don't know what it's like," Amy said.

Emily wasn't so sure anyone in Amy's family had ever found gold here. For one thing, they were a bunch of liars. She wasn't going to say this to Amy. Amy's mom made promises all the time and didn't keep them, Amy's brother AJ wasn't considered reliable at school, and her dad ... Emily felt both disdain and pity for Amy. She wrapped her arm around the girl's shoulder.

"Come on," Emily said, "let's go home. You can both take a hot shower at my house before Melissa's mom comes to pick you guys up. You can borrow my pink sweater …" Amy stopped crying and began to chatter about clothes. As they climbed up the riverbank, headed back into town, Emily shot a glance back at the water. Tomorrow was Saturday. She'd be back. And she'd find that dang gold if it took her all weekend.

People called it the Annual Sixth-Grade Gold Rush, because the students did a unit in their History class with Mrs. Albright on local history, and each group had to write a paper about whether or not there had been an authentic gold strike sometime in the 1870s.

In spite of the lack of any geological evidence that there could have been gold in the flatlands, somewhere hidden in the rock between the topsoil and the Ogallala Aquifer beneath, churned up by the gradual shaping and reshaping of the slow-moving, and often nearly empty, South Loup, the students—indeed, the entire town—believed that gold was once found there in the river outside Harmony. Once in a while you'd see an older person hiking along the banks of the river, stooping to pan occasionally without much hope. It was considered a legitimate "hobby." Men with metal detectors had been known to make decent money finding chunks of steel, bits of copper pipe and hundreds of aluminum cans, then scrapping the stuff out for cash. There was a lot of valuable metal in the South Loup, but gold was elusive. Usually a week of searching in sixth grade was enough to convince the Harmony kids that whatever piles of gold might have been there a hundred years ago were gone now. But it didn't stop some people from the irrational vision of finding piles of gold coins—like the crew of the Hispaniola does at the end of *Treasure Island.*

In her classroom, Mrs. Albright had a way of bringing history alive. Her white hair in a bun, her carefully pressed slacks swishing, she briskly stepped from her desk to the blackboard where she pulled down a map of Nebraska. Children immediately recognized the shape of their state. It was a butcher knife, chopping down on Kansas, the way the Cornhuskers do when they play football against the Jayhawks or the Wildcats.

"The South Loup originates outside Stapleton," said the teacher, warming to her subject. "Our small communities dot the banks of this river: the villages of Arnold and Callaway in Custer County, Harmony (we are right *here*), Pleasanton, and Ravenna in Buffalo County. The South Loup joins the Middle Loup—that's called a *confluence*—just outside Boelus, and only a few more miles downstream the North Loup joins in. The three Loups, like a wolf pack, flow as one, running silent in the night, keeping low, from where they join together just outside the tiny town of Cushing until the waters join the Platte near the much larger town of Columbus. The Platte meets the Missouri at the Iowa line east of Omaha, which flows on to join the Mississippi at St. Louis and then on down to New Orleans and into the Gulf of Mexico.

"Like the biblical genealogy about a baby born in some backwater of the Roman Empire, this series of rivers is more significant than it seems on the surface. Why?"

"Because there weren't any roads back then?" a girl named Erica said.

"Very good. If you were a French trader in 1862 who wanted to take a canoe *up the river* from New Orleans to what we now call Colorado by way of the Platte to look for beaver pelts and gold, why might you make a wrong turn at the Loup?"

Emily's next-door neighbor Ben raised his hand. "Because the rains had made the confluence of the Platte and Loup into a swamp about two miles wide."

"That's correct. So if you come out of the swamp and you're on the Loup, and you kept staying to your left, or south, every time you came to a branch because that's the way to Colorado—or it would be, if you were on the Platte—you'd eventually be only twenty miles north of the Platte, and your primitive navigational system of sextant and compass might seem slightly off. It's telling you you're roughly on the Platte near where Fort Kearney is supposed to be, but you can't find the fort, because instead of being on the Platte, you're really now on the South Loup. Does anybody know what that is called?"

Emily spoke up: "It's called *being really lost.*" The class found this amusing.

"Yes, exactly, Emily, you'd be completely lost. And if you were very stubborn, you wouldn't admit that you had gone astray, and you'd insist that your location was *the* Fort Kearney. All this happened to Louis St. Martin, who made this journey and this mistake in the winter of 1862, saw that winter was coming and didn't want to admit he was lost, so he built a fort and spent the winter alone."

Louis St. Martin didn't spend his winter entirely alone, but Mrs. Albright, for all her other strengths as a teacher, didn't relish explaining certain aspects of history, especially the details that are sketchy. According to St. Martin's rather blunt journal, one can infer that St. Martin was out fruitlessly checking his traps for beaver one day, and he came across a woman and a small child huddled together, waiting to die of starvation or by freezing, whichever came first. The woman was a Santee Sioux. Her tribe was not from the area. Her husband had been convicted of murder and was one of the thirty-eight men executed in Mankato, Minnesota, following the Sioux War of 1862, and her brothers had been sent to a prison in Iowa. She had simply wandered. It had been days since she'd had the strength to snare even a rabbit. But Louis St. Martin had shot a buffalo, and he had plenty of meat; he attempted to nourish the mother and child with some buffalo jerky. He took them to his fort where the woman gradually recovered and began to see him as a kindhearted man who could help her stay warm at night. After she conveyed her openness to such a possibility, her rescuer wasted little time responding in kind. The child, sadly, did not recover. St. Martin's journal referred to the child only as *l'enfant,* which means "the child" but never as *il* or *elle,* "he" or "she." *"L'enfant"* was too far gone from starvation or perhaps scurvy. *L'enfant* died the day after Louis found them.

Nowhere in the history books is it written down, but one can surmise that this Sioux woman, whose name was Ptaysan-Wee, found her love for the rather hairy Frenchman bittersweet, comforting only in the way a good bearskin rug is comforting, sweet to the skin but not as much to the soul as one might hope. In the middle of the night, some hours after their lovemaking, she awoke from nightmares that would not go away. Her eyes staring into opaque darkness, she could still see her husband, her handsome first love, swinging by the neck from a rope, according to the mandate of a man named Abraham Lincoln. In front of her face, in the depths of the night, the ghost of her dead husband appeared, a man who fought to defend his land and protect his child.

"I failed you," he said.

She loved him for trying.

The woman soon had another child. The daddy was quite pleased—and named the new boy Louis, after himself.

It's not hard to imagine why Mrs. Albright skimmed this part of the lesson. First of all, there was the interracial, childbirth-out-of-wedlock issue, not a topic she wished to explore too deeply with sixth-graders. Second, there was the fact that the town matriarch's first husband was given the death sentence by an American icon and one of the town's three most popular presidents, right after George Washington and Ronald Reagan. And third, the kids in her classes were more interested in the gold-strike part of the story anyway. Regardless of Mrs. Albright's personal thoughts on capital punishment and extramarital sex, she knew what was best for her if she wanted to keep her job.

The Rock of Gibraltar

Owen

Harmony, 1985

Some days, Owen Thibodeaux remembered the earliest things quite clearly. Other days, he struggled to remember whether or not he'd had lunch. Today was a good day.

Coastal Maine, 1898

His grandfather shoved off from shore, little Owen clinging to the sides of the rowboat with both hands. Immediately the earth disappeared, the boat swallowed in the mist like a great fish takes a hook into its belly. No nibbling. Grandfather sat down, set the oars in their locks, and began to row out into the void, which was the little bay called Bailey's Mistake. Grandfather knew where all the rocks were with his eyes closed; he called them *petits rochers.* Even so, Owen worried they would hit something. He turned and faced the bow and peered into the fog, searching for the horizon, aching for the dawn to break into day.

But little Owen, a budding scientist, had many questions for his grandfather. "Except when it's foggy, I can see right through the air; it doesn't have any color. So why is the sky blue?"

"Well ..."

"But, Grandpapa, when you pour water in a cup, it's clear. Why is the sea green?"

"Well …"

"Grandpapa, are all lobsters red?"

"Most of them are. Once I caught a blue one. And I knew an old man who caught a gold one, once."

"Was it really made of gold, or did it just have a gold skin? Do they taste the same as the red ones?"

"I imagine they would. But you don't eat them. They bring good luck if you throw them back."

"I want to catch a gold one, Grandfather," Owen said then, scarcely missing a beat, "Why are you going backwards?"

His grandfather laughed. "How can you tell we're going backwards in this fog? Perhaps we're really going forwards."

Owen watched as Grandfather pulled up the first few traps, empty. In the last trap, he pulled up a fourteen-pound lobster. Owen was disappointed to see he was a regular old red. Grandfather dumped the disoriented creature from the cage into four inches of bilge water at the bottom of the boat, and the lobster scuttled into the dark under Grandfather's bench.

"Grandfather, he goes backwards too!"

This time Grandfather was serious. "My boy," he said, "the lobster goes backwards to keep his enemy in sight. Always in front of you is your past. The dangers you can see and know, but the things that hurt you, those are all behind you. That's why most people find their way into the future headed backwards. They're keeping an eye on the dangers they've faced before, because even if they could see the dangers the future holds coming, they wouldn't recognize them as dangers—until it's too late."

The crustacean was so deep under grandfather's bench he was now tucked in a bucket that had been left on its side. It was the pail they hauled their catch home in at the end of the day. Nothing could sneak up behind him, surprise or ambush him. Feeling much safer with his tail against a wall and his pincers in front of his face, the lobster peered out from his newfound cave and waited.

Harmony, 1985

Owen sat in his wheelchair in a thickening visual fog brought on by cataracts, feeling as confused as a trapped lobster might. He wasn't in Maine. *I'm in Harmony. Where is Harmony?* Mentally, he was never idle. Owen was dropping traps down into the darker spaces of his memory, hoping to pull up a catch. But on days like today, his work was futile. *Did I ever catch a golden lobster?* He decided he'd like to have a snack. Perhaps at the kitchen they'd give him something to munch on. Sometimes they have graham crackers.

A woman was talking. Her voice was vaguely familiar. She sounded like someone he'd once known … who? He thought she'd said her name was Jean, but he never knew a Jean. Whom did he know? He knew … someone named Edith … she was talking. He tried to focus on what she was saying. "… and so, I brought you this stone. I found it on the beach in Nova Scotia. It was sitting on top of a much larger boulder, all alone, as if someone had come and put it there just for me—just for you." Jean took his hand in hers and slipped the stone into his palm. It was about the size of an egg, but flatter.

Owen was quiet for a long time. He rubbed the little rock with his thumb, and it was pleasantly smooth to the touch, worn down over millennia by waves and sand. Finally he said, in a strangely rich baritone for one so old, "You said your name was Jean, Miss?"

"Yes," she said.

"Ah." He thought for some time again. "This stone you brought me: Am I correct in understanding that it comes from the beaches of Nova Scotia?"

"Yes."

Owen rubbed it repeatedly with his thumb. "It's very smooth," he said several times before lapsing into a deep silence. She shared his silence for a minute or two as he pondered whom he'd known with a voice like hers, as he considered the smoothness of the stone.

He spoke again: "Does it have a spectacular color?"

"It's gray."

"Ah. Then it's the same color as everything I see, so it's all for the best. If it were a lovely red granite, or green serpentine, it would do me no good. I'm nearly blind, you know." He rubbed his chin. "I'm sorry I didn't shave before you came. My chin isn't smooth like this rock, or perhaps you'd kiss me."

Jean laughed. "You are more than presentable," she told him, then cupped his rough chin in her hand and kissed his cheek as though he were a little boy.

"Thank you," he said formally, lapsing again into silence.

Jean sat down. She glanced out the window momentarily, her eyes soon returning to the old man. Although his body was broken down, which she expected, and his mind was not altogether sharp as it once had been, about which she had been warned, his voice was rich and powerful. She felt that instead of a scientist, he could have been in radio or perhaps television—if he had been handsome. It was hard to tell now. His ears were comically large, and the skin of his face a floppy clock that, sagging, told time in decades. As a professor, his lectures must have been captivating: his passion for all sorts of mineral deposits, his flair for the drama of the upheaval of layers in the earliest days of the formation of earth as we know it. Each time he opened his mouth, that voice came as a shock, as though the past itself were speaking. The sound of that voice was disconcerting. In contrast, the silence had been the easier part of her visit.

Jean had been looking around the room for a while, and when she looked at Owen again, she saw that his chin was on his chest. She pondered him for a long moment and then, not knowing what else to do, she stood to leave.

He heard her stand up; the chair creaked, and his peripheral vision was just good enough to tell him that she was blocking the light.

"It pleases me more ..." he mumbled. She wondered if he'd been asleep.

"What?" she said.

"Jean." He looked up suddenly. He hadn't been asleep, after all. At least he wasn't now.

"Yes, that's me." She took a step forward.

"Jean … brought me this rock from Nova Scotia. It pleases me more than the Rock of Gibraltar," he added, with conviction in his voice. Then his head drooped again in fatigue, and his chin rested on his chest.

"It was good to meet you, Mr. Thibodeaux." She nearly whispered it.

"Who's there?" Owen said with a start. He felt he'd had a beautiful dream, but he couldn't remember what it was. This smooth stone in his hand, now that was real. Empirical evidence. Perhaps it was a dream, but it was real too.

Of Teacups and Tractors

Melissa and Randall

Harmony, June 1992

Early in the afternoon on the day they graduated, Melissa jumped into Randall's pickup for a short ride over to the home of his grandmother, whom he called "Nana" with a great deal of affection. It amused Randall that Melissa assumed that Nana had invited them. In fact, Randall had called Nana and told her he had a surprise. He drove almost too fast, as was typical. Melissa rolled down the window and let the breeze whip her hair back and forth, the slapping strands of hair nearly stinging her face. When they arrived she was as disheveled as could be. She pulled a scrunchie out of her pocket and pulled her hair back in a simple ponytail, and Randall knew she considered herself as presentable as she needed to be; she grinned at him, and he smiled back.

Randall's fingers felt thick as he fumbled at the laces and removed his boots on the screened-in porch before rapping at the door. Melissa had been peppering him with questions about Nana, and as usual, he hadn't gotten a word in edgewise. Knowing Melissa, she'd chatter all the way through tea with Nana, who was bound to fall in love with her. "One more thing, Melissa. I planned to tell you before—" he began, but just then Nana opened the door. "Hello, Nana." He stooped, allowing her to kiss his cheek.

"My darling boy," she cooed. "And who is this lovely young lady?"

Nana knew who the young lady was, of course, but she wouldn't pass up the opportunity to force Randall to give her a formal introduction.

"Nana, this is my, er, friend, Melissa Stoltzfus." Randall felt himself blushing. "Melissa, this is Nana Martin." He gave a little bow awkwardly in the doorway. Even though Nana made him practice these British formalities at her house, he had never used them anywhere else. One day when he was nine, he told her, "But, Nana, we live in *Nebraska*, not England," and she gave him a look that plainly told him that where they actually lived made no difference to her; he was expected to behave like a gentleman from London, Ontario, her place of birth.

"Let me see you, Melissa Stoltzfus," Nana said, pausing a moment to hold her by the forearms and look her in the eyes for a long moment. Nana touched her own lips lightly, and then her fingers flitted over Melissa's forehead in a quiet blessing. Finally she spoke. "If Randall has brought you, you are welcome in this house. It's so good to have you here."

Randall noticed gratefully that she didn't ask Melissa who her parents were. That was the sort of thing Melissa's parents might have done; indeed, they had done so the first time he met them. When he'd said his parents were Gerald and Margie Martin, they'd been puzzled. "We knew some ... Martins in Hesston, Kansas," they had said tentatively. Melissa was a Mennonite. If a connection could be found, even if it was "We're third cousins, once removed, on your father's side" or "Oh, your grandparents were on the mission field in India with So-and-So in 1937" or "Yes, I knew your mother's cousin's wife's roommate in college," everyone's place in the community could then be established by inference.

Once he realized why they were asking if he was related to these Martins in some important-sounding place called Hesston, Randall explained that his family's name, centuries ago, had been *Saint* Martin, that the background was French, not German. Melissa's parents' eyes had lit with both understanding and disappointment at the same time. *A Catholic boy*. But, as Randall hastily explained, since Nana came from the Anglican tradition, and Grandpa Louis (God rest his soul) had been Catholic with a healthy dose of Sioux religious influences piled on when it wasn't any particularly important saint's day, Randall and his brother had been raised Methodist. This had confused Melissa's parents even more, so he dropped it.

Melissa preferred to be judged on her own merits; she found Nana's greeting without inquiry into her ancestry refreshing, particularly since she'd never met any woman over the age of fifty who had *not* asked such questions. She shot Randall a quizzically pleased smile as Nana led them into the parlor, as if to say, "You have a cool grandma!"

Randall sipped his tea slowly. He didn't mind listening; Melissa was here precisely so that she and Nana could talk. His agenda could wait. He sat back and inhaled slowly through his nose. The house smelled a particular way—not unpleasantly, but in that way a widow's house can smell that makes you feel like you'd better not bump into anything and hope the brownies will be served before you leave.

"These teacups ..." began Melissa, who always loved having tea parties with her friend Emily when she was a girl. She turned to Randall in astonishment. "These teacups are amazing!"

"They're Aynsley teacups, in the corset style. Nana brought them with her from Canada when she married my grandfather. They're my favorite teacups," Randall told her.

"You like *teacups*?" Although Melissa had been dating Randall for two years now, she didn't know this about him. It wasn't exactly something he broadcast at high school.

"Certainly," he said. "Nana has always made sure that each of her grandchildren knows how to behave at a proper tea. This cup here"—he cradled the item in his thick, calloused hand like a baby bird—"I've been drinking out of it since I was old enough to hold it."

"That's right, darling," Nana told her. "Ever since Randall's grandfather Louis brought me home (God rest his aching soul) they've all accused me of trying to civilize the plains."

"'Anglicizing the plains' is what he used to say," Randall corrected.

"What's the difference? Well. My husband's great-grandfather founded Harmony ..." She looked back at Melissa. "Did you know that? Sometimes I wonder if it was worth it. There are times when my husband's people have—how can I put this?—too much vision for their own good. They can get a little crazed in the head—well, not Randall, but some of them. Why, Louis's great-grandfather, whose name was also Louis—but you know they all called him 'Papa'—he was the one, with his brother Philippe, who built a stockade and founded the little fort. He called it Fort Kearney and persuaded people that his was the *original* Fort Kearney, that the other one was a hoax.

"You know, in 1862 some folks made a wrong turn and came up the Loup here instead of the Platte, thinking they were headed for the gold mines in what's now Colorado, but, of course, it was the wrong trail." She *tsked* and gestured toward the West dismissively, as if anyone headed that direction was insane.

"What happened?" asked Melissa, curious to hear Nana's version of local history.

"They got caught in the snow and wintered at the fort; Papa insisted he was on the Platte," continued Nana, dropping her voice to just above a whisper. "They started ... making babies. So, before you knew it, there was a town—and to everyone who lived here, it *was* the original Fort Kearney— Don't fidget so, Randall," she interrupted herself.

"I'm not fidgeting, Nana." Randall had heard the story of his ancestor's deceptive founding of Harmony too many times. His ancestor was Nebraska's version of Leif Eriksson. Besides, he did have a particular reason for bringing Melissa to meet Nana, and the more he sat, the more he waited, the more nervous he felt.

"It wasn't much of a town, though," continued Nana, undeterred, "until they found the gold in the South Loup in the spring of 1872. Back in 1867 we had to have a different name, when Nebraska became a state, and there was a nasty brawl about whose Fort Kearney was the real one too. The local boys were on the verge of a shootout with the fellows from Fort Kearney, until he backed down at his wife's insistence, and he named the town Old Kearney—for the surveyor.

Now, his wife, Ptaysan-Wee, which meant 'White Buffalo Calf Woman' ... she was a Sioux Indian. Her people were from north and west of here. He must have met her on the way back from trapping beaver up in Wyoming or something, and he brought her along; then she converted to Catholicism and took the name Mary St. Martin." And now Nana's voice dropped to a whisper. "She renamed the town Harmony—though she spelled it with that funny *ie* ending—because of her hopes for peace between Indians and Catholics. She did it that very day in 1876 she heard the news of Little Big Horn. It is said that each day she smoked a pipe and prayed for the birth of the White Buffalo, which indicated the beginning of an age of world peace and spiritual harmony. Even *after* she converted to Catholicism!" Nana rolled her eyes heavenward, then resumed her story.

"But Ptaysan-Wee—well, she *was* a visionary. She's the one who started the utopian commune that lasted from 1902 to 1917, when she died wandering in a blizzard outside of town. Well. When I brought my teacups with me from Ontario, young lady, the place did need some civilizing—starting with spelling *Harmony* correctly." Melissa nodded politely. Randall had warned her that Nana could have some peculiar and very particular ideas about the way things ought to be. It was best not to challenge her. She meant well.

"Well, Nana," Randall blurted, placing his cup with a too-loud clink on his saucer and returning it to the tray, "Melissa here is my teacup girl. I brought her to claim her cup." Nana gave a small squeal and clapped her hands in girlish delight.

Melissa, a question on her face, turned toward Randall, who swallowed hard as he gazed into her lovely eyes. He could spend all day with those eyes. "Your teacup girl? What are you talking about?" Melissa placed her hand inquisitively on Randall's arm.

"You'd better tell her, dear, while I fetch the cup," Nana said, easing herself out of her chair and moving with a slight limp off to the kitchen.

"Nana has a large Aynsley collection, you see," began Randall. "Some cups are more special than others. The one you're drinking out of is no big deal. But she has some special ones she never gets out. They're gifts, for whoever the grandkids choose to marry." He paused a moment, a little smile on his face. "I hope you'll accept one of those?"

"You mean …?"

"It's like an engagement ring you can drink tea out of—" Randall began, but before he could finish, Melissa was throwing her arms around his neck and kissing him softly, the kisses of a woman who would gladly be a wife. Even though they'd kissed many times before, this time was different. He suddenly became aware of that flippy feeling in his stomach.

Nana made a small coughing sound from the door. "You'll accept the teacup then, I presume, luv?"

It was beautiful—a creamy white with tiny flowers of cherry red—and there was a saucer to match. Melissa still couldn't believe it. "You mean I get to keep this?"

"It's the family's teacup, and now it's yours. Of course I hope that as long as I live you'll let me watch over it, and you'll come down for tea now and then."

"That would be wonderful. You know, I don't have a nana," Melissa told her.

"I know, dear. Randall has told me all about you." Nana smiled down at him, and he blushed.

"All about me?" Melissa looked at Randall again. "I can't imagine you telling anyone all about *any*thing! The closest you've gotten to telling me all about something is the Farmall you were restoring for your senior shop class."

Randall smiled. "Nothing else much worth talking to Nana about," he said, "besides tractors, teacups, and you. Um, Melissa, since you can't take the teacup home, I thought you might want to wear this." And he produced a ring with a very tiny diamond on it. "I hope it's big enough," he said. She slipped it on her finger.

"Yes, it fits perfectly." Melissa's smile was radiant; she threw her arms around him again.

"I meant the diamond," Randall admitted.

"Oh, that? Of course! It's beautiful. Oh Randall!" For once, Melissa was speechless. So she kissed him again. Nana suddenly found things to do in the kitchen.

The Malachite Dress

Owen

The night he met his wife didn't seem so long ago to Owen.

Omaha, Nebraska, December 31, 1927

It was New Year's Eve, and Owen had been in Omaha only since August. Nebraska had been good to him so far. His colleagues at the university had been welcoming, and he found their discourses on all manner of subjects—not just geology—entirely fascinating. Owen loved a good conversation. He could remember everything about that evening except her name.

She was standing in front of the gas fireplace in a green dress, holding a glass of pink champagne nervously, when Owen saw her. His first thought was that the dress was remarkable: it resembled a malachite brooch from Egypt he had given his mother.

"Who's the girl over there in that amazing dress?" The first three acquaintances he asked shrugged. He grew more intrigued by her mystery.

Owen found the hostess, a socialite named Mrs. Hendrickson. "Excuse me, Ma'am. That girl by the fireplace—yes—do you know her?"

"Allow me to introduce you," Mrs. Hendrickson said with a smile. As she led him by the elbow toward the woman he'd indicated, weaving their way around a variety of other guests, the hostess briefed him on the woman he was about to meet. "She's an elocutionist, wouldn't you know. She teaches private diction lessons to students who are interested in film and radio careers; she works with those unfortunate souls who have impediments." And now she leaned closer to his ear, confidentially. "The girl has amazing diction, but I've noticed that when she meets an attractive young man such as yourself, she tends to fall apart and mash her words together. Do promise me you'll be kind." Owen nodded, and a moment later the nosy socialite chirped, "Darling, allow me to introduce you to Owen Thibodeaux, the newest professor of geology at the university."

"Yes, well, just an associate professorship," he said, laughing. The girl in the malachite dress was indeed a little nervous; that he could see. She finished her glass of champagne almost too quickly, her face glowing like a rose quartz. She looked as though the fire was warming her a bit too much, and the champagne was making her feel dizzy. She seemed a bit frail. Not altogether plain or pallid, but certainly not altogether vibrant, sensuous or healthy either. Still, her gown, which he somehow knew was borrowed, made her gray eyes green, and she had a mysterious quality about her that aroused his curiosity.

After a bit of small talk, Owen blurted, "I must admit, your dress is stunning, Miss—oh my, I've forgotten your name already. I don't mean to offend, but I'm terrible with names. I suppose I'm one of those stereotypically absentminded professors."

She gave him her name again, and he more or less repeated himself: "The dress is magnificent!"

Blushing, she told him, "Thank you. I very much appreciate your compliments, sir," and in spite of what Mrs. Hendrickson said about her diction when talking to handsome bachelors, she enunciated perfectly. She accepted another glass from a passing waiter, and Owen could see that she did so against her better judgment. Owen watched as her tongue darted perfectly between her teeth when she said "thank" and her lips formed a perfectly round O when she said "you," and perhaps because of the liquor he was consuming, he began to think further about her mouth in other ways. In spite of the drinks, or perhaps because of them, she seemed so controlled when her mouth moved. They both had another round of champagne at midnight, and he walked her home through the snow where she asked him in and he accepted. In the back of their minds, they would later admit, they were both astonished at themselves.

In the morning, Owen was wondering what on earth he would say, when he finally found her in the kitchen.

"Look," he fumbled, "I was wondering … come on, now, please don't cry so …" He paused as her weeping intensified. He was a scientist, and he vaguely understood that emotions were not his forte. It would be more accurate to say that his main and conscious thought at the moment was that he hated crying, couldn't tolerate it one more moment, and had to stop it somehow. Where was the switch? Things were getting uncomfortable. "I was wondering if you could wear that same green dress for our wedding," he blurted, "perhaps on Saint Valentine's Day?"

"Professor," she groaned, "I should throw you out, you rogue. But look, I've even made you coffee, and toast with marmalade. Don't be cruel. Are you mocking me?" She turned to face him, the streaks from her tears making her look ghostly to him.

Owen looked her in the eye and said, "How old are you?"

She bawled harder and couldn't answer.

"Well, as for me, I'm thirty-one, and I've never done that in my life—I swear on my mother's grave." He pressed, "How old are you, dammit?"

"Don't swear," she protested. "I'm thirty-three."

"Well, then. Have you had any other offers lately?" he challenged her.

She looked sullen for a moment. "No." Then she turned bitter. "You *are* mocking me!"

"I'm not!" He felt indignant for a moment, but then rationalized that this was really his fault. "I've made a mess of it, I'm afraid." And as Owen got down on one knee, he continued, "Don't look so astonished, my dear. I've had no offers lately either, I must admit. See here. I'll ask your father properly as soon as you can introduce me to him, and I'll buy a diamond ring this very morning. Won't you let me make an honest girl out of you?"

He might be a rogue—but in a handsome sort of way. He was funny, and his diction! *Nonpareil! That could be why I invited him in,* she mused. She'd never get an offer from a man with such an important job as associate professor of Geology again, that was for certain. "Oh, all right then," she sighed and dried her tears.

"You'll wear the malachite dress?"

"The what?"

"The green party dress. It's so lovely."

"Yes, I'll wear it. I certainly can't wear white." And she began to sob again. Owen groaned inside. *This girl is intolerable unless she's drunk!* he thought. *Dammit. What in blazes is her name anyway?*

She cried all through the wedding and during most of the honeymoon except when he was able to get her to have a few drinks. He couldn't stand her sober, even when she wasn't crying, which seemed like an extremely rare thing to him. For the first few months she cried over her previous wantonness, then for the next few years she was mostly drunk. A few years after that, she sobered up for a last chance to try to get pregnant, only to cry desperately over her ultimate barrenness, and then for a while she was mostly drunk again. He found her cooking bland and lacking in imagination—and her company increasingly lackluster in the way he imagined the company of the woman from Grant Wood's new painting *American Gothic* must be. Lovemaking was a chore akin to wrestling a feisty but undersized trout into a net—awkward and unrewarding—and Owen gradually stopped fishing for it. As his career progressed, he discovered more reasons to travel: lecturing, directing digs. Those were his best moments, the farther flung the better. He became important, published several ground-breaking works, and was consulted by geologists worldwide.

There was one more bout of weeping sobriety when he returned from the Black Hills one summer after a few months of geological exploration with a team of undergraduates, but that was pretty much the whole of it as far as sobriety went, and they lapsed finally into an interminable marriage of inconvenience. Although divorce was discussed several times, they never followed through, because, as she said, "We've already begun this marriage on an improper note. Two wrongs don't make a right." He hadn't the heart to disagree with her. In fact, when he thought seriously about getting a divorce, he realized that for her, it would likely end in either being sent to an institution for the mentally ill or suicide. Already possessed with a deeply repressed sense of guilt, he didn't want to feel responsible for that as well. Besides, a divorce and the subsequent hassles would have been a distraction from his work.

Owen's succinct perspective on the entire situation came out in a candid moment with his good friend and former roommate from Harvard, Professor Stephens of Northwestern University. One day, after Owen had been married for ten years or so, Stephens asked, "How's ol' What's-her-name these days anyhow, Thibodeaux?"

"She's an all right girl, I suppose, but over the years I've found that although she can enunciate well enough, she never has found much of anything interesting to actually say."

Most of the time, Owen could still remember this.

Rarely did he want to talk about it.

The part Owen didn't remember anymore was how Stephens had changed the subject of their conversation to something that interested them both much more than Owen's wife.

"You know, Thibodeaux, I had to drive through Nebraska, of course, on my way to a conference in Boulder last fall."

"I'm sorry," said Owen.

"Oh, it's quite all right. I stopped at a lunch counter in Kearney. You know the place? I got to talkin' to a local boy, a farmer in his early twenties who said his name was Doc. He was telling everyone in sight how much gold they pulled out of the South Loup River, 'piles and piles, back in the 1880s,' up near a place called Harmony. Do you know of it?"

"Near Kearney, you say?"

"Yes. I should warn you, the other locals, the Kearney boys, were all scoffing, and he nearly came to fisticuffs with a few of them. Said his own ancestors found it, and he ought to know."

"It's not possible," Owen exclaimed.

"Hypothetically ..." Stephens broke off.

"I know my own state," Owen said.

"The Black Hills are a geological anomaly. What if you have a smaller anomaly in your own backyard?"

"I wouldn't be a scientist if I didn't investigate," Owen said. "Do you think I could get a grant?"

Stephens shrugged. "If you find anything, or even if you don't, I'd like to hear what you turn up."

With one project after another on top of his normal class load, Owen forgot about Harmony for ten years, until Stephens reminded him of it in the postscript of a routine correspondence between the two men sometime in the mid-forties. This time, Owen scheduled a weekend to drive out to Harmony, at least to turn over a few rocks in the riverbed and maybe interview a few old-timers.

Nobody's Going Anywhere

Amy

Harmony, June 1992

Seventeen students marched into Harmony High's gymnasium. Today would be the last time anyone would use it. The school system in Harmony was consolidating with several other small towns, and bulldozers were scheduled to wipe the buildings from the face of the earth the following morning.

Amy Martin glanced around. She saw her mother in the bleachers, smiling like a baboon, waving at her, trying to take a picture of her. Amy marched slowly next to Randall. He had grease under his fingernails and a smudge by his ear. Under his graduation robe he wore a collared shirt and tie. His face was red. She doubted he could breathe; his neck was probably a twenty-one and his shirt a nineteen and a half. *Good old Randall.*

At the very end of the line, the odd seventeenth graduate with nobody to march beside her was Emily Zimmerman, class valedictorian and the perpetual victim of alphabetical order.

The graduates reached their seats and sat down with a sigh as if the march down the aisle had taken four years. Amy's boyfriend, Brad, was trying to catch her eye, but she pretended to be interested in whatever was happening on stage.

Emily got up from her seat on the stage to give her valedictory speech. Amy sat watching her and felt a surge of nostalgia that gave her goose bumps. Emily was never her best friend; in fact, she always felt that Emily looked down on her. But the tea parties they used to have with Melissa … all those good times came back now, and the catfights were forgotten.

Amy tried to focus on what Emily was saying.

"For the last three years I sat back there with the band and played *Pomp and Circumstance.* I thought about what I would do when it was finally our turn. Not just the speech, but what I would do with my life. The graduates' speeches were always pretty much the same. I don't know if any of you took notes. Call me a nerd if you want; I did. Our first year, the speech was titled 'Where Will We Go Next? We Can, if We Try!' When we were sophomores, the speech was 'Good Old Harmony, I'll Be Back.' Last year our quarterback gave a speech. Remember that? It was titled 'I'm a White Buffalo Forever.' But most of the kids who graduated, even just last year, aren't around anymore.

"I don't know about you, but I can't stand the thought of more sentimental bunk spoken by someone who is leaving town, never to return. The school is closing, and there's a reason for that. This town is dying. Well, everyone thinks I should go off to college and become a doctor or lawyer. Maybe I will. But I'm not ready to leave yet, so I'm not going to say, 'I'll be back.' We all know there was gold in that river. At least, around here we just believe it, blindly; we accept it to be true. I do too, but have you looked at the facts? No trace of gold for nearly a century, not a single nugget showing up in the river, and yet nearly everyone in this gymnasium has tried to find it. All of us tried in sixth grade, and some of us keep trying. There was gold here—everybody knows that—so why isn't there even a tiny bit left out there in the South Loup? …"

Emily went on for some time about the gold in the South Loup. Amy had heard Emily wax poetic for years, and she had no interest in it. Sure, the gold her ancestors found was great. Amy wished she could have lived when the family was flush with cash, living large. Somehow they lost it all. Her great-grandparents had bought land—lots of land—and lost much of it during the Great Depression. Land, Amy thought, was worthless. They should have stashed the gold so she could have enjoyed some of it. It looked like Emily was going to wrap it up.

"I want to finish by reading a poem that was written about ninety years ago by a woman known as Ptaysan-Wee, the founding mother of Harmony, Nebraska."

I am not the earth, nor am I the sky—
I am the place where they meet.
I am not the water, nor am I the sun,
But at the moment of sunset, I am the gold
Birthed of their bedding.
I am deep within the living stream,
As at the shedding of blood when a girl becomes a woman.
Here, in me, men become like children—
Stretching their minds beyond the known—
For I am the seeds at the joining of races, I require a new initiation,
I cause the forming of a new tribe.
Memories of wrongs fade and the future ways are unknown, yet—
In me, now, the purest bison pauses from her wanderlust
To exhale a mist of blessing in the cold, still moment of dawn.
Sparrows and prairie dogs come to rest in my dusk,
And a pack of wolves joins forces with the moon to sing of their Creator.
Then, sated by their love-song, they rest beside the sleeping herd,
With their heads bowed humbly upon their paws.
I am the moment you exit the womb, before your first cry,
I am the moment the air steals away and unleashes your spirit
Free from your bones.
I am the entire universe,
I am nowhere.
I am Harmonie.

"I can't imagine a world without Harmony, because it's the only place I've ever known. I'm not ready to give it up yet, and I know many of you aren't either." She said this to the adults in the bleachers on the sides, not to the classmates sitting before her along the basketball baseline, squirming in uncomfortable folding chairs. They couldn't wait to get the hell out. Amy couldn't think of a single reason ever to come back.

"Good-bye, Harmony High. I'm sorry to see them tear you down. I don't know how this could happen, but … I hope, I wish, maybe someday the White Buffalo will roam on the football field again. Anyway, I can't go anywhere until I find out about that gold. I know it's ultimately an existential question. Why are we here in the first place? But I have to stay here until I find out!"

Emily sat back down on the stage. Someone passed her a box of tissues.

A few minutes later, walking across the stage to get her diploma, Amy shook her head in disbelief. *I never really expected to graduate from high school,* she mused. It wasn't that she wasn't smart. *In fact,* Amy admitted to herself, *I'm actually pretty damn clever. I do deserve this!* Her years of school flashed before her eyes as the line of students receiving diplomas receded ahead of her. After acing ninth grade and seeing no practical application of *Romeo and Juliet,* algebra, mitochondria, or the Declaration of Independence in her future, she had obliged the whims of her disillusionment for the following three years. On the occasions that she was in class, she perfected her bored look. As for things she did find relevant, she tended toward shopping and boys, which worked out particularly well when a boy was willing to spend his money on her. *It's a certain sort of commerce,* she always thought, *that I'm really good at!*

In her final semester, things intensified with Brad, who was cute in a rugged sort of way, like Bruce Willis in the *Die Hard* movies. Brad had a tendency to throw jealous temper tantrums whenever she looked at other boys, which was admittedly pretty often. He was also very interested in sports, which she considered stupid. She knew Brad was looking at her, so she kept looking at the stage. She didn't want to make eye contact. She had other plans tonight.

Unknown to Brad, during the last semester things had heated up too with Jimmy from Kearney. Jimmy was roguish-looking, like the sheriff of Nottingham in *Robin Hood: Prince of Thieves,* but very artistic, even poetic. He was really good with his tongue—on a variety of levels. Nobody seemed to mind that Amy's grades weren't up to potential. Oh, several teachers did chastise her on occasion, but no one went out of their way to really care.

Then, in her last semester, when Mr. Jones found her in the hallway and told her she was failing Algebra and asked her what she wanted to do about it, she came to a crossroads where she had to decide if she wanted the actual diploma or not. Based on her desire to appear normal to the general public—since dropping out was almost unheard of in Harmony—Amy arranged a few private meetings with Mr. Jones for "tutoring." Mr. Jones had been pleased with her progress and agreed to award her a passing grade. By the time she was done with the "lessons," he really didn't have much choice but to award her an A+ if he wanted to keep his job. Anyone looking at her transcript might have found this mark to be a suspicious aberration, but who would ever look at her transcript?

Juggling Brad, Jimmy, and making the grade with Mr. Jones had left Amy little time during that last semester for her best friend, Melissa, and the people who hung out with her: Emily, Randall, and Ben. None of them would admit it, but Amy knew they didn't like Brad. They never said, "Hey, we're all getting together at Melissa's house Friday night. *Why don't you bring Brad?"* Maybe that was because they never knew from one day to the next if she was going out with him or not, but mostly it was because they just didn't like him. None of them even knew about Jimmy. And although they had all taken their math classes with Mr. Jones, they certainly had no idea about the equations he and Amy had been working on. Besides, Melissa and Randall were in la-la land most of the time, even though Melissa swore to Amy that she wasn't "doing it" with Randall. The church Melissa and Randall attended was strongly against sex before marriage, and this had been reinforced at youth conferences, youth camping during the summer—endless functions extolling the virtues of chastity. "Your church talks about sex so much you'd think it was better than it really is," Amy once told her shocked friends.

Ben and Emily were busy competing for valedictorian, doing a million extracurricular projects, and generally being too good to hang out with her. Although Ben didn't go to church much, neither he nor

Emily ever had a serious sweetheart; in fact, neither of them even seemed to care about dating at all.

Yes, high school had been a delicate balancing act, and Amy had pulled it off; she even managed to look good doing it. Bring on graduation! She was self-educated, streetwise, and ready for the real world. She had no clue what she would do tomorrow, but this didn't bother her a bit.

It was all worth it, even the tutoring with Mr. Jones, she decided. Her mother had taken the night off to come see her, taking photos on her old Polaroid. Amy couldn't remember the last time she'd seen her mom looking so proud. All the times she thought about dropping out; now she was glad she hadn't. Taking the high school experience on the whole, it wasn't so bad. In fact, she wondered if things would ever be this good again.

When the ceremony was over, the graduates leapt outside, and Amy threw her mortarboard in the air. She didn't go back to pick it up. Her mother was waiting for her, tears streaming down her face. "My baby," she said, "we did it! We got you through!" Amy didn't feel like starting anything, but her mother had nothing to do with it. She had been a zombie ever since Amy could remember. She'd been though rehab lately, to be sure, but Amy didn't trust that it would take. She let her mother hug her. It didn't matter anymore. She was moving out.

Amy was glad she was short. Brad was having trouble finding her in the crowd. She hadn't realized it until just now: He was clingy. He did find her, wrapped his arms around her, and said, "We made it, baby!"

"Brad, don't kiss me right now, not in public."

"Baby, everybody has seen us kiss a thousand times. Deep kissing. So what?"

"Yeah, well, we're adults now."

"You coming over to my place tonight?"

"You never take me out anymore," Amy said. She stuck her lip out in what she meant to be a signal of distress.

"Come on, we can go out tomorrow night. Tonight I'm really tired. Let's just go back to my place, sneak down to the basement, and … you know …"

"Hey, I'm tired too. And I'm supposed to be hanging out with Melissa and Randall, Emily, and Ben."

"Oh God. All right, tomorrow night then. One little kiss—please …"

She gave him a peck on the cheek and went to look for Emily and Melissa. In the growing dusk of early June, her classmates were milling about—as though for the first time they felt out of place at the high school, like moths hanging around their recently vacated cocoons, flexing their wings. When Amy found them, Melissa and Randall were holding hands. Emily and Ben had their arms linked, and the foursome was quiet, but their eyes were all large, as though they'd seen a ghost. Amy skipped up to them and hugged each in turn, then turned and worked her way back through the group of friends, hugging again and adding a flamboyant kiss for everyone, which deeply embarrassed the boys. Amy laughed.

"Guys, these were the best days of our lives!" Amy exalted.

"So far," Melissa replied hopefully.

"I guess," muttered Randall, wiping Amy's lipstick off his cheek.

"Maybe for you," Ben said. "But that's a sad commentary on the state of things to come, if it's true."

"Whatever, Ben." Amy was undaunted.

Emily was starting to cry. "It's never going to be this way again, Amy."

"Oh honey." Amy hugged her again. "We'll always be here for you."

"No. No, you won't," Emily sobbed.

"Nobody's going anywhere," Amy murmured. "We're friends for life!"

Emily pointed at the other three. "What about them?"

"Randall and Melissa aren't going anywhere, are you, guys?"

"We're going on a trip," Randall said.

"Oh Randall. But then we're coming back. Shouldn't I tell her?" Melissa bounced up and down.

"Tell me what?" Amy nearly shrieked.

"Might as well," Randall grinned.

"We're getting married! August eighth!" Melissa did a little twirl. Amy had never thought of Melissa as particularly pretty—certainly not like Emily—and although the girl brushed her strawberry-blond hair and put barrettes in it, the little Mennonite never got the hang of using makeup to accentuate her eyes and slim her round face. But in this moment she was radiant, Amy thought, and her lack of makeup wasn't hurting her. There were congratulations and more hugs.

"We'll all be there, of course!" Amy said.

"Um ..." said Ben.

Amy looked around sharply. "Where's Ben going? Where are *you* going, Ben?"

"Amy, you haven't been around much the last few months, have you? Of course I'm going somewhere. I'm going to college," Ben said.

"But you aren't leaving till after the wedding, right?"

"No, I'm going tomorrow. To New York City. The Big Apple. I'm going to get an apartment with Phil."

"Who is Phil?" Amy was getting confused.

"Ben met Phil at the State Chess Championships last fall in Lincoln," Emily offered.

Ben nodded. "We both got accepted to Columbia, prelaw, and Phil said if I decided to accept admission, he'd room with me, and we're both going out early to find jobs for the summer and try to get used to living there and make some friends before classes start when we really have to knuckle down. I'm not going to be able to make it home for the wedding, Randall. Sorry, Melissa," Ben finished.

"That's OK," Melissa said, "we understand." Randall nodded.

"Wow"—Amy put her hand across her forehead—"things *are* changing fast."

Some other classmates came by and said good luck. Randall's older brother was there, as well as Melissa's three younger sisters, and eventually Randall and Melissa drifted off to pick up some pizza from Pizza Hut. But first they reminded everyone to start heading for Melissa's house. "Sorry, I'm not gonna make it," Amy called after them. "I have a date."

Ben's parents came by and congratulated Amy and Emily. "We're all hanging out at Melissa's for a while tonight," Ben told them. "You can bring me home, right, Emily?" She nodded. Ben and Emily went everywhere together in her ratty little car.

"That's fine," said Ben's father, "but could we drop you off? We'd like to chat with you a bit. We have a graduation gift …" Ben nodded, then turned to Amy. "Stay out of trouble, now," he smiled and let her hug and kiss him one more time.

"You're a sweet boy. What trouble would I get into?" Amy laughed after him. She hadn't felt so magnanimous in a long time. She was even ignoring the fact that Emily had always been a stuck-up snob who treated Amy like she was some kind of slut. *Anyway, I might never have to talk to her again,* Amy thought. *I can handle being with her for ten more minutes.*

Amy and Emily stood watching the red taillights of pickup trucks rolling out of the parking lot, some headed west into the country and some east along Main Street.

"I'm not ready to leave," Emily said quietly. "I don't know what to do next."

"Aren't you going to college this fall? You got good grades."

"Yeah … I don't know," Emily sighed. "I don't know if I want to, or if I want to do something different."

"Like what?"

"Like start my own business or go somewhere just to go. Maybe college, yes, but I want to do something … good."

"What, like Mother Teresa?" Amy said. She began to giggle.

Emily said, "Yeah, maybe something like that. But first, you know, I have to find that gold."

"Right," Amy said, rolling her eyes.

Amy had told Emily many times that while Amy's own ancestors had found the gold, they had found it *all.* There was an awkward pause, until Emily said, "What about you, Amy?"

"What about me? I can't get into college if I wanted to, and I'm no saint."

"Yes, but what are you going to do?"

"I'm going out with Jimmy tonight."

"Jimmy?" Emily's eyebrows went up. Everyone had assumed Amy meant Brad when she told them she had a date.

"Right. He's from Kearney. He's twenty-two. He's really funny, and he says he loves me." Amy decided she didn't care anymore if Emily judged her.

"But what about Brad?"

"Oh Brad." She looked at her shoes. "I'm going out with him tomorrow. But … he's kind of immature, don't you think? He really doesn't want to do anything but work out and make out. And, he's so broke he can't even take me to a movie. Everyone knows he's playing for the Cornhuskers this fall. Well, he's good at football, but even he admits he's not good enough to get rich playing it. I'm probably going to dump him. I'm so, like, *done* with high school relationships. These guys are all losers."

"Not Randall and Ben," Emily pointed out.

"Well, yeah, except Randall and Ben. Randall's been farming so long, he's already, like, Mr. Responsible. He's kinda boring, but Melissa adores him," she went on, "and Ben is classy. Too classy for my taste. Might be just right for you, but then"—she leaned close to Emily—"I think he might be gay. Don't you dare tell anyone I said that, though."

"Oh?" Emily was surprised, then added quickly, "Oh no, I wouldn't tell anyone you said that. Look, Amy—"

Just then Amy saw Jimmy, pulling into the school's driveway in his red Camaro, barely slowing down as he turned the corner. "Ooh. Here comes my rock star," she squealed.

"What do you mean, 'rock star'?" Emily asked.

"Oh, he's in a band. They cover a lot of Guns N' Roses, Poison, Whitesnake, Alice Cooper, you know. Jimmy's the lead singer. He writes some of his own songs too. They're really good!"

When he pulled up, he didn't turn down his radio, but just yelled over the throbbing sounds of Bon Jovi. "Hey, Amy, baby." His arm hanging out the window, he slapped the car door and, cigarette askew, sang with the radio. *"Your love is like bad medicine; bad medicine is what I need!"* His long, curly hair was parted in the middle, and he was trying to grow some hair on his chin.

"Isn't he cute?" Amy gushed, heading for the car, but Emily rolled her eyes. *Snob,* thought Amy.

"Mmm, Jimmy." He took the cigarette out of his mouth as Amy bent at the waist to kiss him through the window, intentionally giving him a glimpse down her T-shirt as she did so. She kissed him a long time. She was in control.

Here I Go Again

Emily

Jimmy looked exactly the way Emily suspected Amy's next boyfriend might look: like a rock star wannabe.

"Wow," Jimmy said, when Amy finally got her tongue out of his mouth, and then he noticed Emily standing there as Amy went around the car to get in. "Who are you?" he said, and his eyes said he'd leave Amy in the dust in a minute if Emily would get in the car. He looked her up and down while Amy pulled his rearview mirror around to reapply her lipstick.

"I'm just Emily," she shrugged, wondering if he could pry his eyes off her chest long enough to drive away. "I'm just one of Amy's friends," she finished lamely.

"Well, Just Emily, you can come along. Three's company," Jimmy said, and he winked at her.

"Um, no thanks, I have to work in the morning," Emily said. She had never dated, and she was naïve, but not so naïve as to miss his innuendo.

"OK, but you're missing out. We always have a good time," Jimmy said, and parted his lips, put his tongue out ever so briefly and far too lasciviously, and took a drag on his cigarette. Emily turned away from him. Jimmy shrugged. "You ready, baby?" he said to Amy, and when she nodded, he left Emily standing in a smoky cloud of burning rubber.

"Here I go again on my own," Emily sang ironically to herself, and walked slowly back to her car, the last person to ever graduate from Harmony High School.

At the post-graduation party Randall and especially Melissa talked about their wedding so excitedly and so long that eventually Emily and Ben, who were genuinely happy for their friends, grew tired of the subject and excused themselves. As day was giving way to night, Emily drove them back into Harmony. Still in her car, they sat in his gravel driveway and looked out the windows on the north edge of town. Most people would say it was in the countryside, but to be in the countryside is an ambiguous condition in Harmony.

The fluorescent glow of the yard light penetrating the fogged-up windows cast shadows that divided Ben's face. He looked like a phantom, as if he were wearing a dramatic mask so that half his face represented good and the other half-evil. The condensation gave the Chevette an intimate feel, like they were alone in their own little world—a sweat lodge with a steering wheel and bucket seats. Somewhere outside, a cricket chirped loudly. Emily rubbed condensation off the glass with her sleeve, looked at her father's perfectly mown lawn, and waited for Ben to say something.

He took his time. She looked at him carefully. He was growing a little beard on his chin. When had he started that? It was cute, somehow less pretentious than Jimmy's attempt. It was … experimental.

Now he twisted the edge of his flannel shirt. Finally he spoke. "I don't care anymore, Emily. I have to tell someone." He groaned. "Everyone has always tried to put us together, as a couple; well, you know that. And you're smart … and gorgeous; I know that. But at the same time there are moments when I see certain guys … I just don't know. Sometimes I think I might like guys. There. I said it."

She'd been bracing herself for this, but she still gasped. "You're gay?"

Ben took a deep breath. "Maybe I am, and maybe I'm not."

"Bi … bisexual?" She had never said this term out loud before.

He shrugged. "How should I know?"

"You just should. Didn't you say I'm gorgeous?"

"Well, yeah, everybody says so."

"Then how's come no boys ever asked me out?"

"Well, you never flirted with anyone, I guess, even though you're way prettier than any girl around. I've heard lots of guys say you're out of their league. A lot of them thought about asking you out, all the time. But you were so quiet, they all assumed you thought you were too good for them, so they never tried. And they all figured that you and I were together."

Emily looked at him quizzically. "You let them believe that?"

"Yeah, sometimes. Better than letting them know I was gay."

"You *told* people we … ?"

"No, I just never denied it when they razzed me about us—"

"Why didn't I ever know that guys liked me?" She said this to herself as much as to Ben.

"Did you ever have a crush on any of them?" Ben asked.

"Of course."

Ben looked surprised. "Well, bottom line, none of them had the balls to ask you out." He rubbed condensation off his window. "You know my theory, right? The one about living in a small town?" He turned to look her in the eye.

Emily sighed. She looked out the window where she had rubbed with her sleeve; the glass was already fogging up again. *Tomorrow is like this window,* she thought, *misty and unknowable. Sometimes tomorrow happens today, and you're really in trouble, because it's still unknowable, but you're in the present.*

"You mean," she said, "that everybody is either a good kid or a bad kid, and there's precious little room to be in the middle. That theory?"

Ben nodded. "Which one am I?"

She didn't answer.

"This is not a rhetorical question, Emily. Oh, I know I've cultivated a certain image. But which one am I?"

"You're one of the good kids." She was determined to believe it.

"And when people find out I'm ...?" His tone was bitter.

"I don't know," she said. "Is there any way to just know ...?"

Ben shrugged. "I appreciate your trying to help, but just forget it. I've been over all these questions in my mind a million times, and I don't have an answer."

"OK." Emily suddenly realized that Ben looked pathetic. She had never seen him look so defeated. Emily leaned across the emergency brake and kissed him softly on his left cheek. At that, he began to cry, and she gently pulled his head onto her shoulder. She kissed his eyelid. "I love you, Ben," she said, "but both of us know we don't have a future."

"I know," he sobbed, his beautiful bass voice cracking as though he were in sixth grade again.

There was a long moment of silence. Finally Emily broke it. "So what are you going to do?"

Ben took a deep breath, wiped his tears and sat up a little straighter. "Well, you know, until today, I've been trying to decide between the Air Force Academy and Columbia." He laughed. "Don't you remember? I'm going to New York, to room with Phil. As much as I'd like to fly—well, if I *am* gay the Air Force doesn't seem like such a good idea. Thank God that's decided," he smiled.

"Oh," Emily said, surprised, "so is Phil gay too then?"

"I haven't really asked him," Ben said, "but he hinted at it. He asked me to room with him; I'm pretty sure."

That was plenty logical. She nodded. "You'll come back to Nebraska and see me, right?"

"I wouldn't count on it, Em." His voice sounded serious and grown-up all of a sudden. *Being eighteen is about being wedged between twelve and twenty-four,* she thought. Ben continued: "I guess I've been pretty wrapped up with my own crap, and I haven't been paying attention." He looked up curiously. "So where are you going to school in the fall? I'm embarrassed to say I can't remember what you decided."

"Well, actually, I haven't even submitted any applications," she began.

"But Emily, we just graduated." Ben sat up straight.

"I know …"

"Well, then?"

"I got a job at the nursing home, starting tomorrow," she said, hoping this would be enough. It wasn't, and she could see it all over his face. "Well, I like taking care of people," she mumbled—and then added more brightly, "I'm thinking of becoming a nurse, or maybe a social worker. Possibly even a doctor, like Lori." Her sister, ten years older, had just recently finished her residency. Emily wasn't sure if she could stand going to another seven to ten years of school and training.

"Well, you ought to make a decision." He looked disappointed. "It's the gold thing, isn't it?"

"Oh, come on, Ben, don't be like my mom. It's just temporary until I decide what I want to do. There's no point going to school if you don't know what you want to study. Mom thinks I should be a doctor, and Dad says nursing is good, and of course Aunt Beverly thinks I'd make a wonderful social worker. Truth is, I could be any of those. I just don't know what I want. Maybe I'll wait a year and go into the Air Force!" He didn't laugh this time.

"Emily, you have to do something. You're one of the smart ones, like Melissa says. One of the natural beauties, like Amy says. Brains, looks, and talent. Sky's the limit, sister."

"Now you *do* sound like my mother. Look. I'll figure it out, Ben. It just might take me a little while— You don't believe there's any gold left, do you?"

"Emily, we've all been waiting for you to drop it since Christmas break in sixth grade. Really? The gold was there, and they found it all, and it's gone and you won't find any. I know I've never said it before, but it's what everyone is thinking. Everybody in the whole damn gymnasium tonight was thinking it. Yeah, I know there are guys who go down to the river with their metal finders, but none of them actually *expects* to find *gold*. You seem to think there should be some trace left. Well, there isn't. Move on. I'm only saying it because I love you."

"Nobody believes in me," Emily said, her voice barely audible.

"I *do* believe in you; that's exactly what I'm saying: I believe in you!"

Emily stared out the window for a while. She wanted to follow Ben's advice and let it go. But she couldn't.

Ben decided to take another tack. "I'm just tellin' ya, time's a-tickin'," he finally said in his best Randall imitation. She started to laugh. He followed it up with some Randall-like hand motions—the ones that always made her laugh—and then did impersonations of Melissa, Amy, and four other kids from their class. Soon Emily was laughing so hard she was crying. For a moment, she completely forgot about the "homosexual thing," and it seemed like good times with Ben again, but when he stopped his mimicry, she remembered everything they had been talking about. She stopped laughing but kept on crying.

"What is it?" Ben asked when he saw her laughter had fled like a good dream when the alarm goes off.

"It's never going to be the same again, is it?"

"No. Of course not." He sat up straight. "That's why I told you about—"

"I realize that," she sniffled. Now it was her turn to put her head on his shoulder.

"Emily, I'll always have a place in my heart for you," he said tenderly.

"Ben, you know I feel the same." He leaned over and kissed her lips. It wasn't like a kiss a brother would give. It was the kiss a boy gives to a girl he has always secretly loved who is dying of a strange disease. If he had kissed her any other way, she decided, she would have minded. But this kiss eased the tension and decreased the confusion in her mind. After a moment, he said, "It's time for bed."

"Yeah. Good night," she said. They sat still for a long moment. Finally, Ben opened his door and walked across the dewy lawn to his house. *It's not Ben's house anymore,* Emily thought. *He's just staying there for a few more days is all.* She began to cry again.

When Emily woke up at five thirty the next morning to go to her first day of work at Harmony Halcyon Home, she noticed that her pillow was still damp.

Harmony Halcyon Home

Emily

Even though she still felt ambivalent about some things, Emily plunged headlong into the world of work. She was on time—well, a couple of minutes late, but not so much that they would care. Even though six in the morning was a lot earlier than the start of school, Emily felt sharp mentally and focused on everything that was going on.

The north wing in Harmony Halcyon Home was perpetually understaffed, so Kate, the head nurse on the first shift, commented as she introduced Emily to the staff that she was glad the director had hired a new girl. Kate noticed that Emily was attentive during morning report—a good sign. Kate planned to have her work with Paul. *Her first tasks shouldn't be too hard, so that she won't quit on Day One,* thought Kate.

"These progress reports aren't done properly," Alice, the night-shift nurse, was grumbling. "I spent all night organizing this paperwork; I swear the girls on second shift are so sloppy. Look at this charting!" Alice waved the offending binder under Kate's nose. She was a little too close, a little too loud, and Kate knew that what she smelled on Alice's breath was a combination of Diet Coke and rum. "I'm going to write those girls up!" Alice muttered. Kate wondered how many times she'd heard Alice threaten this. Alice was the one who ought to be written up. Kate snickered to herself. "What are you laughing about? This isn't funny!"

"No, of course not, Alice. It's terrible. I was just thinking about how easy it is to get away with things around here."

"Like what?"

"Oh, you know, Alice," and Kate made a swift motion with her thumb, indicating a bottle.

"You can't prove anything," Alice replied, glaring. "Look. I have a headache. You finish the report. I'm going home." She left quickly, not looking particularly steady on her feet.

"OK, Paul, I need you to train Emily today. You guys have the north wing, and I'd suggest you get Doc and Owen up first. Break her in gently before you start with the heavy lifting." Kate said with a smile.

Paul looked at his toes and ran his fingers through his hair. He shot a glance at Emily, then studied his kneecaps. The humidity made his thick, coarse shock of sandy-blond hair stand up straight. "Sure," he said after the slightest hesitation.

A few moments later the break room was vacant except for Kate. She finished her coffee as slowly as possible and sighed. "Well, old girl," she said to herself, "one day closer to retirement," and she went to the nurses' station to begin her day.

Doc was up and dressed, walking around backwards and doubled over at the waist when Emily followed Paul into Room 143. The signs by the door were easily removable placards that could be replaced any time a resident was moved to a different room or deceased. The top one said Owen Thibodeaux, and the bottom one said Theodore "Doc" Martin. *Martin,* thought Emily. *Probably someone Amy and Randall are related to somehow. I wonder if he knows about the gold.* She made a mental note to ask him about it sometime.

"Where's my coffee? Where's my coffee?" Doc was shouting to no one in particular. Paul, who came prepared, handed him a mug and guided him to a chair. "That—ow!—goddam doctor," Doc groaned as he sat down.

"Are you OK?" Emily asked.

"A-course I ain't OK"—Doc increased his volume—***"that doctor got his hands on me yesterday and I swear, he does everything all ass-backwards!"***

Kate, hearing the commotion, had been hustling down the hall, and she rushed in, out of breath. "Good morning, fellows. Doc, you must've seen Dr. Hostetler yesterday afternoon."

"Damn straight I did. Ass-backwards, ass-backwards." Doc got out of his chair again, increasingly agitated and waving his arms about, sloshing coffee on the floor.

"What did he say this time?" Kate seemed indifferent to his answer before he gave it.

"Ass-backwards. Said I have 'colon.' Course I got a colon. He said on account I got 'colon,' I can't have no beer. I'll be damned. What a quack! I didn't live to be a hundred years old on water. I got my rights!"

"You're a hundred? That means you were born in … 1892?" Emily was astonished. "You're so … vigorous!" Doc paused a moment in his doubled-over, backwards-walking, coffee-sloshing dance with eternity to wink at her.

"He's actually seventy-eight," said Kate. "He just likes to pile on the years to get pity. These guys pretty much take care of themselves. They both self-potty. Even though Owen over there can't see too good, he can get to the bathroom. Some mornings I help them shave if I have time."

Looking at Emily, she said, "So what did you do last weekend? Do you have a boyfriend? Did you go out?" Kate looked up and saw Paul ducking out to help Mrs. Murphy, who was screaming ghoulishly a few rooms down the hall.

Emily looked around for an answer, trying to focus. There was so much noise here. Old people screaming, rattling the aluminum rails on the sides of their beds. Aides running up and down the hall with clean linens. It was bedlam. "No, I just stayed home and read."

"You … read? Didn't you finish your exams already? You graduated on Monday, right?"

"Yeah, but I had a book I couldn't put down—not schoolwork, just pleasure reading." Kate shook her head at this, indicating incomprehension. Emily went on. "Besides, all my friends were busy. Doc, do you walk around backwards like that every day?"

Doc paid no attention to Emily. "Ass-backwards. Ass-backwards! Stupid doctor! Dr. Hostetler—hell, more like Dr. Frankenstein!"

"Well, I'm sure the doctor knows—" Emily began.

"Actually, that doctor …" Kate was shaking her head in a sad way.

"Oh?" Emily was confused, Kate could see. She'd learn soon enough.

Doc continued his rant. "Ass-backwards, no doubt. Let me tell you something. I knew his daddy. Now *he* was a decent feller. Man could hold his liquor. But all his kid ever says: 'You have colon.'" Peering at Emily, he added, "If you went to see him, no doubt, he'd want to do a pelvic exam, pretty little tail like yours."

"Never mind him," said Kate. "All right, Doc, so ass-backwards yourself down to breakfast."

Doc left, quacking like a duck, still walking backwards and doubled over like a piece of rumpled paper.

"He'll get some coffee, and Judy will put a tiny nip of whiskey in it, and he'll probably be calmer all day, and he'll go forwards again. We tried to get him off booze for a long time, but nobody could work with him. He likes pretty girls, but he won't try to pinch or grab you or anything like some guys around here do. You have to be careful with some of them because they'll even sneak up on you. You'll get along with Doc just fine, 'cause you're cute. Good morning, Owen." Emily noticed that Kate had a way of being able to change the subject abruptly and efficiently.

Owen was stirring. He sat bolt upright at the sound of his name. Swinging his legs mechanically out of his bed, he said, "Good morning, Nurse. Is there someone new here?"

Kate raised her voice. ***"This is Emily,*** the new ***aide."*** Then, whispering to Emily, she added, "He's blind—and almost deaf."

"I knew an Edith," Owen began. "She was my Scottish nurse. When I got shot in the war, I was shot in the *derriere,* you see, it wasn't serious. When I got shot, I went into the hospital and this Scottish girl came over to me and said, 'I'm Edith, your nurse. Did you just come in here to-die?' And I said, 'No, I came here to live,' but, you see, that's how Scottish people talk."

"It's actually ... my name is Emily."

"I knew another Edith," Owen continued, "a beautiful, intelligent girl, but she was too forward ... you aren't of lax moral integrity, are you Edith? No, you're a nurse. Wholesome girl. Are you Scottish? Well, I didn't come in here to die. But I probably won't have much choice when all is said and done. Is the Metamucil coming?"

"What?" Emily was confused. Kate smiled to herself. *She'll catch on quick. She's taking it all in.*

"He wants his Metamucil; it's a nasty, orange-flavored fiber drink," Kate explained.

"Nurse, it's been a fortnight!" Owen sounded astonished.

"Remember, Owen, they give it to you at breakfast now," Kate practically yelled into his ear.

"Ah!"

"Two weeks since you had Metamucil?" Emily wondered aloud.

"No, since his bowels moved," said Kate. "He says that all the time. He gets rather uncomfortable. But even if he had a poop yesterday, he'd still be asking for the Metamucil. He can't remember shit." Kate laughed at her own joke. *I get funnier every day I work here,* she thought. But Emily, still in focus mode, didn't laugh or respond in any outward way.

"Oh" was all she said. She was watching Owen carefully. He had groped his way along the edge of the bed, nearly tripping over his wheelchair, and now was rummaging in the drawer of his nightstand.

"What are you doing now?" asked Emily, leaning close to Owen so he could hear.

"I ought to clean out that junk in his drawer, but he'd probably be lost without it." Kate said. "Where the hell did Paul go anyway? We need to get housekeeping in here to mop up this coffee."

Owen found a small, plain, smooth, gray beach stone in the drawer. "Jean brought me this rock from Nova Scotia," he intoned.

"Who's Jean?" asked Emily.

"It pleases me more than the Rock of Gibraltar," he declared as he held it, palm up, so Emily could see it.

"You didn't like the Rock of Gibraltar? I heard it was—"

"It was dark, and craggy," Owen continued. "It was ugly. This one is smooth." With his empty hand he caught Emily's arm, and put the stone in her right hand.

"I see," Emily replied, rubbing it with her thumb and index finger. It wasn't much to look at, she thought, and then she remembered he was blind. "Yes, it's lovely." She decided it would be if you were blind. She rubbed it a moment longer, then put it back into his hand.

While they had been talking, Kate combed Owen's hair, made his bed, closed his drawer, called the housekeeper, and rebuttoned his shirt. She wasn't bothered that Emily hadn't done any of it. It was Emily's first day on the job, and she had lots to learn. It was best that she get off on the right foot with the residents anyway. "Come on, Owen, time for breakfast," Kate said.

"Is the Metamucil coming?"

"At breakfast, Owen." Kate was finally getting exasperated. *Where is Paul?* she wondered again. *I can't handle this Metamucil crap over and over, not to mention this Rock of Gibraltar stuff.*

Owen wasn't moving toward the door. He wasn't sitting in his wheelchair. Instead, he was putting on an old army helmet, with a hole cut in the top, and talking to nobody in particular. "I was in the Great War. My best friend ... a shell exploded ... all that was left was his *brains* in his helmet. What time is it? Is the Metamucil coming?"

"You get it at breakfast, Owen," Emily said gently, but just loudly enough so he could hear.

"Ah! Is it time for breakfast? I had breakfast with Edith," Owen continued sadly. "I gave her two hundred dollars ... she went to Denver on the train ..." He sat down in his wheelchair and Kate wheeled him out, thinking to herself, *This girl is gonna do fine. She has the magic touch.*

Salt Caravans in Morocco

Paul

Emily was expected to have a pretty good grasp of the job by the end of the week. It's not complicated being a nurse's aide. It isn't easy—anyone who tries it for a day can see that—but it's certainly not complicated.

When Kate and Emily came into the break room for lunch on Emily's second day, Paul stifled the urge to jump up and run out. *For a guy who works mostly with women,* he thought, *I'm such a chicken when it comes to talking to the pretty ones. I guess this is the first time a pretty one ever worked here, but still.* Paul noticed that Kate was talking to him. "What?" he said.

"I said, 'Have you gotten a chance to talk to Emily yet?'" Kate said this almost as though Emily was not in the room. He glanced at Emily. She was young, just out of high school. She had a cute, blond haircut—not long, but not short, and fashionably bouncy. Her face had just a few freckles around her cute, little nose; a mouth that seemed to always smile; and straight, white teeth. She was neither tall nor short, neither fat nor particularly skinny; her body was well proportioned in every way. Although Paul only glanced at her, whenever she walked away from him, he took some liberty to notice her absolutely perfect rear end, possibly her finest feature. No, that wasn't it. It was her eyes. You couldn't say exactly what color they were—somewhere between green and gray, sometimes bluer, and other times flecked with gold. You might even say they were an ocean, or a mountain stream. In any case, no matter what color they appeared when Paul happened to be looking at them, they were her best feature. However, her butt had to be a close second.

"Yeah." Kate looked at him as though she expected more. "Yeah, we talked a little bit after morning report, when Alice left in one of her moods."

"Alice was mad because I was two minutes late. Is that normal for her?" Emily wanted to know.

"She's always mad," Kate said, and Paul nodded.

"Oh well. Hey, Kate, when we were working this morning, Paul introduced me to Mrs. Murphy. She's just ... amazing!" Emily was trying to take the focus off Paul, and he appreciated her for that.

"Mrs. Murphy has been here ever since I started working here twenty-two years ago," Kate said.

"She's a hundred and twelve, right?" Emily was clearly in disbelief.

"It *is* phenomenal," Paul said. "She's currently the fourth oldest person in the world—on record, that is. I can't quite get over it. She'll even tell you: 'I was born in California. Not every state had birth certificates back then, but California did!' Yep, it's authenticated. A hundred and twelve years old—and still in her right mind."

"That's debatable," Kate said under her breath.

"Well, she's in pain." Paul insisted.

"She's a hypochondriac," Kate shot back.

Paul wasn't so sure. "That's what Dr. Hostetler says. But he also says she has 'colon.'"

"She's addicted to pain medicine. Valium, morphine. God knows what her granddaughter sneaks her." Kate rolled her eyes.

"You would be too, if you were a hundred and twelve," Paul protested. He loved arguing with Kate; it was easy to get her riled up. He could see Kate was warming up to a good rant.

"Damn straight I would. God forbid! When I came here fresh out of nursing school we all expected her to be gone before her next birthday. She's so frail, and her bones are so brittle, but she never gets an infection or anything. But the craziest thing was that when she was a hundred and two, she was walking out in the parking lot—she used to go out for a walk every day—she was walking in the parking lot when old man Charlie, who was here visiting his wife (she died, oh God, a long time ago). Well, you know Charlie, he's right down on East Hall now (this was before he moved in, of course; she always said he drove like a bat out of hell) … Anyway, he backed his pickup over old Mrs. Murphy, and Charlie thought he'd killed her. There were tire tracks on her nylons, and it broke both her legs, and she was in the hospital, fading away, so the doctor even started filling out her death certificate, and then she just bounced back. Her legs never healed too well, but she has lived another ten years!"

"Wow! What's her secret?" Emily was fascinated.

"She has secretly got the cellular structure of a turtle," Paul said with a chuckle.

"Actually, if you ask her, she'll say it's because she got rid of her husband early." Kate wasn't done gossiping.

"Oh! How long was she married?" Emily was eating it up; Paul could see that.

"Twenty-one days," Kate went on. "He was killed in a mining accident out in Colorado. Died saving four of his buddies. Everyone else thought he was a hero, but she says they were the worst three weeks of her life."

"That's horrible!" Emily shot a sly grin at Paul, and he realized that she was on to how he was playing Kate—who was shaking her head sadly, enjoying the importance of being the bearer of this sad story.

"She never remarried. Such a pity. Well, to hear her tell it she was lucky not to have a man poking about all the time. I suppose maybe she's right, come to think of it. But she's been a widow since 1898," Kate said, finishing with a tragic flourish.

"But that's … ninety-four years!" Emily exclaimed.

"So," Kate said, leaning forward, "what about you, Emily? Why are you really hanging around this godforsaken town? You don't expect to live here for a hundred and twelve years, do you?"

"No, but … you might say I'm still trying to figure out where the gold went," Emily said.

Kate and Paul looked at each other for a moment. Kate began to laugh. Unsure if Emily was serious, Paul tried not to smile for a moment, but then Emily giggled, and he joined in.

"I can laugh about it too," Emily said, "but I'm dead serious. Everyone thinks I'm nuts, and obviously you do too, but that's OK with me. I know it's kinda wacky, but something about the whole thing doesn't make sense."

"Honey, most of life don't make sense," Kate said. "Especially around here."

The door slowly opened, and Mrs. O'Toole stuck her head in. "Where are we? Where … where are we?" she said as though it was some kind of meditation mantra. Paul thought, *Maybe it* is *some sort of special chant, and she's just fooling us.*

"Oh dammit, Mrs. O'Toole, you aren't supposed to be in here; it's staff only. Do you have your locket, or did you leave it on your pillow again?" Kate was feigning exasperation.

Mrs. O'Toole reached to her collar and began feeling her neckline for the locket, which was missing. "Mother?"

"Never mind," Kate said as Paul made a move to help the lost resident. "I'll take her down to her room. You two get better acquainted," and she left to help Mrs. O'Toole find the locket, which somehow helped her orient herself in Harmony Halcyon Home.

"Usually she makes me do that kind of thing," Paul confided to Emily, "but Mrs. O'Toole is the only one she'll get off her butt for during her lunch break." He wished Kate had let him go; *what would he say to this girl?*

"Why not?"

"Ah, Mrs. O'Toole is her favorite resident. You're not supposed to have favorites, but it happens."

"Really? Who's your favorite?"

"I don't have one," Paul mumbled, kicking himself. *Dude, you are pathetic,* he berated himself.

"You just said everybody has one," Emily teased.

"I'm just … not that kind of guy," Paul said with a shrug. "I try not to get too attached to people, I guess."

"So, how does a guy like you end up working here then?"

"How does anybody? This nursing home is the biggest employer in town; did you know that?" Paul wondered why this girl wanted to know so much about him.

"I never thought about it," she said pensively.

"It's like half this town is hanging around here, sitting in a wheelchair waiting to die, and the other half is changing their bedpans, and they don't realize it, but they're just waiting to die too … they just have a little longer to go," Paul explained.

"Come on, that's pretty fatalistic."

"Hey, that's how it looks to me. But case in point: Look at Kate. She's miserable. She's convinced that the day she quits work here, she'll have to move in. She even talks about what a mean bitch she'll probably be when she goes senile."

"And she's probably right," Emily said, then giggled. A moment later, she looked at him more seriously. "So why are you still here?"

"I'm saving up to get out of here. I'm not spending my whole life this way." Paul could sense he was starting to say too much. He tried to stop himself, but the words kept coming. *Damn! Why did Emily have to be such a good listener?* "I'm leaving as soon as I can. I mean—but I'd stay in town, like, if there was a good reason."

"Like what kind of reason would be good enough to stay?"

"Well, you know, like I meet a girl or whatever." *Oh shit, oh shit,* he thought, *not what I want to be talking about at all!*

"I'm a girl—and you just met me. Does that mean you're staying?"

Paul was seriously flustered, and he knew it was his own fault. "I mean, like, someone who is—she's … not just *meet* her …"

"I know what you mean; I'm just teasing. I'm sorry," she said as though she meant it. "Where would you go?"

"Huh?" This girl wasn't laughing at him. That was odd. Paul realized he was relieved.

"When you save up the money and leave town, where would you go?" she pressed.

"Look, it's, never mind." he said.

"Come on. You can tell me," she urged.

He turned away. "My mom doesn't even know."

"Please!" She begged so sincerely he had to look at her again. Her eyes said she could keep a secret, and they were very, very beautiful too. Slowly, Paul opened his mouth.

"One day when I was a kid—I remember it like it was yesterday—I was riding my bike down Main Street and not paying attention to stuff. All of a sudden I realized this rainstorm had blown in and there wasn't time to get home. So just as the drops started to fall, big and fat, I pulled up at the library, threw my bike down, and ran inside."

She acted hurt. "Paul! Don't change the subject on me! Seriously, where would you go?"

"I'm not changing the subject!" he said, a little indignantly. "I'm getting to that. So I went in the library and picked up the first thing I saw, and it was a *National Geographic* magazine. Well, ever since then …"

Emily noticed a faraway look in his eye. He was a curious man. Funny and funny-looking, and smart in the way that makes people memorize useless facts just for something to do with their active brains, and so lacking in self-confidence—but sure of what he did know. A strange combination.

"What?"

"There's just some places I want to check out," Paul said softly. "In Morocco. Casablanca, for sure, and Fez, and I just … I don't know. Maybe …"

"Maybe what?"

"I guess the best thing would be if I could go with a salt caravan across the Sahara." Paul was nearly whispering.

"Wow, a *salt* caravan?"

Now that it was out there, Paul got excited. "Yeah, they've been doing this with camels for hundreds of years; it's the ultimate—" Just then Kate came back in, still shaking her head.

"That Mrs. O'Toolio. Crazy old bat."

"You say that, but we all know you love her," Paul said, shooting back.

"I don't know why," Kate wondered aloud. "She's just as insane as anyone else around here. So … you guys get to know each other?"

"A little," Emily said. "He's not much of a talker—" She smiled and glanced at Paul.

"I don't believe that for a minute," Kate interrupted. "What do you think, Paul? She's cute, isn't she?"

Poor Paul was reduced to saying "Uh, um … well, come on, I mean—sure, but ..."

"But?" Kate said. "But what?"

"Oh come on, Kate, leave him alone." Emily looked as though she might be embarrassed for him. Paul was grateful for her intervention once again.

"She tries to hook me up with everybody that works here," Paul told Emily.

"He's twenty-seven, he needs a girlfriend. All he does is play Super Mario Brothers and some Zelda thing. Sits at home playing with his joystick all night," Kate said, grinning at Paul, who blushed a deep red.

"He doesn't go out because he's saving his money—right, Paul?" Emily was being helpful again.

"Yeah, I am." Paul was relieved, but it was time for an escape from Kate. "I'm putting money away all the time, every paycheck. Look, that reminds me, I … uh, I need to call the, um, call the bank." Paul was up and gone before Kate could say anything else.

"You embarrassed him," Emily said.

"He ought to ask you out," Kate grumbled.

"What makes you think I'd go out with him? He's so much older, and he's—"

"He's a nice guy. Go have a drink with him; give him a kiss; see what happens," Kate persisted.

"Kate! I just met him yesterday!"

"Well, *I* think it wouldn't hurt for him to try a little more—" Kate paused, looking at her watch. "It's about time to start our afternoon rounds." Emily felt relieved to be done with this conversation. Paul was strangely interesting. Beyond that, she wasn't sure, but having a drink and giving him a kiss? That sounded more like something Amy would do. *Yes,* Emily decided, *perhaps I'll introduce them. Paul is a decent sort of guy, and Amy would be better off with a guy like him*. Even as she thought this, Emily knew it would never happen.

Independence Day

Doc

Harmony, 1992

Some might be surprised that Doc could remember this story because he was heavily inebriated, but nobody ever knew that he remembered it because it wasn't a story he enjoyed telling. It was the worst Fourth of July ever, when it should have been the best; it was a day he'd waited twenty-four long years for—ever since he'd had a revelation, a vision, back in '52. He secretly thought it might be the day the world would end, and in a way, at least for him, it was.

Harmony, July 4, 1976

The bicentennial on the Fourth of July in Harmony was bigger than the one in Kearney. Maybe even bigger than the ones in Lincoln and Omaha, some people said. Those Harmony folks whose everyday work wasn't enough to keep them super busy—and who found themselves drawn to volunteer to organize the local festivities—were determined that this bicentennial Independence Day celebration would not be equaled for another hundred years.

Every renovated tractor and refurbished antique fire truck in three counties was there for the parade, and anyone who owned cart-pulling miniature ponies or a few llamas would not have considered staying away. Political candidates—from those running for county assessor all the way up to those running for US Senate—were packed in convertibles, signs soliciting votes decorating the doors. The pork queen, beef queen (the reigning beef queen had also won the shot put at the state track meet earlier that spring), and poultry queen each had a huge float pulled by a spotless new tractor just off the lot at the dealership. To be fair to all local businesses, the three queens were pulled by tractors from different dealers; the pairings were decided by lot. John Deere drew pork; Holland drew beef. Fortune smiled on Case International. The poultry queen was a top-ten finalist for Miss Nebraska; she was much admired by many a farm boy. They also had the best float by a long shot.

Doc drove a convertible for the Republican US Senate incumbent, a distant cousin. He could never remember how he was related to the senator, but nevertheless, the parade was his proudest moment of the year. Doc drove down Main Street muttering and grumbling at miniature ponies, Democrats, T-ball teams throwing out handfuls of Bazooka Joe, and Shriners alike. None of them were nearly as important as his honored passenger, and yet they cluttered the streets with nasty bubble gum and horse droppings. He might not have driven faster had the senator's convertible been the only vehicle on the road, but it still seemed that everyone was in his way. The senator had important places to go, like the Annual Republican Fourth of July Hog Roast Fundraiser; therefore, so did Doc. The best part of July Fourth, of course, was the barbecue. Anything that stood in his way, even for a moment, was a personal insult.

When Gerald found Doc at the senator's barbecue it was before dusk, but Doc was half-gone. He couldn't count how many sheets he was to the wind anymore. He had a Coors in either hand and a third one bulging in his shirt pocket with a soda straw sticking out of it, grazing his stubbly chin.

"Uncle Doc, you gotta come with me. Something's wrong," Gerald spoke softly. He had to repeat himself when a deafening round of firecrackers interrupted him. ***"Something's wrong,"*** Gerald said louder. As plastered as he was, Doc could see the seriousness on

Gerald's face. Reluctantly he followed his nephew to the Ford pickup parked out front, sipping out of his straw for comfort.

"What's the matter, son?"

"Get in."

"There's a boy in the truck," Doc observed.

"Yep. Randall, scoot over so Uncle Doc can get in."

The toddler obeyed. Doc got in, and little Randall said, "Eeeeh, Wahs p'up, Doc?" Even though he would eventually stop identifying himself as Bugs Bunny, Randall would always think of his great-uncle Doc as Elmer Fudd.

Doc grunted as he reached for his seatbelt, then let it drop. It would crush the beer can in his shirt pocket if he fastened it. "Howdy, Randall. What's up? That's what I wanna know."

"Caroline called and told me to get you and bring you out to the house," Gerald said slowly.

"Caroline? She hates my guts!" Doc rolled his tongue around inside his mouth, trying to get a taste for what was going on, but all he got was the flavor of beer. Why would his daughter-in-law summon him, especially on a day she ought to know he'd be drinking?

"Maybe so. She wouldn't say what the trouble is, but I reckon something's wrong with Arnie ..." Gerald trailed off. He was worried. Doc's son—Gerald's cousin—Arnie had always been Gerald's best friend.

Doc shook his head, trying to sober up quickly. His son must be in some kind of bad trouble if his daughter-in-law would ask Gerald to come for him. Doc was sober enough to grasp this.

Doc attempted to put one of his beers down on the seat, forgetting that Randall was sitting there. He spilled a little, which made him cuss. "Why'd you bring your boy, anyhow?"

"Can't leave him at home. He screams bloody murder if I get in the truck without him. Tells his mom he wants to go farming with 'Gerald.' It's pretty funny, actually. My boy calls me Gerald instead of Dad, and calls his mother 'Margie.' His older brother never did that."

"We ain't goin' farmin', kid," Doc told Randall, who only grunted, his face flushed and his body straining with internal effort. The child was filling his diaper, Doc realized, and he rolled down his window, gagging.

At Arnie and Caroline's farm, Gerald changed Randall's diaper on the hood of the pickup truck while Doc went to the pump in the yard and drenched his own head in an attempt to sober up. Finally they went inside where Caroline was sitting tight-lipped at the dining room table, peeling potatoes mechanically. It looked to Gerald as if she was getting ready to sell mashed potatoes at the county fair; she had peeled nearly an entire ten-pound bag. Doc stumbled in behind Gerald, and Randall stayed in the yard chasing the cat, hoping to pull her tail.

"What's the matter," Doc said. "What do you want?"

"Arnie's gone," Caroline said stoically. "He left this morning."

"He was in the parade, you know," Gerald said softly.

"Yes," she agreed, "he was in the parade, drove his tractor, drove it straight home, got in his pickup, and left again."

"He's probably just having a few extra pops with the boys," Doc slurred. "Relax."

Caroline sat a moment longer. "You won't believe me? Why don't I just show you?" She got up and went to the desk in the corner of the kitchen, overflowing with bills and all sorts of papers. "See for yourself. Read this. He left it on the tractor. He's gone." She handed a note to Gerald, who read it out loud.

Gerald, I can't take this buffalo shit no more. Caroline don't need me, she's been raising the kids by herself anyway. Don't anybody wait up nights, I ain't coming back. Let the land lie fallow and collect the money from Uncle Sam if you don't want to farm it all.

There was no signature, but Gerald knew Arnold's handwriting.

Gerald looked out into the yard. Randall was laughing hysterically as Caroline's boy, AJ, took a stick and began knocking green apples off the apple tree, hard and mechanically. But AJ wasn't doing it to be funny. AJ was old enough. He knew his daddy was gone, and he was angry. Gerald could tell all the way from the kitchen window. Caroline's little girl was sitting in the sandbox, crying. She had been crying for a long time, Gerald knew, because there were no tears, only fatigued wails now and then, whenever she hoped someone might notice.

"Shit," Doc said. "Shit, Caroline, that no-good—"

"He'll come back in a few days," Gerald said. Doc and Caroline looked at him. This was no time to be diplomatic. Things were exactly as they seemed. "No. He's not coming back at all," Gerald stated flatly, then sat down. "Sorry, Carrie. This is bad. Damn. Real bad."

"It's not your fault I married a lousy bum," she replied. Caroline stood up. "You own this farm together," she reminded Doc, "but Arnie did all the work. He also owes some people. The bills are on the desk, mostly. If you want to keep your farm, figure out how to pay these bills. Your farm is no longer any of my concern." She slapped her hands together sideways as if dusting them off.

"What are *you* going to do?" Doc asked, still trying to take everything in.

"I'm packing clothes and moving into Kearney. I'll get a job there somehow," she went on, "and, Gerald, thanks. I know you would help—and Margie too—but I'm not going to put that on you. I've thought it out, and it wouldn't be right—you with Caleb and Randall already and probably more kids on the way someday. Better for me to try and manage on my own."

Gerald tried to protest, but she wouldn't hear it. "Why did you call us out here then," he finally asked, "if you won't let us help?"

"I never learned much about farming," she said, "but that wheat doesn't stop growing when you walk away from it. You boys will have to take care of that part. I figured I oughtta let you know." She said the last phrase looking at Gerald. Doc would have to pay the bills, but Gerald would end up bringing in the harvest, she knew, and the fall was going to be a lot more work than he had planned.

It was sinking in for Gerald. He began to shake his head. "Arnie can't *do* this," he said.

"He's got his rights," Doc muttered. "He's got his rights. Statue of Liberty, that damn-fool kid."

Doc was sufficiently sobered up by the evening to help the volunteer firemen set off fireworks over Municipal Park. The county pops orchestra, led by the high school's enthusiastic marching band director, played woeful renditions in the band shell. Doc's head felt like it was going to explode.

Doing a Bad Job

Melissa and Randall

Randall was happiest in a pickup truck running an errand. He'd been driving tractors home from the fields since he was eleven, started taking to the back roads in a truck at thirteen, and gone into town for tractor parts well before he had his driver's license—a fact that Gerald easily hid from his wife, Margie, because it worked better to have Caleb's help at the farm. Margie didn't realize Randall was driving so much, at least for a while, until Margie's brother Ryan, who was *the* police force in Harmony, mentioned to her at a family dinner that he wondered if he'd seen her boy driving in town the other day. He knew Randall didn't have a license, and the boy he saw was unmistakably Margie's younger kid, but Ryan had looked the other way. "I reckon maybe I saw wrong—maybe it was Caleb," he said. He knew that if it really *was* Randall, Margie would put a stop to it. And she did, for the most part.

Now fully legal, Randall drove constantly. With gas at ninety-seven cents a gallon, sometimes he and Melissa would just get in on a Sunday afternoon and drive straight down US 183 to Kansas and back, just to be able to say they took a trip together out of state over the weekend—for shock value—at school. They talked and listened to country music. They got hamburgers in Woodruff, Kansas, and sometimes picked up something for Gerald or Margie, or Melissa's folks, along the way. They drove home at dusk, and Melissa would doze off while Randall roared along. He would turn off the radio and watch the sun set out to his left.

One Wednesday evening, just a few nights after graduation, Randall was coming home with a couple of gallons of milk, a few other groceries, and a sharpened blade for the Bush-Whacker. The CB crackled. "This is Kitchen," came Margie's voice, "calling Jolly Green Giant. Got your ears on?"

"Roger," Randall said.

"Melissa called. Wonders if you have time to swing by her place. It sounded like something important. Gerald can wait a little while for the mower blades, but don't let that milk go sour while you're smoochin' your gal. Over."

"Ten-four," Randall replied.

Randall didn't need much convincing to go see Melissa, and he pushed his foot down on the gas. *Probably some question about what color flowers should she put on the table by the book where people sign their names that you never look at again after you're married.* A lot of this wedding stuff was pretty silly, and it amazed him how much effort a girl could put into it. His tires threw up gravel and dust as he took the back way to Melissa's from town.

Melissa was sitting on the couch inside the front door, with tears running down her cheeks. In between sobs, she was choking out something about how *bad* it was. Randall couldn't quite make it out. He was never quite sure what to do with her when she was crying. Should he hold her close, or would she notice when he got aroused and then be irritated at his maleness? Or should he pat her hand? That's what grandmas do. Finally, not knowing what to do with his hands, he just found a tissue and handed it to her. That seemed to do the trick; she blew her nose and settled down.

"What is it, Melissa? Did I do something wrong?" he asked for the fourth time, and she shook her head no again.

"It's Amy," she began. "She started this new job."

"Well, good for her. That doesn't seem so bad," he said. "If she works hard, she'll make it." Randall had never seen Amy work at anything, but graduating high school had different effects on different people. Maybe Amy had suddenly discovered how to work.

"It's bad, Randall," she explained. "Because it's a *bad* job."

"Doesn't pay good? Well, maybe she can work her way up, right?"

"No, it's bad because what she's *doing* is bad." Melissa began sobbing again, suddenly.

Randall sat down and waited for her to stop crying. *I don't know too many jobs around here that are bad just to do them,* he thought, puzzled.

"Is she dealing marijuana?"

"She's working at that place by the interstate, west of Kearney. She's a live girl," Melissa said.

"What do you mean? Alive, not dead? What's her job? Talk sense, Melissa."

"You know—the signs that say Gunner's Live Girls. She's an … exotic dancer," Melissa whispered at last, then slumped over on the couch. Now *she* was blushing. Melissa exhaled slowly.

"Really? Amy is?" Randall didn't know anybody who had ever done that. In fact, now that he thought about it, it was hard to imagine that anyone who lived in Nebraska *could* do that. Everyone would know about it in a few hours. But the signs off the interstate had been there for years, so somebody must be working there. He had always wondered what live girls looked like, and now he knew. They looked like Amy. "Are you sure? How do you know?" Randall pressed.

"She told me herself. I was at the mall in Kearney this morning looking for something for the wedding—I can't even remember what—and I saw her, and she was picking out some really expensive jeans, and lots of other things, and I kind of hinted that all those clothes would cost a lot of money, and she paid with cash. She had a lot more than what she was spending—I peeked in her purse—and I said, 'Where did you get all that?' and she said, 'Work.' I said, 'You got a job?' and Amy said, 'Yeah. Come on, I'll buy you an ice cream and tell you about it.' She actually seemed *proud* of it."

"Huh," said Randall, shaking his head. "Amy dances naked for money. Imagine that."

"You better *not,*" Melissa said, and smacked him. She laughed in spite of herself.

"I'd *rather* not. Does Emily know?"

"Not until you call her."

"Me? No way. I'm not calling Emily," Randall replied, folding his arms.

"I'm just messing with you," Melissa said. "Amy actually asked *me* to tell her. She said, 'Call Emily, and tell her she can make some real money instead of wiping nasty, old butts at the nursing home.' I'm calling her now. Can you imagine what Emily will … never mind." She went to the phone and began to dial. "Thanks for coming over, Randall. You're so sweet."

"OK, well, I gotta get back to the farm," and Randall excused himself, unsure of how he'd been helpful. The situation was definitely defused, though. And he did it all before the milk went sour. He hopped back in the pickup, urged it back to life, and headed north toward the farmhouse thinking about women.

The thing about girls is that you love them and you can't really stand them either. They talk so much, and they cry so much, and then they sort of look at you a certain way and make you want to melt into a puddle. And then they touch your hand, and your beanpole salutes, and you have trouble thinking about anything else but getting to see them naked, and I can see why these guys are paying to see Amy naked, not because Amy is so amazingly beautiful in particular—in fact, she's sort of regular, with kind of a too-big butt and too-little boobs and a few teeth crooked. Nobody would ever mistake her for a beauty queen, but guys would pay to see her get naked just because she is a girl. *These guys drive their trucks, and they run from Iowa to California or New York to Colorado; and all they see is that lonely highway. It's the idea of seeing a girl naked, not so much the idea of seeing* Amy. *In fact, I wouldn't want to see that at all. It would be embarrassing, to say the least, if I saw Amy without her shirt on—actually kind of gross. She's almost like a sister to me anyway.*

Gerald was waiting patiently. "It's going to be a long summer," he said.

"Why, Gerald?" Randall asked.

"'Cause you're getting married. Every time I need a part, I gotta wait while you go to town, get the part, but then you stop by Melissa's, talk a while about lacy dresses and flowers and whatnot, smooch a bit, and finally get on back." His dad was laughing at him, Randall realized, but he also knew it wasn't in a mean way.

"It's going to be a long summer," Gerald said again.

"Yeah, well, no smooches this time."

"Did she call it off?" Gerald joked with a straight face.

"No. It's just she's all worried about Amy. She's a dancer, see."

"Like the waltz?" Gerald was confused.

"Naked. Nude. Or at least, topless. I'm not sure. In that place down by the interstate."

"Oh." Gerald took the mower blade and looked at it with satisfaction. Randall hoisted the mower into place so Gerald could reach the bolts.

"You don't seem surprised."

"Should I be?" Gerald asked.

Randall thought about that while they secured the blade.

"I guess if you think about it, nobody should be surprised, considering this is Amy we're talking about," Randall finally said.

"Nope," said Gerald. "I oughtta go tan her hide, but she's a big girl now, and she's gonna make her own decisions."

"Do you remember when my cousin Arnie left?" Gerald asked his son at dinner.

"No," Randall admitted. He knew a little of the story, but Cousin Arnie was not a regular topic of discussion at the Martin dinner table.

"Ah, he was little," said Margie, serving up a stew of roast beef, potatoes and carrots.

"Well, Arnie left one day, and everybody who thought they knew him was surprised," Gerald shrugged.

"He ended up fishing salmon in Alaska—or was it crabs?" Margie explained. "Then he met a woman from Florida, and they started living together, and eventually Caroline divorced him, and he married this Florida woman. She sends a card every Christmas—you've seen 'em; it's like she thinks she's a member of the family. It's very odd. They have two kids together."

"You weren't surprised when he left?" Randall said.

"Nope," said Gerald. "Disappointed? Yes. Angry. Downright pissed off, even. But not surprised. You could tell something was bothering him, if you were paying attention. But nobody was paying attention."

"Do you think he'll ever come back?"

"People who aren't happy with life in Harmony, they should get out early. Like your pal Ben. Some reason, I could tell he didn't feel like he fit in. The ones who are smart enough to go, they never come back," Gerald replied.

"What your father is trying to say," Margie went on, "is we want you to know you don't have to farm all your life if you don't want to. If you need some adventure, better to get it over with before you leave Melissa with a couple kids and a bunch of debt."

"I wouldn't do that, Mother!" Randall said. As levelheaded as he was, he was pretty close to getting mad.

"Don't get us wrong, son. We'd be surprised if you did," said Gerald, "but you're the one who needs to be sure. You gotta pay attention to yourself. Know your gut, and go with that."

"I'm sure. I love it here in Harmony, and I love Melissa. I got no need to go fishin' to try to find something better. It doesn't get any better than this," Randall said, and he smiled as Margie served a fresh strawberry pie.

No Place Like Nebraska

Emily

Shortly after everyone returned from the dining room, Emily's job was to help people into bed for afternoon naps. She worked her way down the hall, coming at last to Owen and Doc's room where they were sitting quietly. Owen was puttering with a few mementos in his drawer while Doc was watching Jerry Springer. A trashy redneck couple were screaming at each other over parental rights. The woman looked like she lived on Coca-Cola and potato chips, and the man looked like his diet was heroin and his beverage of choice was tattoo ink. Doc was glued to the screen, laughing at the brawl. Kate was still explaining the rhythm of the home, and Emily wasn't really paying attention.

"... so once you have these two settled for the afternoon, you get a fifteen-minute break if you're done early enough, and then you have to chart before you punch out. I'm going out for a smoke," Kate was saying.

"I don't smoke—" Emily turned around, but Kate was already gone, leaving her to deal with her last two residents. Doc moved away from his twelve-inch, black-and-white TV set, and cornered Emily near the bathroom door.

"You shouldn't smoke, you know. Dr. Hostetler says it'll give you 'colon.' What a goddam quack!" Doc was feeling belligerent.

It's the TV show, Emily thought. *It gets him riled up. Besides, he's predisposed to orneriness.* "Well, I don't know about your colon, but it can give you lung cancer and kill you."

Doc became more perturbed and began waving his cane. "I'll smoke if I want to! I got my rights! Statue of Liberty! Smoking never killed me! They won't let me smoke anymore. But I got some chaw nobody knows about." Yelling tired him quickly, and his arm dropped. Emily had been afraid for a moment that he would strike her with the cane—more by accident than on purpose—but she relaxed a little.

"Well, I don't know about that; it's all down your shirt. You dribble ..." she sighed. It seemed like she ought to help him change his shirt, but her shift was almost over, and she doubted he would cooperate.

"So what if it is? Can't a guy have tobacco? We used to throw coffee grounds and spit out our chaw in the sty and the hogs'd eat it. Good enough for a pig, it's good enough for a man, I always say. Them hogs never got 'colon'!"

Emily sighed again, and got out a new shirt. To her surprise, he seemed not to notice that she was unbuttoning his flannel. "You had hogs?" she asked, trying to keep his mind busy.

"Now I suppose you'll say bacon'll give me 'colon' too. This country ain't *Iz*-lam. The Good Book gives us permission: Peter's revelation! We eat pigs 'n' seafood, and in the Depression we ate plenty of groundhogs—see there, them are hogs too—but we never made no bacon out of them, and we even ate 'possum, but you gotta cook it longer; it's gamy. This is America. Why, I preached out to the Baptist church for years about This Is America, and We Got Our Rights, and if I'd near as suggested you don't eat pork I'da been kicked outta there before you could spit across the South Loup in a drought. Course most Baptists don't smoke, or drink, but they got a right to anyways if they wanted to. This is Nebraska! United States! Remember the Alamo!" Doc was on a roll.

"But ... the Alamo was in Texas!" Emily fastened the last button.

"I know that," he said, waving his hand dismissively. "You got any chaw? I'm almost out."

"No."

"Why don't you bring me a beer?" Doc lolled his tongue out of his mouth to show how thirsty he was. He really looked like a basset hound just then, she noticed, his lower eyelids drooping and red.

"I'm the nurse's aide, not a waitress. I can't bring you beer; they'd fire me," she said with a smile and waved her hand, mimicking him.

Doc ignored her. "You got a nice ass; you could make good tips at that place down by the interstate," he observed.

"Ugh! That strip club? My friend Amy works there. She used to be my friend, but I never see her anymore. She's been a … she's been, um, well, I haven't talked to her much for a year or so. No way. I'm not …" She wasn't quite sure how to tell this dirty, old man her friend was a slut, especially since Emily presumed Doc and Amy were related somehow, but *slut* was the only word she could think of at the moment, so she let her sentence end midstream. To her relief, he didn't pursue the matter.

Doc looked at her slyly out of the corner of his eye. "Well, I'll allow you're a good girl. But what are you doing in this hellhole? Why don't you get married and have some babies?"

"I just got out of high school and needed a job, so here I am. And one other thing: People say I'm nuts, but I'm still trying to find the gold down in the river."

"Gold?!" Doc yelled.

"Well, I'm still hoping—" Emily ventured, but Doc cut her off.

"Shit, young lady," said Doc, whereupon he unleashed a string of profanity and vulgarity that would make your hair stand on end and keep you awake all night, like strong coffee. He mixed vulgar metaphors, and he blasphemed everything from the Catholic Church to the Washington Monument. He called for copulation between the most disparate beings and objects. He questioned the sanity of a variety of town officials and the ethnic purity of religious individuals from his entire eighty-some years in Harmony. He cursed his ancestry, particularly the "Injun" side because of their "witchcraft." The upshot was that he knew the gold was right under everybody's nose—his own especially—and try as they like, it was hidden by some spell. "That gold …" he finally wheezed, "that gold is haunted. Don't you worry yer pretty little head about it; you'll never find it. I've looked everywhere. It's gone. Damn, it's gone."

When he was finally quiet, catching his breath and tucking some chaw in his cheek, Emily wondered if she should be offended, but then she remembered that Kate had said the residents were ninety-nine percent harmless, so she replied, "I don't think I would've said it the way you did, but I hate to admit you're probably right. Maybe I should just give up. I'm not sure it's all that important anyway." She paused and let out a long sigh.

As Doc was looking for a cup to spit in, Emily suddenly looked at him and said, "You were a doctor. What do you think about me going to UN Kearney this fall and starting a pre-med program? And maybe I'll learn stuff about being a doctor—or a nurse—around here this summer …"

"You won't learn anything if you hang around with Dr. Hostetler, except that he's a quack," Doc said with a growl. He went on. "And don't do the night shift! Those idiots! I put my light on at night, but they don't come. I timed 'em one time, and it took 'em forty minutes to see what I needed. I coulda died. Now I don't even use it. I just go talk to Alice, but she won't get off her lazy ass. But that Dr. Hostetler takes the cake. No bacon? Doctors and nurses. Huh." Doc turned to get into bed.

"Well, I think bacon *is* bad for your—" Emily stopped. There was no use arguing with Doc.

He turned around again and raised his voice a notch. "I don't care. 'Colon.' Huh! We ain't *Moos*lems. I got my rights!"

"Statue of Liberty?" Emily added, trying to make peace.

Doc was surprised. "Yes! Statue of Liberty! I believe … you're on to something. I'm liking you more and more, young lady."

At that, he went back and sat down to watch Jerry Springer and the "mobile home park residents," as Emily's mother would have too delicately put it. Emily slumped in the empty chair by Owen's bed. "Is that Mademoiselle Edith?" Owen's nearly blind eyes searched the space in front of him.

"Yes, Owen, it's Emily," she smiled despite her fatigue.

"Are you Nurse Edith? Or the one with the lax morals?"

"Emily. My name is Emily. I'm morally upright, sir, although I'm not a nurse, but … I might be someday. I'm thinking about starting at the University of Nebraska this fall. Or maybe—"

Owen startled her when he began singing, suddenly and very loudly:

"There is no place like Nebraska,
Good ol' Nebraska U.
Where the girls are the fairest,
The boys are the squarest,
That ever the world knew ...
So take me back to Nebraska,
Good ol' Nebraska U.
Where the girls are the fairest,
The boys are the squarest,
That ever the world kne-e-e-e-e-ew."

"That was lovely! Did you go to Nebraska?" She poured him a glass of water and put it in his hand.

"Thank you. I went to Johns Hopkins and Harvard. But I taught geology at Nebraska. Can I have a graham cracker?" Owen sat back in his wheelchair, which he normally got around in by walking it along with his feet, and held out an expectant palm.

"What?" Had she heard him right?

"Can I have a graham cracker?" he repeated.

"Uh, sure. I don't see why not." She looked around, and he seemed to sense that she was lost.

"They're in the drawer, Nurse Edith." He gestured vaguely toward the bed stand.

"Oh!" It took her a moment to get the cracker out of the box. "Here you are," but as she turned to Owen she saw that he had fallen asleep. Suddenly, her mind was racing. *A professor of geology! Maybe he knows something about the South Loup.* Emily determined to look for her chance to ask Owen if he knew anything about it. She gently removed his cup of water, put the cracker in his open palm, and left. It was time to do her charting and head home for the day.

Brothers

Paul

Paul could go to work at Harmony Halcyon Home and just about turn it on autopilot and cruise through the day. At the end of those days he couldn't tell you what happened. He cleaned people, fed people, helped them use the "facilities." He let his mind wander other places as he pushed chairs on wheels down long, musty hallways. While we all go through days like this, certain other days are etched in memory like the ruts of a wagon train. Anytime your mind travels near them, it slips down into the old ruts and follows the track traveled so many times before. You may not want to relive it, or go where it's going, but the grooves lock your wheels in.

Harmony, September 30, 1978

Back when Paul was a kid, he and his younger brother, Tony, had a Saturday routine that was both simple and elegant. This particular Saturday, when Paul was twelve, somehow stuck in Paul's mind; he played it over and over. Whenever he caught himself talking to himself about it, he had to laugh, because September 30, 1978, was also the day the famous Edgar Bergen died, and Charlie McCarthy with him.

They got on their bikes and went to the Valley Grocery.

"I'm getting a *Spiderman* comic," Tony bragged.

"I'm getting the new *Batman*," Paul told Tony as they rolled along, their allowance jingling in their pockets.

"I'm getting baseball cards—George Brett, oh please, oh please," Tony said.

"I'm getting *football* cards—Lyle Alzado, oh please, oh please," Paul replied.

"Aw man, yeah," Tony grinned. Tony was a good brother. He knew when he'd been one-upped; he didn't fight it.

"Watch this," Tony said, accelerating as they approached a stop sign. He hit the brakes hard at the last second and spun sideways, leaving a thin, gray, rubber streak on the sidewalk.

"Watch this," Paul countered, and ramped his bike over the curb, catching air.

"Wow," said Tony. Paul popped a wheelie. Tony let out a low whistle. "Awesome!" he cheered.

They got their comics and cards. The pink gum, which had been packaged in the wax-paper Topps packs for several months, was chalky and brittle, and Tony wouldn't chew it. Paul had a huge wad in his cheek. He traded his George Brett to Tony for three Broncos, but nobody got Lyle Alzado. They put their cards in their hip pockets, instantly dog-earing the corners. They knew whose cards were whose at home because Tony always drew a big *T* with a yellow marker on his. Today, Tony was thrilled to have a brand-new George Brett card. As they rode along, Tony chattered about how he hoped the Royals would be able to beat the Yankees next week in the American League Championship Series. "You watch, Paul; George Brett is going to be awesome!"

Next, they sailed on their bikes to the empty lot behind the Farmer's Supply to look for treasures among the weeds.

"Paul, I found a piece of blue glass!"

Tony called out his finds from time to time. Paul had found a magazine a few weeks back that he kept hidden and dry in an old tire, and once Tony was occupied looking for glass, he would sneak it out and look at the nearly naked women in dazed awe. "That's great, Tony," he called back to his brother.

They proceeded to the library, carefully skirting several blocks to avoid Wade Wright's house.

"If we see Wade, do *not* stop to talk, no matter what he says to you," Paul cautioned.

"Why is he so mean?" Tony wondered.

"Mom said it's because he's sad."

"Sad isn't the same as mean, though," Tony puzzled. "Why is he sad *and* mean?"

"His dad died."

Tony thought about this for several blocks. "Our dad died too," he finally remarked, "and sometimes I'm really sad, but we're not mean, are we Paul?"

"Our dad had an accident, but Wade's dad shot himself with a gun—on purpose," Paul explained weakly.

"Why would he do that?" Tony was really confused. He was only eight.

"I don't know," said Paul. *Our dad really didn't* mean *to die. Maybe that's the difference. Wade is* mean *because his dad* meant *to die.*

This didn't seem quite right, so he decided not to explain it to Tony.

At the library, Tony looked at kids' books while Paul went to the periodicals. From the televised news, he already knew what he would find. The paper was bursting at the seams with details about Pope John Paul I—his life and the details surrounding his upcoming funeral. Paul found the official obituary and began to copy it into his notebook. It was almost too much for a boy to handle—being named after his father *and* the pope, both of them dying in the same year. His hands trembled, and he bit his lip. He flipped through the notebook. January 9, 1978: his father's obituary. January 13, 1978: both Hubert Humphrey, the vice president, and Joseph McCarthy, the Yankees manager. January 25–27, 1978: seventy souls lost in the Great Blizzard, most of them in Ohio. On and on it went. He read the obituary for the pope once again in the paper, checking to make sure he'd copied everything word for word. It was his longest entry to date—September 28, 1978. Finally, Paul drifted to the magazines and picked up the new *National Geographic,* but there was nothing about Morocco in it this time.

"Looking for some pictures of African girls with their shirts off?"

Paul looked up. It was Evil Wade. He was even wearing his trademarked Evil Grin and laughing in a hissing way to keep the librarian from hearing.

"No," said Paul sullenly.

"What else would you be looking for in there?"

"Nothing." Paul decided not to explain his interest in Morocco. "I'm just waiting for my brother to pick a book."

"You're a liar," Wade said, "and a jerk-off."

"No I'm not," Paul said, denying the first half of the accusation—the only part he understood.

"As soon as you get outside, I'm going to kick your butt," Wade threatened.

"I'll stay here all night," Paul retorted.

"I'll be here when they open in the morning," Wade insisted. "I'll beat up you and your little brother too."

"Tony's pretty tough for an eight-year-old," Paul lied.

"Ha. Then I'll shoot you."

Paul gulped, and his bubble gum went halfway down his throat and lodged there uncomfortably. *Wade would do it,* he thought. "Look," Paul temporized, "you can do whatever you want to me, but leave Tony alone."

"I'll do whatever I want to *both* of you," Wade said. He had made his point, and he knew he was in charge. "Is that the new *Batman*?"

"Yeah," Paul admitted.

"Let me see it," Wade demanded.

"No," said Paul. Wade rolled his fingers slowly into a fist. "No!" Paul said, louder.

The librarian came over. "We keep our voices down in the library," she said, but before Paul had a chance to explain, she went back to her work. Paul felt his face flush.

"That was your fault," he hissed at Wade. "You're going to get me kicked out of here. My mom will be mad then! She'll … get you."

"I'll shoot your mom," Wade said. "I'll shoot her tits off." He grinned maniacally.

Paul wanted to grab Wade's throat and strangle him right then. But Wade was much bigger and far too strong. Paul wanted to cry with frustration and anger. Crying was a bad idea; it would only make matters worse for the future. He wanted to be Batman—or, better yet, Superman. *POW,* he thought. *THUD. SLUG! SMA-A-ACK!* Biting his lips, he did nothing.

"Just go away," he said, struggling in vain to keep the whimper out of his voice. "Leave me alone."

"No," said Wade calmly, "let me see *Batman*."

"If you steal it, I'm telling." Paul reluctantly handed over the magazine. *How am I going to get away from here?* Paul wondered. Tony came around the corner. He was looking at a book and didn't notice Wade.

"Paul, I found this book about George Brett," he said, "and look, I can use my George Brett baseball card as a bookmark!"

"Let me see that," Wade said, dropping the *Batman* comic.

Tony was so astonished to see Wade that he just handed the book over. The George Brett baseball card was sticking out the top. Wade opened the book and casually put the card in his back pocket. He made a show of looking at the book for a few moments, then dropped it next to the *Batman* comic. Then, just as casually as could be, Wade walked out of the library.

Tony began to cry. He worked it up into a solid wail. The librarian came over to see what was wrong, and Paul tried to explain, but Tony was bawling so hard, everything was just a mess. The librarian was flustered. She asked Paul to help calm Tony down. Tony's anguish flooded the library. Paul was nearly in tears himself. He looked out the window. Wade was gone. Paul gave the three Bronco cards he'd traded for back to Tony. Then he said, "You can have my *Batman* comic too. Come on, Tony, let's go home." Tony cried all the way back to the house, and the rest of their Saturday routine was scrapped—which is to say, they neglected their standard search for genuine arrowheads and huge nuggets of gold in the South Loup riverbed.

That night, as Paul lay in his bed, he experienced waves of hatred mixed with guilty relief. Ultimately he was relieved that Wade had not asked about his special notebook, but he decided he ought to hate Wade more just for what he did to Tony. He made a solemn vow. *To my dad and God and Pope John Paul, R.I.P., and Jesus and Mary and Joseph and all the saints: As God is my witness, someday I will* get *Wade Wright—before I go to Morocco. I swear it on my mother's grave. Cross my heart and hope to die.* He left out the stick-a-needle-in-your-eye part. It seemed superfluous—and not nearly painful enough.

Staying for Good

Arnold

Anchorage, Alaska, 1979

Arnold was what they call a drifter out West for a long time after he left Harmony, but eventually, one morning, he woke up in the back of his pickup truck to find himself penniless in Anchorage. It was the kind of place where you could get a job and still feel like a drifter. So he found a job fishing—very seasonal, very challenging, but plenty lucrative. Eventually he found an apartment.

Arnold couldn't quite remember how it happened that Judy had moved in, or when they had even met. It must have been sometime last year, he figured, not long after he arrived in Alaska. They had mutual friends, or at least acquaintances. They had met casually several times at a variety of social events, and Judy was friendly enough toward him—at least as friendly as a guy like Arnold could hope for. He wasn't particularly good-looking or bright. He didn't have a lot of money. He wasn't sure what brought them together; rather, you might say, he wasn't even sure they *were* together. Sometimes, when nobody else they knew was available to go out, they'd have dinner together, and then he'd drive her home in silence, listening together to whatever was on the radio. She didn't seem to have to talk all the time, and he liked that.

Then one day her lease was up. She showed up at his apartment with her aromatherapy kit, acupuncture needles, an economy-sized box of tampons, a small suitcase of clothes, a toothbrush and comb, an ergonomic pillow, and a goose-down sleeping bag, which she rolled out on the couch. Everything sat in a heap on the floor, and Arnold looked it over. He looked Judy over too. She moved the way he imagined a palm tree would move—never breaking, gracefully bending to accept whatever the wind threw at her. She was a good eight inches taller than he was and very long-legged; when they stood facing each other his eyes looked directly ahead and fell on the place where her delicate collarbones nearly touched above her sternum, a soft depression between them he wanted to touch.

"I'm giving my rent money this month to hurricane victims in the Dominican Republic" was all she said to explain her presence in his house. She looked in the fridge, made no comment or facial expression, and left again without a word, her pile of belongings still on the living room floor. She came back a half-hour later with a bag from the health food market and proceeded to cook something incredibly flavorful, which turned out to be made of soybean curds. It also had cumin and garlic, plus a bunch of things he'd never heard of before.

"Did you like it?" she wondered.

"It was good. Different, but really good. Is that what they call health food then?"

She laughed. "It's not healthy for your wallet, but it'll cure what ails you. Tomorrow I'm making asparagus bisque."

The bisque was much better than it sounded. She placed fresh, crumbled goat cheese on top of it, flown in from Switzerland at great expense. As it turned out, she had only to cook for Arnold for a week before his constipation was gone. He went to the freezer and threw out a bunch of things.

"What happened to your frozen Salisbury steak dinners, hash browns … ?"

"It wasn't worth it," he said.

"Worth what?"

"Not bein' regular," he said.

Judy smiled back at him. With her last man, she would've nagged. This time around, letting him figure it out for himself had been almost too easy. She had expected it to take two years for him to see things her way.

She slept on the couch for a month, until Arnold went crab fishing. He more than half-expected her to be gone when he came back a few weeks later. A bit surprisingly, not only was she still there, but her ergonomic pillow was now on his bed, her sleeping bag was rolled up in his closet, and the smell of ginger, fresh bread, crushed black pepper, and garlic permeated the kitchen. She was serving eggplant.

"You know, when I came home from fishing," he told her, "I used to like to have a big steak. But this stuff is really good."

"I missed you too," she smiled, and brought out yogurt parfaits with sliced almonds, homemade granola, and wild blueberries. He nearly went to sleep at his plate, but made it to his bed before crashing in his clothes—and slumbered for fourteen hours.

When Arnold woke up, Judy was sitting in the bay window, looking out over the bay. She turned to face him, and he saw something different in her eyes.

"I'm still technically … married," he said as she pulled off her T-shirt.

"I suspected as much," she replied, shrugging, undoing her brassiere. "What are the kids' names?" She pointed to the photograph by his bed.

"AJ and Amy. They live in Nebraska with their mom—or maybe with my cousin and his wife."

"I guess we have something in common. I'm still technically married too, as far as I know. But by now my husband has probably overdosed one too many times in a back alley in Miami somewhere. I'm giving my rent money to UNICEF this month," she told him later as she lay toying with the curly hairs that crept like kudzu from his collarbones up to his neck. Arnold was feeling a little dizzy.

"That was intense," he said.

She put her fingers on his forehead. A warm, tingling sensation swept over him as though he were enveloped by an electric blanket. Her fingers found a tender place just below his pectoral muscle, a lymph node, and pressed hard.

"Ouch! That's sore!"

"I know," she said, "but trust me. You'll feel great tomorrow. Just concentrate on breathing in and out, deeply. In and out." She massaged a variety of pressure points on his work-fatigued shoulders and torso and then found some very sore spots around his knees and along his thighs.

Aroused again, he reached out to touch her without a word. She grinned and playfully warned, "If we do this often, I just might conceive."

"I thought you were a women's libber," he said, eyeing the unshaven hair on her legs. "Don't you take the pill?"

"It disturbs my electromagnetic meridians," she explained obliquely. "Besides, while you were gone I decided I *want* to have a baby."

"Are you staying for good then?" Arnold hoped she'd say yes, and realized how ironic it was for him to be asking this.

"I'm giving my rent money to the Red Cross next month," she smiled as she pulled him to herself, "and the month after that to the March of Dimes. And so on," she sighed as they joined together.

She came home one day a few months later and informed him that she was indeed carrying his child. He had not seen his other children in three years, and the news of a new one was joyful. But it reminded him of the painful briar patch he had left behind. She saw these things in his eyes.

"Why don't you just call them?" Judy asked softly.

She's perceptive, spiritually, Arnold thought. "I don't know," Arnold said. "Please don't ask me about it again." So she didn't.

Arnold spent a lot of time thinking about how she knew what he was feeling. He never told her; she just read it on his face. She learned when not to mention what she saw too. He hadn't really been around other people who could perceive things this way, and he found it strangely comforting. His own father, who called himself Doc, always claimed to be able to judge things in the spirit world. He even fancied himself a type of medicine man in the Sioux tradition, but Arnold—and pretty much everyone else—figured Doc's "spirituality" was the delusional result of a horrible illness some time ago.

Our Lady

Doc

Harmony, 1992

Doc had always hoped that one day he'd be a shaman or medicine man. He was fairly young and hoped that sometime he'd have a vision that would guide him for the rest of his life. Sometimes, when a man hopes for a vision hard enough, the universe conspires to give him his wish; or maybe it's just the moonshine talking. In any case, whatever it was he saw, or however it came about, there was never any moment afterward when he was ashamed to tell people what he'd seen. But the most likely explanation for his vision stemmed from an incident when he was sober.

1952

Doc lost his left thumb one day when feeding the hogs. They panicked or stampeded, smashing up against a steel gate, which he slammed against them just in time as they pressed against it in a crush, and his thumb was caught between the hinges somehow. It was wedged so tight it couldn't bleed, but it pinched a nerve and he passed out from the pain. When he came to, the thumb was gone, clean eaten off by a curious sow who smelled the blood and went a little crazy once she had a taste. If he'd been on the other side of the gate, sure as shootin', those pigs would've eaten him lock, stock, and barrel.

He wouldn't take the penicillin shot the doctor told him to take, and as a result went into a delirious fever in which he had two dreams. Later, even after the fever subsided, the dreams would recur.

In one of them the Statue of Liberty would appear to him. In the dream, Doc would be a little boy sailing into New York harbor on a ship full of people awed to silence. He would stand by his father, who never would say a word. Everyone else would fade away, and the Statue of Liberty would become flesh in his dream, and speak to him.

"Greetings, American. Welcome to our humble shores; rights that are ours are now called yours."

"Thank you," he always said in this dream. He also removed his cap.

"From now on, my child of liberty, know these rights, and always be free."

The statue would then pause, put down her torch, take her book out from under her arm, and produce a pair of reading spectacles. While she did this, Doc always found himself standing at attention, waiting patiently.

"First Right: You can say what you want to say, but don't cuss a lady.

"Second Right: It's better here than anywhere else, and you don't have to go there to find it out either. Trust me.

"Third Right: Eat up and drink up whatever you want—tomorrow you die.

"Fourth Right: Get a gun when you need one to shoot bad guys, which is anybody who doesn't agree with these rights.

"Fifth Right: Go to church, but it doesn't matter where. God knows, Christians protect this land from Democrats, Communists, and other heathens.

"Sixth Right: You don't have to work for nobody if you don't feel like it. You can get money from the government any time; they print it for people every day.

"Seventh Right: If your country needs you, by God, you better join up. Bring your gun—you're going to need it to keep the peace.

"Eighth Right: Send your kids to school as long as the teachers aren't morons.

"Ninth Right: Nobody can tell you what to think or what to do. Be a good Republican.

"Tenth Right: Get these rights tattooed on your arms so you'll never forget them.

"I am the Statue of Liberty, and I will protect you. Live a long and healthy life, my son."

It was a comforting dream in a strange sort of way—and powerfully real. With a few minor variations, the dream was always the same—and Doc always remembered it when he woke up. After he'd had the same dream three or four times, Doc figured he needed to take the lady at her word, so he went into Kearney and found a fellow who used to be in prison and got him to do a very nice tattoo of the Statue of Liberty on his right arm, but he decided it was overkill to have the guy do all ten of the rights, written out word for word. Instead, he just had the guy put *"I got my Rites"* on his left arm. It's not like he was going to forget the list.

As for the second dream, Doc couldn't remember what it was, but it was terrifying. All he could recall whenever he awoke was that it didn't have the Statue of Liberty in it. These dreams both ended up recurring often, even after he recovered from the infection in the stub of his thumb. The one he couldn't remember haunted him, and yet he was glad to have them both. He knew he was carrying an important spiritual message, which he attributed to being Sioux through his great-grandmother. His father had dreams, and his sister had dreams. Mother was German, and she didn't have dreams, but then, she didn't have any Sioux blood either.

"After all," he told Reverend Miller, the Mennonite minister, whom he loved to consult but whose advice he rarely followed, "not just anyone has a personal relationship with Our Lady."

"Mary?" Reverend Miller was puzzled by Catholicism in general, and Doc wasn't helping.

"No, dammit! The Statue of Liberty!"

'I Found the Gold'

Emily

Emily worked hard, and within two weeks she knew what to do. She could listen to morning report for a few minutes, catch up on the incessant gossip and bickering between Alice and Kate—and the occasional actual news—and then go do her work without prompting. Emily was an extremely valuable employee making six dollars and ninety-five cents an hour.

It appeared that Owen had slept in his clothes, so Emily helped him get out of bed, wash his face, change his clothes, and get into his chair. While she was doing these things, she chatted—loudly—with him. ***"Tell me again about the war, Owen."***

Owen sat up a little straighter and considered for a moment. "We were in the troop transport ship headed for Marseilles. The Strait of Gibraltar loomed dark against the northern sky. Many men would die …" Owen was searching for something in his pocket. "Jean brought me this rock from Nova Scotia," he said when he found what he was looking for. "It pleases me more than the Rock of Gibraltar. In a fortnight … my best friend … a shell exploded … all that was left was his *brains* in his helmet. Is the Metamucil coming?"

Kate entered the room in a hurry, as usual, and shoved a cup full of Metamucil into Owen's hand. ***"You're supposed to get your Metamucil at breakfast now, Owen!"*** Owen made a pleased face and began to swallow his fiber. "That ought to shut him up for a few minutes," Kate muttered into the air. Next, bustling over to Doc, she shook his shoulder, but Doc rolled away from her. Kate left him for a moment, getting clothes out of his closet.

"Have you ever been to Florida?" Owen asked.

"No," Emily said, intrigued.

"The frogs—I don't know how they do it," Owen continued. "Before midnight, they chirp in a high voice, 'Qui-nine, qui-nine!' Just like that. And at midnight, right at midnight—and I don't know how they know what time it is—they change over to a low voice, and they say, 'Double-de-dose, double-de-dose.'" He paused as she pulled his shirt over his head. She didn't get the joke. "Have you ever been to Hawai'*i*?" he continued, naming the fiftieth state with an accented third syllable.

"No, Owen, tell me about it." It was easier to work with people when they weren't preoccupied with how much it hurt to move. Emily already had learned to keep them talking.

"You should go to Hawai'*i*. It's beautiful! The beaches become mountains! Honolulu! Oahu! Maui! Kailua Kona! Kaunakakai!" The words came out as a poetry recital.

"I'd love to go there," she sighed.

"You must go." He was adamant.

"I've never been out of Nebraska. My family never had much money."

"You haven't lived if all you've seen is Nebraska. You can't know the beauty of Nebraska if you never leave. You must go to South Dakota, at least."

She almost laughed at this advice, but everything he ever said was delivered with such seriousness. She helped him into his wheelchair. "You sound like my sister. She's always telling me I need to get out of Nebraska. She travels all over."

"Go see the Black Hills; it's a place of mystery; there's gold in the Black Hills. What time is it? Is the Metamucil coming?"

Emily stopped in her tracks. "There *was* gold in Nebraska once, wasn't there?"

"Well, Colorado used to be part of the Nebraska Territory."

How Owen remembered this, Emily had no idea. "Yes, I know, but I mean here. In Harmony. There was gold here, did you know that?"

"No. We always knew that ... geologically, it's impossible ... but I did find gold ... yes, I found the gold. Did I find gold in Harmony? In the South Loup? Where was it? What time is it? Is the Metamucil coming?"

Emily sighed. Owen was no help after all. "Let's go down to the breakfast room. You might get some more Metamucil there, but Kate just gave you some," she said, gently removing the empty Dixie cup from his hand.

"Is it time for breakfast now? Good." He leaned back as she began to push his wheelchair down the hall toward the dining room. Owen began to ramble. "I had breakfast with Edith ... I gave her two hundred dollars ... she took the train to Denver ... she shouldn't have gone ... I'll have to get some Metamucil."

Kate had gotten a few more people out of bed in the meantime, but she was now back in Owen and Doc's room. ***"Doc, aren't you awake yet?"*** She was nearly yelling, as he was nearly deaf too.

"Leave me alone." Doc pulled the blanket over his head.

"You're usually up early. What's the matter?" Kate was worried. Although everyone in the Harmony Halcyon Home had some sort of ailment, mental or physical, anything out of the ordinary could mean a lot more work and stress for her staff.

"Just leave me alone!" Doc was angry.

"Are you sick? Do you want me to call Dr. Hostetler?"

"No! Oh God, no! Just go away."

Kate pulled his blanket off and tugged his arm. ***"It's my job to get you up in the morning, and you—"***

"Over my dead body! I got my rights! I know I still got 'em—this is America! Boston Tea Party! Mount Rushmore!" Doc was building up a good head of steam. With Owen now chewing away cheerfully in the dining room, Emily was back to lend a hand with Doc. She wondered if she could help somehow, but she kept quiet. Kate had been here so long, she knew what she was doing.

"Doc ..." Kate was a little bit at a loss too, it seemed.

"Leave me alone, I tell you! I'll sue! I can't sleep in peace, and I don't want to get up! I'm already dead! Scatter my ashes over the amber waves of grain! I got a will, and my will says, 'Let Me Die in Peace and Scatter My Ashes over the Amber Waves of Grain'! Statue of Liberty! The Grand Canyon!"

Kate shrugged and gave up the physical struggle, and decided to try a different approach. "Whatever," she said. "But you're going to get bedsores. If you don't get up right now, I'm calling Dr. Hostetler. Pelvic exam!"

"No! Ass-backwards. This country is ass-backwards. Since when does a doctor tell you when to get out of your bed?" Emily wondered if he wasn't right about that, but suddenly he sat up. "When I was a kid, if you felt bad, doctors said to stay in bed. I got my rights! Golden Gate Bridge! It's *my* goddam gold!"

"Statue of Liberty!" Kate yelled back at him in frustration.

"Doc," Emily ventured, "everyone's asking about you at breakfast. They want to know if you're sick. Mr. Melbourne asked if you're dead!"

"I'm coming, I'm coming," Doc grunted and finally hauled his carcass out of bed. "Gotta get my coffee and bacon. Besides, I can't wait to disappoint that old crackpot Melbourne. Crazy Pentecostal preacher's kid. Oh, I knew his daddy. Man played with rattlesnakes. He's got his rights, a-course, but crazy is as crazy does." Doc shook his head.

"I thought you were kind of a preacher yourself." Emily was confused.

In a stage whisper, Kate said, "He was a construction worker, preacher, and hog farmer—but always a drunk and never a doctor. Now he's just senile." Doc got his clothes on, took his cane, and headed for breakfast.

Abnormally Optimistic

Harmony Halcyon Home

The next day, a little before noon, Kate sat down in the empty break room and exhaled. She could feel an ache in each individual bone. *I work so hard,* she told herself, *a little extra break time won't hurt today*. Mrs. O'Toole wandered in.

"Hi, Mrs. O'Toole." Kate managed a smile.

"Is this the place?" Mrs. O'Toole was even more confused than usual today.

"Sure. Have a seat." Kate pulled a chair out.

"We haven't had anything to eat; the beans are gone," said Mrs. O'Toole, pacing.

"Is it the Great Depression again?" Kate asked kindly.

"Nobody in the county has anything left. Dust, dust, blowing away." The old woman's face was lined with concern.

"Here, I brought you a peanut-butter sandwich." Kate handed her a triangle of bread. Mrs. O'Toole crammed the whole thing in her mouth.

"Oh, the goob Lorb bleff 'ou. The boys—I shoob safe some for the boys, but I don't 'ow where they are." She swallowed the sandwich and began looking under chairs. "Andrew? Andrew?"

"Why don't you sit down, honey?" Kate got up, gently held Mrs. O'Toole by the shoulder, and found her locket around her neck. "Look, here's your locket," and she showed Mrs. O'Toole the photograph of "Mother." It was actually a photo of Mrs. O'Toole herself, as a young woman, but she didn't seem to recognize herself. Even so, looking at the locket seemed to help her find her center.

"Hello, Mother. Everything tastes like dust, blowing in the wind …"

She wandered out, reoriented, as Paul came in for his lunch. "Did you give her a sandwich?"

"Yeah," Kate admitted a little sheepishly.

"Where's Emily?" Paul asked.

"I don't know. She might be down talking to Owen. You like her, don't you?"

"Everyone likes her." Paul mimicked Kate, "You like her, don't you?"

"She's a sweet one," Kate replied. "I can't figure her out, though."

"That's because she's caring and optimistic," Paul suggested.

"And I'm not?" Kate was a little hurt.

"Um … I mean, she's *abnormally* optimistic," Paul quickly added.

"Huh. She's naïve, is what she is," Kate said, pouting.

"I think she knows more than you think."

"She told me she's never even kissed a boy," Kate said.

"So?" Paul wasn't going to admit he lived under a similar hex.

"She's almost nineteen, Paul, and she's never made out."

"And if she wasn't that way you'd probably say she's a slut."

Kate laughed. "You got me there. So do you like her?"

"Yeah. Of course." Paul wondered if she would ever stop.

"She's a fox, isn't she?"

Paul was getting fed up, but he had something to say. "Of course," he said. "Look at her; everyone can see she's gorgeous. Even Mrs. Murphy noticed that. She goes, 'Did you see the knockers on that girl?' I tried to ignore her, but she kept after me. 'She's got knockers; you aren't a man if you haven't noticed.' So I finally said, 'Yes, Ma'am, she *is* a lovely girl.' Mrs. M said, 'Her breasts, Paul!' I said, 'Yes, Ma'am, they're very … feminine.' She goes, 'You dirty boy.' I roll my eyes, and turn around to leave, and she pinches my butt!"

Kate chuckled. "She's a little young for you, don't you think?"

"Mrs. Murphy?" Paul played dumb.

"No, idiot, Emily!"

"You're the one trying to hook us up!" Paul was exasperated. What was Kate's problem? Half the time she was trying to get them to go out, and then she was saying Emily was too young. Maybe Kate was just being Kate, but Paul didn't think Emily was too young. The real problem was that Emily was on a different level—and he knew it.

"But she's hot, right?" Kate practically leered at him.

Paul's mouth started moving. "She's so hot, she's like bare feet on asphalt in hell." He shook his head, realizing what he was saying and who was hearing it. "But Kate, don't tell her I said so ..."

It couldn't have been a worse time for Emily to come in. "Hey, guys," she said, "whatcha talking about?"

"What's up?" said Paul, trying to give Kate a warning look.

"Paul says you're hot," Kate told her, grinning.

"Kate, you're so full of crap. Paul would never tell you that even if he thought so. You'd just blab it all over," Emily said smoothly. Paul thought, *Man, this girl is something else. Most women would have laughed in my face right there.*

"God, these hot flashes," Kate said. "I can't sleep these days 'cause of these hot flashes."

Paul was glad for the topic to change. "Geez," he grinned evilly. "That's gotta suck. The Wicked Witch of the West, in hell, melting into the asphalt. 'Toto, it's menopause! We're not in Kansas anymore!'"

"Paul, you can't take a joke." Now it was Kate's turn to be annoyed.

Emily didn't want to know what the joke was, so she picked up on what Kate had said. "I had trouble sleeping last night too," Emily commented, to Kate and Paul's surprise.

"Really?" Kate was suddenly interested. In disbelief she repeated herself. "Really? What keeps a girl like you up at night?"

"I was just thinking about ..."

Emily was thinking about what Owen said. He said it was impossible, geologically. But he also said he found it. *If only I can figure this out ... maybe then I could worry about what's next.* "I was thinking about my future." Emily looked out the window as though she could see it in the lawn.

"Thinking about a boy? Who you're going to marry? Prince Charming?" Kate teased.

Emily, as usual, didn't take the bait. "I'm thinking about studying nursing in Kearney. Of course, Kearney is where high school kids and townies hang out; maybe I'll go to Chicago."

"Chicago for … nursing?" Paul was curious too.

"I don't know. School, or … get a job working for an ad agency." Emily continued to gaze out at the lawn as though it were a crystal ball. She was making things up now, just to say something.

"Would you model?" Paul wondered.

"I bet you'd like to see her in a bikini," Kate said, honey in her voice.

Paul just glared at Kate.

"You know"—Emily stared out the window, then turned abruptly—"I've always wanted to model … scarves."

"Scarves?" Kate and Paul said the word together, looking at each other in bewilderment.

"Yeah," Emily said, suddenly feeling a bit feisty. "You know, winter on the prairie at forty below. It's beautiful, my favorite season, but without a scarf … I hate having a cold neck."

"I know!" It made sense to Kate. "It's the worst feeling in the world, like when you're unlocking the door and there's a drip, and it goes down your back."

"And besides, everyone has boring, brown or black coats. A colorful scarf is what says, 'Winter be damned, here I come!'" Emily went on, encouraged.

"Maybe you could even start a scarf company!" Paul was getting into it now, relieved that they were done talking about bikinis.

"Maybe. I mean, I was thinking of modeling first and saving up to start my own line," Emily said.

"That's a great idea. You have a beautiful neckline," Kate gushed. "You'd be awesome."

"I don't know," Emily said, sitting down. "I have so many ideas, I don't know where to begin." *I've scoured the river, looked at every document I can find in the historical museum and the library, talked to all the old-timers—the sane ones and the … confused ones too.*

"We'd better *begin* by doing afternoon rounds," Paul said, glancing at the clock.

"Oh, look at the time!" Kate realized she had taken a much longer break than she had intended. She jumped up and hurried back to work.

"Hey, Emily, do you have a minute?" Paul asked tentatively.

"Yeah." She looked at him curiously.

"Um, do you want to go … I mean, I thought you wanted to go into medicine, or nursing ... and you'd be good at it. Why the sudden shift?"

"I still might," she said. "I have so many ideas going through my head. I guess I'm just trying to figure out what my dreams are. Then maybe I'll worry about what to actually do!"

"Yeah, I know what you mean. Well, I was just wondering if you wanted to go … I mean, I was just curious." Paul stood and watched her turn to leave, kicking himself for his cowardice. *She's so amazing. She'd never fall for me. I'd be crazy to ask her out. I can't do it!*

"No, that's cool," Emily said, "it was a good question. Come on, let's get to work."

The Setup

Paul

Paul wasn't really doing much—rereading the cover article "Pilgrimage to Mecca" in the November 1978 *National Geographic* and listening to Chopin on an old vinyl record—when the phone rang. Before he answered it, he turned down Chopin and turned up the volume on his TV where Super Mario was waiting for players.

"Hey, Paul, it's Kate at the home."

"Aw Kate."

"What?"

"Don't tell me you need me to come in," Paul moaned.

"No, we have plenty of staff," Kate lied. "I was just talking to Emily on break, and she said her friends aren't doing anything tonight. She said she was hoping you would ask her out," she lied again, "and was wondering if I had your phone number to see if you would go get a pizza tonight with her. I called for her because, well, you know, she's shy." Kate smiled to herself.

"Um …" *Think fast,* Paul told himself, but then he realized he had no context for knowing what to say in this situation. *Is Emily really that shy …?*

"Well?" Kate interrupted his thoughts.

"OK, I guess." Paul groped for words.

"Pizza Hut at seven." Kate closed the deal.

"Sure."

Paul combed his hair and got to Pizza Hut at 6:30 that night. He sat in his car and waited. At 6:51 he turned his car on again and drove out of the parking lot, went down the street two blocks, turned around, and went back. It was now 6:56. *What the hell am I doing here?* He noticed that he was pulling at his hair, so he found a comb and combed it back into place. It was now 7 o'clock and no sign of Emily. Paul decided to leave. Then he decided to stay; then leave; then stay. 7:02. *Leave.* He reached for the key, and looked in the rearview mirror. Emily's Chevette pulled into the Pizza Hut lot, and she parked beside him.

Stay. He exhaled slowly and got out of his car.

"Hi, Paul," she said. "Sorry I'm late. Thanks for inviting me. Um, just as long as we're clear, it's just as friends."

"I thought *you* invited *me,*" Paul said as he held the door open for her. He struggled to keep the note of disappointment out of his voice, but he thought she picked up on it.

They exchanged puzzled glances—then: *"Kate,"* they said simultaneously, laughing. Paul shook his head.

"Don't worry, we'll find a way to get her back," said Paul. "So, why did you come?"

"My friends are all busy. My mom is driving me crazy asking me if I'm going out, so I finally said, 'Yes, Mom, I'm going out.' She thinks I should be more social," Emily said with a shrug.

"That sounds exactly like my mom," Paul agreed, pleased to find some common ground so quickly.

After they were seated and had ordered Cokes and pizza, Paul asked, "Well, um, how do you like work so far?"

"It's OK, I suppose. Today was a long day without you to help lift."

"Yeah, that's what all the gals say when I have a day off."

"We didn't get everything done. Why do we have to chart so much?" Emily wondered.

"It's stupid, but eventually the state will come in and want proof that you changed people's clothes, brushed their teeth, made sure to turn them so they don't get bedsores." Paul explained.

"I didn't have time to do half of those things today," she worried.

"I know." Paul was glad to talk about something he knew about. "But I figure, it isn't my fault that Mr. Kinross didn't get his dentures cleaned. I can't do everything. I'm not Superman. Maybe the Master Jailer," Paul laughed a little too loudly at his joke, but Emily looked confused.

"Uh ..." continued Paul, "that's a minor character in *Superman* comics. First appeared in '38; they brought him back just last year. Um ... never mind ... I'm sort of a comics collector." *I should keep the conversation to work-related stuff,* he thought. *I'm an* idiot, *like Chris Farley. My hair's probably sticking up already.*

"Apparently," she said.

"You've never read a comic book, have you?" Paul suddenly felt childish.

"Sure I have," Emily replied to his surprise. "*Sheena, the Jungle Queen; The Phantom Lady; Wonder Woman* too. I found them in my grandma's attic, and read them all. I was really into that stuff in seventh grade."

"Yeah? I know, it's kinda kid stuff." Paul wished they could forget the whole thing.

"Oh well. I mean, so you still like it. So what? My dad still plays with trains. And I'm still looking for gold in the river like I did when I was in sixth grade. You went to Harmony, right?"

"Yeah," he smiled.

"Did you like school?" she asked.

"Not really—I'm ADD. And I was scrawny. I took a lot of beatings. There was this jerk named Wade ..."

"You aren't scrawny now," she pointed out.

"I grew a ton right before my senior year—grew eight inches and put on sixty pounds in seven months. That year wasn't so bad. I was a linebacker on the football team that went to State."

"I remember that year," she said, with more enthusiasm than he expected. "I was in fourth grade, I think. It was a big deal; all the kids and teachers at the elementary school were talking about it, and you *had* to have a Harmony Football Boosters sweater. Wasn't the quarterback named Jimmy-something?"

"Yeah, Jimmy LaFleur. Sells dental equipment in Denver now." Paul shrugged. "Here's Jimmy's idea of small-town heroism: 'It's like old coffee. It used to be a rush, but it gets more and more bitter, just cold and stale, and you wish you could throw it out and start something fresh. But you can't. Somebody always remembers.' He's right, you know. I come down here to the Pizza Hut, and people still call me 'Ninety-Five.' That was my jersey number. It's been years!"

"Yeah? If you were so good, why didn't you play in college?"

"Grades. ADD, remember? Besides, I was just average for a high school player. What about you? Did you like school?"

"Yeah," she confessed, "I did. I liked it a lot."

"You were popular, though." *A girl this pretty had to be popular,* he thought. *In fact, she's so much younger than me and so sweet that I still can't believe she's sitting here talking to me.*

"Not really. I'm sort of a bookworm. I had three or four friends."

"What do you mean, 'you had'? You just graduated two weeks ago, right?"

"Well, Melissa—she's my best friend, and she's marrying Randall in August. So we always hung out with Randall. He's a good guy. Farmer. Works for his dad." She shrugged again in that funny, sexy way she had.

"All of a sudden you don't see them anymore, right?" Paul was getting it.

"Yep. And then Amy—I just found out she's been working at Gunner's for a while now, ever since she turned eighteen." Emily didn't look happy about this.

"What does she do there?"

"You don't know what Gunner's is?"

"Oh … *that* Gunner's … along the interstate. Is she a … does she …" Paul didn't know what you called it in front of a lady.

"Yeah. She's an 'exotic dancer.' We've mostly just been friends because of Melissa for the last while anyhow."

"Wow." Paul ran his fingers through his coarse hair. It stood straight up. Emily had to admit that Paul was cute in the way a St. Bernard was cute.

"Well," said Emily, "I told Melissa a couple of years ago that I thought Amy was a slut. Amy found out from Randall. He's not always the smoothest. I apologized later, but Amy always knew I meant it. Things have been sort of strained between us since then."

"So … is she a fox?" By her look, Paul knew that was the wrong thing to say. "Uh, never mind. Sorry." There was an awkward silence. Paul tried hard to think of an innocuous topic, but he froze.

"Anyway, our group was Melissa, Randall, Amy, me, and Ben." She sipped her Coke and thought for a while. He wondered what she was thinking. It would help so much.

"Who's Ben?" Paul could smell competition. Not that he thought he had a chance.

"Good question," she shrugged. "Ben has to figure that out."

"What do you mean?" Paul asked.

"He was my next-door neighbor all our lives. I grew up with him like a brother."

"So?"

"Well, the night we graduated, we were talking, and Ben said he might be in love with me, or he might be …" Emily shrugged again. *She shrugs a lot,* Paul thought.

"He's gay." Paul knew he was right on the money when he saw her jaw drop.

"Don't tell anyone. How did you know?" Emily was deadly serious.

"Lucky guess, I s'pose. Relax. I won't tell a soul," he soothed. "Especially not Kate."

She crossed her arms. "Of course not," she insisted, and he laughed. She started chuckling too.

"Ben just left town," Emily went on, "because even if I was in love with him, he'd still need to figure it all out anyway, and so he said he might never come back."

Paul sighed as the pizza arrived. "Uh-huh. I would guess not," he said. "My brother, Tony, never came back." Paul picked up a piece of Supreme. "Even after I called and told him that I'd broken Wade's arm over there in the arcade," he said as he took a bite, pointing toward the video games, "Tony just said, 'Good for you, Paul; I'm glad you exorcised your demon.'"

"Who was this guy? Didn't you get in trouble for breaking his arm?" Paul was such a teddy bear; she couldn't see him hurting someone. "Or was it an accident?"

"Oh, it was no accident," he smiled. "It was my senior year, and all of a sudden I was bigger than he was. Wade was just a bully, that's all. He came in here and was giving me crap again, and I realized I didn't have to take it anymore, so I busted his arm. Then I told him ..."

"What?"

"Well, it wasn't exactly polite."

She gave him a look as if to say, "We've wiped dirty rear ends together; you can tell me anything," and so he went on.

Paul lowered his voice. "I told him if I ever saw him in this Pizza Hut again, I'd cut his nuts off with a rusty pizza slicer."

Emily winced. "Wow. But you didn't get in trouble for ... assault or something?"

"We were winning a lot of football games that fall, you know. Quarterbacks get all the press, but Sergeant Ryan knows a decent starting linebacker is a pretty valuable part of a winning team. Plus, everybody knew Wade was an asshole."

"What happened to him?" she asked.

"I have no idea," Paul said. "Nobody's seen him around since then. The last anyone knew, he went to Dr. Hostetler to have his wrist set in a cast."

Kate had the weekend off while Emily and Paul worked, but she was itching for some gossip Monday morning. Paul and Emily been laughing at the Harlequin novel Kate had left in the break room over the weekend. When cornered, Emily finally hinted at a torrid affair with all-night lovemaking in a moonlit glade by the river. It took Kate longer to get Paul to confess, but he eventually told her the sun had risen upon their firm, still excited bodies glistening with perspiration in the middle of a wheat field after a starry night of passion.

"Emily said you were down by the river," she said.

"Oh, right, that was Saturday night. I was talking about Friday night."

"What about Sunday?" she asked, wide-eyed.

Paul considered intimating something about a long horseback ride and a lonely castle on the moor, pearly bosoms sparkling in the moonlight, heavy breathing followed by exhausted cries of ecstasy, but he decided not to push his luck. "I was too tired Sunday night," he said. "You can ask my mom. I swear I was home in the basement playing Super Mario." Kate bought the whole story for a few hours, until she picked up her Harlequin novel during her lunch break and realized that Emily and Paul's sensual tales were taken nearly verbatim from Chapter Seventeen.

Wonderland

Amy

1984

For eight years, Caroline bounced her two kids around from town to town. Sometimes, shortly after Arnie left, AJ and Amy stayed with Gerald and Margie for months at a time, even though Caroline had sworn she wouldn't impose her children upon her ex-husband's cousin and his wife. Sometimes they had an apartment in Harmony, but after a while she settled in Kearney where there was more low-income housing.

The years passed, Caroline's father died, her mother went to live in Harmony Halcyon Home, and something needed to be done with her parents' home. Her brother in California agreed that she should have it. He was making tons of money selling arcade games, so he didn't need anything for it. He told Caroline if she would just sober up, she could have the house. So she threw out her prescription pills as August rolled around, and she moved her kids into her parents' house. Soon it was time to send the kids to school. Her hiatus from drugs lasted all of three weeks—from the day they moved in until the day she went to meet her kids' teachers.

That summer, when Amy was ten years old, she and her brother started going to Harmony Community Schools. On the second day, she sat with AJ, on the school bus. AJ was desperately trying to conceal that he wished he was at the back of the bus showing the other boys how tough he could be. He had been far too tough the day before (an older boy had gone home with his nose still bleeding, and

Dr. Hostetler had to set it), and the driver had consigned him to the front of the bus with a threat that he would walk home if anything like it happened again. Amy had sat there with him for solidarity's sake; she knew he hadn't started it. Besides, without him, she might have trouble herself on the bus—being new and all. She could smell the tobacco on the back of the bus driver's head, in his clothes. She wanted a cigarette. She stared out the window. She'd have to wait a few more minutes.

Looking out the bus window, Amy saw a tractor sitting idly in a field. Her earliest memory was of a tractor sitting without a driver. Mama was holding a piece of paper. Her mother's heels dug into blackest dirt, her back curved, shoving against those big tires, as though she were trying to push the tractor back to the barn. Amy, who had been only two, remembered how she had pressed her own back up against the other tire in imitation, but Mama didn't smile at her antics. Now, whenever she saw a tractor sitting idly in a field, the farmer having left it like a pair of pants that didn't fit anymore, she felt the same panic starting again. Something was wrong with Mama, so something was wrong with Amy.

Across from AJ sat a girl she recognized from her new class.

"Your name is Amy, right?" the other girl said. Amy saw that she wore lip gloss. *I bet she pretends that's lipstick,* Amy thought. This made her feel bolder. The girl was being very brave—to talk to a loser like Amy on Amy's second day of school. "I'm Melissa. People call me Missy sometimes. But I don't like to be called Missy. I think Melissa is much better, don't you?" The girl stuck out her hand in an awkwardly formal fashion. Amy decided to try a little smile meant to patronize Melissa.

"Sure, much better," Amy agreed.

Melissa smiled back at her, revealing a mouthful of metal. Her hand was still outstretched, never wavering, reaching for Amy.

Amy took her hand and suppressed a sigh; she could use any friend she could get. "Hi, Melissa," she said. Amy was unsure how long to shake hands.

"Come over to my house tomorrow after school?" Melissa blurted. Then she added, "I have a secret. I can't even show it to my best friend, Emily." Amy looked around the bus for Emily. "She walks. Lives in town," Melissa explained.

In spite of herself, Amy was curious. "OK." She shrugged. Melissa's hand smelled like artificial cherry flavoring. Lip gloss.

When the kids got home, Amy saw that Mom was on the couch. She didn't bother to say hello. Amy would make some Kraft macaroni for dinner. Mom wasn't really asleep, but then she wasn't awake either. *Valium again,* Amy thought. She lifted a cigarette out of Mom's purse and went outside. AJ got a Coke out of the fridge and went to his room to lift weights. He wouldn't smoke. He said the Navy SEALs training would be hard enough, even if he was in great shape.

The next afternoon, Amy rode the bus another mile down the road to her new friend's house. Melissa's mother greeted them both at the door. "Hello, Amy, I'm so glad you could come. Your mother didn't mind?"

Amy tried not to laugh. "No, she didn't care." It was true. Her mother might not notice if she didn't come home all night.

"Will she pick you up, or do I need to run you home later?"

"She'll pick me up," Amy lied. Her house was just a mile down the road. She'd walk.

Melissa was eager to show Amy her room. She ran ahead, and Amy followed, feeling like a puppy being brought home from the pound. Amy said "Wow!" in a way that she hoped would make Melissa feel good, but Amy tried not to act too impressed. Melissa's room was full of pink stuff. All of it looked new. "It's really … nice," Amy added. None of Amy's own things matched. Melissa smiled shyly.

"Look," she whispered. She led Amy to a writing desk, upon which lay a Bible in a cloth cover made of pieces of pink material quilted together.

"A Bible?" Amy was incredulous.

"Yes … and no." Melissa opened the Bible, then extracted it from the cloth cover. Inside the cloth cover was a hidden pocket, from which she pulled a regular piece of lined notebook paper folded in quarters. Without another word, Melissa handed it to Amy, who unfolded it.

"Dear Melissa, I like you do you like me? From Randall. P.S. don't tell anyone."

Once again Amy found herself trying hard not to laugh. If she laughed, Melissa might be offended, and Amy decided this was a friend she might want to keep. "Well," she said, "do you like him?"

"I don't know," Melissa said. "I thought I did, until he gave me this. Now I think maybe I don't."

This made no sense to Amy. "When did he give you this?"

"Last Valentine's Day."

"What did you tell him?" Amy asked.

"I didn't tell him anything."

"But … this is September!"

"Yeah …" Melissa inspected her toes. Everything smelled of artificial cherry fragrance. It was almost heady. "Yeah. What should I do? Should I like him back? And if I do, does that mean we're 'going out'? And if we're 'going out,' does that mean I have to kiss him or—" Melissa blushed a deeper pink than her pillowcase.

"Well, I don't know if you should like him or not," Amy protested.

"Do you think he's cute?" Melissa wondered.

"Uh … I don't know."

"You *do* know which one Randall is, right?"

"Yeah. He's my cousin, sort of. I never thought about whether or not he's cute."

Melissa looked mortified. "He's your cousin?" The words came out as though she were dying.

"Well, his dad and my father are cousins."

"You're not going to tell him about this, are you?"

Amy had to swear four different ways that she wouldn't tell Randall whatever it was that Melissa ultimately decided she thought about him. They discussed it at such length—at least Melissa did—that Amy soon became sick of the topic. Melissa was obsessed. It wasn't that she *did* like him but certainly not that she *didn't* either. She seemed to relish the purgatory of doubt much more than any solid evidence she could conjure for or against having a boyfriend. But beyond the hypothetical and general concept of Boyfriend, the specific concept of Randall as a target of affection made everything much more confusing. All his traits were analyzed, and to Amy's astonishment this girl saw her cousin Randall in a completely different light. *Of course,* she reflected, *Melissa has built an entire mystery boy out of absolutely nothing.* She didn't have the heart to tell Melissa that Randall was nothing like anything her imagination had constructed.

"I used to live with them, you know, for a while, when my mom was, um, sick." Amy finally admitted. "He's like a brother."

Melissa nearly shrieked. "So you've actually talked to him?"

"You mean, you haven't ever even talked to him?" Amy chewed on this news.

"Well, yes ... but not ... well, just, like, 'Excuse me, you dropped something,' or whatever. Is he nice?"

"He's nicer to me than my brother, AJ, is. His mom and dad would probably kill him if he was mean to me."

"Why?" Melissa wondered aloud.

"Because everyone is always extra nice to me." Amy decided to divulge her own secret, which wasn't much of a secret in Harmony anyway, and plunged ahead. "I had to go stay with them because my dad left, and my mom was ... you know, depressed. Everybody is nice to me because they feel sorry for me. AJ and I had to live with Randall's family until right before I started kindergarten. Then we went back to stay with Mom in Kearney, and now Mom decided to move us all back to Harmony because—well, I don't really know why, but my grandma's house was empty. Mom had a job working at the old people's home for a while mopping floors and stuff, but she got fired. Now she just ..." Amy stopped. "I think Randall is perfect for you," she decided.

"Really?" Melissa looked frightened. She leapt onto her bed and buried her face in the pillows. After a moment Amy realized she was sobbing.

"What's the matter?" She went and patted Melissa very tentatively. Melissa broke off crying and sat up.

"Don't you see? Since Valentine's Day I never said anything to him. Seven months! He probably doesn't like me anymore. Besides, I got braces since then. And he probably thinks that I hate him because

I never answered," she half-wailed, "and he probably likes some other girl by now!"

"You could just ask him," Amy shrugged. She knew Randall; it wasn't really a big deal.

"Can you do it?" Just as quickly she changed her mind. "No. No, I don't want you to say anything."

Eventually Amy walked home, shaking her head. Her new friend, Melissa, was hard to figure out, though to Amy she was just weird. Melissa's entire life reminded Amy of *Leave It to Beaver* reruns. Everything in the Stoltzfus house was in its place, including Melissa's father at the dinner table, promptly at six o'clock. Melissa's obsession with Randall baffled Amy. Why couldn't the poor girl just decide to either like him or not? Amy had never met anyone who so desperately needed a daisy to pull petals off until the final petal revealed an answer. Maybe a girl who lived in a house with a mom who actually wore an apron to cook *needed* something to feel unsure about.

When Amy got home and entered the kitchen, she saw that AJ had made himself a bologna sandwich. The mayonnaise was on the counter going bad. He hadn't closed the bread bag; it was already stale. She sighed and put everything away. *Jeopardy!* was on, but Mom wasn't really watching it. There was a Double Jeopardy answer about Madonna that none of the contestants knew the question for, and Amy would have made two thousand dollars. Her knowledge was useful only in the right place at the right time—which was never. Amy decided she wasn't hungry and went to her room without supper.

After Dad left, Amy's mother never cried; she just shrank into herself like a turtle pulling her head back into her shell—and never came out. She began to take sleeping pills. In the dark of her bedroom, Amy closed her eyes and saw her mother's head slowly sliding down between her collarbones. Sometimes her mother was Marie

Antoinette, other nights the Headless Horseman, but in her dreams her mother always lost her head one way or another. Amy decided when she was five that people looked much more normal without their heads. She sometimes found herself laughing at people in public because their heads were so funny. Some of them were too big. Others were too small, or too bald. Still others, too hairy, the noses too piggy or too horsey. Heads were not normal. Mama was better off without one.

In the middle of the night, Amy grew hungry and went to make a fried baloney sandwich with ketchup, ate it, and went to the bathroom to pee. Since she wasn't tired, she inspected her face in the mirror, then her body.

She knew how Alice felt when she arrived in Wonderland and drank a cordial, only to find herself looking up at a table with a key on it far above her head. Her longing for being the right size haunted her. When her father left, she had been too small to help Mom. Now that her body was changing, she worried that her breasts would become too big, or never get quite large enough to be more than buds. In fact, she had barely begun to develop. She spent many minutes wondering if one wouldn't end up just a bit bigger than the other. What if one grew and the other one didn't? She wasn't worried so much about being too small or too big, it was just that she had always felt lopsided. Lopsided was worse than anything in the world. Melissa wasn't lopsided at all. Except for the part about Randall.

The next day, when Melissa climbed off the bus at school, she left Amy and ran to find Emily right away. "I have a new friend! You have to meet her!" Melissa was soon pulling Emily, who went along reluctantly, through the halls at school. Bigger kids were staring at them, but Melissa didn't notice.

"She's over there," Melissa pointed. Emily knew which one she meant: The New Girl Who Wore Makeup. Amy was sitting by herself on a bench, waiting for the bell to ring. Emily offered resistance, finally jerking Melissa backwards with her until they elbowed their way into the girls' room.

"Do you think she saw us?" Emily wondered aloud.

"No … what's the matter with you? She's fun. Come on, let's go meet her!"

"Remember our pact?" Emily dropped her hands to her sides in exasperation.

"Oh. Yeah, I guess so," Melissa said.

"You do? What is it then?"

Melissa looked at her hands as if they were not her own and she couldn't be held responsible for her own actions. "We don't let anyone in the club without con- … con- …"

"Consensus," Emily prompted her.

"Right."

"So she's not in until we both say." Emily looked hard at Melissa.

"It's kind of too late." Melissa mumbled.

"What do you mean?"

"I already told her she could be in."

"What?"

"I sort of … forgot." Emily gave her a hard look, and Melissa searched for a way out. "Anyway, she's really nice and she knows—" Melissa stopped. She hadn't told Emily about her crush on Randall. This information would complicate the current situation, because revealing it would also reveal that she had told Amy, further proving her disloyalty to the club.

"She knows what?" Emily's curiosity was aroused.

"She knows … how babies are made," Melissa finished lamely.

"So?" Emily let this most biting of comments hang in the air. After a long moment Emily repeated it. "So-o-o-o?"

Just then Amy walked into the bathroom. "Hi, Melissa," she said as though Melissa were a lazy housecat who was just in the way, as though she had important business to attend to and Melissa had nothing to do with it at all. Emily thought this was no way to treat a member of the club—if you wanted to be in it—and glared at Amy.

"Hi, Amy," Melissa piped up, cheerfully oblivious to the new girl's sour attitude. "This is my friend Emily!"

Amy looked Emily over for a moment. Her assessment was succinct: *This girl thinks she's perfect. She certainly* looks *perfect, so she must think she is.* Amy decided she might not want to join the club after all—too many perfect kids. She looked at Melissa and replied with extra layers of scorn piled up like a triple-decker birthday cake. "So?"

Melissa was devastated. Everything had gone wrong; she desperately wanted these two to be friends, all in her club. Instead, not only did they hate each other on sight, now they both hated *her* for trying to expand the circle. In Sunday school they talked about sharing and made it seem as though everything was clear skies when you were friendly to newcomers. Sharing was definitely harder than they made it sound at church.

Melissa barely made it out the bathroom door before the tears began to tumble over her eyelids and down across her sweater. She ran to her classroom, still five minutes early, found her desk, and buried her head in her arms, pretending to be asleep. Her quaking shoulders belied her true situation, but the teacher, who was preparing for class and saw her distress, decided it was probably a squabble that would take care of itself.

"What do you mean, 'So?'" Emily looked hard at Amy.

Amy shrugged.

"You hurt her feelings," Emily pressed.

"So?" Amy turned to the mirror and, withdrawing some lipstick, applied it liberally for effect. Emily and Melissa weren't allowed lipstick yet. Applying lipstick was part of Amy's calculated power grab.

"She wants you to be in our club," Emily said simply, "and you treated her mean."

Amy shrugged again. "Sor-ry. Maybe I was trying to hurt *your* feelings, not hers," she admitted casually.

"You *are* mean. Maybe you should apologize," Emily suggested, ignoring Amy's cavalier attitude.

"Maybe *you* should apologize," Amy mocked.

Emily wouldn't be moved, now that she was standing up for Melissa instead of tearing her down. She was too loyal to be drawn into an insignificant skirmish with this new outrider. "You know what? You're right," Emily said. "I was mean to her too, just before you came in."

"Why?" Amy was suddenly curious.

"Because I didn't want you in our club, that's why."

"Why not?" Amy asked. She tried to pretend she didn't care.

"I don't know." Emily knew it was because she was jealous. But she wouldn't admit this to Amy.

"Because you were jealous?" Amy wondered.

"No," Emily lied, then added sullenly: "Just because ... it's a secret club."

"Well, I know some secrets about Melissa," Amy said.

"You do?" The words came out before Emily's could stop them. "*What* secrets?"

"I can't tell you unless I'm in the club"—Amy crossed her arms—"and then only if Melissa agrees."

Emily was furious but recognized the justice in this statement. "OK," she sighed. "I guess you can be in."

"What about Melissa? Don't you have to ask her?"

"She'll say yes."

Amy had the upper hand now, and she wasn't going to waste it. "Well, maybe I don't want to be in your club. Maybe I want to make my *own* club."

"You can't have a club by yourself," said Emily with some exasperation, "You have to have some other people in it. You have to have at least two people. Otherwise it's just Lonely Heartsville. Like Sergeant Pepper."

"What?" Amy's brow furrowed in confusion.

"Sergeant Pepper's Lonely Hearts Club Band. You know," Emily explained. "The Beatles."

"Oh yeah," Amy nodded wisely; she had heard that song before. "Well, then," she continued, "You can be in my club, and so can Melissa. Then I'll have a *real* club. You can be secretary and Melissa can be vice president."

Something was wrong here, but Emily decided not to push the issue. "OK," she said, "but only if Melissa really does have a secret."

"You don't believe me?" Amy asked, feigning incredulity. "Let's go talk to Melissa, and we'll see about that."

Melissa was the only one who didn't care *whose* club it was, as long as her friends could be in it, sharing their secrets—which is why, without any exertion on her part (except the continual effort she put into peacemaking between Emily and Amy), it became unofficially known by their classmates as "Melissa and Her Friends." Melissa wasn't the vice president or secretary, she was the boss.

A New Brother

Arnold

Anchorage, June 1989

Arnold was pretty well settled in. Anchorage nearly felt like home. He didn't have many friends, but the few he had were close. He and Judy had two girls; they'd been together ten years now, and most of the time he could live his life without remembering why he was here. He was fairly stable—for a drifter.

Coming home from running some routine errands one Saturday morning, Arnold pulled into the driveway and saw a Honda motorcycle blocking his access to the garage. Arnold glanced around. Someone in aviator sunglasses, a leather jacket, jeans, and cowboy boots was sitting on the front steps.

"What can I do for you, young man?"

"Arnold Martin?"

"That's my name." Arnold peered at the youth suspiciously. "And you are?"

"Arnold Martin. Ha-ha! That's my name too; what a *fuckin'* coincidence," the boy said casually.

"Oh," said Arnold, "you came to see me." What else was he supposed to say to his grown son? Arnold was well aware that AJ was eighteen, and though Arnold reproached himself often for never contacting his own children in Nebraska, it hadn't occurred to him that they might one day come to find *him*. Shocked, he said it again, with the emphasis on the last word. "You came to see *me*."

"You sure your name isn't Mr. Obvious?" AJ sneered.

This pissed Arnold off, but he took a deep breath before responding. "Did you come all this way just to try to make me feel like crap? Because I've got two things to tell you, if you did: I've felt like crap for a long time, and I have better stuff to do if that's all you want from me."

"Huh. Nice speech, 'Dad.'"

Arnold also let that one slide. "It's good to see you. How did you find—?"

"Margie gave me your address." AJ looked at him sideways. "It was a long ride. Do you mind if I camp out in the backyard tonight?"

Arnold nodded. "Yes, I do mind. We have a guest room; you can sleep in a bed. You must be hungry, and thirsty. You want a beer? I might have one in the back of the fridge," Arnold told him as he opened the door and motioned his son into his house.

"Um ... sure." AJ was disarmed momentarily. He imagined a lot of things he might say to his father once he found him, as well as a lot of things his father might say in return, but "You want a beer?" wasn't one of them.

"Who's that, Papa?" Little Beth peered into the hallway, holding a naked Barbie doll.

"Your brother," her father said matter-of-factly as he passed her in the hall. Beth dropped her doll and opened her mouth in astonishment. *For once,* Arnold thought, *she can't think of anything to say!*

It didn't last long. Beth ran to her room screaming delightedly. ***"Amanda! Amanda! Papa brought us a brother from the grocery store! We have a new brother!"*** Amanda didn't believe this, but Beth persisted. "We have a new brother, and he's big, and he has a motorcycle! I saw it out the window," she exclaimed.

Amanda pulled her little sister's hair. "Stop lying, you liar!" she said, and Beth burst into tears.

"Look out the window, you stupid-head!" Beth screamed at her sister, and tried to scratch at her face, but Beth's arms were too short. Amanda pushed her back. Skeptically, and without letting Beth see her do it, Amanda glanced outside. Sure enough, there was a very shiny blue bike out there.

"Brothers don't come from grocery stores," she instructed Beth, "and babies can't ride motorcycles."

"But Papa said he was our brother—the man who came on the motorcycle. He's not a baby, but he's our brother. Go ask Papa yourself."

Amanda approached the kitchen cautiously. She heard a strange voice talking to her father. She peeked through the doorway. Her father was sitting at the kitchen table with his back to her. Across from him sat a younger man in a leather jacket was fiddling with a beer and talking.

"I didn't mean to be such an asshole. I guess I hoped you'd be a jerk back to me, and then I'd just get on my bike and leave again."

"Never mind," Arnold said. "Have you seen Pa?"

"Grandpa Doc? Yeah, I went down to the home a few weeks ago to tell him that I joined up, and all he could do is yell about how the gold was stolen."

"Oh, that fortune his grandfather supposedly buried?"

"Yeah, that's all he talked about that day. That and the Statue of Liberty; you know the drill. I don't know why I bothered. He's a senile old bastard. And I don't say that with disrespect, but more as a statement of fact, you know?"

Arnold nodded. AJ suddenly felt eyes burning the back of his neck and swung around toward the door.

"Those would be my girls. Your sisters. Amanda is nine, and Beth is five," said Arnold with a smile and more than a little pride.

Amanda stepped out shyly, but Beth ran right around her, jumped up into AJ's lap and kissed him right on the lips. His eyes widened in astonishment, and Arnold had to restrain himself to keep from laughing.

"I've always wanted a big brother," said Beth cheerfully. Then she peppered a rapid-fire interrogation at her new brother. "What's your name? You're handsome, like Tom Cruise. Amanda has a crush on Tom Cruise, but I think boys are *yecch*, except you, of course. You're wonderful, because you're my brother. This is my Barbie. Do you play Barbies? I guess not. Boys don't play Barbies, they're *yecch*. My friend Nikki has a new baby brother, but he's really little. He can't talk; he just goes, 'Blblbllbblblb.' He's really cute, though. He's only nasty when he goes pooey. I can't wait to tell her I have a big brother who is all grown up and handsome like Tom Cruise with sunglasses and a motorcycle. Do you fly airplanes too?"

"Whoa, whoa, slow down," AJ smiled, completely disarmed by her enthusiasm. "One question at a time."

"What's your name?"

"AJ."

"That's a funny name. Where did you come from?"

"Harmony, Nebraska," he said. Beth shrugged. He could have said he was from Dar es Salaam, and it would have been the same to her.

"Is that *really* your *own* motorcycle outside?" Beth's eyes were wide.

"Yes." He thought he would hate his half-siblings on principle; they got his dad, and he got a prescription-drug addict for a mom. AJ hadn't spent time with five-year-old kids, though, and he was completely charmed by this little girl. *More younger sisters, huh?* He hadn't thought much about the fact that his father would have another family, and he would have been shocked, had he thought about it, that it might be a family that would accept him at face value. After all, he had ridden the entire way with bitter venom in his heart, rehearsing cruel speeches. *The girls do both look like Amy around the eyes, although these two are long and willowy, with much more spindly legs than Amy has.*

"I like motorcycles a lot! Will you take me for a ride?" Beth asked, bouncing up and down on AJ's knees. "Please, Papa, please, oh please?"

"Um ..." AJ looked at Arnold, who was nodding. "Sure," AJ said.

"Good, let's go now!" Beth jumped off his lap and headed for the door. But now Amanda stepped further into the kitchen.

"Did you come out of my mom's ... *uterus*?" Amanda tried to look fierce, to demand an answer. This sudden brother thing didn't suit her nearly as well as it suited little Beth.

"No." AJ looked to Arnold for help. Arnold shrugged. Amanda scowled. Her face told the men that there were questions that must be answered.

"Who is your mom then?"

"His mom's name is Caroline," Arnold cut in. Amanda looked suspiciously from one man to the other.

Beth was bouncing off the walls. She couldn't contain her excitement and took no interest in the details of his parentage. ***"AJ is going to take me for a motorcycle ride, Amanda!"*** she shouted.

"Go ahead," Arnold said, "take Beth around the block."

Relieved, AJ got up, leaving his beer half-finished, and went with Beth to zip around the block.

Amanda sat down, her arms folded in front of her, and Arnold knew he had some explaining to do. He sighed. *Little girls don't stay little forever.*

"Sometimes," he began, "grown-ups don't really know what to do. We make mistakes too. But sometimes the mistakes come out for the best in the end, because I got you now, Sweetie, and Beth too." Amanda just glared at her father. Her look told him to cut the crap. So Arnold began to tell Amanda who he used to be and where he came from. How he grew up on a farm near a place called Harmony. How in 1967 he took a girl named Caroline to the prom …

After AJ met Judy, had dinner with the family, and the girls were in bed, Arnold and AJ took a few beers to the deck overlooking the bay to the west. They sat and waited for the sun to go down. It was nearly midnight. Finally Arnold began to speak.

"The sun stays down south in the summer time. The nights are so short, and then the winters are so long. Even after all this time, the seasons are strange to me. I kinda feel like time ain't passing the way it should. In my head I know I've been gone for thirteen years, but in my heart, well, I haven't seen a single wheat field ripen.

"You might find this hard to believe, but I came up here to escape from … something I couldn't fight. Not something normal, like fighting with your wife, something simple you can deal with and get over it. It was something, well, paranormal. I wanted to fight it, but I didn't know how. So I left. What can I say? I was a coward. But you: What brings you all the way up here?"

AJ looked off into the distance, squinting after the dying sun. "I came to tell you I'm joinin' the Marines."

"The Marines?" Arnold was silent for a moment. "Well, whaddya know about that. Good for you, Son. Gotta say you're off to a better start than I was at your age. All I did was chase girls and—" He stopped himself. He was about to say, *"—get your mom pregnant."*

"And I wasn't very disciplined," he finished.

AJ slipped his jacket off, revealing a gray T-shirt he'd gotten from a Marines recruiter, with that single, potent word lettered across the front: MARINES. The sleeves bulged around huge biceps. He pulled the bottom of his shirt out of his jeans and showed off a rock-hard abdomen.

"I'm in top condition," AJ said, flexing unconsciously. "I can run four miles in just under twenty-two minutes."

"That's pretty solid," Arnold admitted, wondering if the boy could run that fast in boots, humping a forty-five-pound pack under hostile fire.

AJ went on: "I drove all the way up here to tell you how much I hate you, what a shithead you are. And some of that is still true. But now I see, I mean, I realize, you love your kids. I really just wanted you to be proud of me, but you can't, because you don't even know me. I'm not your kid. So if you're a shithead, you're somebody else's shithead."

"I wish I could say you're wrong," Arnold said. He stood up. There was a long, uncomfortable silence. "So, how's your ma? And little Amy?"

"They're … You should go ask them yourself," AJ replied.

"OK. You're right again. I haven't been able to do that yet, and I don't know why." Arnold stood and looked toward where the sun had set, where the light was still the strongest. He didn't find any answers in the twilit sky, nor in the bay beneath it.

"Maybe I should go," AJ said, standing up unsteadily.

"You've had a lot to drink," Arnold reminded him.

"Yeah, I'll sleep it off," AJ said. He went to the guest room and crashed on the bed, fully clothed, but he was gone before sunrise.

Prom

Melissa

May 1991

Their freshman year might have been the best year the three girls had as a clique. They were mature enough to not have fifth-grade squabbles, but not so mature that they were going their separate ways. But by the time they were juniors …

"It's just a matter of time," Amy said as the girls checked their hair in the bathroom mirror, "and I'll probably let him. After all, he *is* taking me to the prom," she explained. Amy had been going out with Brad since homecoming, and things were heating up. "Anyway, what about you, Emily?"

"What *about* me?" Emily was looking at Amy with astonishment.

"Who's taking you to prom?"

"I can go by myself." Emily replied, trying not to sound defensive.

"Oh come on," Melissa cut in, "even I have a date!" Amy and Emily squealed, which was the reaction she was hoping for. She acted coy.

"Melissa, that's, like, awesome," Amy gushed. "Who is it?"

"Randall." She beamed.

"Randall?" Emily hugged her.

"He finally asked you?" Amy was astonished.

"No. I asked *him.*" Melissa hopped on the counter by the sink with a smug look on her face.

"What? Why?" Amy pressed.

"Why not? Is there something wrong with him?" Melissa sounded offended.

"No, no," Amy hastily demurred, "but … well, usually the boy … oh well. He's so quiet." Her cousin annoyed her sometimes.

"Just because he's quiet doesn't mean he's not nice," Emily pointed out.

"I know that, but, I mean …" Amy was uncharacteristically at a loss.

"I sit next to him in Biology," Melissa explained, "and I was really dreading dissecting the fetal pig, and Randall just … helped me. He showed me how everything works together in that little body. And all the other girls were, like, grossed out, and I realized it was just part of nature. It was really kind of, well … interesting. Besides," she gushed on, "well, *I* think he's cute. I always have. So I finally called him and he said yes." She smiled proudly while Emily and Amy congratulated her again.

"What about Emily, though?" Melissa finally said. "Hey, Emily, what about Ben?"

"Why does everyone always put us together? Just because I live next door to him?"

"No, not *just* that," Melissa said. "You're also the two smartest kids in class."

"And the best-looking," Amy added. "At least, everyone says you are. And while I admit that Ben's the best-dressed, Brad is still the best-looking, and he's mine!" Already as a sophomore, Brad was the starting tight end on the varsity football team. "And he's got great hands," Amy added with a sly smile. Melissa giggled nervously, and Emily rolled her eyes.

"Amy, you should be careful," Emily said.

"Careful about *what*?" Amy reacted, a defiant flash in her eyes.

"Getting yourself into a situation … getting stuck with something."

"Getting pregnant, you mean?" Now Amy was mad. "I won't get pregnant. Brad has condoms in his wallet; I saw them"—Melissa gasped at this—"and anyway … anyway, I'll be careful," she added.

"Oh come on, Amy." Emily was exasperated. "Don't you know what the boys say about you?"

"Like what?"

Emily looked at Melissa for a moment. Melissa shook her head no. Emily plowed ahead anyway. "Ben says in the locker room they say you're easy. That's what. You know what comes after easy? Then they start calling you a slut. Once you get that label, it's hard to get away from it, Amy."

"Oh well, aren't you just perfect, Emily Zimmerman? I know some boys who say you don't know how to have fun, that your idea of good time is reading *Jane Eyre* by yourself at the library. So just shove it." Amy tossed her head and slammed out of the bathroom and headed down the hall.

"Wait, Amy." Melissa trailed after her, and when Amy allowed her to catch up she added, "Don't worry about Emily. She means well."

"I'm not talking to her. Ever again," Amy declared as she stormed off.

In the spring, when prom got closer, nobody asked Emily, not even the older boys. In what might be termed an arrangement of convenience for both, she and Ben showed up together in her rusty car, but they didn't slow-dance. It wasn't really a date. *He looks so relaxed in a tuxedo,* Emily thought. She actually felt pretty good in her gown; she knew she looked great, but she was a little shy about showing off her shoulders. She was glad she had brought a shawl. They each had a Pepsi and, on a slight caffeine buzz, spent much of the evening debating whether *Huckleberry Finn* or *To Kill a Mockingbird* was the greatest American novel. This passed as a really good time for Emily and Ben.

Amy showed up with Brad, and they slow-danced very closely, but they didn't stay long.

Randall picked up Melissa early; he gave her a beautiful corsage. He looked a tad uncomfortable in a tuxedo, but his old truck was carefully washed and waxed. They went to a little Italian place in Kearney, and Randall showed Melissa which silverware to use for which course. There was a different fork for salad, main dish, and dessert. His huge, calloused hands handled his fork as though it were a surgeon's instrument. He paid for the meal with his own credit card. His refinement surprised her. He said very little on the way back to the school. As they slow-danced, she started asking him questions.

"How do you know so much about silverware?" she said.

"Margie—that's my mother." Randall thought for a moment. "She says a fork is not a shovel, and her food is not manure. We can shovel manure in the barn where Gerald's in charge—that's my father. But in the kitchen, Margie is boss, and we have to use manners or else."

"Or else what?"

"She stops cooking."

"Has she ever done that?" Melissa was incredulous.

"Once, when I was about five, my brother, Caleb, came in hungry and started eating before Gerald said grace. He was in fact using a spoon like a shovel; he dribbled food everywhere. Without a word Margie got up, took his plate outside, and threw it to the hogs, then sent him to bed. She didn't cook the next day at all. Gerald came in for dinner and tried to make some waffles, and they were as hard as bricks, and we all chewed and chewed them because we were so hungry, and I've done my best to have good manners ever since. And Caleb? He's downright refined!"

"Wow," Melissa said, "your mom must be pretty tough."

"Yeah, but she's all right," Randall agreed. "Tonight she fixed my favorite: Swedish meatballs and mashed potatoes with gravy, cauliflower with cheddar cheese, and chocolate ice cream." Randall smiled.

"Too bad you had to miss it to go out with me." said Melissa, moving a little closer in his arms as they swayed to the music: *"Every rose has its thorn ... Just like every cowboy sings a sad, sad song. Every rose has its thorn."*

"Miss what?" Randall looked puzzled.

"Your mom's meal," Melissa explained.

"Oh, I didn't miss it. She made supper early."

"But … you ate that whole lasagna." Melissa was confused.

"Oh yeah. I went easy on Margie's meal and had only one helping of everything."

"Why don't you play on the football team anyway? Mr. Benner said in Biology they'd love to have you on the line. Seems like you'd be pretty good."

Randall considered his answer. It seemed to Melissa like he didn't say anything without thinking about it carefully first, and she liked that. "Yes, I suppose I could be. I'm bigger than everybody in the school. Gerald needs me during the harvest, though. I'd rather get the harvester ready to pick corn than knock some guy down on his backside. What do I have against him?" He looked at his knuckles over her shoulder. Several of them were skinned up and sore. One had a Band-Aid on it, and he was making sure it wouldn't fall off. He wouldn't want to bleed on Melissa's dress.

They danced as Melissa thought about his rejection of fame in favor of farming. "Are you always going to be a farmer?" she finally asked.

"Can't imagine why I wouldn't," he said, and she suddenly realized she was starting to picture herself as a farm wife—a handkerchief tied around her head, babies running through the kitchen, men in chore boots coming in muddy for hot coffee with smiles on their faces, sitting up late together in midsummer watching the thunderstorms roll in across the prairie, going to church to pray, asking God Almighty for just the right amounts of rain and sun—and it seemed good to her.

"That's really nice," she said and surprised him by resting her head against his chest as they danced. His heart sped up and bounced against his ribs like a basketball on the side of the barn. For her part, Melissa surprised herself by how far ahead her mind started racing that evening.

Randall had her home ten minutes before eleven that night. He went into the house and said good night to Melissa's parents. Randall shook her father's hand and thanked them for allowing him to escort their daughter to prom. As he drove away, Randall thought to himself, *One of these days I'm gonna take this girl to Nana's for tea.*

Daily Bread

Doc

Toward the end of her shift, at the end of a monotonous day, Emily went in to check on the old men in Room 143. She knew they appreciated having a little help getting into bed for an afternoon nap sometimes. Owen was sitting in his wheelchair, quietly puttering with an odd assortment of mementos in his dresser drawers with one hand, and holding his Nova Scotia stone in the other. She decided to let him be for the moment.

"Doc, you ready for a rest?" He nodded, and she held his elbow, fluffed his pillow, and generally fussed over him. "I noticed you slept *in* this morning," Emily said conversationally.

"Yeah, I slept in. I wanted to be dead," he grumbled. She saw him glance to see what kind of a reaction he was getting.

She feigned astonishment. "You wanted to be dead?"

He was pleased with her reaction. Seeing that she wasn't in a hurry, he went on. "Right. I had a dream last night. I'm waiting on the train platform to catch a boxcar. It was a sunny day, too goddam hot for me. The grain was all ripened; I don't know where the town went. It was just a train platform in the middle of a field so wide you couldn't see the end of it. The tracks came up to the platform and went a few more feet and disappeared into the wheat. I waited all day, and the day went on and on like they say it does up in Alaska in summer. We never shoulda bought that godforsaken land, you know."

"Did your family have a wheat field?" Emily was confused.

"Alaska! We never shoulda bought Alaska. And the train never came, and I didn't want to get on it anyway, and I knew if it came I would have to jump in a boxcar with a bunch of corpses like what the Krauts did in the Second War. Those bastards—not that I care much for Jews. We shoulda killed them first."

"The Jews?" Emily was definitely lost.

"No, no, no, no. The Germans," Doc exploded. "God, even the Jews have rights! The Ten Commandments! Mount Sinai! Jerusalem! Don't you know that? What do they teach you kids these days? I never went outside the *YOU*-nited States, and I know that! They said I had flat feet and couldn't go. Hell, I'd have been dead for sure then." Returning to his dream, Doc railed on: "So I waited for the train on that platform and the sun was beating down and I thought my skin would blister, and I kept feeling my lips, and they wouldn't ever blister, but my mouth tasted like a campfire after you cook your beans and piss on the fire to put it out." Doc finally took a couple of deep breaths. He was winded and starting to get more than a little worked up. Emily wondered if he was going to give himself a heart attack.

"I don't ..." Emily wondered if it was wise to continue the conversation.

"Beans and piss. So I started in to preaching, but nobody was there to hear it, and I looked for something to eat in the depot, but all I found was a dirty piece of bread—and it hurt to swallow." Doc grabbed his throat and stuck his tongue out. "Bread is pain, and in French, *pain* is bread. That's what the people said."

"What people? I thought you said there was nobody to preach to," Emily said, trying to stay with him.

"Hell, I don't care about that." Doc waved his hand dismissively. "Just the wheat—you know, sometimes the heads of grain were people's heads all screaming, and the train never coming, and me never wanting to get on it if it did come. And where would it go, anyhow? So I told God—I said, 'I'll just preach to you. Look here, God, I got my rights, and I don't have to get on no train if it comes, and I don't have to wait here all day if it doesn't. And I don't got to eat bread if it means pain, and I don't have to swallow any more pain even if it *is* my daily bread.'" Doc was nearly yelling now.

"Did God talk back to you?" The more Emily listened, the more she wondered if the dream might be significant, or if Doc was just crazy.

"Then I woke up, and that nurse was telling me Dr. Hostetler was going to come take away my bacon and coffee and God knows what other regular, American-raised food—bananas next, no doubt—and give me a pelvic exam and I said, 'The hell with it. I'll get up even if I don't want to.' But the station is still there with all the wheat—reddish gold around it like a branding iron. And all you can make of it is pain, *le pain* anyway. If I close my eyes, I can see it."

"Kate says you're crazy, but you don't fool me." Emily folded her arms and called his bluff.

At that, Doc winked at her. "Dr. Hostetler says I've got 'colon,' but *he* doesn't fool me. Anyhow, I got a right to be crazy if I want."

"I believe you do. After all, the Brooklyn Bridge, right? Have you ever been to New York City?"

"You think I'm going to tell you stories like him?" Doc jerked his thumb in Owen's direction. "I'll tell you something. I never been out of Nebraska. There's nothing wrong with Nebraska. We raise everything we need right here. Coffee, pork—"

"The Statue of Liberty is in New York."

"I got me one of them right in here." Doc threw off his cover, swung his legs out of bed, and reached for his nightstand. Pulling open a drawer, he withdrew a miniature Statue of Liberty, and a crucifix. "And I got a Jesus too. New York City? What's wrong with Nebraska? We got everything we need here: pork and beans and coffee. And not too many Krauts or Jews or Mo-ho-mmade-ans."

"And railroads to take away the wheat and bring back the bread," Emily summarized. *In some strange sort of way,* she thought, *this old man makes his own kind of sense.*

She underestimated the power of his dream, however, and Doc, reminded of the horror, reacted swiftly and violently, swinging his cane at her. "Don't you talk to me about no goddam wheat! I don't want to hear about wheat! I ain't waiting all day for a train that never comes! I can't see beyond the end of all that screaming wheat! It hurts, it hurts! 'Give us this day our daily bread,' not 'Give us so much wheat it makes our head hurt to try to see past it all!' I want my lawyer! I can't stand any more bread—can't take the pain, *le pain.* ***I got my rights! I'm getting out of this filthy hellhole. I'm going home!"*** He nearly leapt out of bed and tottered toward her, his cane lashing out like a rapier and actually landed a glancing blow on her left shoulder.

Emily backed away quickly. ***"No,"*** she yelled, ***"look out!*** No, I'll get—" To her immense relief, Kate and Paul were just down the hall and had heard Doc yelling. They came running, or rather, they hurried in the sort of way that says everyday emergency. Emily was rubbing her shoulder and backing away from Doc as they entered the room. Soon other staffers followed.

"Doc, what are you doing?" Kate put her body between Doc and Emily, while Paul snatched his cane from him.

"I want to go home!" Doc raged.

"You can't hit the girls! You want to hit somebody, hit me! It's me, Paul! Doc, you were hitting Emily." Paul soothed him. "You can't go home, Doc; it burned down. Remember? That was five years ago now. There's nobody to look after you out there; who would cook your meals or bring your chaw?"

Hearing Paul's voice, Doc was shaken out of his temper. His eyes watered. "Oh God, was I hitting a girl? I ain't got a right to do that. I just wanted to go home … I just wanted to go home …" He retreated to his bed, his wrinkled mouth pulled down in a sad way.

"Yeah, and now you hit girls!" yelled Kate, keeping after him. "You coward, you hit girls!" She seemed genuinely upset.

Emily pulled her back. "It's OK, Kate, I said something wrong, I think."

"I just want to rest," said Doc. "Leave me alone now, girls, please?" The excitement over, all the staff began to drift out to their other chores. As they left, Emily heard him mutter, "I want to die. Just leave me alone to die." Doc's voice drifted to a whisper. "'Scatter My Ashes on the Amber Waves of Grain.' That'll shut 'em up."

Dresses and Boys

Melissa

On an average Wednesday afternoon Amy was sitting in her little apartment on the west side of Kearney watching *Montel* and painting her toenails, when the phone rang. She sighed and wondered, *Why the hell do I even have that thing? It does nothing but interrupt me.* She answered it anyway.

"Hey, Amy." It was Melissa.

"Hey, sweetie."

"Do you have a minute?"

"Yeah, but I gotta go soon." Amy wasn't sure if she wanted to talk. "Back to the daily grind, you know." She laughed at herself, but Melissa didn't even get the joke.

"Well, it's about Randall. I guess I called you because you, like, understand men."

"Men are pigs," Amy said. "They're pretty simple. All they want is to eat, drink, and screw."

"Not Randall." Melissa sounded hopeful.

"Oh sweetie, Randall too." Amy chuckled. "I've seen how he looks at you. It's the same way he looks at a plate of steak and home fries. He can barely keep from drooling."

"Well, that's the thing. Randall, he's so polite. But when he kisses me, I know that underneath is this …" Melissa broke off. Amy let her twist in the wind for a minute before she completed the sentence.

"… big-boner, massive sex drive, right?" Amy was smiling.

There was a moment of silence while Melissa contemplated how to respond to this.

"I'm not a very good cook," Melissa said, "and I'm worried that after we're married, like, that he'll be unhappy. What if I don't *please* him?" She really sounded worried. Amy sighed and decided to help.

"I guess you guys aren't *doing it*, huh?" Amy was direct.

"No!" Melissa protested.

"You're going to wait, like, until your honeymoon?" Amy allowed the slightest incredulity into her voice.

"Of course!" Melissa was adamant.

"Well, I don't know about cooking. Maybe you can ask his mom about some of his favorite recipes, but I think you're a better cook than you'd ever admit. God, your mom is a Mennonite ... You don't even realize how much you know compared to me about cooking," Amy said, thinking about fried baloney sandwiches. "But screwing isn't that hard. You'll catch on quick."

"But what if *I* don't like it?" Melissa worried.

Amy laughed. "You like Randall, don't you?"

"I'm crazy about him!"

"You'll be fine. You'll like it sometimes, and sometimes you won't. That's all there is to it."

Melissa sighed. "Have you seen Emily lately?" she asked.

"No." Amy looked at her nails.

"She went out with this guy, Paul," Melissa offered. "He's, like, twenty-seven or something."

Amy was suddenly interested. "Where did she meet him?"

"At work," Melissa gushed. "She said he's funny. But she also said he wasn't really an option."

"Huh," Amy grunted, just as quickly losing interest. "She's too picky."

"All she ever does anymore is work. We should all get together sometime." Melissa put on her hopeful voice again.

"Yeah." Amy hoped this conversation would go away.

"What are you doing Saturday night? We could all go see *Batman Returns*. Michael Keaton is in it," she said, trying for a nibble.

"I have to work," Amy said. "Saturday is our biggest night. Besides," she said, "Jimmy says that movie sucks. How's the wedding planning going?" She wasn't very interested in Melissa's wedding and was going to be glad when the whole thing was over.

"Well, the menu is set with the caterer, we've got to pick bridesmaids' dresses, and then we're really just down to the last details," Melissa said.

"How about your bachelorette party?" Amy was still miffed that Melissa hadn't allowed her to plan it.

"We're not really having one. I'm going to have to be up at five on the big day to do my hair and makeup. I don't want to look tired."

Amy wondered if she would sleep at all the night before her own wedding—that is, if Jimmy ever got around to proposing. "Yeah," she said, "I guess not." After a pause, Amy excused herself and hung up.

Melissa dialed another number.

"Hello?" Emily sounded bored. This was a good thing.

"Hey, it's me. I was just talking to Amy. Have you talked to her lately?"

"No. Not since graduation. I'm not sure what I would even have to say to her. How's the bridal thing going?"

"Great. Can you come with my mother and I this weekend? We're going down to Kearney to pick out bouquets and dresses."

"Saturday?" asked Emily.

"Yeah, late morning."

"I guess I could."

"Emily, what do you think of men?" Melissa twisted a strand of hair around her finger.

She was used to Melissa's directness, so she didn't really miss a beat. "I think they're complicated."

"Is it the men who are complicated, or is it just us?"

Emily thought about it for a moment, then smiled. "Yeah, I think we're the ones that make it complicated. Do you think we confuse them?"

"I'm pretty sure we do," Melissa agreed, "but do men confuse you? I mean, even a little?"

"I don't know. I guess I don't think about them that much." Emily had never been in love, but this statement wasn't exactly truthful either.

"Right." Melissa sighed, not wanting to disagree too overtly with her friend. She thought about Randall constantly.

"The first thing we have to do is pick out the bridesmaids' dresses," Melissa said as soon as Emily jumped in the pickup. Melissa gunned the engine, and soon they were driving south on 183 toward the shopping center in Kearney. Melissa and her mother chatted excitedly about the wedding. For some time they seemed unaware of their surroundings.

"Melissa, you're driving like Randall," Mrs. Stoltzfus said. "By the way, where *is* he? Isn't he coming along?"

"He's still choring. He's catching up with us later for sandwiches." Melissa directed her attention to Emily. "Mom has to get back home when we're done, so Randall will take us home. So, how's Paul?"

"He's good," Emily said absently.

"Are you guys going out again?"

"I don't think so, Melissa," Emily sighed. "He's really sweet, but he's not my type, really."

"Randall is bringing Walt along today," Melissa said.

"Walt who? The guy who drew Mickey Mouse?"

"No. Walt Ropp. He's a guy from church. He's part of the young adults group. He's not too old, just twenty-four. He's really nice; you'll like him."

"OK," Emily agreed with a shrug. Somehow she already doubted Melissa on this one.

Melissa pulled Emily along as she bounced into the bridal shop. "For the bridesmaids, here's the one I like the best." Melissa and her

mother showed the dress to Emily before Mrs. Stoltzfus went to look at another section of the store. The dress had way more ruffles than Emily would prefer. It was the type of dress you laughed at in the photo album seven years later.

"It's perfect. Make it easy on yourself. Let's go with that."

"The only problem is the price. Look." Melissa turned over the tag, and Emily's eyes got big.

"You only get married once," Emily said. "If that's the one you like the best ..."

"I have to buy four of them, though—my sisters, plus one for you and one for Amy." Melissa shook her head.

"Let's look at something else," Emily said, relieved. "Here's something simpler ... but the price is only ten percent less than the one you like best."

"Ten percent is still a lot of money." Melissa's Mennonite frugality was kicking in. "Oh look! Emily, this one is half-off! Plus, it covers more, which would really make my mom happy. She's not into showing very much back, legs, or ... bosoms." Melissa nodded to herself as though she could hear her mother's lecture on modesty.

It's half-off because it's horrible, Emily thought. *Victorian. Lace up the neck to our ears. Melissa's church in Broken Bow has no air conditioning. The fabric is not light. Without any breeze, we'll be sweatin' like hogs.* But she couldn't think of anything to say. As far as Melissa was concerned, there were far too many pluses.

"Let's go look at shoes over there next," Melissa said as her mother returned and approved her dress selection. Emily groaned inside. Melissa was sure to pick something cheap and uncomfortable again.

At noon, Melissa's mother headed home, and Randall and Walt met them at a Subway that had just opened. Randall and Walt were already eating. Emily and Melissa got their sandwiches and joined the boys.

"Hi, Emily," Randall said briefly, "this is Walt."

Walt's suspenders curved snugly around his belly, tenuously clinging to his jeans, which wanted to escape the grip of the tiny, metal clasps and surprise everyone by dropping to the floor. His short-sleeved dress shirt, buttoned all the way up, was too small, and he mopped his brow with a very damp, red handkerchief with black paisleys on it. It appeared that Walt cut his own hair and shaved without a mirror.

"Hi." Walt looked Emily over frankly as though she were a heifer at the auction barn, his gaze finally coming to rest on her toes sticking out of her sandals. She wondered if he had a fetish or was just shy. Perhaps he'd never seen a girl with painted toenails before. She tried to curl her toes, and finally slid her feet back into her sandals so nobody could see her neon-orange nails.

"Walt farms up between Harmony and Broken Bow," Melissa said helpfully.

"Beans and wheat, but I got chickens. …" Walt launched into a tirade about his chickens. *Clearly,* Emily thought, *he has a love-hate relationship with these chickens*. Several of them had won prizes at the state fair, but some of them had nasty personalities, and the roosters sounded like Amy's boyfriends and their drinking buddies. There were codependent hens and chicks so stupid and neurotic, they drowned themselves in two inches of water, aggravating Walt to tears, and as he told the story his eyes watered again. He mopped at his eyes with his hankie. He was eating a meatball sub with extra mayonnaise as he talked. There was marinara *and* mayonnaise on his face. He mopped his brow again but neglected his chin.

"Emily works at the nursing home in Harmony," Melissa interrupted when Walt swallowed.

"Yeah." Emily said.

"How do you like that?" Walt asked, remembering his manners.

"It's OK." *How do you tell someone about people like Doc and Owen, Mrs. O'Toole, Mrs. Murphy, Kate, Alice, and Paul? It would take a whole book.* Emily didn't want to talk about it to Walt. After all, he talked about chickens as though they were people. She didn't want to appear very interested in him—because she wasn't.

"Huh," Walt grunted, inhaling some sandwich in the lull in conversation.

Randall shifted on his bench and cleared his throat. "Walt's … single," he said apologetically, almost as if he were getting paid to say it.

"I can see that," Emily said, then covered for herself. "He's not wearing a ring."

"Oh, us Zion Mennonites don't wear rings," Walt said. "Too worldly—jewelry." He finished his words that ended in a *-y* more with an *-eh. Worldleh. Jew'reh.* As if only Jews wore it.

"Right," Emily said.

"I could use some help. I burn my dinner 'cause I fall asleep waiting for it to cook. Sometimes I don't get all the chores done until nine or later. Need someone to help feed the chickens. Ma says she's tired of starching my shirts; time to get a wife."

"I hope you find someone," Emily said and shot a look at Melissa.

"I'm working on it." Walt said through a mouthful of sandwich, looking pensive as though it were tax time and he had several W-2s complicating the matter.

"Randall owed him a favor," Melissa explained when they finally went back to shopping.

"Oh, so I'm a favor? Well, now you owe *me* a favor," Emily said, shaking her head. She'd think of something *good.* Or maybe she'd let it go. Her friends meant well.

The Big Apple

Ben

New York City, June 1992

Ben and Phil explored the Upper West Side of Manhattan together. They had perhaps been the only two people in the state of Nebraska who were playing chess on something called the World Wide Web as early as 1991, and they'd gotten to know each other pretty well that way.

They had a talk early on, each admitting to the other that he wasn't sure if he was gay or not. They decided that even if they were, they had better not be lovers, and they both appeared to be immensely relieved by this decision.

Across the hall from Phil and Ben lived two guys who had one year left at Columbia and became the Nebraskans' first close friends: Guy, who was from Paris but had a flawless British accent, and Michael, who came from Mobile, Alabama, and was more difficult to understand.

They laughed when Ben worried about muggers and ordered in some delicious *pad Thai* the night they moved in. They showed Ben and Phil the artwork in their apartment; they even loaned them a couple of paintings, which were very modern looking and possibly quite valuable. "Michael buys them," Guy explained, "but I pick them out. You may think they're very expensive, but we usually buy at senior exhibitions or from other students." Ben liked most of the artwork, but Phil admitted to Ben that he found the pieces "alternately disturbing and confusing."

Guy called Michael "Me-shell," which was really just the way a French guy would say *Michael* anyway. Ben decided that it sounded flamingly homosexual, and his heartbeat quickened. You could be a flamer here if you wanted to, and nobody would even bat an eye. Ben didn't think he'd ever act that way—but it was nice to know he could if he wanted to.

"Come on, lads," Guy said one night, "you've been here two weeks. It's time to celebrate! There's a small party at our flat tonight." Phil wondered if they should bring something, perhaps a casserole, and Guy replied, "Everything is arranged. I purchased a whole lorry full of Bordeaux."

"A lorry?" Ben and Phil laughed.

"Don't y'all 'member Guy learnt English while he was in London?" Michael told them.

"Y'all? *Learnt*?" Ben and Phil laughed harder. Michael tried so hard to be sophisticated, but he couldn't shake his Southern speech patterns when he got excited.

At the party, Ben took a glass when Guy offered it, and started to drink it like it was Kool-Aid. *"Non!"* Guy exclaimed. "You'll get too drunk too fast! Besides, *smell* it before you *taste* it. It's from Le Puy in Haute Loire. First, fields of *jonquils* ..., can you smell them? Now sip. A mountain stream, rocks covered with moss, mushrooms in the middle—*Ah Champignons!* Finally, a spicy kick of freshly crushed black pepper and melted butter on a croissant. Not used for getting pissed. *Tu vois?"*

Ben did not see. It tasted horrible, but he had the sense to smack his lips a little and say, *"Ah Shamp-een-OH!"*

Guy was telling him everyone's name—this fellow, that chap, and the other bloke. Guy was also moving around the room with an arm around Ben's waist, and his hand on Ben's hip, and Ben felt a little excited at the attention, but also a bit uncomfortable with it, since it was known that Guy and Michael weren't just *living* together. Besides, Guy was drinking the Bordeaux like it *was* Kool-Aid. As soon as he could, Ben peeled away from the Frenchman and found a quiet corner where he began to sniff and taste the wine carefully, noticing a variety of flavors, some pleasant and others a tad raunchy, wondering what a *jonquil* was. Even if Guy wasn't going to practice what he preached, Ben was determined to understand this wine as much as he hoped to understand the modern art hanging in so many of the apartments where their friends had these parties. Ben's parents had collected several Midwestern impressionist paintings that were nice, but they didn't *mean* anything. They were mostly of cows in pastures looking well fed but still eating. Metaphors for buffet restaurants or church potlucks.

"Do you mind?"

Ben looked up. "What?"

"Do you mind?" A guy who looked to be in his mid-twenties was holding a camera, gesturing at Ben, then at the Nikon in his hand. It was a really expensive piece, Ben could tell, even though he knew very little about cameras. For some reason this guy looked vaguely familiar, but Ben attributed that to the wine. Everybody looks a little more familiar with wine.

"No, I guess not," he replied. The man indicated he should act reflective, so Ben sipped his wine and looked out the window at the Hudson River and the George Washington Bridge. The man shot several photos of Ben, then stood by him at the window.

"I'd like to have you come to the studio, if you would be willing," he said. "I'll pay well."

Ben felt a little dizzy. "Right now?" he said, incredulously. "I'm a little drunk. Just because I'm a country boy doesn't mean—"

"Oh no," the man laughed, a little embarrassed. "In the daylight, of course. This was just for fun. I'm talking about a serious, artistic photo shoot. Not the full monty. Just … beautiful. Something you could show your mother. You know?"

"I don't even *know* you," Ben protested, "but if Guy says you're OK—or, better yet, Michael—then maybe …" Ben looked around but couldn't see Guy or Michael.

"Sorry. I should have introduced myself. I'm Tony Milano, but my friends all call me 'Caravaggio.'"

"'Caravaggio'? Interesting. Whence the nickname?" Ben smiled to himself. He felt sophisticated for using the word *whence.*

"Maybe it's the way I view darkness and light through the lens; maybe it's the way I view darkness and light through the rosary," Tony said. "Maybe it's both. Lots of my friends think it's crazy that I still go to Mass. But then lots of my artist friends say I'm crazy to love black and white in an age of color! Never mind. Neon pink and phosphorescent green is a fad, and fading quickly too. Watch and see. Black and white is eternal; it'll be back in vogue in five years. Black and white is like a tuxedo: always the classiest way to go, never out of style. Did you say you're a country boy?"

Ben nodded and stared westward across the river. He could see New Jersey. Beyond, there was Pennsylvania, then Ohio, Indiana, Illinois, and Iowa. Out there somewhere, half a world away, was Harmony, Nebraska.

"Did you say 'Harmony, Nebraska'?" Tony nearly dropped his camera out the open window.

"Huh? Did I?" Ben was unaware he had spoken.

"You did. You're not from Harmony, are you?" Tony was squinting at him.

"Yes. Originally," Ben added. He wanted it to sound like it had been a long time ago.

"I'm Tony Milano," Tony told him again. "I'm from Harmony too."

"Wow, really? Anyway, did I mention my name? I'm Ben." He stuck his hand out awkwardly. He thought it should be extremely surprising to find someone from Harmony in the middle of these millions. But it wasn't. "It's a small world," he smiled.

"I'm Italian," Tony said. "We hug." He held his arms wide.

"I'm German," Ben countered, "but I'm not even sure what I am. Can I pass?"

Tony, shrugging, laughed at this. He held out his hand for Ben to shake. "So you're from Harmony. So, do you know—?"

"I'd rather not talk about Harmony," Ben said, and shook Tony's hand. Then, in a surge of homesickness, Ben hugged him anyway. It was comforting to find someone in this huge city who knew where he came from. *It was familiar, like finding a brother,* Ben admitted to himself.

Tony was pleasantly surprised, and when Ben let go, he touched his cheek. "You're beautiful, kid. But I can't have you. You do need to be careful," Tony informed him. "There are guys who will try to get you drunk, then get you to go home with them. A lot of us won't get tested because we don't want to know. But everybody knows somebody who ..." Tony turned away.

"Somebody who what?"

Tony lowered his voice. "Somebody who died of AIDS. It isn't the seventies anymore, Ben. The Village isn't a 'village' the way you think of it if you're from Harmony. Everyone's very friendly, but they're also potentially ... lethal."

"Not ... you?"

"Yes, unfortunately I'm HIV positive, and I'll appreciate if you don't tell anyone back home. Just ... be careful." Tony swallowed hard and turned away from him.

"I'm sure of it now," Phil told Ben. They had returned to their tiny apartment as the sun cracked into the sky like an egg yolk peeking over the edge of a gray skillet. "I'm straight, Ben." Phil looked sad, which Ben thought was counterintuitive. Being sure of being straight would make life so easy.

"How do you know?" Ben realized this was a stupid question as soon as he asked it.

"Don't ask," Phil told him, "but I know."

"Well ... that's great, isn't it, Phil? I mean, why are you so down?"

"I don't want to talk about it." Phil rolled his eyes. "It's not that simple," he grumbled, and went to put on his pajamas. Ben heard him vomiting in the narrow bathroom.

Himself dizzy with wine, Ben said, "Did you drink too much?"

"No," Phil said, "I didn't drink at all."

"Do you have the flu?"

"No," Phil said as tears ran down his ashen face. Refusing to look at Ben, Phil turned and went to bed.

Still feeling buzzed, Ben went down to the street and found a place to buy a postcard and picked one with a nighttime view of the Statue of Liberty. He wrote:

> *Dear Emily,*
> *I'm having a great time here, and yes, I'm being careful. I met a guy from Harmony. Tony Milano. He's going to take pictures of me. I wonder what you're doing for fun these days. Mom told me what Amy is doing, and I bet I know what you think of that. I'm making friends here. I guess Melissa and Randall are excited, huh? Miss you!*
> *Ben*

He didn't have a stamp, and the breeze that came in the window that night blew the postcard under the bed. Ben couldn't sleep. The wine was catching up to him, so he went into the bathroom and retched. *So that's what* jonquils *are,* he thought wryly.

'Medic!'

Owen

Moments of lucidity still came to Owen now and then. It felt to him as though the helmet he sometimes wore helped. He wondered if this was because the hole he cut in the top of it allowed radio waves to hit his brain at the very top of his skull.

He lost his train of thought, then regained it.

Amiens, France, August, 1918

"Medic!" A young British soldier was screaming as the Germans retreated from Amiens. The wounded man's unit moved on, urged by their lieutenant forward into the fray and encouraged by the success of their assault. *"Medic!"* His voice began to carry over the din of artillery thuds and the pop of lighter weapons carried by the infantry as the battle surged eastward. Trenches were being abandoned at an alarming rate, and Owen knew that somewhere nearby, a man needed immediate attention.

"We've got to go find him," Owen's best friend and fellow medic, George, urged.

Owen lifted his head above the lip of the trench just high enough to see the battlefield. "I don't know where he is," Owen said, hesitating.

"He's losing blood, I guarantee it," George insisted. "We've got to find him. He sounds really hurt."

"We can't help anyone if we get shot ourselves," Owen worried.

"Look, the Germans are pulling back." It was true. The firefight was receding. It *looked* safe to go out.

"Medic!" The cry was frightened now, but no less animal than before. *"Au Secours!* Help me! *Medic! S'il vous plait!* I don't want to die!" The soldier out there was just lucid enough to use some French in his plea, in case the nearest medic was a local boy.

George grabbed the stretcher and threw it out of the trench. "He's just south of us, come on!"

"No! He's to the north!" Owen grabbed George's arm.

"South. We're going south first!" George broke away from Owen's grip and leapt out of the trench. Staying low, he grabbed the stretcher at one end and began dragging it.

"Medic!" The fainter cry was of a man who didn't want to die alone. He was beginning to weaken. Owen had no choice but to follow George, who would need help with the stretcher. Cautiously, Owen crawled out of the trench. For much of the war, he'd been unafraid, but now, suddenly and inexplicably, Owen felt as though he was about to wet himself. George was already twenty yards away, dragging the heavy stretcher by himself. Crouching, Owen started to run after him, but he took only two strides before a whistle stopped him in his tracks. George stopped too, looking back at Owen in surprise for a moment, and then the earth leapt up about George and became the sky around him. Owen dropped flat on his face with his hands over the back of his neck for many long moments.

When his ears stopped ringing, he realized someone was still crying for a medic, swearing in English and then in French. Owen remembered saying those French curses in front of his father when he was very young. They had been fishing, and Owen had caught his finger on his hook. He used some words he'd heard Grandfather say one day when Grandfather caught his own finger on a hook, and Owen's papa slapped him across the mouth. He fell and tasted dirt and blood on his tongue. "You should not use such words," his father told him in their Acadian dialect, "not even if you are dying. God hears." The scream came once again, and he looked up to see if it was George. But George's body had no mouth with which to call out. His helmet was spinning like a top. *Nobody should have such a gap between their chest and their brain,* Owen thought. *It isn't natural.*

Blinded by his own tears, Owen eventually found the screaming British soldier in a slight depression forty yards to the north. "Thank God, Medic," said the soldier weakly when he saw the red cross on Owen's helmet.

Owen put a tourniquet on what was left of the man's right arm, and injected him with morphine. "George," Owen cried over and over. "George!"

"No," said the dazed soldier in his care. "No, I'm Godfrey. Tell my mother it's Godfrey. George is at home; he's just a lad. He's too young to fight …" The morphine overcame him, and he fell asleep. His heart rate fell, and Owen applied pressure with all his might until he stopped the bleeding. Godfrey was saved. *He will have to learn to write and use a fork with his left hand,* Owen thought.

There were other screams now, and Owen worked through the haze of his tears and through the numbness of his grief. Moving precisely and efficiently, Owen was oblivious to the occasional fire from the front. Mechanically determining at a glance whether or not a wounded man had a chance to survive, and callously leaving those who didn't, he worked until he was utterly exhausted, even delirious. That day, Owen saved the lives of four more British men, seven Germans shot while fleeing, and two Americans, none of whom was named George.

A few days later, Owen awoke in a field hospital where he convalesced with a deep shrapnel wound in his left buttock, sustained he knew not when, but probably from the same shell that killed George. He stayed there until after he had survived a pretty bad strain of the influenza virus that killed thousands all over Europe. Having been awarded several medals, which Owen was predisposed to accept graciously, he was finally sent home to Maine in January of 1919. He enrolled in the Geology Department at Johns Hopkins University that fall.

1992

Owen remembered it all vividly; he wanted to tell someone before he forgot.

Everything was dark, and then he recalled he was blind.

"What time is it?"

Nobody answered. Perhaps it was one in the morning. Perhaps they were all out smoking. Perhaps he was already dead, and this was the afterlife. He couldn't remember dying, though. He inhaled, and noticed the oxygen tickle the bottom of his lungs. Proof.

Brains in His Helmet

Owen

Something was wrong when Emily and Paul went into Room 143 the next morning. Emily didn't pick up on what it was right away. "Good morning, gentlemen," she said brightly. "Doc, your hair looks nice." Doc sat in his armchair. He was combing his hair carefully, and he was dressed in clean clothes.

Paul turned. "Owen?" The professor was curled up in his bed, moaning.

"Doctor, is that you? *Medic*?" Owen tried to get up, collapsed back on his bed, and said weakly, "Is the Metamucil coming?" He began to moan louder. "*Medic,*" he said. "Uu-u-u-h-h-h-h-h."

"He's sick!" Emily had a penchant sometimes for stating the obvious.

"Dr. Hostetler is on his rounds today, he's just down the hall. Maybe we should see if he can come and see Owen," Paul suggested.

"You get him comfortable, I'll get the doctor," Emily urged as she hurried out.

From across the room, Paul heard Doc. "Did she say, 'I'll get the doctor'?"

"Yes, Doc, he happens to be in the building right now, so we're fetching him for Owen," Paul replied.

"Like hell I'm going to be here when that ass-backwards, sorry excuse for a doctor shows up. I'm going to get my coffee. Frankenstein!" Doc left for breakfast faster than Paul had seen him move in months.

Emily was back as quickly as she had left. Taking Owen's hand, she soothed him, murmuring, "Dr. Hostetler said he'd be just a minute. Owen, I have some cool water to put on a washcloth for your forehead. You're sweating! Paul, do you know where the K-Y Jelly is? Owen, it's going to be OK."

Finally, Dr. Hostetler sauntered in with what Emily thought of as his far too precocious air. Kate hustled in right behind him. "Well, Mr. Thibodeaux, not feeling well?" The doctor was aloof.

"A fortnight!" Owen groaned. "Is the Metamucil coming? A shell exploded … my best friend … all that was left was his brains in his helmet. *Medic!*"

Dr. Hostetler probed around Owen's middle. He grunted. "Hmm. Distended, tight. Could be compaction. Do we still have him on Metamucil?"

"He asks for it every day until it drives you crazy," Kate exclaimed. "How can we not give it to him!"

"No more Metamucil," the doctor ordered. "No coffee, juice, tea, milk, or soda. Just water. He's compacted; we'll have to help him."

"What can we do?" Emily was wringing her hands.

"We'll have to dig him out," Kate said curtly as she began to put on her gloves.

"You mean …" Emily was horrified.

"Manually, yes." Kate's look was grim. Clearly this was not her favorite part of the job.

"Mr. Thibodeaux, we'll have to do a pelvic exam," Dr. Hostetler explained.

"Is that the doctor?" Owen's hand waved in the air, searching for the body with the voice.

"Yes," the doctor went on, grasping the old professor's hand for a moment. "Owen, you have colon. We're going to have to do a pelvic exam to help you have a bowel movement."

"It's been a fortnight." Owen let out his longest, saddest moan. Emily suddenly realized that even though he was indeed in great discomfort, he was also, in a strange sort of way, thriving on all the attention. "Is the Metamucil coming? Nurse? Nurse Edith? Are you there? *Medic?*"

"I'm right here, Owen. Dr. Hostetler and Nurse Kate are going to help you," Emily said, but Dr. Hostetler turned and left the room without a word.

"Nurse Edith," Owen moaned, "I'm afraid I've come here to die."

"Paul, don't go. I have a feeling we'll need you to help hold him over on his side. He's not going to like this," Kate directed.

Emily held the old gentleman's hand, while Paul put his shoulder against Owen's back to keep him from rolling over—like a blocking sled in football practice. Owen howled as Kate began to work.

"I *definitely* need to get out of this town," Emily heard Paul mutter under his breath.

White Buffalo Football

Paul

Although Paul might not want to admit it, some of the proudest moments of his life were on the gridiron. He devoutly wished that one day he could say he'd participated in something greater than the football season of 1983, but so far it was still the best thing he could remember. The more time passed, the more that season of glory glowed with the polish of careful retelling, but he would never forget the way that year *really* started.

August 8, 1983

On the fourth afternoon of camp, Paul finished his laps with the herd of defensemen, all of whom staggered to a halt by the water cooler and drank deeply from gallon milk jugs filled with lukewarm water. Coach Hartman's three-a-days were putting the fear of God into the Harmony White Buffalo. One of the junior defensive backs had gotten heat stroke the day before and was still on intravenous liquids; everyone was drinking three or four gallons a day and still losing weight.

"Milano, Coach wants to see you in his office," somebody yelled. Paul groaned with relief and headed for the locker room.

"What's up, Coach?"

"First of all, congratulations, you're my starting middle linebacker this fall. Don't tell anyone I said this, but you're the best defensive player we have. Usually I don't announce starters until a few days before the opener, but I need you to be a leader this fall. Between you and me, I think we have a chance to go to State. You're inspiring your teammates with your work ethic and improvement." Coach smiled.

Paul would've killed for Coach Hartman. There was a reason why he'd stuck it out for three years, riding the pine, waiting for his body to catch up to his peers. Coach Hartman was the best coach a guy could have. He talked to kids in the hallway instead of retreating to the teachers' lounge. While he was tough as nails, he never missed a chance to applaud his boys' efforts. He refrained from using phrases like *one hundred and ten percent*—and, gratefully, the kids did their best to give him more than they had. Today, Paul was rewarded for his patience. No longer would he be a second-stringer.

When camp was over, the whole team convened in the locker room. "This is one of the proudest moments in a young man's life," Coach said. "Don't take these colors lightly. Every one of you had to earn the privilege of wearing them, with your outstanding behavior on the field and off. The other coaches and I, we watch you, and we've found those of you in this room worthy. Oh look at these," and he opened the first cardboard box.

A white helmet with a single navy stripe. No decoration of any kind—Penn State-style. Two jerseys for each boy—a navy shirt with HARMONY emblazoned across the chest in white for away games; a white shirt with WHITE BUFFALO printed in navy for home games—and, for Paul, the number *95* on the back of both. White pants, no stripes. White socks. There was a special shipment of all-white cleats from Nike paid for by the Boosters. This year Paul's was the biggest pair in the batch.

"There shouldn't be a single white jersey by the end of the year," continued Coach. "On my teams, everybody gets to play—varsity or JV. And everybody better get some mud, some grass stains—maybe even some blood—on these pretty white shirts. That's how people know when they've seen a football player from Harmony. Are you ready to be White Buffalo this fall? If you are, let me hear you roar!"

The boys, some of them nearly men, did roar through eleven straight opponents that year before falling to a much bigger school in the State Championship by a score of 34 to 16. In 1983, the town of Harmony held its head high.

Only a few years later, in both the seasons of 1990 and 1991, the White Buffalo compiled a record of zero wins, eight losses. As painful as it was for everyone to admit, there just weren't enough kids around anymore to make a high school financially viable. The district could've hung on a bit longer if it were just about the money, but when the only thing to do on Friday night is watch high school football, and you lose every week, it makes the tough pill of consolidation easier to swallow. Perhaps after the consolidation of school districts, the team could win a few games. But even that wasn't enough for Paul. All he could make of it was that the whole town was going down. *I can't stick around to find out if that's the way it's gonna be. The opposite of critical mass. The moment before extinction. If you're the last guy standing, nobody writes your obit. I gotta get outta here.*

Demons in the Black Hills

Emily

A light breeze brought the earthy smell of growing wheat in from the fields as Emily climbed into her beat-up Chevette to drive to the home at half past five on Tuesday morning. The sun had not yet risen, but the wheat fields were lit by a full moon to the southwest and the first light of dawn to the southeast. It had rained in the night and was still humid. Emily was grateful for air conditioning in the workplace, even if the units were old and initially blew a foul scent up into your face when they kicked on. Even before her morning report was finished, Emily was sent to check out a ruckus in Room 143. Doc was dressed, but Emily found Mrs. O'Toole milling about in the room, confused. The poor lady was standing in the room wearing a nightgown over a blouse and slacks, babbling to herself faster than ever. "So cold—I'm so cold. Help me! Help me! I'm lost!"

Doc was the one making most of the real noise, Emily quickly realized. He was yelling at the intruder. ***"Get out of the room! You're not going to steal my Jesus again! I know you!*** You're that crazy Mrs. O'Toole! Where's that young man? What's his name? Paul, I think." Doc yelled out the door. ***"Doctor Paul, where are you?"***

"I've got to melon, melon, melon. I've got to peach, peach, peach. I can't find my way," Mrs. O'Toole explained.

Owen sat up. "Is that Mrs. O'Toole, the blue-eyed, Irish, red-headed beauty?"

"Mrs. Chip O'Toole, Mrs. Chipper O'The-Toolio. Oh-oh!" she introduced herself. "So cold—my feet. Chip? Where are you, Chippy?

Chipper?" She followed Doc to the doorway, and their voices echoed in the empty corridor, waking the rest of the residents. "*An*drew? Andrew O'To-o-o-o-ole?" she called out. "You come in right this second! Andrew is lost!"

Owen burst into song. "*When Irish eyes are smiling, oh the world seems bright and gay—*"

He seemed to forget why he had started, and stopped as abruptly as he had begun. But Mrs. O'Toole was pleased, and, clapping her hands, she cried, "Yes! Yes! He always played it. He had a lemon, and we would pickle. I would dance! But now I am cold—so cold. Cheddar—onions! Which way is north?"

Somehow Emily got everyone dressed and ready for breakfast, but that afternoon the scene repeated itself. Doc again called for Paul to help him remove the offending Mrs. O'Toole, who seemed hell-bent on stealing his crucifix.

This time it was indeed Paul who came to Doc's rescue. "Mrs. O! What are you doing in Doc and Owen's room?" In spite of how confused the lady was, she evaded him for a moment or two before he caught her gently by the elbow. "Come on, dear," Paul said, "it's time to go to bed. Afternoon naptime before the second shift comes in—"

"Augh! I'm not going to bed with you! Why you"—Mrs. O'Toole swatted him playfully—"you're a naughty one. I bet you'd like to get melons, peaches, grapes, apples. But I won't let you! Not today, anyhow!" She slipped out of his grip, and Paul spent several more moments chasing her. He was trying to catch her without causing injury, which was difficult, considering the frailness of her bones.

"It's not like that! Come on, I'll help you find your room. Is Andrew lost again, Mrs. O'Toole?"

"Lost?" she said as she dodged him again. "Well, I'm not sure. 'I'm cold,' I told her. 'I'm cold, and can we have another corncob? And what does the cat do in there, creeping through the corn, coming through the rye? New York and after all we're just … cold. Pumpernickel. It's got barbed wire,' I said. 'I need a fire,' I said. 'He might be dead,' I said, 'or he might have left when I was just a girl. Or both.' Chipper? Are you out there? Andrew? Are you baking? Did you leave the oven on? Which way is north? Everything's so cloudy.

Mother? Mo-o-o-other?" She stretched out the first syllable. Finally, Paul got her arm and guided her toward the door. Doc was clapping and jeering.

"Come on, now," Paul directed. "North is that way. Get your locket; it's around your neck." As soon as Mrs. O'Toole saw the picture of herself in the locket, which she thought to be of her mother, she settled right down and headed meekly back to her room on her own accord.

"Doctor, she's just crazy as a bat in a bottle of beetle juice," said Doc, addressing Paul. "A drunk skunk wouldn't be more sunk if he drank piss from a monk and fall down dead *ker-plunk*. Loony." Doc was grinning, clearly pleased with his rhyme scheme. Paul could tell he was glad *he* wasn't crazy.

"Yeah, Doc, I know. Look, I'm no more a doctor than you are. Come on, you know me. I'm Paul. The nurse's aide. I'm *not* a physician." Paul sighed and headed out the door.

"Whatever you say, Doc," said Doc.

A moment later, Emily stuck her head into the room. "You guys need anything? What's the ruckus, Doc?"

"Make sure that crazy lady didn't pinch my Jesus or pilfer my Statue of Liberty. She's a thief, that one. Keep her out of here! Trespassing! I want my lawyer!"

"Yeah, I know. You got your rights," Emily said as she checked his top drawer. "Everyone is here—Jesus and Lady Liberty—all mixed up over who's who."

"She's a burglar, that Mrs. O'Toole. Andrew never did come back. Some say he died ridin' the rails, but I know better," he winked.

"Really?" Emily noticed that Owen was struggling to get out of his wheelchair. "Owen, do you need help getting into bed for a rest?"

"Thank you, nurse," Owen replied.

"I have a few minutes for a story if you'd like to tell one. I hear you have a lot of stories. It's time for my afternoon break."

Owen didn't need to be asked twice. "Did I ever tell you about teaching at Nebraska?" he asked. Then he sighed as his bones sank into the mattress.

"No, but you did sing the song for me." *There could never be enough music in this sorry place,* she thought.

"I did?"

"Yes," she smiled. "I love to hear you sing."

"What do I sing?" Owen couldn't think of any songs.

"Let's see, I've heard you sing three songs: the Nebraska fight song, 'Irish Eyes Are Smiling,' and 'Trust and Ob—'"

"*Allons enfants de la patriiiie, le jour de gloire est arrivé. Aux armes, citoyens, aux armes, citoyens—*" Owen broke off. "Can I have a graham cracker?"

"'*La Marseillaise*'! Wonderful!" Emily found a cracker. "You're French, aren't you? Thibodeaux."

"My family was '*acadienne,*' we say, but when they drew the borderlines we ended up in Maine."

"What about teaching at Nebraska?" she reminded him.

"Ah yes. When I taught at Nebraska, there was a girl. Edith. Not like you; she wasn't a nurse. But she was smart. My best student. Sharp as a tack and the most beautiful girl I ever met. She loved the earth—stones, boulders, pebbles. She found some amazing belemnites. But she was too forward. Jean brought me this rock from Nova Scotia. It pleases me more than the Rock of Gibraltar."

"Did you marry her?" Emily wondered.

"I was married …" he said pensively.

"Did you marry Edith?"

"Edith was a Protestant girl …" It was as if he were paging through a mental scrapbook with pages missing.

"How did Edith come to love the rocks so much?"

"Ah!" He remembered something. "Edith went with me to South Dakota. The Black Hills! Do you know why they are called the Black Hills?"

"No."

His face fell. "I don't remember. There may be evil spirits. Some old Indian told me that, but I don't know. We explored those hills several times. I would take a team of students for a summer internship. But Edith was the brightest student. She loved the hills. She could dig like nobody's business, and she could identify any little trace of mineral in the stone by sight, by color. Basalt, rhyolite, pegmatite, and precambrian schist. A brilliant girl, read books all the time. By the end of the first summer she knew as much as I did, or nearly. What time is it? Can I have a graham cracker?"

Emily handed him another snack. "It's … 1:42 in the afternoon. What happened in the internship with Edith?"

"The last year … it began to rain so hard that we couldn't work. The students played cards in their tents. Edith had bits of chiseled granite in her black hair; the quartz minerals became jewels in the lamplight. She came to my tent pulling the braid out of her hair. Her skin was golden like summer wheat. Her eyes were grayish green, like the clouds before a tornado. Maybe it was the demons in the Black Hills. The pioneers tamed Nebraska, but the Black Hills are wild. She never did anything like that at the university. Have you ever been to Hawai'*i*? It's beautiful. The beaches become mountains. I went to Hawai'i many times."

"But … how did it end?"

"How did what end?"

"Your time with Edith," Emily prompted patiently. Owen's eyes lit up—a revelation. He remembered something he usually couldn't remember.

"Ah! It rained for a whole week. The Indians said they'd never seen anything like it. The other students were playing cards and drinking; Edith and I were … *studying* in my tent. Finally, the rain cleared up and we all went back to work. Then one day she said she … well, I gave her two hundred dollars to go to Denver. It was the only thing to do."

"Why did she go to—?"

Owen remembered something else. "My wife … she knew immediately when I returned."

Emily thought she was putting some pieces together. "You mean, you were married to someone else at the time?"

As if just remembering, Owen exclaimed, "Yes, I was! It's too easy for a man to forget he's married. He has to see what is before him night and day. I'm blind, Nurse Edith." He paused for a long moment, and she thought he was going to fall asleep. She noticed that

Doc was snoring. Finally, he whispered, "The Black Hills' beauty blinded me. I never wanted to see anything again after I left." Then, loudly, as if trying to jar his own memory, ***"Jean brought me this stone from Nova Scotia.*** It pleases me more than the Rock of Gibraltar …" But he trailed off.

"Who is Jean anyway?"

"Jean? Who is Jean? I'm not sure … I can't remember. Jean is the wonderful girl who brought me this rock from Nova Scotia. It pleases me more than the Rock of Gibraltar." Owen held the small stone out to her as if she'd never seen it before.

Emily's shoulders drooped in frustration. "It's a lovely stone. My break time is over, Owen; I have to go chart. I'll see you in the morning."

"*Good-die,* Nurse Edith," he said in his best Scottish accent.

"Good-die, Professor Owen." Emily reached over and squeezed his hand before she left.

Regrets

Emily

After Alice gave her morning report, Emily went down to Room 143 and quietly slipped in. *You're supposed to knock,* she told herself, *but don't wake Owen just yet*. Owen was indeed asleep in his bed, but the other bed was empty.

Kate had seen which direction Emily went and followed her. Entering the room, she found Emily sitting on Doc's bed. She put her hand on Emily's shoulder. "Hard to believe he's gone," she said.

"I thought he'd live a long time yet," Emily said, shaking her head.

"He was a heavy drinker, you know. His liver was trashed, hard as a rock," Kate pointed out.

"Ugh." Emily shuddered at the thought of a limestone liver lying lifeless in a corpse. "What time did they say it was?"

"About 3, maybe 3:30, this morning. He usually got up real early, around that time, and would go down to the nurses' station to beg for whiskey for a few minutes, or pester Alice with his stories when she was trying to wrap up her charting for the morning. Anyway, when he didn't show, they checked on him, and he had the death rattle," Kate said.

"I never heard that. It sounds creepy."

"It is. You never get used to it, even if you hear it lots of times. The breathing gets rattly, and each time they inhale it gets farther and farther apart—and you start waiting for the next one, and you wait a little longer each time, and finally you realize there's nothing left to wait for, because the next one is never going to come, and it's over,"

Kate said. Her delivery made Emily think that Kate was actually quite used to observing death.

"It seems so sudden that Doc's gone," replied Emily. "I mean, he was walking around yesterday just fine, grumbling about his knee and Dr. Hostetler. And then you get someone like Janet down the hall. Lies in bed, all catatonic, and you feed her with a spoon and she never says a word, her eyes all glazed over. And she stays like that for weeks, somehow just hanging on."

Kate sat down next to Emily. She smiled and took Emily's hand. "Some people come in, and they stay for two weeks, and then they die, and you never got to know them, but when they're with us for ten years like Doc, you start to think they'll never die. Everyone does eventually. I mean, of course they do—Listen to me ..." Kate laughed at herself. "What I mean is, you don't notice them getting weaker and weaker because it's so gradual. And then one morning you come in and the night nurses have cleaned them up, and the funeral home has already been over to pick 'em up, and it's like they were never there."

Emily looked around the room. "The bed is made and his stuff is cleaned out already!" Emily was having trouble believing this.

"Well, the night aides don't have much to do. We'll probably have a new resident by this afternoon, and they know we don't have time to do it. It's part of their job. Most people go between midnight and four, you know. Why do you think they call it the graveyard shift?"

Emily nodded. In her mind, she knew it was all part of the job. But there was someone else in the room whom this death might concern. "What about Owen?" she wondered.

"He never paid Doc no attention anyway," Kate shrugged and went to wake him up. It was time to start the day's work. "Owen?"

Owen's eyes opened and, blind as he was, he saw enough light to know that it was daytime. "Good morning, Nurse," he said politely.

"Owen, there's bad news," Emily said as she went to help him get dressed.

Owen looked worried. "Are we out of Metamucil?"

Kate helped him up. "Owen, your roommate, Doc, is gone."

"Where did he go?"

"He died in the middle of the night," Emily said as she escorted him to the toilet.

"Why didn't you say so? What's the bad news? Do I have to see that doctor today?"

"No, Owen, Doc passed away." Kate was getting frustrated.

"That's a shame; such a young fellow." Owen said, looking stricken.

"Not Dr. Hostetler. Your roommate, Theodore Martin. They all called him 'Doc,'" Emily explained.

Owen's face lit up with understanding. "Ah! Theodore!" He was thoughtful for a moment. "I wondered why things were so quiet. Is the Metamucil coming?"

Kate turned to Emily. "Well, I guess that's about the extent of it," she said wryly, and then, looking with annoyance at Owen, "Metamucil at breakfast."

"Didn't Frankenstein say he shouldn't have any Metamucil?" Emily laughed.

"Yeah, but do you want to try to keep him from it? 'Is the Metamucil coming?' All day long! As Doc would say, Owen's got his rights, you know," Kate said.

"Statue of Liberty!" Emily replied.

Owen sat alone in his room most of the morning. He couldn't remember why things were so quiet. He kept himself company with his thoughts, rubbing a small stone someone named Jean had brought him from Nova Scotia.

"Nurse?" ... Owen listened for some time to see if anyone would come. "Have the nurses gone to lunch?" he wondered aloud. "Nurse? Can I have a graham cracker?" Nobody came. Owen had a buzzer on his nightstand, but he seldom remembered to use it. He felt his way to the nightstand, but he wasn't looking for the buzzer. He wanted a graham cracker. He fumbled in one of the drawers for a moment.

There was a box, but as he picked it up the weight of it told him it was empty. His stomach growled. "Nurse? Is it dinnertime yet?"

A wave of memories washed his hunger away for the moment and kept him busy talking to himself. "My best friend … all that was left was his *brains* in his helmet … his brains in his helmet … I can't remember … something … we had a foxhole, and when it seemed safe to go … did I go first?" He thought about this. *Surely,* he thought, *I would have had the courage to go first. I was brave that day, was I not?* "All that was left was his brains in his helmet." He could not remember it all, but some. Some days he could remember more. Did he want to? There were dead men, and there were ones who lived, and this, he was certain, was the way it had always been and would always be.

Continuing his soliloquy, he said, "Jean brought me this rock from Nova Scotia. It pleases me more than the Rock of Gibraltar. Who is Jean?" He called out louder. "Jean?" He waited, but Jean did not come. More quietly, he reprimanded himself. "No, Jean is not the nurse; Edith is the nurse." He thought about this.

"Nurse Edith? Nurse? Edith?" Edith did not come. Edith, who had been so beautiful. He remembered something now.

"That night with Edith the student, in my tent … she was so beautiful, quartz crystals sparkling in her hair. She smelled wild, like the Black Hills air. Everything was wild. There was a moment I thought I was devolving. I forgot … I forget …" He struggled to stay focused. It was there in his long-term memory, for sure. The challenge was getting past the failing short-term memory, the part that reminded him what he was thinking about. A little thing like his stomach growling would take it all off track, and he'd have to start over again. "I was wild, like the gorillas of the eastern Congo. We found an important fossil, a beautiful specimen of belemnite, the little squid tentacles perfectly laid out like a well-pressed pair of pants. Edith did it. She found it, after the mudslide, and it kept on raining. The whole thing was so exciting. Do the female gorillas cry? I didn't study the gorillas; I studied geology, and Edith studied geology, and I studied … Edith? Nurse?" He listened for a moment. No nurse came.

No, not the nurse, the other Edith. Too forward, but when she came to my tent I decided … I became the gorilla. After breakfast, I gave her two hundred dollars. She boarded the train for Denver, crying. My wife … she knew what had happened. Was she angry? I can't remember. She must have been angry …

This was where it usually began to break down for him. He pushed deeper into the recesses of his mind. *I began to go blind that day. I got mud in my eyes from the landslide. Did it hurt my eyes? Why can't I remember? I think … she said there would be a baby … unless … Yes, she* had *to go to Denver …*

The whole time I thought I might die. The whole time with Edith the student felt like a mudslide—dangerous … powerful … dark … and something uncovered at the end, like a beautiful belemnite specimen. You can die in a mudslide, and I thought I would die … Was I in the mudslide?

Suddenly frightened, he cried out loudly. ***"Nurse Edith? I didn't come here to die!"*** More quietly, he wondered, "Is it breakfast time yet? Is the Metamucil coming?"

Hearing Owen yell in what sounded like pain, Emily left what she was doing and hurried to Room 143. "Hello, Owen! What's the matter?"

"What time is it? Is it time for breakfast?"

"No, Owen, you just had lunch a little while ago."

"It's my eyes; it all seems darker every day. I can't remember what time it is. What time is it?"

"It's one thirty in the afternoon. July 4, 1992."

"Oh. How late it's gotten! Did you say the Fourth of July?"

"Yes."

Owen placed his hand on his heart and began to sing. "*Oh say, can you see, by the dawn's early light … ?* I can't see you. Are you Nurse Edith?"

"Yes, Mr. Thibodeaux." He heard the smile in her voice.

"What happened to your Scottish accent?" He was confused again. Past and present blurred. He hated that.

But Emily had a sense of humor. "What happened to your French-Canadian accent?"

This astonished him. It was a wonderful question. "I don't know! I was born in Maine ... I was in World War I ... my best friend ... all that was left was his brains in his helmet ..."

She helped him remember. "Did you get an education?"

"Yes, yes! I believe I did! I studied at Harvard and Johns Hopkins!" He was so happy to remember this.

"How did you get to Nebraska?"

"Hmm. I don't know." But he was all right with this. Even if it wouldn't all come back, this nurse would care for him. He showed her the best thing he had. "Jean brought me this rock from Nova Scotia—"

Emily cut to the chase. "Do you prefer this or the Rock of Gibraltar?"

"This one small stone ... it's simple and uncomplicated. It has been around just as long as the Rock of Gibraltar, but there are no regrets in a pebble. The Strait of Gibraltar is dark, craggy, and fraught with danger ... the Moors, the Romans, the Spaniards ... the British. You're not British?" He couldn't quite believe she wasn't the same nurse who had cared for him as he convalesced during the Great War.

"No, I'm from Nebraska. Harmony, Nebraska."

"Ah! I used to teach at the University of Nebraska!" This was a good memory too.

"Yes, Owen. You did. By the way, we're bringing in a new roommate in a few hours; I thought you'd appreciate a little warning."

"What happened to the other fellow?"

"He died in the night, remember?"

In the night. Yes. "My best friend ... all that was left was his brains in his helmet ..."

"You look tired. Would you like to lie down?"

He nodded and leaned on the arm she offered him. "Nurse Edith?" He was just checking.

"Yes?"

Why does she not sound Scottish? Oh well. "Sometimes I can see the beaches of Hawai'*i*, or perhaps it is Florida. The white sands hurt my eyes. But they are so lovely. Almost like the Black Hills. Do you think death will look bright, like the beaches; or dark, deep darkness, like the blindness I've had since I returned from the Black Hills?"

What do I know about death? Emily wondered. "Oh Owen. You've done so much in your life, I don't even know how to compare death to all the amazing places you've been."

"I did have great adventures, but the ones I remember— I can't seem to remember how they ended. I didn't come here to die, Nurse Edith. But I will anyway."

"How do you know you're living?" Emily asked.

"Ah! Did I die? Is this heaven? I can still see the beaches. In Florida, you had to wait for the turtles to cross the road, and the little frogs in the swamp would sing at night ... 'Qui-nine!' Is this heaven?" He hoped it was, and he hoped it wasn't. Even blind, constipated, and confused, there were things he loved about living.

Emily was laughing, "No, no, it's Nebraska! We don't have much in the way of beaches. You are still alive, Owen; you didn't die. What I mean is, how do you know you're *really* living?"

This jolted him again. "I don't know. That's a hard question ... philosophical."

Emily sat down next to him. "Yes. It is. It is philosophical." She sat quietly for a while. "Do you have any regrets, Professor Thibodeaux?"

"Yes."

She didn't ask what they were. He wasn't sure anyway. Regret was looming like the Rock of Gibraltar, but what for? He didn't know anymore.

"Do you have any regrets, Nurse Edith?" He doubted she would.

"My friend Amy ... I might have been more helpful. She doesn't talk to me anymore. I regret some things I said. And Ben— I don't know. I've never had a boyfriend, and I don't really regret that, but I could have kissed him. Maybe I should have."

"I knew some university girls who didn't mind having lots of boyfriends." Some of them were quite sexy, as he recalled. He remembered the feel of velvety skin.

"Well, that's one thing I know I'd regret: having too many boyfriends. Regrets come from ..." She didn't know.

Owen nodded. *He* knew this one. "Ah! Regrets come from doing exactly what you want to do, and finding out later how wrong it was. Other regrets come from … being right and watching other people suffer because you weren't able to convince them they were wrong."

Emily nodded, forgetting that he couldn't see her, and continued pensively. "Another thing I know: I don't want to live in Harmony forever. My uncles all left, but Daddy stayed here. When I was little I thought I'd stay a country girl and marry a farmer—or a woodworker like my father. But now I think I would regret that. Doc—I mean, Theodore—lived all his life here. Do you think he had regrets?"

"Was he old?"

"He was pretty old."

"Oh, then he had regrets," Owen said.

Paul stuck his head in the door. "Hey, Emily, can you help me get Anna Mae off the john? She's not heavy, but she swears and claws at me real nasty if I try to do it alone."

Emily's break was over. "I have to get going, Owen. I'll see you tomorrow. It looks like they'll admit your new roommate on the second shift. I'll be curious to meet him." She eased her way out of the room.

Owen thought about this for a moment. A new roommate. What did that mean? His stomach growled at him. Distractedly, he said, "Can I have a graham cracker? What time is it?" But this time nobody answered.

Heyoka

Arnie

1975

The first time Arnie saw the White Buffalo was sometime in 1975. The most striking thing he noticed was that the big girl was hungry. Something in the beast's eyes said, "Feed me," which Arnie thought was preposterous. After all, this buffalo was only a bison from her shoulders to the tips of her horns. Just a big, dumb head, living, yes, and breathing, exhaling huge puffs of misty carbon dioxide, which steamed in the air as if from a warm set of invisible lungs that existed only in another dimension. Arnie was afraid at first. The White Buffalo acted as though she wanted to tell him something. Indeed, he thought she should have spoken, but she didn't; she simply gaped at him in a sort of forlorn way that indicated he ought to do something: feed her. Bison have an insatiable hunger for grass, which drives their entire ecosystem. Once the grass is consumed, their hunger drives them to new pasture, leaving manure to nourish the soil. The prairie dogs living alongside them aerate the soil, which in turn produces acres of lush, green grass for another herd to consume. But here before Arnie's astonished eyes was a vision of a white bison without a body.

Disconcerting, to say the least, and as some weeks went by, the White Buffalo, her red eyes staring through him like Superman's X-ray vision, appeared to Arnie more and more often. When the vision began to follow him around, Arnie secretly began to try to fool her.

One cold night early in '76, while planting wheat in the fields his father owned, Arnie had gotten out of the tractor to inspect a banging noise that came from under the front axle just a moment before, and found himself standing in the headlights of the tractor, surrounded by a vapor from the White Buffalo's nostrils. He saw prisms of color dancing about him.

He wished that he'd been on something, but he wasn't so fortunate to have been drinking absinthe or popping mushrooms. In fact, the White Buffalo, Ptaysan-Wee, whom he'd come to think of as Great-grandmother—at first secretly in his mind, then later out loud—followed him mostly when he was sober. Well, that wasn't quite true. She was there just as often when he was drunk, he knew; he just didn't notice as much. Not only did she seem hungry, but she acted as though something was *expected* of him. Something bigger. Something self-sacrificial, upside-down, and of epic importance. Something unspoken but not unknown.

"Heyoka," Arnie's grandfather used to tell him when he was very little, "is the medicine man who does things backwards to remind us how foolish we truly are. *Heyoka* sees things nobody else can see, but he is more real than the earth, the sky, the water, or the animals. The things *heyoka* sees are terrifying and bring with them strong medicine. Your father thinks he is *heyoka.* He has had strange visions, it is certain." Grandfather didn't say it, but everyone knew Arnie's dad for what he truly was, and so did Arnie, a few years later. About the same time he realized that Santa Claus was a guy at the mall with a fake beard, he realized that his pa—Doc—was no medicine man, in spite of his nickname.

On this particular spring night, surrounded by the salty mist of the White Buffalo's breath, Arnie felt deep in his belly that he had to shake this thing off. He did not want to be *heyoka.* So he removed his clothing, and walked away from the lights of the tractor, across the field into the darkness. The tractor grew smaller and smaller until its light made it appear no larger than a firefly, and the bison did not follow Arnie. Stupidly, the cow stayed close to Arnie's clothes, huffing and snuffing, as though she were a confused pizza delivery boy who couldn't find an address. Something was out of order for the poor, mute spirit. Arnie stifled a chuckle. Arnie spent some time on his back, stark naked, smelling the earthy soil underneath him, feeling goose pimples on his skin in the chilly night air, completely relieved to be alone without the White Buffalo hovering about.

Now it dawned on him that his bison had been there when he woke up, hung around the kitchen with him, gotten into his face when he tried to play with his little children, and even hovered near the end of the bed when Arnie attempted to make love to his wife, Caroline, which generally did not go well. Indeed, it hadn't been going well before the White Buffalo appeared. Now, naked in the field, taking a break from planting wheat, Arnie sighed. How nice to have a moment to himself. Eventually, though, Arnie grew tired of the company of nothing but stars, and, a bit too cold for comfort, he returned to his tractor. He sighed. The apparition remained, snuffing about his clothes. He pulled on his briefs, jeans, and shirt, moving toward his idling tractor, while the White Buffalo followed behind.

Arnie began to take walks at night even when there wasn't work to be done. He'd go out into a field, remove his clothing, leave the buffalo, and run for a mile. It was the best he'd felt in a long time. He reveled in the freedom but eventually realized that all he could think about when the bison stayed with his clothes was the bison herself, and in a sense she was with him even more when she was gone. ***"What the fuck does she want?"*** he screamed at God one night.

A few days later, on an errand in Broken Bow, he noticed that the White Buffalo was around only part of the time, and once, when he went farther from home—south beyond Kearney, and out of the tri-county area for a farm estate auction—he returned with the realization that the bison had not pestered him all day. Finally, about a year after the first time he'd ever seen the specter, on that fateful July Fourth of 1976 when he drove his tractor in the parade, the White Buffalo brought some friends along: a fox's head, a rabbit, and an eagle, all peering at him from the fourth dimension. Arnie had had enough. Here he was, riding his antique tractor down Main Street in

Harmony, behind a hay wagon with a T-ball team, in front of a guy leading three llamas, and a menagerie of spirit-world animals nobody else could see was dancing around him as though he were the missionary in the kettle—and they were the cannibals. If the White Buffalo was trying to tell him something, why wouldn't the damn thing speak? Why did she have to bring friends?

January 1992

Off the coast of Alaska in the boat that he owned and captained, Arnold and his crew worked with a focus that would put a microscope to shame. He felt a wave of pride. The snow crab were hungry, and the pots were filling fast. He knew they'd only be out on the Bering Sea a few more days. *This year,* he promised himself as he crawled into his bunk for three or four hours of shuteye, *will be my last*. Crabbing was lucrative, yes, but fishing for snow crab was one of the most dangerous jobs in America, and if you let your guard down for a moment, you were likely to die; death could come in any number of ways. There would be plenty of time to think about selling the boat when he returned home. Margins were going to be good this year—and maybe for a few more. No point in trying to time the market, though.

Arnold shook his head. He'd promised himself he wouldn't think about it. He needed to get to sleep.

Above decks, the crew hustled. The exhausted men realized they were on their last few shifts before heading home. They'd had scrapes, cuts, and bruises, to be sure, but nothing life-threatening this year, and everyone viewed that as a miracle in itself. Arnold's crab trawler, the *Ptaysan-Wee,* was known for her safety record, and Arnold's crew was top-notch. He drifted off to sleep, smiling to think that once again, the hold was nearly full of succulent and very valuable crab.

As he slept, the decapitated head of a salmon appeared.

Arnold woke up, and the fish did not vanish. What was even more surreal, the Salmon's gills fluttered easily; its eye fixed on Arnold.

Arnold had never seen a salmon in a vision. For that matter, he hadn't seen anything from the spirit world in years. Most days, he was oblivious to why he'd come to Alaska in the first place. This was not a good turn of events. "What do you want?" Arnold said angrily.

"The White Buffalo has found her voice," the Salmon replied.

"Well, holy shit," Arnold said sarcastically. "At least the Salmon talks. It's like a bad joke. A salmon walks into a bar and says, 'I'll have a red-eye,' and the bartender says, 'Holy cow, a talking fish!'" Arnold did a double take. "What did you say?"

"The White Buffalo has spoken," the Salmon repeated.

"Well, it's about time," Arnold said, becoming more furious. "What does she say?"

"She'll have to tell you herself," and the Salmon winked at him and slowly disappeared, grinning like a Cheshire cat.

"No! What did she say? Come back!" Arnold yelled as the Salmon faded. "Salmon don't wink! Salmon don't have teeth! ***Come back!"*** he nearly screamed.

"What did you say?" Someone stuck his head in the cabin. It was Dave.

"I must have been talking in my sleep," Arnold replied.

"But you're wide awake," Dave objected. "Are you all right?"

On land, Dave was a preacher. Arnold and Judy went to Dave's church now and then, mainly because he was part of the crew, and the crew was like family. He worked so hard to care for people, and they recognized in him a genuine altruism that, as Judy said, "is deeply puzzling to see in a Christian."

"I'm … No. I'm not all right," Arnold confessed. "I miss my kids."

"Yeah," Dave said, "me too. But we'll be home in a few days."

"No," Arnold countered, "I mean my kids in Nebraska."

The boat was in a trough sideways, and the waves were rocking it hard. *It must be storming topside; it's always storming on the Bering Sea.* He remembered the story of Jonah that Dave had talked about once in a sermon. The man ran away from his responsibility—and from nothing beyond that, really—and so he had to live in the belly of a fish. Arnold had seen enough fish guts to know that must not have been pleasant. *I ran,* he thought. *I ran from nothing, really. So what if I saw the ghost of a White Buffalo breathing hard and looking hungry? Maybe I thought I was going to go crazy, but even that isn't worth leaving your kids over. Everything smells rotten. AJ came to see me, and that was OK. But I've been gone a long, long time. Amy probably won't want to talk to me now. Even so, I ought to go back and try.*

"Well, I didn't know you had kids back in Nebraska, but I think she'd be glad to hear from you" was all Dave said.

Arnold wondered whether he'd been thinking out loud. "Besides," Arnold moaned, lying back in his bunk, "I can't help but wonder what that damn White Buffalo wanted to tell me all along. Probably something pretty simple."

Dave nodded. He had no idea what Arnold was talking about. When he didn't get something, he knew enough to keep his mouth shut. It's the first thing pastors learn if they want people to think they are far wiser than what they themselves know to be true.

Back in Anchorage, nothing really changed. Months went by. Sometime in the middle of June, Arnold realized that his daughter had graduated from high school. That night he tossed in his sleep. Whenever he thought of Amy, he had trouble getting to sleep.

Arnold dreamed he was fishing in the Athapascan style, trying to spear a sockeye salmon heading back to its natal lake. He would kill it and devour it before it had a chance to spawn. He thrust his barb into the river, and when he withdrew it, the disembodied salmon head burst violently into his consciousness. Arnold dropped his spear, which appeared not to have harmed the sockeye. It didn't speak, but its gills fluttered, and its mouth opened and closed several times, stupidly. Arnold quickly became impatient and even outraged with this spirit. He decided to badger it.

"Are you the Ghost of Christmas Past?" There was no answer. "Are you … the Statue of Liberty?" He wasn't sure if he meant this as a joke. There was no laughter, so perhaps it wasn't funny. "Are you Buddha, Joseph Smith, the Prophet for Allah, Moses, the Virgin

Mother, Jesus Christ?" Silence. "Are you Wakan Tanka, the Great Mystery?" Nothing.

Arnold felt sick for a moment. Then the Salmon slowly shifted shape, until it became a man clad in buckskin, an outfit that looked a lot like his great-grandmother's clothing in the old daguerreotype his pa used to have on the kitchen wall before the house burned down. This man, Arnold noticed, had rough, scarred hands and a knowing smile.

"I am. It may be that I have been in or touched many of the lives you speak about, but in your case, the question is not so much what I am, Arnold, as what you are. You are *heyoka,* the spiritual clown. You run when you should stay. You belong to the plains, but you went to work upon the sea. You personify many paradoxes. The people in your hometown say that when you leave you can never return, so you must go back. You have done horrible things, but now you will do something right. Do you love me? Return to Harmony—and feed my buffalo."

"I'm a black sheep," he objected. "I'm sure my father has disinherited me."

"That may be true, but it doesn't mean you can't lead other sheep to new pasture."

"Are you suggesting I form a new religion?"

"There is no need for new religion, only for new commitments."

"I can't go back. Harmony is the opposite of Hotel California."

"According to whom?" The spirit was angry.

"Well ..." Arnold decided to drop it.

"According to whom?" the spirit insisted.

There was no avoiding this question. While the spirit allowed Arnold the luxury of rhetorical questioning, it expected a response. "The beast?" Arnold guessed.

"Is what the beast says true?"

"No?" Arnold decided to stop guessing. "No," he said again, with conviction.

"In this sense Harmony is the opposite of Hotel California: You can kill the beast. Whom do you know who came back?" the spirit asked.

"I can't think of anybody," he admitted.

"There's always a first."

"Nobody will accept me ... as *heyoka*. How can they accept someone who left his wife and kids, never called, never wrote, as a spiritual leader, a backwards, clowning medicine man?"

"Isn't that the point? The White Buffalo has spoken, but you have not yet heard what she has to say. Go. Learn to be comfortable in her silence, should she lose her voice again."

Arnold woke up in the morning, surprised to find himself well rested. He rolled over and saw that Judy was up, sitting in the east window. She often woke up early to meditate. Even though he wasn't a religious man, Arnold always suspected that her prayers had something to do with the fact that he'd spent so many years fishing on the Bering and North Pacific but had never been seriously hurt.

"Judy?"

"Yes?"

"When you meditate, or pray ... um ..." Arnold scratched his head and stretched. "When you pray do you hear a mysterious spirit ... or Jesus ... or anything?"

"You mean with my ears?" Judy turned to see if he was serious. His face said he was. She knew that Arnold and his crewmate Pastor David had talked about Jesus—and that Arnold had even gone to a few Bible studies. But Arnold also made fun of church folks on a regular basis for their hypocrisies and routine narrow-mindedness. "I ... not really. It sounds dumb, I guess, but I never hear anyone talking to me. Once in a while I have a really strong sense that God, or some great spirit, is listening to me. I guess it must be God. Most of the time, though, I'm just glad to have a moment of quiet before everybody else gets up and nothing important really happens."

"Well, he talks to me," Arnold said, feeling foolish. "A couple times he did anyway."

"Who is 'he'?" asked Judy, intrigued.

"God, or somebody, I guess," replied Arnold.

"How long has this been happening?" Judy squinted at him.

"Off and on, you know. I see visions. We get them in our family. Usually ridiculous, sometimes very powerful. My great-grandfather was *heyoka,* a Sioux prophet with a deeply spiritual perspective on the absurdity of life, and death … and life again," Arnold explained briefly.

Judy could see that he wasn't mocking her. "What does this Great Spirit tell you?"

"Well, I don't know if you're going to like it."

"Maybe not. But if you're sure it was him, Arnold, I'll do my best to go with it. Are you sure?"

Arnold considered this for a long time. Staring at the ceiling, he realized he had almost fallen asleep again. Judy left him alone and turned back to the rising sun. She seemed to have forgotten what they were talking about. *Anyway,* Arnold thought, *am I sure? Or did I eat something funky last night? Am I going crazy like my old man, hearing voices?* The dreaming was so vivid. But he remembered the look on Pa's face after he had the Statue of Liberty dream—and that other dream he could never remember. Pa always looked wild after those dreams. Like he might hurt anybody who disagreed with him. Arnold didn't feel that way.

He went to the bathroom. He looked carefully into the mirror, but didn't see a wild man. Just a guy with morning breath. He brushed his teeth and showered. He took his time on the john, then even trimmed his beard. When he was dressed, he found Judy in the kitchen making toast, eggs, and sausage. She poured him a tall glass of orange juice. Even after all these years, the price of orange juice in Anchorage still shocked him. Back in Harmony, breakfast was cheap; that was for sure.

Halfway through his first egg Arnold put his fork down. "I'm sure, darling," he said, looking Judy in the eye. "I'm sure. It's a mysterious thing. It's a great spirit, and he is Jesus, but he wears buckskin trousers, but he's not what the Mormons think either. Sometimes he talks to me as a salmon. Tells me there's a white buffalo who finally has something to tell me—back in Harmony." He swallowed hard. "I thought I could never go back. I missed those kids this whole time, you know. My little Amy …"

A tear ran down his face.

"Also, I want to hear what *Ptaysan-Wee* has to say."

"I know, honey," Judy sighed with relief. "I know."

They decided not to waste any time. Pastor Dave's wife, Wendy, was a Realtor. She was willing to deal with their furnished house, broker the boat, and sell their second car for them as well. Renting a U-Haul trailer and hooking it to their Jeep four-by-four, they encouraged the girls to pack lightly, with promises of a whole new wardrobe upon their arrival in Nebraska. Amanda, the twelve-year-old, was angry about leaving her on-and-off boyfriend and her mob of girls "to go to a hole in the wall in the middle of nowhere," as she put it. As if Anchorage were the center of the universe. But Beth, who was eight, was eager for adventure.

"As long as we're going east," Beth said, "we ought to see the redwoods in California."

"Can we go to Yellowstone?" Judy chimed in excitedly.

"I hate camping," Amanda pouted. "Can't we stay in a nice hotel at least once, Daddy? With an outdoor swimming pool? Maybe in Las Vegas?"

"I've always wanted to see the Grand Canyon," Arnold laughed, "and it won't hurt to take our time getting there. Yeah, we'll find some things to see along the way."

And so, on July fourth, when Arnold had been gone from Harmony for sixteen years to the day, they rolled out of Anchorage, ready to see as much of the West—which was southeast—as they could in a little over three weeks.

The Journal

Paul

Very little was going on at the Halcyon Home at one thirty in the afternoon. Owen was asleep, and Emily didn't have much to do for the last half-hour of her shift. She sighed and headed to the break room where she found Paul scribbling in a small notebook.

"What's that?" she said. Paul looked up in surprise, then flipped his notebook shut.

"Nothing," he replied.

Emily shrugged. "Well, it must be *something,*" she reasoned, "or you wouldn't say it's nothing."

"Yeah. It's a secret," he frowned. "Can't a guy have a secret?"

"Does Kate know about it?"

"Oh, she knows it *exists,* but I'll never tell her what it is," he said. "She would ..."

"... laugh?" Emily smiled. "Come on, let me see it."

"No. She wouldn't laugh," Paul said.

"What, are you writing a Harlequin or something? She wouldn't laugh at that." Emily smiled again. She broke his defenses down. He knew it, but he couldn't help it.

"No," he admitted, "she would *diagnose* me."

"Your hit list?" Emily probed.

Paul's jaw dropped. "Almost." She held out her hands commandingly, and he gave her the journal, which she opened to the last page.

"June 29, 1992," she read. "Mohamed Boudiaf. Algerian president. Assassinated at age 73.

"July 4, 1992: Joseph Dwight Newman. Jazz trumpeter with Count Basie. Age 69.

"July 4, 1992: Theodore 'Doc' Martin. HHH. 'Statue of Liberty! I got my rights!' Age 78."

"It's my obituary journal," Paul explained, suddenly feeling stupid. "Kind of a morbid hobby, I know."

"Huh," she said, thumbing through it. "It goes all the way back to January." She placed it back on the table in front of him.

"Yeah." He looked at the floor.

"You have others?" She raised one eyebrow.

"Uh-huh." Then it all came out. How he'd started when his father died in '78. How he checked the papers every day. Famous people, local people. There were murders, assassinations, mysteries, and routine farming accidents. Heart attacks, strokes, and … "Well," he said, "somebody dies every day, you know. Not necessarily in this nursing home, or this town, but somewhere."

She didn't laugh. Emily thought about it for a while. "This helped you cope, huh?"

"Yeah, I think so. I think it still does. After I did it for a year, Mom wondered if I'd ever quit. She took me to a shrink in Kearney, and he told her, 'Don't worry about it,' but now I think it's a little compulsive."

"Who else died this year?" Emily's curiosity was piqued.

"Look in the book," Paul said.

"I have to admit, I *am* curious," Emily murmured as she picked the book up again and flipped through it, skimming over the entries:

January 7. Richard Hunt. The Muppet Movie. *Died of AIDS, age 40.*

February 10. Alex Haley. The Autobiography of Malcolm X, Roots. *He was 70.*

March 28. Hazel Anderson. Broken Bow. 90.

April 6. Isaac Asimov. Prolific science-fiction author. 72.

May 14. Lyle Alzado. NFL defensive lineman, died of a brain tumor at 43.

May 17. Leonardo del Ferro. One of the "Three Tenors."

May 22. Tony "Big Tuna" Accardo, mobster known for St. Valentine's Day massacre. Age 86.

Emily shut the notebook and handed it back to Paul. "Don't let Kate see this," she smiled, "ever."

"Emily," he said, "I know my hobby's kinda strange. You should be laughing at me, but you're not." He cocked his head to the side, considering. "You're a good person," he finally said.

She could tell he didn't mean, "a good girl as opposed to a bad girl," the way Ben thought about it. His tone said something more like, "a person who is good no matter where she is or what she's doing."

Emily didn't know what to say to that. So she shrugged.

Shamikah

Ben

New York City, July 1992

One thing Ben hadn't anticipated was actually feeling homesick for Harmony within six weeks of moving to New York City. For the last three years of high school, he occupied himself with ever more difficult tasks and challenges because if he slowed down for even a moment, he could think of nothing but leaving town. It turned out his parents were ready to leave town as well. A few weeks after he moved to New York, they called to say they were putting the house up for sale, having decided they would move to New Mexico. Ben's father had been hired by a law firm in New Mexico and would make a lot more money there than he ever could in Harmony. The hardest part about being homesick for Harmony was that Harmony wasn't home anymore. To see his parents, he'd have to fly to Albuquerque now. Most of what he missed about Harmony had to do with a few scattered moments in time, but the nostalgia was strong. However slowly time seemed to move in Harmony, it wasn't static. He knew he could never go back and find it the way it was, and this fueled his homesickness like nothing else could.

He and Phil had settled into a routine, working two jobs and eating ramen noodles. On the first Sunday Ben had off, he took a long run down the west side of Manhattan, past the World Trade Center, and down to Battery Park, from whence he could see the Statue of Liberty. Life was a journey full of whither and whence, but most importantly, why. The statue, with her back to him, offered no immediate explanations.

Then, turning, he ran north again, waves of heat baking him between pavement and sky. His muscles became rubbery underneath him as he surged up the last hill to his apartment. *Looking at a map, you'd never realize how hilly Manhattan is,* he thought. He had expected it to be just as flat as Nebraska.

After his run, Ben found Phil sitting in the chair in their apartment.

"What's going on?"

"I went out to Central Park this morning while you were on your run," Phil said.

"And?"

"Two guys were playing chess at a table there. I realized that growing up in Nebraska I'd had this stereotypical assumption that blacks just didn't play chess, which was clearly wrong."

"Yeah, I've seen some black guys playing over there before," said Ben.

"Well, I watched these guys for a while, and when they were done, they invited me to play. I played one guy, a huge dude named Cornelius, and he won two out of three. Then this other guy named Da'Shawn asked me if I could shoot hoops. We shot around for a while, and they invited me to come play with them in a three-on-three tourney next weekend. Da'Shawn is amazing, and it turns out that Cornelius, for all his weight, can play pretty well too."

A few weeks later, Phil told Ben they were winning some basketball tournaments. "It turns out that Da'Shawn has this knockout older sister, Shamikah," Phil sighed, gently accenting the second syllable. "She doesn't see me as white, or nerdy, or a hick farm kid, or effeminate, or anything I've ever been labeled. I never expected love at first sight like this."

Ben didn't see Phil much after that. Phil continued to pay rent and drop in from time to time, but his toothbrush no longer cluttered the bathroom sink.

An Ecumenical Conference

Emery

1970

Young men find comfort in the arms of their wives, but the longer they stay married, the more they realize there are things a woman will never understand about them, and so they congregate in places where the coffee is weak enough that it won't make them pee any more often than they already have to. As men in Harmony got older, they found solace in a little place that had a name but was mostly referred to simply as "the café."

Some people might even say it was Reverend Emery Miller's office. In any case, he met Doc there periodically, as they got older, and he humored Doc.

"I've been having more dreams," Doc confided in the reverend.

"What do you suppose they mean?" Emery stirred his coffee.

"Damned if I know (pardon my French). You know I'm half-Irish, half-French, and half-Injun," and Emery nodded, ignoring Doc's poor math. Doc went on. "No offense, but I can't talk to the priest this way. He says my dreams are on account of my ancestors. Meanin' the Sioux blood. Which is true," he added, and continued emphatically after a dramatic pause. "He wants to 'exercise' me. I tol' him, 'Hell no. The Wakan Tanka, the Great Mystery, is bigger 'n you think. I'm *heyoka.*' The Statue of Liberty, for crissakes."

Doc peered across his mug to see how the Anabaptist preacher would take all this. The reverend wasn't put off by Doc's pidgin religion, and his accepting attitude was conveyed to Doc in his demeanor. The minister had no doubt that Doc did have spiritualistic dreams. They might be induced by alcohol—or any number of hallucinogenic plant matter—but you could never be sure about these things. Generally Doc didn't need to be messed up to have wacky ideas. After a time, the reverend asked, "How's your family?"

"Haven't heard from the boy," Doc muttered. "Don't see the grandkids a-tawl. My wife—she sends money over to Caroline time t' time. That wife o' mine: She talks too much—blows smoke up my ass about how I oughtta go find the boy. Hell, I don't know where he is; he could be anywhere. My sister-in-law just says, 'I *knew* this would happen, I saw it coming.'" Doc shook his head but continued, "And Gerald and Margie have been real good to Caroline, watchin' out for her little ones, but that Caroline is a goddam waste o' space. I'da left too."

Reverend Miller could see the pain in Doc's eyes, but he knew neither of them would never acknowledge it out loud. It would destroy the semblance of what Doc considered an ecumenical conference, or, in Doc's words, "two medicine men gettin' together for a coupla cups of bitter, black medicine."

"You oughtta run for representative," Doc said. "We need a good man in Lincoln."

"Oh, I appreciate the thought," Emery said, "but my work is here in these parts. Besides, most of my people don't believe in being politicians. It goes back to the roots of the Anabaptist movement—"

"I used t' think we could trust 'em," Doc admitted, completely uninterested in the roots of the Anabaptist movement. "But who can we trust if we can't trust Richard Nixon?" They pondered this for a moment or two. "You always talk about God …" Doc began.

"I hardly *ever* talk about God with you," Emery pointed out.

"Well, but suppose y' did then. I know you talk about God all the time with your people at the Mennonite church. What else would you talk about? And you 'terpret what he says. Why would God talk to you especially? Who made you the one to speak for God?" Doc asked this simply for information. It was not a challenge, though it could have been. Reverend Miller could tell that Doc was wondering why the spirit of the Statue of Liberty had chosen Doc as her vessel.

"Some days I hear God ... when I take a walk out through the fields. I hear the wind in the wheat."

"Like a vision," Doc nodded. "What's he say?"

"Oh, it gets all muddled when I try to say it later," the minister said.

Doc nodded again. "The spirits tell me we got the greatest country on earth, but I cain't seem to say it how they do," he said, shaking his head again. Doc figured they were two of a kind.

The Gig

Amy

Kearney, Nebraska

Jimmy woke Amy up at noon; she threw one of her pillows at him and rolled over.

"I gotta leave for this gig we're playing in Omaha tonight," he said. "Why don't you come along?"

"Jimmy, I can't. I have to work the late shift. Let me go back to sleep."

"You never come to my gigs anymore," he complained.

"I would if you made enough money for both of us," she snapped, "but no, I'm the one paying the rent. Do you want me to pay the rent next week, or is your stupid band going to have some money left over after you party with the boys?"

"Those guys work hard! They deserve a beer or two after we play," he grumbled.

"Bullshit," she said. "They're lazy. They don't show up for rehearsal on time—and they won't use their own money to buy equipment, so you end up paying for strings, sticks, drumheads, whatever they break. They're a bunch of slobs. They don't shower. They don't brush their teeth. They're as bad as the filthy truckers at Gunner's. And besides," she jabbed, "two of them are musical morons. Brett couldn't find the beat if his drumstick was in his pants, which is where he looks for it most of the time anyway, and Joey can't keep his guitar tuned because he's fucking deaf. Fish has no discipline, but he at least knows music."

"Pipe down," Jimmy said. "They're *out* there!" He pointed to the living room. Amy didn't much care *what* they thought. She pulled the pillow over her head and went back to sleep.

"What's she bitchin' about?" Joey asked Brett, but Brett was paying no attention to the argument because he was watching a porn video.

Fish, the talented bass player, was there too. His bass was in his hands, and he was doing arpeggios perfectly, unplugged. Nobody could hear it over the moans on the screen, but it didn't matter; he knew it was right. "She said you're deaf," Fish told Joey. "You stand too close to your amp. It's true. And Brett gets off rhythm even when he beats his meat."

"What?" Joey said again. Fish just laughed at him.

Jimmy came out of the bedroom. "She's staying home," he said glumly. "Let's go."

"You know what?" Fish said, pulling Jimmy toward the door and lowering his voice. "Amy's right, Jimmy."

"Screw you, Fish," Jimmy snarled.

"No, man, screw these fools," Fish said with a laugh. "You can play lead guitar like a maniac, Jimmy, and you sing OK," he went on, "but these guys … they suck, man. They're makin' us look bad."

"Oh well," Jimmy sighed. "We got a gig tonight, we gotta go play it. Besides, they're our friends. Let's load the van." He threw the apartment door open and grabbed his guitar case.

"No, man," Fish told Jimmy as he followed him outside. "They're *your* friends. I quit, dude. Or you can fire your friends."

"Bullshit," Jimmy laughed. Then he saw that Fish meant what he said. "Aw shit, Fish, come on."

Fish put his arm around Jimmy's shoulder. "Look, man," he said in a conspiratorial tone, "we can do better tonight by ourselves."

"Without a drummer? You can't rock if you don't have a drummer."

"Wrong. You can't rock if you don't have a *good* drummer. You definitely can't rock if you have a bad one." Fish crossed his arms and leaned back against the side of the van. "That's the point Amy's making; I couldn't have said it better myself. In fact, I tried to talk to you about it last week, but you just walked away. Jimmy, we don't make any money because we don't *rock*. We suck. Your drummer sucks, and your rhythm guitarist is deaf. Jesus, you have to tune his guitar for him!"

"Where are we going to get a good drummer?" Jimmy said, suddenly feeling a wave of despair. Fish was undeterred. He tapped his own chest, causing Jimmy to protest, "But you play bass!"

"Yeah, I play bass. But I know a great drummer in Omaha; hey, I already called him. We pick him up on the way to the club. Tonight, Stone plays drums, we rock the joint, we crash at Stone's place—no partying—and we find a rhythm guitarist in Omaha tomorrow or the next day ... easy. Maybe we find a true tenor who knows how to work a crowd too, but that's a long shot in Omaha. We stay with Stone, save some money, and in a week we'll be tighter than this band has ever been. We'll practice until your knuckles ache, but in a month we'll be the best band in Nebraska. Then we drive to California. Let's take a chance. I'm not going as part of this band anymore, so if you take those losers, I guarantee you will suck."

Jimmy took a deep breath and shook his head. It was a lot to absorb all of a sudden. "They're my friends." Jimmy said, looking back toward the door.

"Friends don't always make good business partners," Fish insisted as he put his bass amp in Jimmy's van.

Jimmy was starting to weaken. "What about Amy?" he wondered aloud.

"Dude, in a few weeks you'll have dozens of chicks hotter than her anytime you want," and Fish jumped into the driver's seat and slammed the door. "Besides," he continued, "no more playing covers after tonight. These guys I know will be able to handle the intricate shit you've been writing lately. Your songs are going to be hits. Let's go rock and roll," he commanded.

Jimmy wasn't quite convinced. Leaning in the passenger window, he said "Dammit, they oughtta be out here by now with their stuff, it's past time to go. We gotta at least tell 'em, don't we?"

Fish just laughed. "They'll figure it out. Sometime next month. Get in the van."

"No, I'm serious, they've been like brothers since, I don't know when," said Jimmy, but he did what Fish told him to do. Fish thought Jimmy's songs could be famous, and that's what mattered.

Fish groaned, jumped out, and jogged to the half-open apartment door. "Gig's been canceled," he lied. "Me and Jimmy are going out for burgers. Want us to get you something?" Neither Joey nor Brett even looked at him.

As Fish got back in the van, Jimmy shook his head again, but now he was starting to smile. He looked at the notebook in his hand; he never went anywhere without it. The songs he wrote were his life. He grinned at Fish and said, "This is nuts," as his friend floored it.

Amy woke up again at four. Wearing nothing but a long T-shirt, she headed toward the bathroom. Halfway across the living room, a groggy voice said, "Oh yeahhhh, shake that booty."

She screamed, startled, and turned to see Brett looking at her. "Oh, it's you." She felt a little embarrassed at how much leg she was showing, even though she recognized the irony. Joey was asleep on the couch. He had been drinking whiskey straight from the bottle, and he'd be out for a while. Brett kept staring at her. She was used to having strangers do that to her, but Brett should know she was off limits. "Hey, why aren't you guys at the gig?"

"There's no gig tonight," Brett said, "except me and you." He began to unzip his pants.

"I don't think so, asshole," Amy told him and went into the bathroom, locking the door behind her. *This is turning into a nightmare,* she thought. Jimmy didn't like how she earned a living, but he couldn't make any money. Now he had left his horrible, perverted friends in her apartment while she was asleep. Did he care at all if they raped her? She wasn't sure how to get them to leave. They didn't seem inclined to do it on their own. She finally decided she could stay in the bathroom until they got hungry and went to get something to eat. But that could be hours. She decided she hated Jimmy. Vaguely, she wondered where he was if there was no gig, but he often took off for a while without telling her where he was going. *When he gets back, I'm going to give that boy a piece of my mind,* she thought.

It was indeed three hours before she heard the guys start talking about leaving, and Amy had waited it out in the bathroom. She didn't really think Brett would try something, especially with Joey there, but she couldn't be sure. Brett was creepy.

She painted all ten fingernails. She plucked her eyebrows. She shaved, being careful around her knees. She did her hair and makeup. Amy was ready for work, but she didn't know if she wanted to go. Finally, she heard Joey's Oldsmobile pull out of the parking lot. As they came around the front of the complex, she watched them through the bathroom window to make sure they were both in the car, then ran to lock the back door.

That's when the tears came. Amy wanted to call somebody and be told everything would turn out fine, but she couldn't think of anyone. Her mom would be at work by now, mopping floors or emptying trash cans in an office somewhere, and she wasn't calling Melissa or Emily about this. They wouldn't understand. They'd never felt this used or lonely, she was sure of it.

Brad? Training for his freshman season as a Cornhusker.

AJ? In Iraq fixing Humvees.

Randall? She *could* talk to Randall if she had to. She might call him later.

Amy called Gunner's and said she was taking the night off. The manager went ballistic, but he couldn't fire her. She was too valuable an employee, and they both knew it. She told him where he could shove it if he didn't like it. And hung up.

Owen's New Roommate

Emery

1974

Emery Miller's Mennonite congregation in Harmony loved him. He easily navigated the politics, the differences of opinions the church board and congregation had from time to time. Indeed, throughout several counties he was known and respected. He knew that he might soon be asked to take a position of leadership in the Great Plains Region. Even local ministers from other denominations sought his counsel. But the day in August 1974 that Nixon resigned, everything changed. His beliefs, especially those that lay at the intersection of politics and faith, were shaken to the core. Never again would he align himself with a political party.

"Who can we trust?" his wife, Clara, had lamented.

"Only God," Emery said with humility, looking at a dollar bill. "Only Almighty God." He felt as though he wanted to rip the money in half.

He called his second son, Bruce, who was away at college. Many in the next generation had eyes to see and ears to hear—and were being introduced to something called "post-modernism." Emery and Clara had lost their older son, Warren, in the Vietnam War. The boy had ignored his Mennonite roots, the pacifist calling to be the "quiet in the land," and instead of refraining from military service by any means possible (many of the Mennonites alternatively served in programs such as Pax or the Peace Corps or dodged the draft by moving to Canada), Warren was drafted and drifted with the waves of popular opinion: When your country calls, you go. He went missing in action and was now presumed dead. Emery hadn't really been listening to Bruce, but now his worldview shattered, and it was time to listen.

Bruce was glad to talk and have his father truly listen for a change, instead of interrupting to suggest that he get a haircut. Emery suggested that he'd like to visit the campus of the Mennonite college Bruce attended in Hesston, Kansas, on the following Saturday to discuss some of the new ideas with some of the boy's more radical professors. Bruce agreed to arrange some meetings.

When Emery got home very late on Saturday night, he told Clara he'd still have to be up late to pray and prepare his sermon.

It was as though he had flipped a switch. Sunday morning dawned, and still he prayed in his office. The elders were wondering where he was, and debating how they ought to proceed, since none of them were prepared to preach. The song leader led an extra hymn, then another. On a signal from one of the deacons he led a third, something people could sing from memory so he wouldn't have to flip through his hymnal to select it. Finally, the reverend came rushing up the aisle, wearing neither his plain coat nor even a buttoned-up shirt, but rather, he still wore a sweater that said HESSTON COLLEGE. It was apparent immediately that he hadn't shaved for several days. He mounted the platform and caught his breath. A gleam was in his eye, and he began speaking extemporaneously, taking on the look and demeanor of an Old Testament prophet.

"My beloved congregation: This week, the man I admired most has been humbled, and all those of us who followed him are therefore humbled with him. No longer is Richard Nixon the president of the United States of America, and no longer shall I hunger for the respect that is accorded a minister of the Gospel in this town. For, just like Mister Nixon, I am a sinner. Without the respect typically accorded one of my social position, a minister's life is misery. I've counseled many ministers of various denominations who've lost their flock's respect, and I know this to be true. Since I have no desire to continue to attempt to earn your respect, nor a desire to hold a position where your respect is essential for my sanity, I hereby resign as your pastor. What I don't resign, however, is my love for Jesus and his teachings.

"My heart and my life now align with a higher quest; that of seeking the surpassing love of God above all earthly respect.

"I must leave you today with this warning: As I confess the sin of placing my faith in the president, in a man, I exhort you to be cautious. For one party is no different or better than another. No town, no other nation on this earth is better than the next, each has its corrupt individuals and each has its Godly ones.

"We are not better than God's children in China or Russia or even Vietnam. Even a headhunter in Papua New Guinea is more honest in following his beliefs than we often are. We have had the arrogance to think that simply being 'Christians' in name makes us better than followers of Buddha, Muhammad, Marx, Mao, or Darwin, yet if we have not truly followed Jesus, we have done nothing more than devour our own flesh instead of partaking of Christ's body. If they follow their false gods, and we refuse to follow our True One, who is the better? Indeed, all have sinned and fallen short of the glory of God."

There was much more; it was his longest sermon ever. The Mennonites of Nebraska are not inclined to shout anyone down in mid-speech. They much prefer to deal with such matters decently and in order. Within a few hours, following a potluck meal at the church, the church board and elders had met to accept Reverend Miller's resignation. The vote was unanimous. As those who were in the meeting recounted the discussion later, their pastor had indeed gone off the deep end in saying they were no better than Communists or cannibals. Some thought he ought to be committed to an institution, but this motion was considered extreme. Anything "extreme" was frowned upon; indeed, that was why Reverend Miller's resignation was being accepted.

Emery Miller never preached from a real pulpit again. He found a job selling Bibles at a Christian bookstore in Kearney. He soon bought and ran the store himself, adding a selection of titles aimed at educating local readers about a wide range of religious thought to enhance their understanding of spirituality in its infinite variety. For many years Reverend Miller (he still held the title "Reverend" because, although he resigned, he wasn't defrocked by the larger Mennonite conference) conducted small Bible studies and led a "house" church, which met in his store instead of in a home. This group of idealists and seekers and misfits would come to the store early on Sundays to help move shelves back so they could sit cross-legged in a circle on the floor. It wasn't unusual for one of the young people to find an interesting book while moving the shelves, and the next thing they knew, the entire morning was spent comparing Taoism to the teachings of Jesus—and finding many similarities and a few differences.

Gradually, however, Emery went from radical Anabaptist to merely quirky and eccentric. General consensus among people who knew him was that Reverend Miller was suffering from early-onset dementia. His customers, and even those attending his Bible studies and small gatherings of thinkers, dwindled because he began to yell scriptural quotations at them when they walked in, quoting obscure verses as "'I am a prophet also as thou art; and an angel spake unto me by the word of the Lord, saying, 'Bring him back with thee into thine house, that he may eat bread and drink water.' But he lied unto him. First Kings, chapter thirteen, verse eighteen."

One day in 1989, some years after Clara died, Bruce found his father in the bookstore surrounded by several inches of water sobbing about Noah. He had been trying to fix the bathroom sink, but there were pieces of plumbing on bookshelves and in the cash register. The family began to understand that he wasn't simply eccentric; he was truly incapable of living on his own. Soon he was invited by Bruce's family to move in. After a few months of resistance from a humble yet independent man, Emery did.

Harmony Halcyon Home

July 6, 1992

Alice, Paul, and Kate were sitting around the table in the break room as the sun came up, when Emily came in to begin her shift. "Morning, everyone," she said cheerfully.

"You're late," Alice grumbled. "I should write you up."

Kate smirked, and Paul rolled his eyes.

"Hi, Alice." Emily said cheerfully because she knew she had the majority in the room behind her. She glanced at the clock on the wall. "You're right! I'm late by two minutes! Just like always!" She shrugged. "Rough night?"

"The usual. C'mon, let's get this over with." Alice was waving a stack of second-shift paperwork, done incorrectly the previous afternoon before Alice's night shift, and Kate had been trying to placate her. Emily sat next to Paul.

"The usual," Paul whispered. "Surliness."

Alice glared at Paul a moment and made a harrumphing noise. "New guy in with Owen arrived yesterday afternoon; he's a preacher … Reverend Emery Miller. Early stages of Alzheimer's. His son, Bruce Miller, the attorney, brought him in. They can't handle him at home; he gets hold of tools and 'fixes' things. Bruce said that a couple days ago he 'fixed' the bathtub with a pipe wrench and flooded the basement. That was the last straw. He's very creative, so we'll really have to watch and make sure he doesn't get into any of the housekeeping closets or maintenance room or anything. He also moves furniture around. There's nothing worse than a dining hall chair screeching across the floor at three in the morning, and it's like fingernails—" and she held up her claws and drew them down an invisible blackboard.

"Paul will keep an eye on him," Kate offered. Paul shot her a quick look that said, *Since when am I being volunteered for the shit work?* Kate ignored his look.

"I'd like to get a restraining order on the reverend and strap him in his bed," Alice said, half under her breath.

Emily was incredulous. "Can you do that?"

"Is he likely to hurt anyone? Himself?" Kate pressed.

"No, but he hurts my ears moving that furniture," Alice complained.

Kate interrupted her. "Well, too bad, 'cause you can't do it. I don't care if he walks down to the nurses' station every five minutes stark naked like old man Jackson used to do. If you go to Dr. Hostetler on this one for a restraining order, I'll—"

"Forget I even mentioned it!" Alice barked.

"If I come in here early one day and find him tied down, I'll—" Kate looked serious.

Alice knew what Kate could do if she wanted to. ***"I said forget it!*** God, I have a headache!"

"Sometimes I wonder ..." Kate shook her head.

"I just haven't had to put up with anyone bothering me at two in the morning since Doc passed, OK? At least he'd just ask for whiskey and go back to bed." Alice's mood wasn't improving.

"Well, look, Reverend Miller can get up in the middle of the night just like Doc did if he wants to, so I don't want to hear any more about that. The preacher's got his rights—Statue of Liberty—OK?" Paul and Emily snickered into their hands, but Alice was fuming.

"You—you're not the boss here. I could make your life a living hell, you know."

"Maybe it already is," Kate mumbled under her breath, so that only Paul and Emily could hear, "since I have to deal with you every day."

Paul was trying not to laugh. His was the voice of reason. He could hear residents beginning to stir and knew it was time to get on with the morning routine. "All right, chill out, ladies. Alice, anything else?"

"No. I won't say it was a quiet night, but everyone else was calm enough. My head is killing me. I'm going home." Alice left in her usual huff.

"She probably drugged everyone else," said Kate "Anyone that gets up at all, she goes, 'Here, Tylenol with codeine. Go back to bed and sleep forever.' Dr. Hostetler lets her do it too. Of course, he's hopped up on all kinds of prescription meds himself."

"Kate, I remember how I thought you were a bitch till I met Alice," Paul laughed.

"Yeah. She's been here forever. She's probably drinking Doc's portion on top of her own these days." Kate sighed. "Well, time to get people up for breakfast, everyone. I'll go down to Owen's room and check on the reverend right away. We'll make sure he's not tied in bed."

Kate found the reverend perched in a new recliner brought in by his family and placed by Doc's old bed. He was wearing a sweater, shirt, and tank undershirt in reverse order. Owen was digging about in his dresser.

"Good morning," Kate said briskly, "you must be Reverend Miller. You're dressed already. Um, but let's get those switched around. I'm Nurse Kate; I work the morning shift, and if you need anything, call Emily, all right?" Kate attempted to help the reverend change his clothes, but he didn't cooperate.

"Why did my son bring me here?"

Kate was brutally honest. "It's a nursing home. Your son couldn't care for you anymore, I'm afraid."

"Well, what do I do? I can't sit in this chair all day. Early to bed and early to rise ..." The reverend slipped away from her, one arm out of his shirt, the shirtsleeve dangling at his waist.

"Emily will be along in a moment, and she'll show you where the dining hall is. You can go there for breakfast—and also at lunch and suppertime," Kate instructed him.

"What do I do in between?"

What does anyone do in between, Kate thought, *but sleep and make messes in their pants?* "Well, Joe, the activities director, has things to do for a half-hour at 2 o'clock if you aren't napping," she told him.

"I can't read the Bible anymore; the letters blur. I have no pulpit. What should I do?"

Kate was irritated with this guy already. He was worse than most, she could see. "I don't know what you're supposed to do, Rev. Maybe Emily will think of something."

To Kate's relief, Emily came in with a cheery "Good morning!"

"Good morning!" said the reverend just as brightly.

"Emily, this is Reverend Miller; he just moved in yesterday," Kate told her as if she had just started the job that day. "Can you show him to breakfast? He can go along when you take Owen down." Kate left, and Emily rolled her eyes.

"So you're a preacher?" Emily quickly finished changing the gentleman's clothing around so that his tank was on the bottom, then his shirt, and finally his cardigan. For some reason he allowed her to assist him.

"I *was* a preacher. I don't know what I am now. My son brought me here, but I don't know why. What am I supposed to do? Do I feed the chickens in the morning—or collect the eggs?"

"No, we don't have chickens," Emily smiled.

Paul stuck his head in the door. "Where's the new guy?"

"This is Reverend Emery Miller. That's another aide; his name is Paul." She introduced them.

"How you doing?" Paul grinned.

"Hello, Paul," said the reverend. "Do *you* know what I'm supposed to do next?"

Paul laughed. "Put your feet up, sir! Boy, I wish *I* could."

"Well, I can't do that, son. Idleness is the devil's workshop," the preacher declared.

Paul shook his head. "Well, I don't know then."

Paul and Emily began to help Owen get dressed. "Is the Metamucil coming?" Owen wondered aloud.

"You get it at *breakfast* now," Paul said flatly.

"Ah!"

"Reverend Miller, are you tired?" Emily wondered how a man could stay up all night bothering Alice and look so alert. Even perky.

"No."

"Well, everyone needs the proper amount of rest," she reminded him.

"Well, of course. We work six days and then the Sabbath."

"Yes." she said absently.

"Is this the Sabbath day?"

"No. It's Thursday," Paul said, "but we really don't have any jobs for you. At least not yet."

"You know," Emily told Paul, "perhaps he could take a little cart with a pitcher of water around and give people drinks. I mean, we're supposed to do that to make sure they stay hydrated, and we never seem to have time."

"It's a good idea, but I think it's against regulations for a resident to work for the home."

"That's ridiculous," she said.

"Maybe so, but it's true."

Owen interrupted. "Nurse Edith? Is the Metamucil coming?"

"It's not Edith, Owen, it's Emily," Paul corrected him.

"Never mind, Paul," said Emily. "I've given up on that one a while ago." She waved dismissively. "Let's get moving. Come along, Reverend. Follow us; we'll show you to the cafeteria."

"What shall I do after breakfast? Do you have a list of projects? Is anything leaking? I know how to fix a leaky faucet!"

"No, Reverend, there's nothing to do. It's Sunday," Paul lied.

"Then I should have a place to preach …" And the elderly minister launched into an exceedingly radical sermon that continued all the way down the hall.

Harmony's Gold Rush: A Professor's Analysis

Owen

August 22, 1948

Professors Johnson, Liddell, Case, and Lopez
Esteemed Colleagues,

As you are already well aware, it became necessary in the course of natural scientific inquiry for us to confirm or deny the claims that Harmony, Nebraska, had in 1882 been the site of a minor gold rush, with some $15,000 in gold (or around $40,000 in today's dollars) panned from the South Loup and several feeder creeks one to two miles west of town. Because no map contained any hint of geological aberration that might indicate any remote possibility that there could be a vein or deposit, I traveled out to Harmony this summer and inspected the South Loup myself.

To be sure, in the South Loup there remain indications that much gold-panning activity did take place in 1882 and 1883. Sixty-six years later, artifacts related to the panning are still in evidence along the banks; you'll find a catalog of them in the following report. In my estimation, however, gold was never found here. Nor would any experienced miner have stayed for long if indeed any were even enticed to come in the first place. The geology precludes any possibility of a gold deposit.

While the public librarian did little to help me, I did locate a woman from the Harmony Historical Society, a Mrs. Martin, who allowed me to look at her most precious documents: the journals of her husband's great-grandfather, who was called "Papa." Having taken careful charge of them, I returned to Omaha and began to read them. These journals are fascinating precisely because they contain a riddle. Writing in English, Louis Saint Martin also encoded some of his entries; it took me some time to break the code, but once it occurred to me that the wily pioneer had encoded his message to be broken down into French*, rather than English, the simplistic code was broken rather quickly.*

The upshot of his encoded journal entries then is that Mr. St. Martin was a charlatan of the first order. Not only did he attempt to convince passers-by that his fort was Ft. Kearney, he also created a scam, with the assistance of his brother, Philippe, who had returned from the Civil War after wandering afield and striking some small fortune in gold—but not in Harmony, a hoax these two brothers seem to have perpetrated.

The brothers spawned a story that they found this gold in the South Loup some six years after Philippe returned from war. Until then they kept this bounty to themselves as a carefully guarded secret. They staked a claim immediately and continued to find gold on their claim for a few months, in the meantime setting up a general store at the fort and making a killing supplying last-minute necessities to the hordes who rushed to the site. They also opened a saloon where they hosted droves of thirsty, but unlucky, miners. Eventually the newcomers' money would dry up, and they'd either leave town or buy a small plot of land (from the Martins) and begin to farm.

Of course, it was mandatory to authenticate a new strike, and the brothers appeared to have done everything on the up-and-up, but Louis's coded journal indicates that the government assessor was given a fairly hefty bribe to authenticate the strike! While the rush was short lived by virtue of its very fraudulence, the brothers appear to have quadrupled their fortune in just a few short months.

They were intelligent criminals and quit while they were ahead. This cessation of felonious action seems to have been precipitated by Louis's squaw wife, one he called Mary but her descendants refer to as Ptaysan-Wee. It seems she had a vision of Louis hanging on a gallows, and it frightened her so much that he was convinced to turn away from his criminal ventures.

But the brothers promoted the town via all legitimate means known in their day! They hosted rodeos and baseball games against barnstorming teams from the East. Teddy Roosevelt arrived and gave speeches lauding the pioneer spirit, circa 1899. They built a theater and converted it to a moving-picture house when they were very old men—but not so old that they could not see the magnetic attraction money has to technology. They capitalized on it!

The fortunes of the Martin family have dwindled by dispersion over several generations of families, but the remaining (St.) Martins in the area are middle-class farmers whose main wealth lies in farmland holdings.

A carefully prepared copy of all encoded journal entries, the broken code in French, and my translation into English, as well as detailed geological and archaeological maps of the South Loup starting at Harmony and covering terrain to the west for four miles, follow.

Yours truly,
Owen Thibodeaux
Professor of Geology
University of Nebraska
Lincoln

The Real Gold Mine

Emily

It was turning into a lazy summer in Harmony, Nebraska. After work, Emily showered, attempting to get the smell of the nursing home out of her pores, then turned the faucet to COLD and tried to bring her body temperature down a notch. She found a Popsicle and soon drifted out back to her father's woodshop. It smelled like his kiss—the earthiness of oak and maple shavings, the intoxicating, misty haze of varnish. "What are you working on, Dad?"

"Sorry, Em," he said, turning toward her and removing his earplugs. "I didn't catch that."

"I asked what you're working on."

"Oh, still building that dining room table for Melissa's wedding." He gestured toward the workbench.

Emily walked around him, observing his work with admiration as he picked up a piece of fine sandpaper and worked a table leg to its final smoothness. Ever since she was a little girl, her dad had shown her the flaws in his work, so that one day Emily would know the difference between great and just OK. This piece was being done to perfection. "So far," she knew he would say. In the end, nothing was ever deemed perfect, but it was invariably good enough for him to sign his name with a wood-burning tool in some unseen corner of the piece: *JimZim*. She stepped back, away from his bench.

"Melissa always loved to come in here, you know. She was the first one to tell me you're an artist, Daddy."

"I'm no artist," Dad demurred.

"Yes you are," Emily insisted, moving a router and a couple of hand tools, making room on a cluttered workbench to perch. She sat there in silence for some time and watched him work.

"What's on your mind, girl?" he prompted her, placing his sandpaper on the workbench and sitting down to really listen. Jim knew his younger daughter wouldn't have sat there so long if something weren't percolating.

"Do you think there was really gold in the South Loup?" Emily said distractedly, picking up a small piece of rosewood and toying with it. This wasn't the issue bothering her, Jim was fairly sure, but he allowed her train of thought to guide him.

"Sure. The Martin brothers found it up there on their farm in 1882; everybody knows that. Heaps and heaps of gold." He glanced at her with a wry grin and a wink but put down his sanding block when she failed to smile at his humor. "What's eating you, honey?"

"So many people ... all they want is to find a pot of gold and retire comfortably. I don't think that's what I want. If you went down to the river today and found the biggest nugget ever, what would you do tomorrow?"

Jim dusted his hands on his jeans and found a chair. "Tomorrow? I'd get up at five, eat a fried egg and a piece of toast with strawberry jam, drink my coffee, come in here, and finish this table. I've got some work to do on the lathe, quite a few pieces to sand, and, of course, the staining. What do you think—Honey Wheat or Deep Chocolate?"

Emily stood up, approached his bench, and looked closely. "Quarter-sawn white oak? I'd go with a medium value, not too light, but not too dark. Use something that lets the grain really pop; how about Spanish Gold?"

"Good choice. So, Emily, you were already wondering about the gold when you were in sixth grade. Remember when you and Melissa did a history project on the South Loup gold strike?"

"Yes, Daddy. We got an A+."

"Did you do any research?"

"Well ... no." She stopped, a bit embarrassed. She and Melissa had spent an hour writing down everything they had ever heard about the gold strike, but they didn't crack a single book. She didn't know why she felt silly; that was six years ago. She would never do a paper that way now.

"We, uh, went with our gut feeling, I guess," she confessed.

"Which *was*?" Her dad smiled the way she imagined Socrates smiled at his pupils. It almost made her mad.

"Well, we thought, 'Of course there was gold.' Everyone said it, so it had to be there."

"Why do you think Mrs. Albright gave you an A+ when you didn't do any research? When you didn't actually study?" He began to sand the tabletop again, using a very fine grit and taking his time.

Emily took a step back. Her eyes told her father that she had never considered this. "I don't know. Do you?"

"I sure do. She told your mother and me that every year at least three kids picked the topic of Harmony's South Loup gold for their history research project, and they never did a lick of research—at least none that wasn't based on *oral* history. For thirty-five years, Mrs. Albright was able to examine the trends as the history evolved; she's been working on a special, long-term project for the Harmony Historical Society. Anyone who added to her research got an automatic A+."

"Wow, I didn't know that," said Emily. "What's she finding?" Emily felt curiously like an adult, having this conversation with her father about her sixth-grade project. It was an initiation somehow into the world—into the perspectives, of parents and teachers.

"Her theory was that the further removed we got from the actual events in the 1800s, the more solidified the oral history would be—in favor of belief in a myth."

"What do you mean, 'belief in a myth'?"

"There never *was* any gold in the South Loup; we're in central Nebraska, for heaven's sake! All serious studies ever done are conclusive, Emily: There could not have been gold here. Several professors have come out and poked around the supposed site. The more they proved there was never any gold here, the more the people of Harmony became convinced that there had been, as evidenced by the solidification of the myth in oral history."

"Did anyone ever consider that sixth-graders might just be overly idealistic?"

"Oh yes, but at the beginning of Mrs. Albright's career, the sixth-grade groups were much more skeptical, because those kids' grandparents still remembered people who had been bankrupted in their attempt to make it rich here, people for whom the myth led to a very sad reality. Now, nobody remembers those people personally, so gradually the oral histories have solidified into a myth. What's more, belief in the existence of Harmony gold gives the town an inflated sense of self-importance. Gold is the most magical of all metals. The sixth-graders simply regurgitated what they heard at home, and as time went on, they heard only the myth, while their skepticism faded as the first-hand accounts of their grandparents died with them."

"You're saying there was no gold? For sure?" Emily peered at him through the dust rising from his sandpaper.

"It's impossible. It had to be a hoax," Jim said.

Emily's brow furrowed. "Like Santa Claus, I guess we all know deep down it isn't real."

"But we talk like it is." He shrugged then, noticing something in a piece he'd been sanding, Jim bent close to the wood, looking at a nearly imperceptible scratch.

"Well, then, how do we know Harmony even exists?" asked Emily.

"Ha!" her father laughed, then picked up his sandpaper and began to create a new cloud of dust, and shook his head. "So this is what's eating you—an existential angst. Why are we here? and What is life all about?"

"Well, life sure isn't about gold," she retorted. She didn't appreciate him laughing at her.

"No, you're right about that." He was taking her seriously after all, she saw, peering into his eyes again through the dust. He *was* listening.

"Then what *is* it about?" She smiled at her father with a simple, beautiful smile nonetheless edged with just a touch of cynicism. She was a grown woman giving him one last chance to be omniscient, as if she were still a toddler. But the innocence was no longer real, and he knew it.

Jim sat down and looked at her thoughtfully. *She is so sharp, so lovely,* he thought. *She could go anywhere, do anything, or be anyone. She wants to go somewhere, to be someone. She wants to be great, not just OK. And* that *will be a challenge.* She was becoming everything he had ever hoped she would become. He shook his head again.

"Honey, I can't tell you the answer. You're going to have to figure it out for yourself. But when you get it—and let me tell you, it's no myth: You can and you will figure it out. And that's the real gold mine."

Steroids and Ice Machines in Denver

Paul

After Reverend Miller had wandered through the nursing home to deliver the Good News, Paul led him back to his room. He'd been found at the end of the hallway, stark naked. Room 143 was a mess. Owen wasn't there, but his side of the room was trashed, all the stuff pulled out of his drawers, and his bed covers were everywhere. Paul dressed Emery, made the bed and cleaned up Owen's things while he talked casually with the reverend, who kept trying to open the door. "Huh. I wonder if Mrs. O'Toole was in here. Where's Owen? Hmm, I bet he's down getting a box of graham crackers from the kitchen."

"What do we do next?" The reverend found a screwdriver he'd swiped from the maintenance man's toolbox, and began trying to take the door off its hinges.

"Well, this is your room, Rev. There's your chair," Paul said, pointing, not paying attention to the loose screws. "I gotta clean up this mess."

Reverend Miller laid down his screwdriver and sat in the chair. "It's nice! This is a fancy hotel! Look, the bellhop has already put my things here! Why, it's as nice as the hotel I stayed at in Denver! They had an ice machine. Imagine that—a machine that makes ice!" He got up again and resumed worrying the door with the screwdriver.

"So you went to Denver ..." said Paul absently, making conversation.

"Yes, we had a conference there. Ministers from all over the region: Nebraska, Colorado, all the way from Arizona some of them. They had a machine that made ice! I wonder if there's one here."

"Denver. I went to Denver once. I went up there with my dad to see the Broncos play. Just before he died."

"Your father took you to Denver?"

"Yeah."

"What did he do?"

"Dad was a truck driver. It was January 1, 1978. I was twelve years old, but I remember it like it was yesterday. We had Christmas, then a few days later he told Mom he had to pick up a load in Denver on Monday, and he'd have me and my brother, Tony, home in time to go back to school on Tuesday."

"I once went to Denver! They had an ice machine! Imagine!"

Paul smiled and picked up Owen's army helmet. *Crazy old farts.* "Yep. They can make ice. So I went with him up to Denver, and he said, 'Your ma don't know it, but we got tickets for the playoffs!' I was so pumped up. We got to see the Broncos beat Oakland, 20 to 17. It was—"

"Did you ever go to a fancy hotel like this one?" The good reverend looked around in awe as though he were in a cathedral.

This "hotel" is many things, Paul thought, *but it's definitely not fancy.* "No, we slept in the truck. It was the year they started calling them the 'Orange Crush.' I wanted to *be* Lyle Alzado. He was the greatest defensive end ever. Then I hated him when he went to the Raiders. I told my dad I wished he was dead. Then Alzado admitted doing steroids, and now he *is* dead. Just a few weeks ago; brain tumor got him. I put it in my book—May 14. I told my cousin, who's on the high school team, 'Don't do steroids! Look at Lyle Alzado. He was huge, but he was only forty-three!' People shouldn't die at forty-three. My dad was forty-three too."

"Ice machines! It makes ice right on the spot for you! They had one right in the hallway."

Paul shook his head. He knew he was mostly talking to himself here, but the only way to stay sane in this place was to talk to people. "Yep, makes ice. Pretty fantastic. Lyle Alzado could do anything. I always thought it was so cool that he was in *Ernest Goes to Camp*. It was my favorite movie for years. But I told my cousin, 'Look, you can't idolize Lyle Alzado like I did, because he used steroids. No, look at someone like OJ Simpson. He was an awesome football player even without steroids, and besides, the *Naked Gun* movies are way better than *Ernest Goes to Camp*. There's a lot of losers out there, but OJ never did anything stupid like Alzado.'"

"I'm going to go look for an ice machine." The reverend nearly had the door off. Paul hadn't noticed yet. Owen's things were everywhere.

"There's one in the kitchen, but you can't go in there," he told the reverend.

"Does it work? I could fix it." The preacher brandished the screwdriver.

"I don't know, man." Paul finally noticed the door dangling from the top hinge. Emery was crawling into bed on top of a pile of Owen's clothing, which Paul *thought* he had just put away in the closet. That preacher was quick. "Hey! What the—? What did you take all his stuff for?"

"Leave me alone. I've been fixing things all day. It's time for some peace and quiet around here without all these druggie kids yelling at me."

Paul backed off. Senile people were as finicky as prairie weather in winter. "Avoid the violence" was Paul's motto. "Be my guest," he said. "Have a nice nap." As if on command, the old preacher put his head down and fell asleep. Paul picked up the screwdriver and began to rehang the door.

An aide brought Owen back to his room, leaving him in the doorway as was customary, and then she was gone down the hall. Owen was toting a new box of graham crackers. "Is someone there?" he called out.

Paul identified himself.

"Is Nurse Edith here?" Owen asked.

"It's her day off," Paul sighed. Things ran smoother with Emily around.

"Ah." Owen was disappointed. "Care for a graham cracker?"

"No, thanks."

"I'd like some lobster," Owen grunted.

"Graham cracker's a long ways from being lobster," Paul observed.

"I was born in Maine, you know," Owen said.

"I've never even had lobster," Paul said.

Owen was surprised. "Why, you just go down to the docks anytime. You can buy one for a dime."

"Owen, this is Nebraska. We don't have docks. And it's 1992. You can't get a lobster for a dime *anywhere*."

"Ah yes, Nebraska," Owen remembered. "You should go to Maine."

"I've been thinking about that," Paul agreed. "I think it's time to get out of Nebraska. I've got some money saved."

"How much money?"

"You won't tell anyone?" Under his breath, he added, "No, you won't remember in five minutes." He went on: "When my father died, there was a life insurance policy. Mom used some of it to raise us, of course, but when I graduated from high school she split the rest between my brother—Tony—and myself. With that money, plus what I've saved, I have just over forty grand in the bank."

Owen whistled. "That's a pretty penny."

"Yes, it is," Paul concurred. "My grandmother wanted me to go to college. But I'm twenty-seven, and besides, I didn't have good grades."

"Grades have nothing to do with intelligence." Owen knew from experience.

"True," Paul admitted, "but they have something to do with admission."

"Ah." Owen nodded.

"What should I do?" Paul wondered aloud.

"Have you ever been to Florida?" Owen began.

"No."

"In the swamps, the little frogs ..."

I should get the hell out of here, Paul thought.

"In Florida, the little frogs ..."

Paul said it with him, word for word: "... they say, 'Qui-nine, qui-nine,' in a teeny-tiny voice, then at midnight—I don't know how they do it—but right at midnight they change, and they say, 'Double-de-dose, double-de-dose.'"

"Yeah, I know. I've heard it before," Paul sighed.

"You should travel. Go to Florida!" Owen wasn't done.

Paul remembered the next part too—and said it right along with Owen: "The turtles … you have to wait for them to cross the road!"

Again, under his breath: "I definitely need to get out of here—soon." Paul closed the door, leaving Owen with his mantras.

"My best friend," Owen mused, "my best friend. All that was left was his brains in his helmet." He dug in his pocket and found his stone. "Jean … brought me this rock from Nova Scotia. It pleases me more than the Rock of Gibraltar."

Good Girl, Bad Girl

Emily

Owen was asleep in his wheelchair. He looked too relaxed for anyone to bother getting him into bed. The good reverend was sitting in his recliner, wide awake and looking eager for something to do, when Emily knocked at their door on a humid, sluggish afternoon.

"Hi, Reverend." Emily's feet hurt.

"Hello, young lady. What do we do next?" He stood and bounced on the balls of his feet over and over. *Where does this guy get his energy?* Emily wondered.

"Well, you just had lunch. I was going to help Owen into bed, but I'd hate to wake him up."

"Well, I need to do *some*thing," Emery said as he began pacing.

"Isn't it nice sometimes to just sit in your chair?" Emily looked at his chair longingly.

"We work every day, unless it's the Sabbath," the preacher lectured. "Is it Sunday?"

"No, it's only Tuesday. Still a few days till Sunday. And I'll let the chaplain know you're waiting here; perhaps he'll come read some scripture to you." She hoped that would quiet his nerves.

"We don't work on the Sabbath," he said sternly.

"Of course not." Emily sat down. *Just for a minute,* she told herself.

"Do you work on the Sabbath?"

He was so jumpy she was surprised he wasn't doing jumping jacks. All she could do was talk. "Well, I have to work every other weekend, just like all the nurse's aides. Someone needs to be here to take care of you. I don't really like working Sundays, though. I used to always have a friend over every Sunday afternoon: usually Melissa—she's my best friend—and sometimes Amy. When we were little girls, we'd make a tea party, then in high school, we'd just get together and go for a walk or study for a big test together, or Amy would talk about the boys at school. Amy was always so boy crazy. I guess she had, like, one, two ... six different boyfriends. Eventually she started spending her Sunday afternoons with her boyfriends more and more. So now I have to work on Sunday every other week, and Melissa is getting married in August and hoping for a baby."

"One is a good girl, the other is a bad girl," the old preacher summed up. It was remarkable that he'd heard anything she said; he was engaged in a busy yet futile attempt to dismantle his recliner with his trusty screwdriver. Emily helped Emery get seated in his chair and discreetly confiscated the screwdriver.

"That's what people say around town," she went on. "Ben said he couldn't stand it. He said, 'In a small town, you get labeled "good kid" or "bad kid" when we're all really sort of in between.' Amy was lonely; Melissa was lonely until she had Randall; Ben was confused. No, he was probably really lonely too. And we all had each other; that's the irony of it. Now it's my turn to be lonely. I wish—"

But the reverend was done listening to her. "What can I do here?" he muttered.

"You're lonely too, aren't you, Reverend? Isn't this chair comfortable?"

"No. I can't sit while there's work to be done." The door was closed, and he was jiggling the knob. It seemed like he couldn't remember how to work a doorknob. That was perhaps a good development.

"There's nothing to do," she sighed.

"Nonsense. The work is never done. Do you have a screwdriver?"

Emily had an idea. "Could you work a puzzle for me?"

"I don't know ... I've never been very good at puzzles," he replied.

"Well, I'll check with Joe (he's our activities director) and see if he can find a puzzle for you to work on; we might need someone to do that." *Brilliant idea,* she thought.

"I just want to help out. I know how to do quite a few things. I can fix leaky pipes, I can chore—Are there chickens? We always had chickens before. The eggs were so fresh."

Emily hauled herself back onto her still sore feet. "I'm going to go see what I can get to keep you busy, OK?"

The reverend watched her go, suddenly suspicious. "Well, all right." After a moment he went to his drawer where he had managed to stash a hammer. He began to bang on the bed frame.

The racket awakened and startled Owen. "Who's there?" He waved his hands in front of his face.

"These pistons don't look right," said the preacher.

"Hello? Who is it?" Owen was frantic. His roommate dropped the hammer and went to talk to him.

"Why did my son leave me here?"

"I don't know," Owen replied slowly, thinking hard. "Who are you?"

"Emery. I'm Emery. Just trying to fix this gadget here, this thingamabob." He went back to the bed where a piece of metal he'd been hammering had broken off.

"What time is it?" Owen wondered. "Can I have a graham cracker?"

"How's it coming?" Owen's query did not compute.

"A graham cracker," Owen repeated.

"Where are they? How do you fix a graham cracker?" The preacher picked up his hammer.

"You eat them. Are you hungry?" Owen said magnanimously.

"I could eat," said Miller. His mouth began to make chewing motions.

"They're in the drawer," Owen told him.

"Let me check," said Emery, and located the box of treats in Owen's drawer. "Yes! How do you do it?" He was unable to open the box.

"Give them to me, please," Owen requested.

"How does this thingamajigger work?" Emery picked up his hammer but didn't strike the box. He began to nudge at the box tentatively as if that would help him open it.

"Nurse! What time is it?" *None of the nurses are around,* Owen thought.

Finally, Emery put the graham cracker box in Owen's lap. Owen tore it open and gave a cracker to the preacher, who commented solemnly, "Thank you. You are too kind."

"You're welcome."

Reverend Miller pulled back the sheets on his bed. Gently and deliberately he began to crumble the graham cracker over the bed. "In the name of the Father, the Son, and the Holy Ghost. Amen," he said.

"What?" Owen ate another cracker.

"May the peace of Jesus rest upon you all." Emery finished crumbling his cracker and replaced the bedspread. Then, picking up and hefting his hammer decisively, he spoke to it: "Have a good week, Mrs. Schwartz. Thank you. No, sometimes I don't know how the Lord gives me words to speak. He is a mystery. I'll come straight over Monday morning and see if I can fix it." Emery approached the door, managed to turn the doorknob as though he'd never forgotten how. Next, he opened the door, flipped off the light, then exited the room.

Owen was left sitting in the semi-darkness. "Nurse? Who's there? Is anyone there? Is the Metamucil coming? What time is it?"

Confessing to the Mennonite Minister

Owen

1952

Four years after his last attempt to find the gold hidden in Harmony, Owen stood in the doorway of the office marked "Pastor," just inside the main entrance to Harmony Mennonite Church. "Do you know who I am?" Owen asked quietly.

The pastor, Emery Miller, never forgot a face. He nodded graciously. "You're the professor who came some years back to prove that there never was gold in the South Loup."

"Correct."

"Welcome back to Harmony. Have a seat," the minister said with a calm smile.

"Could we go for a drive instead, perhaps out toward Broken Bow?" Owen said, glancing toward Reverend Miller's secretary, who was talking on the phone with someone named Nancy. It seemed that there were many things Nancy needed to know about all sorts of people. Emery, sensitive to his secretary's penchant for gossip, nodded his assent to Owen's suggestion that they head out. It wasn't unusual for people to request to speak with him in private, and that was one thing his office was not. Owen whispered, "I have something to confess." The minister rose from his seat and followed Owen outside.

"I'll drive," Reverend Miller offered. "My car isn't fancy, but I know all the back roads." Owen slid into the passenger side and drew the door shut, while the Mennonite man fired up the car.

"I'm surprised you drive," Owen said.

"How would I get to the church? I live twenty miles west of here."

"I just thought you'd have a horse and buggy," Owen said.

"Oh no, that would be our Amish cousins. We don't go to the movie houses or allow those new-fangled televisions though," Miller told him. "You're a Catholic, aren't you?" Emery looked the professor over as the shorter man rubbed the fingers of his left hand against his kneecaps and gripped the door handle with his right hand.

Owen wished the Protestant minister would keep his eyes on the road. "Yes, I am a Catholic; there's a stop sign—"

"Why don't you confess to the priest?"

"He's out of town," Owen lied.

The reverend nodded. He had seen his spiritual counterpart just that morning; he'd had coffee with the man.

"I haven't been to confession for a long time," Owen continued.

This seemed more truthful. Emery nodded again.

"If I get advice from him, I have to follow it, but with you, I get to choose," Owen finished.

Emery decided that no offense was meant, so none should be taken.

"I've found something that doesn't belong to me," Owen went on, lowering his voice so that it could barely be heard above the noise of the engine, "and I can't decide what to do with it."

Emery raised an eyebrow. "Did you find the South Loup gold after all then?" Even preachers sometimes like to tease.

Owen's lips pursed. He reached into his jacket and pulled out a revolver. If Emery hadn't been a pacifist, Mennonite minister, and therefore completely unfamiliar with firearms, he might have recognized the weapon as a genuine 1858 Remington. As it was, he only saw an eight-inch barrel of death.

"Don't shoot!" The suddenly terrified minister raised both hands involuntarily, the car swerving toward a ditch.

"Keep your hands on the wheel, dammit," said Owen, quickly adding, "Beg pardon, Father." The professor waved his weapon.

After Emery brought the car under control, muttering a Bible verse—"'Call no man on earth *father*'"—Owen reached into his pocket again and continued his show-and-tell.

"I found this old revolver wrapped in oilskin; it was in a crate with this," he said simply. "Look." He held up a satchel made of black leather, loosened the drawstring, and showed the astonished minister several nuggets of what could only be gold.

The wheels thumped on the narrow shoulder, and Emery hit the brakes, bringing the car to a jolting stop on the shoulder, the left wheels still on the edge of the country road.

"Where did you find *that*?" Emery asked, his eyes wide with surprise.

"What, this ancient thing? It's not even loaded," Owen muttered.

"No, I mean the stash. Where was it?"

"You won't tell anyone?" Owen asked with a scowl, brandishing the gun.

"No, I won't tell anyone," the preacher replied nervously. "Are you sure it isn't loaded?"

"Not loaded." Owen pointed the pistol out the open window and pulled the trigger. The hammer clicked, and the driver winced.

Emery motioned that Owen ought to put the gun away. Owen placed the gold back in his jacket, followed by the piece.

"I found both right where Louis St. Martin said it was," Owen sighed.

"Louis St. Martin?" Emery repeated.

"Keep your ears open and your mouth shut," Owen admonished him. "What kind of priest are you anyway?"

Emery smiled slightly, shaking his head, but obeying the command.

Owen continued: "Louis said in code, in his journal, which I borrowed from Mrs. Anne Martin, that the remainder of the South Loup gold was buried three feet down, six feet due north of the sugar maple in his farmyard. There is only one such tree. Oh, I thought I was sharp when I broke that code. But when I went out that night back in '48 and dug a hole in Doc Martin's lawn, I forgot to subtract two feet for the growth of the tree. It took me four years to realize that the sapling Louis buried his treasure near was now sixty or seventy years old, and therefore if he planted the gold six feet away, it was probably now only four feet away from the trunk, the tree having grown out two feet in radius in the meanwhile. Sure enough, I missed last time by a foot or so. This time, I hit the steel box in just a few minutes. The gun was on top, the gold underneath."

"So there really was gold in the South Loup." Reverend Miller shook his head in astonishment.

"Not at all." Owen's dour demeanor brightened as he explained how the St. Martin brothers, hucksters that they were, had created a stampede simply to take advantage of the geologically ignorant, selling them supplies to search for something they would never find—and whiskey after they failed to find it. "But it really isn't my gold," Owen concluded. "I found it on Doc Martin's land. I don't suspect he'd put it to good use, however. He'd probably piss it away. Begging your pardon again, Father."

"Indeed," Emery nodded. "Doc Martin hasn't been himself since earlier this spring when he nearly got killed by his own hogs. The hogs ate his thumb off; did you know that? Sent him into a delirium for a month. If it's possible, if you can believe it, it's made him even crazier than he was four years ago, the last time you came to town."

Owen wasn't interested in the state of Doc's mind—or appendages. All he knew was that he'd gotten the gold by sneaking onto the property of a potentially dangerous man.

"What should I do?" Owen patted his pocket.

"Well, Holy Scripture says that the love of money is the root of all manner of evil," Emery began. "How much is the gold worth?"

"More than enough to make digging around this strange, little town for all these years worth my while, that's for sure. It's a lot."

Emery sighed and thought for a moment.

"It isn't really yours, is it?"

"Not exactly. That's why I came to see you."

"You know what Jesus said about money?" Emery fixed one eye on the professor.

"Jesus said a lot of things about money," Owen replied, noncommittally.

"Well, he said give to Caesar what is Caesar's, and give to God what is God's. He also said you don't want to cast your pearls before swine,"

"Well, then," said Owen, heaving a sigh, "I guess I already know what I have to do."

Crazy, one-thumbed Doc Martin noticed a lump in his lawn a day or two later—where it appeared that someone had been digging. He vaguely recollected having pests dig up this part of his lawn some years ago. Believing there were groundhogs burrowing around his tree, he got his shotgun and sat long into the evening waiting, but well past dusk there was still no sign of any animals. He had his rights—Statue of Liberty!—so he'd be damned if he wasn't going to make the varmint pay for the damage. He decided that he'd sit out there every evening for a month, if that's what it took, to catch the trespasser. A few days later he shot a chipmunk and decided that would show 'em, then forgot the matter entirely after a fifth of vodka.

Exodus

Emery

Paul sat at the break-room table drinking coffee and waiting for morning report. "Full moon last night," he informed Kate authoritatively. "Where's Alice?"

"She went to the restroom." Kate shook her head.

"I hope she's all right," Emily said. "She looked kind of sick."

Finally Alice came back. Sitting down with a groan, she said, "God, I'm going to kill him."

"Who?" Paul and Emily replied together.

"Emery. He's so obnoxious."

"No, Doc was obnoxious," Kate retorted.

"Not like this. Oh, the noise that man makes!" Alice held her head.

"He sleeps all day," Paul observed. "There's nothing for him to do, he says."

Alice was visibly irritated. "Well, why don't you just try to keep him up? He finds plenty to do in the middle of the night."

"Come on, Alice, you know we're busy; we can't just go in there and goose the guy to keep him awake," Paul protested.

"His sleep rhythms are out of whack," Emily said.

"You just have to deal with it, Alice," Kate insisted. "He's nocturnal."

"God," Alice moaned, "I wish he *would* be more like a possum and play dead."

Paul was tired of it. "You shouldn't wish people were dead. Some people die. Lyle Alzado did," he said.

Alice mocked him in a singsong voice: "'Some people die.' Look, buster, everybody dies ... and some not soon enough. And who the hell is Lyle Zaldado?"

"Alzado. He was a football player. Never mind."

"Yeah. That's what I thought," Alice said, and slurped her coffee.

"Anything else? I have work to do if you're just going to sit here and bitch," said Kate.

"Nothing else. Oh— Mrs. Murphy died quietly in her sleep. No big surprise there."

Alice has that way of making someone's death about as exciting as brushing your teeth, Paul thought. *Even when death isn't a big surprise, there's certainly more to it than this.*

"No, I suppose not … She was older than some of the hills," Kate said.

"Even the world-records people were paying attention," Paul reminded the others.

"God," Kate continued. "I've been taking care of that lady since I was twenty-four; that's half my life. I'll miss her. So will Paul; she's the only woman who would grab his rear. Well, OK. Nothing else to report? We'll see you tomorrow morning." And with that, Alice walked out of the room.

As the others were starting to get up, Paul said, "I have something to say before we get to work."

"About Mrs. Murphy? For the report?" Kate was confused.

"Not exactly. I mean, I just wanted to tell you after Alice left." Paul examined his fingernails.

Kate and Emily sat back down.

"Well …?" Kate was trying to be patient.

"I'm leaving." Paul looked up and smiled.

"Leaving?" Kate acted like she didn't know what the word meant.

"What?" Emily was astonished too.

"I'm going to Morocco. I've been saving money. I'm going to miss you guys. I might come back someday, but if I don't, well, it's been good knowing you."

"When are you going?" Emily asked, even though she thought she knew.

"Tomorrow."

Kate, incredulous, again took the lead: "Whatever happened to two weeks' notice?"

"Screw two weeks' notice," said Paul, obviously relieved to be leaving *and* to have his secret out.

"You said you saved some money," Kate wondered. "How much?"

"Forty thousand dollars."

Kate's empty coffee mug clattered to the table. "Working for seven twenty-five an hour?"

"I probably saved a quarter of it since I started here, but my mom started an account for me when Dad died; he had a life insurance policy. You'd be amazed what compound interest can do for you over fifteen years. I'll probably die poor, but at least I'm going to Morocco, join a caravan, and cross the Sahara."

"Lucky bastard!" Kate punched his arm, and Emily just grinned.

"Last day on the job." Paul stood up to get started, then let out a shy "Woo-hoo!"

"Emily's going to miss you," Kate cooed.

"Oh shut up, Kate," said Emily, rolling her eyes. "We'll *all* miss him."

"Good morning, Reverend." Emily's smile lit up the old men's room when she went in.

Emery was gasping like a fish out of water, but he put his hand up in greeting. "Good morning!"

"Need some coffee to get going?" Emily wasn't paying attention at first.

"I— There's an elephant sitting on my chest!"

"What do you mean? Are you OK?" Emily dropped to one knee.

The octogenarian grabbed at his left shoulder. "It's up here—a big elephant."

"I'll get the nurse!" Emily was gone for only a few moments before she returned with Paul. "Paul's not a nurse, but he knows a lot. We couldn't find the nurse."

Paul took a deep breath. "Hi, Rev. Are you hurting? Oh man. Can you hear me?"

The response was a mumbled "Yes."

Paul touched Emery's left shoulder. "Is it here?"

After a moment, the reverend, as if on a telephone connection with a time lapse, said, "Yes," again. But moments later, he relaxed and looked up lucidly. "Ah. It's gone."

"He just suffered a mild heart attack; I'm almost sure," Paul whispered to Emily, then turning back to Emery: "Is the pain gone now, Rev?" Paul's huge paw enveloped the ancient preacher's wrinkled hand.

"Yes … yes, I feel better now."

Emily rushed off to find one of the nurses. *Scared,* she thought, *I'm actually scared right now. I don't want to panic, but that was truly frightening.*

While Emily sought a higher power, Mrs. O'Toole wandered into Room 143 where the scene was one of chaos. Everyone began talking at once, and Paul was left trying to pick up the pieces of a blind man, a very confused geriatric woman, and a heart attack.

"Is the Metamucil coming? What time is it?"

"I can't find That Dog. We called him 'That Dog'; he didn't have a name. Which way is north? I can't see the sun."

"This is a fancy hotel!"

Paul was the master of talking to everyone at once. "Oh God, Mrs. O'Toole, not right now. At breakfast, Owen. It's 6:42 in the morning. Mrs. O, you need your locket. It's around your neck. Talk to your mother. Would you like to see the ice machine, Pastor Miller?"

"Mother? Mother? Where are you?" Paul helped her find the locket. "Oh, there you are. Everything's fine now. I'm going to school today; perhaps Milford will notice my new stockings. Oh Mother, he's a good boy; he doesn't just stare at my ankles. He does well in school too. But I'll go get my breakfast now, Mother. It's just down this hallway …" Mrs. O'Toole headed out into the hall, but she was back in a few moments.

"My best friend … a shell exploded … all that was left was his brains in his helmet. What time is it?"

"Is there something I need to fix today?"

Paul found it hard to take anyone at Harmony Halcyon Home seriously. The home held in-services from time to time about how every time you entered a room, and every time you dealt with a different resident, you should wash your hands. Right now he was dealing with three residents at a time, none of whom were, in the strictest sense of the word, clean. Owen sported graham cracker crumbs on his flannel shirt. The reverend, who had been drooling during the heart attack, had saliva not only on his face and neck but on his hands as well. And Mrs. O'Toole smelled like she'd had trouble keeping her dress out of the toilet when she urinated. There was no telling whose room she had chosen to look for a toilet in. Yet he should wash his hands for ninety seconds after dealing with each of them? He was half-tempted to walk over to the bathroom and just wash his hands of the whole situation.

"Is the Metamucil coming?"

"Are they here? I was here before I think, but I don't know for sure."

"Why did my son leave me here? This sure is a fancy place."

Paul saw it coming. There had been a full moon—in fact, even rarer, a blue moon. The earth's electromagnetic field was wacky, and so, it seemed, was everyone in his care. He worked carefully to help the preacher get a shirt on. No doubt there would be an ambulance trip to the hospital. He would need loose clothes. The radio buzzed in the corner. Owen was messing with it. Owen never messed with the radio. *"Stock market down ... December hogs up a quarter ... and September wheat off fifty percent overnight."*

"Jean brought me this rock from Nova Scotia. It pleases me more than the Rock of Gibraltar."

"I've got to get peaches, oranges, melons ... How do you get to town? The outhouse? Where is it?" Mrs. O'Toole wasn't leaving.

Owen was becoming frantic. "Somebody ***help me!***"

"What should I do next? I could fix any dripping faucets."

"Talk to Mother, Mrs. O'Toole," Paul urged, hoping she'd go away.

"What time is it? My best friend ... a shell exploded near him ... nothing was left but his brains in his helmet!"

"How will I collect the eggs? Can I still work?"

Mrs. O'Toole looked at the preacher. Some distant memory was sparked, and she began stroking his hair. "Eggs? There was the little red hen, you know, and she planted and collected the wheat and baked the bread, and then she was lost and couldn't find Andrew and he wasn't coming in all night and could they have some bread, please? Andrew? I'm hungry! *An*drew-w-w-w!"

"Who are you?" Emery was trying to knock her hand away.

Paul stopped, stuck his head out the door, and called for help. "Emily! I'm putting out fires over here! Hurry up!" Under his breath, he added, "Morocco, here I come …"

Finally, Kate hustled around the corner, with Emily trailing behind, both looking concerned. Kate checked Emery's pulse, then his blood pressure, and everything was quiet for a moment. There was something awe-inspiring about the ritual application of a blood pressure cuff and the omnipresent stethoscope that went with it. "Not good. Paul's probably right; you most likely had a heart attack. I'll call the doctor. He may want to get you on some nitroglycerin or something," she prescribed.

Paul guided Mrs. O'Toole out of the room as Kate left to call Dr. Hostetler.

"What do I do now?" the reverend said, trying to get up. Emily saw the look in his eye that said, *I'm going to get naked and pace the hallways*.

"I'm afraid you'll have to slow down a bit now," Emily chided gently.

"Do you need someone to feed the chickens?"

"No, Reverend, the chaplain is scheduled to come read you something this afternoon." Gently but firmly, she helped him sit back down in his recliner.

"Aaah! Drowning … Psalm … Psalm … 18," the preacher said emphatically.

"Yes, I'll have him read that," Emily said.

"The Lord is my Rock … The cords of death encompassed me … In my distress I called upon the Lord …"

Emily turned to see him grunting and clutching at his shoulder again. "Emery? Emery, can you breathe?" She realized she was barely breathing herself.

"What time is it?" Owen wondered for the four hundredth time that day.

"It's another heart attack!" Emily gasped.

"My Rock …" quoted the preacher.

It reminded Owen of something. "Jean brought me this rock from Nova Scotia."

"… and my fortress, and my deliverer. My Rock …"

"It pleases me more than the Rock of Gibraltar," Owen said solemnly.

"… in whom I take refuge … my stronghold … He drew me out of many waters …" And with that final quote, and one last, long exhaled breath, the reverend slumped in his chair and ceased to live.

Emily sat for a few moments. She didn't at first know quite what to do. But after a minute passed, Owen sensed that something was wrong. "Nurse? Nurse Edith? Are you there?"

Emily checked Emery's pulse, carefully. She thought she felt something. Yes, indeed she did. But the body seemed lifeless. She checked again. There it was, racing and strong. No. If he had a pulse at all, it would be fluttering like a wounded moth. Something was wrong. Surreal. Then she realized the strong pulse was in her own thumb. "Yes, Owen. I think Reverend Miller is … dead. He's had another heart attack, but I think this time it's over."

She looked up. Kate and Dr. Hostetler were standing in the doorway. Kate's arms were crossed. "Oh," said Kate in a clinical way.

"I think he's …" Emily was shaking.

"Let me see." Dr. Hostetler checked the pulse himself. There was nothing. "Is he DNR?"

Kate nodded. Most of the residents' files were categorized as "Do not resuscitate."

"Well, that's it then." The doctor sat down on the bed next to the corpse. "Time of death," he said, glancing at his watch, "6:55 a.m. Can you get the paperwork?"

"Certainly," and Kate headed for the nurses' station.

"Are you all right?"

Emily didn't realize at first that the doctor was talking to her. "What? Oh. Yes, I think so. It's just—it's the first time I ever saw …"

"You've had quite a shock, young lady," said the doctor. He got up and put an arm around her shoulder. "I can have the nurse give you half a Valium. Shock can do some bad things to you … gives you colon. If you need a checkup …"

Emily felt sick. She grabbed his wrist and pulled it away from her. "I'll be fine without any medication. I'm just … it isn't what you expect first thing in the morning."

"Certainly not," said the doctor with a smarmy smile.

Emily's skin was crawling. She had work to do elsewhere. As she left, she heard Owen begin to talk to the doctor.

"What time is it? Can I have a graham cracker?"

The graham crackers were lying on his nightstand in plain view. Dr. Hostetler got a graham cracker out for Owen, put the box down, then decided to retrieve a cracker for himself as well. "Here you are, Professor," he said.

"Thank you, nurse," said Owen, munching away.

Dr. Hostetler chuckled and sat down next to Reverend Emery Miller's now soul-less flesh. As the spirit of the deceased wandered off, naked as he had come, down a long and brightly lit corridor on his final journey toward eternal rest, the doctor sat munching his graham cracker, waiting for Kate to return, and worrying about his own colon.

Edith the Student

Owen

Black Hills, South Dakota, Summer 1934

Owen sat in his tent late at night, looking over the few notes he'd taken. They were dry, which was about all you could say for them. The first week of summer had not gone well, in terms of research. For the most part, the team's geological survey had not gotten very far before the rains came, forcing everyone back to camp. Owen looked up when he heard feet sloshing outside the tent; the rain drumming on the roof juxtaposed against the realization that someone might be outside made his tent seem all the more a safe haven.

Why was someone coming now? Was a student feeling ill?

His best student, Edith, ducked into his tent, laughing.

"Oh. Hello, Edith. I thought you were all sleeping by now."

"Of course not. They're playing at cards and drinking. I tired of it and came to talk to you. They're all so drunk that I suspect any minute they'll doze off for the night. I wasn't sleepy." Edith had not been drinking, at least not much. Owen was sure of it. He knew a sober woman when he saw one.

"I'm tired of thinking about geology," he said, "since we haven't been able to actually *do* much."

"Oh, that's all right," she said. "We can just talk about nothing."

"I'm not much at small talk." Owen twisted back and forth on his camp stool and pulled at his earlobe for a few moments, looking at the girl, wondering what *nothing* meant.

"No? My, but it's wet out," said Edith, and she began to unbraid her hair. It glistened in the lamplight.

"It is?" he said lamely. The rain did qualify as nothing, he supposed.

"It's so wet I'm afraid I'll catch pneumonia," she said with a shiver.

"Well, you shouldn't have run through the downpour," he chided.

"Perhaps not, but then I wouldn't be here, would I? No matter. I'll just need some dry clothes."

"I don't—" he began, but then, standing in the light of his lamp, Edith began removing her clothing. Owen swallowed hard, watching, transfixed, as she removed her blouse and slacks.

"You haven't averted your eyes, have you?" she challenged. His eyes locked with hers, and she smiled at him with a captivating directness.

"No, I haven't. Ah, should I?" Owen hoped she wouldn't say yes. He'd feel an awful fool if she did.

"These are moist too," she commented, slowly removing her undergarments in a hypnotic striptease, "but I suppose if I remove them in your tent, I can hardly complain if you lay eyes on the remainder."

Edith sighed as he took her on his cot. She had been waiting for this moment since midway through the previous fall semester, when she snapped herself out of a daydream. That day, she was watching Owen, a professor for whom gneiss was an exciting topic, lecture in class, when she realized her deep desire for him had been growing for some time and she was actually aroused. She bided her time, signed up for the internship in the Black Hills, maintaining eye contact with Professor Thibodeaux for months.

For Owen's part, as the fantasy, which had been subliminally shared in his mind for months as well, took a sudden and powerful leap into the realm of reality, he was initially worried that she would experience some physical discomfort, but she reached for him eagerly and begged him to get closer. He realized it wasn't her first time. That realization surprised him momentarily, and he nearly stopped.

"This tryst," he said, "isn't innocent at all. You've seduced me. Or else I've become a simple primate. Evolution in reverse."

"Seduction," she said, "is only a concept in human thought. If you're an animal, you can't be operating from an immoral perspective. Therefore, I haven't seduced you; we've simply done what our instinct compels us to do." He shook his head, unable to engage this line of logic—or any thought that could be expressed linguistically—until they had finished the act.

There was some coffee in a Thermos that was still warm, and they shared it, talking about anything and everything, except for geology and his wife, while the rain continued to fall. He had never known anyone he could talk to like this. Small talk ... and big talk too. Philosophy. Edith had ideas. She was full of passion for life, and she satisfied much of what was wild in his soul. Meanwhile, his social and moral obligation to his wife was thrust aside, and he failed to ask himself the question: "What ape instinctually discusses the esotericism of modern painting?"

Later in the night, as the storm raged at its strongest and threatened to knock the tent down around them, she groaned excitedly as she slid on top of him and aggressively filled herself with him; and then yet again, after they had dozed and the storm abated, she reached for him and coaxed him gently to a final, more tender encounter, which, he thought later, might have been the best of all. His opinion on the matter was simple. She hadn't been drunk, and she hadn't wept. It was fantastic sex and even better conversation. As a primate, he was sexually, relationally, and intellectually satisfied with the experience. As a human, his conscience was overrun with the toxicity and torment of immorality. Due to this dissonance, he would be at odds with himself for the rest of his days.

Every time it rained at night, for the rest of the summer, Edith went to his tent. The patter of water on the tent roof kept the other students from hearing their lovemaking, yet everyone knew.

The summer wore on. There were some sunny weeks at last at the end of July. Then one clear, starry night she returned to his tent.

"Everyone knows about it anyway," she said in her matter-of-fact, scientist voice.

"There's no rain to muffle the sound," he protested in a whisper.

"We'll just sleep," she said. "It's been a while now, and I miss your arms. I'll be up extra early and get out before anyone notices."

Owen nodded, and she joined him on the cot fully dressed. He stroked her hair as they talked, and she gradually stretched out on the bed and fell asleep. It was lovely to have her there. In the diffused moonlight, he held her close as she slept.

Eventually his arm began to go numb from being under her body, and he had to pull it out and wave it around to get his circulation going, his little finger tingling in pain. She woke up and saw him flapping his hand and nearly burst out laughing. Covering her mouth to smother her fit of giggles, she exited the tent to urinate, and when she returned, she grabbed a blanket and pulled him out into the dark, leading him silently beyond the encampment, up into the hills, where they became a couple of crazed, coital chimpanzees under the stars.

The next morning they both awakened very early and hurried back to camp where Owen fired up his camp stove. She made coffee, and he made eggs, but they didn't eat.

"Owen," she said, "I'm carrying your child."

"I'm infertile," Owen replied. "It's impossible."

"There's no other explanation," she reasoned.

"What are you going to do?"

"I'll go to Denver and find a doctor who can … terminate it, and I'll be back in time for school to start," she said.

"That seems logical," he nodded, not realizing he was calling her bluff.

Suddenly she was angry. "I thought you loved me! How could you—"

"Wait a minute," he interjected. "You just said that's what you wanted to do."

"No," she argued, "I said that's what I'm going to do. But I was hoping you'd present a better alternative."

"Like what?" Owen was mystified.

"For example, you fool, you could say, 'Oh dear Edith, we could never do that to our child!'"

"Just a minute here," he said. "How do I know it's mine?" There had been nights she hadn't come to him.

"Oh Owen. How *could* you?" For the first time all summer, she seemed close to tears.

Owen was undeterred. "You were no maiden when you came to me, so how should I know? When it comes to being unfaithful, *I'm* the one who bears that guilt."

Now her tears flowed. "No! I came to you because I love you! If you don't love me, why did you accept me as a lover?"

But then the story came out. There had been a student in the camp who coerced her on one of the nights she had not gone to Owen's tent. She had been a little drunk, and the boy had threatened to blow the whistle on her torrid escapades with the professor if he didn't get in on the party himself. With anguish, she admitted her one disloyalty to Owen, hoping he would see how much she had sacrificed to prolong their summer of passion. Ever the scientist, she pointed out that her menstrual flow had begun the day after she had allowed the younger man to have his way with her—and that she had come to Owen again later, when her ovulation cycle was at its most fertile. The baby was Owen's, beyond a doubt.

Instead of having the effect she'd hoped for, the explanation disgusted him, and it strengthened his resolve to be rid of her.

The entire affair was riddled with holes, like the fuselage of a biplane over the Rhone in the Great War. All Owen could think was that his career stood as the bedrock of his life, while this wildflower romance was doomed from the start. The scientist in him made a painful but rational decision: He chose his career over his lover and opted to send her away. He gave her two hundred dollars, and indeed she headed for Denver.

Owen never saw Edith the student again. His nights posing as a lower primate were over, and his days of painful, human regret began.

Alone in the Crowd

Ben

New York City

As the summer of '92 wore on, Ben spent more and more of his spare time at Tony's studio. He modeled a little, but he wasn't considered particularly versatile. That is to say, there were a lot of guys who looked better modeling jeans without a shirt. His runner's frame was a bit too wiry for current tastes.

Whenever Tony was shooting other models, Ben hung around, helping with the lights. He found himself fascinated by lighting techniques. He learned quickly, and soon Tony was paying him a decent rate for the work he did, even surpassing his wages at his steady job waiting tables. Sometimes, Ben could even anticipate how Tony would want to light a model, and this made shoots run more efficiently. Ben quit his other job and became Tony's full-time assistant.

One particular Saturday, Tony was shooting a female model, and things weren't going well. She was angular, and Tony wanted more curves. They worked on that by tightening and loosening various portions of her garments. Tony was still dissatisfied. Next, she was too dark, then too hard, too casual, too peppery, and Ben had to play tricks on the camera with the lighting. "You're so beautiful, just gorgeous," Tony cajoled her, trying to get something authentically feminine out of her, but she couldn't seem to get past that aloofness that plagued most models Ben had met. Finally the model took a break and went out to smoke some cigarettes, which she often did to stay skinny. In frustration, Tony pulled his film out of the camera without winding it, ruining the entire roll. Angrily, he threw it in the trashcan. "It was ruined anyway. These women have no imagination. They don't believe in their own beauty anymore," he grumbled.

"I know a girl in Harmony who is more strikingly beautiful than any of the models we've ever shot here," Ben told him. "She's voluptuous, and her only problem is that she has so many ideas that they nearly stifle her."

"I'm sure we could go to Nebraska and, within a day, shoot half a dozen women with more beauty and less pretense," Tony agreed.

They sat and talked about Harmony for a long while. They had avoided it before. As they talked, Harmony seemed like a book they had both read; they remembered various characters—and what they were known for doing … or not doing.

"Did you ever go to Dr. Hostetler?" Ben asked.

"Of course," Tony said. "He used to do the school athletic physicals."

"What sports did you play?" Ben asked.

"I went out for football, all four years."

"Were you on the State team?"

"No, but my brother, Paul, was a starting linebacker … played behind that guy Ryan, the deputy's kid."

"Yeah. Officer Ryan always busted kids for making out under the bleachers. My classmates Brad and Amy got caught making out at halftime; Brad kept his pads and jersey on but had his pants half-off. Nobody could figure out why he wasn't in the locker room." Ben laughed at the memory.

"Yeah," Tony laughed. "My senior year I quit the team, and Sergeant Ryan caught me and my girlfriend making out just about every home game."

"You weren't very smart about it then, I guess," Ben smiled. "Ryan wasn't that hard to hide from."

"On the contrary. I wanted to get caught," Tony said.

"Why?"

"Because the girl was seriously horny. She would kiss me all over. I could barely stand it. When she started talking about going all the way, breathing hard in my ear and everything, I had to put a stop to it. It was disgusting. I broke up with her after the last game of the season because I was starting to realize I didn't want a girlfriend ..."

There was a long pause.

"Ever had a boyfriend?" Tony asked.

"Uh, no," said Ben.

"Have you even had a fling?" Tony wondered.

"Not really," Ben said. "I used to wonder if Phil and I would develop some kind of relationship; we're still roommates, but we've never been lovers. Phil decided he wasn't gay after all—and that was the end of that. Besides, I never did have a whole lot of passion for him. He's too much like me ... Is that crazy, stuck-up model ever going to quit smoking out there?"

They poked their heads outside. She was gone; she had walked off the job.

Tony laughed. "Good riddance," he told Ben, who nodded.

That night Ben would meet quite a few people. They rolled back the tripods, backdrops, and odds and ends in Tony's studio. Then Ben helped put up some of Tony's best work in large frames hung from the studio walls, and a caterer and deejay came in and began to set up around six. By a quarter to ten, a group had gathered. Models, both male and female, other photographers, and some art patrons, as well as advertising execs, were there in abundance.

Ben was as excited as he'd been the first time his father had taken him camping. He thought there would be bogeymen in the woods out there; that's how intimidated he felt at first. But in the middle of the party, he discovered that he felt himself to be in a little cocoon, feeling as at home and comfortable as he did in his little sleeping bag so long ago. He found other young people to talk with, trendy people from every spot on the globe, and they all had such a good time. At two in the morning, Ben went out with six other guys for Thai food (which Ben had decided was the best food in the world), and he found himself talking to a guy named Casey, from California, who was smart and very funny. Others drifted off, but Ben and Casey talked on into the night about art, advertising, money, and philosophy. When they parted ways, Ben leaned over and kissed him on the lips. Casey looked surprised. "I'm sorry, Ben; I didn't mean to mislead you tonight. I'm straight." Even though Casey was very kind about it, Ben was deeply embarrassed, but when he woke up in the morning, he knew beyond a doubt that he was gay.

Phil, on one of his infrequent visits back to the apartment, was making a big farmer's breakfast in the kitchen as Ben's eyelids began to flutter open. Ben glanced at the clock, and his head hit the pillow again. It was Sunday, and there was absolutely no reason to get up. Ten minutes later, Ben's eyes popped open when Phil sat down on his bed and handed him a plate of fried potatoes, bacon, onions, bell peppers, and scrambled eggs. It smelled fantastic.

"Thanks, man," Ben smiled, drowning his plate with ketchup, using the bottle Phil handed him.

"You're welcome," Phil said. As Ben ate, savoring the chow, Phil sat there for a while in silence then: "I'm going home," Phil said.

"What? Why?"

"I'm sick," Phil said.

"You mean homesick? I felt that way a few times," Ben confessed, "but I've been so busy."

"No, Ben. I had a test. I'm HIV-positive."

"What? I thought you decided you weren't ..." Ben scratched his head.

"... gay? How do you think I finally knew I *wasn't*?" Phil interrupted.

"Oh, right." Ben didn't know what else to say.

"Yeah." Phil sat again in silence. Ben began to wonder how long it would be. "Yeah," Phil finally went on, "I called my parents yesterday and told them everything. They didn't really understand anything. Mom thought I was going to die today. The doctor told me I could have several good years left, or I could get sick and die in only a few months. It just depends. So, Mom said, 'Honey, we don't understand why this happened, but we'll always love you. And you're welcome to come on home.' And that's just what I'm going to do."

"OK," Ben said.

"I'm packed up," Phil said.

"You mean you're leaving *now*?"

"Right," Phil nodded but didn't get up.

"What about Shamikah?"

Phil swallowed hard. "Shamikah ..." His voice trailed off. "My beautiful Shamikah," he whispered again. "I can't tell her. I can't do it, Ben. Can you tell her for me? She might be infected too, you know." Phil choked on the last words as though the truth of what he was saying was going to strangle him. Then he stood up and left.

Phil had not thought to leave a phone number, and even if there was one at Shamikah's apartment, her place must have been under someone else's name—a roommate's, perhaps—because she wasn't listed. Ben, ever responsible, went to the park several more times on Sundays over the following weeks to see if he could find Da'Shawn or Cornelius, but they were never there.

Finally, after a month had gone by, Ben called directory assistance to get the number for Phil's parents' house.

"This is Ben," he said, "Phil's roommate. In New York. I came from Harmony. I need to know—"

"Phil ... took his own life," Phil's father said, almost inaudibly, and hung up the phone.

Ben sat still for a moment. He had to try again. He had to ask if Shamikah had even been mentioned. He picked the phone up again and dialed the number. The phone rang and rang.

In desperation, he went back to the park for one last attempt, but nobody who played chess there seemed to know Da'Shawn, Cornelius, or Shamikah.

Shamikah, a woman he felt deep compassion for, had disappeared among the waves of humanity that washed the sidewalks of Manhattan, leaving a wake of cigarette butts and the occasional discarded condom. Since Ben had never met Shamikah, he might pass her on the sidewalk every day for the next year and never know it.

Homecoming

Arnold

At midday, a Jeep four-by-four pulling a U-Haul trailer pulled into Gerald and Margie's driveway a few miles northwest of Harmony. Margie, who was learning to do bookkeeping on their new personal computer, heard the gravel crunching and went to see who it was. Gerald was a few miles down the road taking soil samples. Nobody was expected.

Four members of a family—a man, a woman, and two girls—got out of the Jeep and stretched their muscles.

"You folks lost?" Margie wondered, and then, noticing the Alaska plates, she added, "You're a long ways from home."

"On the contrary," the man replied. "I believe I'm as close as I've been in a long time."

"Do I know you?" Margie shaded her eyes with her hand and peered at him. The man's voice was familiar, but he was wearing shades, and had a full, red beard. It took Margie a moment to put it together. A short man with a full, red beard. Alaska plates. Close to home. "Arnie," she gasped.

The woman stepped forward with her hand extended. "My name is Judy Baxter; I'm Arnold's wife. Our girls, Amanda and Beth." She waved her hand—long fingers like a willow tree in a breeze—indicating her children. "You must be Margaret. I'm aware that there may not be a place for me at your table, but it was important that we come—for his sake."

"Yes. I'm so sorry we didn't get the news to you sooner. I need to sit down," Margie said, leading them to the porch and seating herself on a chair, her hands pressed against her forehead.

"What news?" Arnold shot a quizzical glance at Judy.

"Doc's gone to be with Jesus—if St. Peter recognizes him. If not, he's haunting Ellis Island. He passed, just a few weeks back—on the fourth, which everyone says was fitting. They held him at the morgue while we tried to locate you, but finally we just had to bury him. The dirt out there at the family plot is still fresh. I reckon in a week or two it'll be nothin' but nettles, even though we planted grass."

"The fourth? That's the day we left Alaska. We've been vacationing, seeing the West. Maybe we should have called to let you know we were coming," Arnold said.

"You didn't really tell anyone you were leaving either. I mean, back in '76," Margie sighed. "Come on in, girls," she told the lanky youngsters who were still hanging back by the trailer, looking uncomfortable. "I was just thinking about making lemonade. Would you like some?"

Amanda shrugged, but the younger one, Beth, nodded eagerly to indicate that, yes, she would like some lemonade. As the five of them went into the house, Arnold asked, "Where's my cousin?"

"Gerald? He's down the road taking soil samples. I'll get on the CB and tell him to come home." When Margie did this, she found out that Gerald had run to town for something, but he could be back in two hours. So, as promised, she stirred up a batch of lemonade. She set out five glasses and poured the drinks, adding a spring of mint for the girls.

Arnold cleared his throat. "When Gerald gets here, I'll explain why I left *and* why I came back—" Arnold began, but Margie cut him off.

"Explanations are usually excuses," Margie said curtly, sitting down. There was a brief silence. The girls looked at their father. In that moment, Arnold nearly pushed his chair back and bolted. Judy gazed helplessly at him. He was obviously wondering how fast they could get back to Alaska.

Fortunately, Margie knew the difference between an awkward silence and a normal one: Nobody was drinking her lemonade. "I'm sorry," she said. "This must not be easy for you. What I meant was, well, like my mother said, 'Nurse a little baby grudge, and it will grow into a giant hatred.' I haven't nursed a grudge about it, Arnie. Honestly, I haven't, even when I was caring for my own two, plus AJ and Amy. But you know me, Arnie. I usually say what I mean and mean what I say."

Arnold let out a little sigh, but he didn't say anything.

"Actually," Margie continued, "I'm so glad to see you and these beautiful young ladies," With that she got up and brought out a crock full of chocolate-chip cookies. Amanda took one and nibbled it, while Beth grabbed four and stuffed them quickly into her mouth. "Gerald will be glad to see you too. Welcome home," Margie finished.

There was another silence, a little less awkward this time. Judy handed Beth a napkin. Beth wiped her chin, and they all laughed when Amanda pointed out that there was still melted chocolate on Beth's nose.

"Now," Margie said, "about your explanation. Don't worry, we'll hear you out. And is it OK if I call Randall and his fiancée Melissa—and see if they can come over?"

"That's fine," Arnold said. "And would you mind showing the girls around the farm, while I go pay my respects?"

The lot on which Doc Martin's house had stood was empty. The charred timbers of this place where Arnold had grown up had settled into the cellar. The farm was still in the family. An old barn and crumbling silo stood off to the back; beyond them a patch of weeds grew around rusting farm implements. The land was fallow. Through a glitch in a federal farm subsidy program, the federal government had been sending just enough money to enable Margie, who had been the executor of the estate since Doc went to the nursing home, to pay the property taxes every year. Gerald didn't have time to farm it all, even with Randall helping.

Arnold went out to the barn to see if the old Honda four-wheeler was still there and, if so, to find out if he could get it running. The ancient machine was indeed there, and it looked as though Gerald or Randall used it from time to time. He fired it up and headed out down a lane past his father's fallow fields leaving a cloud of exhaust. Even the lane was nearly overgrown, really just a tractor path without a tractor. Crushed weeds leading back toward the South Loup River were evidence of one vehicle coming through, and Arnold followed that path. It had been a hearse.

At the family cemetery he found Doc's fresh grave.

"Sorry I'm late," he told the old man's headstone. He sat there for a few minutes trying to think of something else to say. "You old bastard" didn't seem proper. "I miss you" wasn't true. "I'm going to right what I done wrong" smacked of ornamental platitude, and it probably wasn't possible even if he meant it.

"I got no excuses," he finally said. "I ran from my own dreams like a coward. What's worse, I stayed away; I didn't even call the little girl on her birthdays. I don't know why. I regret that more than you would ever imagine. But there's no reason not to come back and try again. They say you can't go home again, but I got my rights, don't I?"

As Arnold kicked the engine to life, he turned for a last look at the headstone and said, "See ya, Pa," then roared back toward the barn, leaving a huge cloud of blue exhaust hanging over Doc's grave.

The specter was waiting for him at the barn. The albino buffalo cow looked hungrier than ever. Arnold parked his vehicle and stood facing the spirit with his arms crossed. "The Salmon said you wanted to talk to me. But I'm guessing you're hungry. Want to eat something first?"

Ptaysan-Wee snorted; steam came out of her nostrils as though the air were cold. Arnold looked around the old shed. There was plenty of grass outside, but the animal seemed to want something else. Methodically, Arnold searched the place. Finding something to feed a ghostly buffalo seemed about as unlikely as getting the four-wheeler to work. After a few minutes of careful investigation, however, Arnold found a fifty-pound bag of wheat. He ripped it open and found it dry and free of mold and moisture. None of it had germinated. It was, in fact, perfect. Next, he found a trough and, with a glance, noticed that the cow had begun to slobber. Arnold grabbed the bag and dumped all fifty pounds out for the beast. Then he stepped back.

She stuck her head into the wheat and began to eat. Arnold found a five-gallon bucket and went out to the pump. He filled the bucket and brought it back for the spirit, who drank deeply, ate some more, drank again, ate a little more, then looked up at Arnold and said, "Thank you."

"You're welcome," Arnold said.

"There's a pebble in the wheat," she told him. "I always have to move it aside with my tongue."

"What? Oh." Arnold looked. Sure enough, a small stone lay in the trough, nudged off to one side. "Sorry," Arnold said.

"No, it's quite all right," she mooed. "A pebble makes you slow down a bit, makes you remember why you're eating. I haven't eaten in a hundred years. Food's so deliciously temporal," she said, winking.

Arnold laughed. He overturned the now empty five-gallon bucket, sat down, and laughed until his sides ached, and the ghost bison laughed with him.

"All right," Arnold said when their glee subsided, "I understand you have something to tell me."

"Yes. Come with me," she said.

"Where are we going?"

"You'll have to take hold of my horns," she replied.

Arnold did as he was told, and the spirit immediately jerked backwards, jolting Arnold off his feet. In the next moment, he saw not only the Buffalo's head but her entire body; the Buffalo's flanks shimmered with sweat, and her back hooves stirred the dust. The barn was gone, and in its place stood a vast prairie. Arnold felt the cuff of his flannel shirt, then looked down suddenly, surprised to see buckskin fringes. He was covered in supple clothing festooned with porcupine quills.

The grasses, ablaze with thirst, waved to Arnold, and a herd of bison moving past slowed occasionally to glance at him like gawkers staring at a freeway wreck.

A prairie dog approached Arnold, sat on his boot, and, looking up, said, "Where have you been?"

"I went to Alaska," Arnold told the rodent, who cocked his head quizzically. "I was afraid. I'm not sure what I was afraid of. I ran away. It was wrong. But I came back."

The little creature scurried over to the cow, and sniffed the air. "Ptaysan-Wee," it said sadly, "is the man-creature too late?"

"No, my burrowing brother," the cow said. "He's right on time." Raising her head, she called to Arnold. "*Heyoka,* come look deeply into my eye."

Arnold saw many things. Some of them were chilling; some of them were of such extreme beauty that he dropped to his knees.

"What is my … task?"

"Simply put, you must care for your children, offspring of the creatures Adam and Eve. Warn them when you see danger, as you have just seen in my eye. Guide them to be just and to love mercy. But as a symbol of this caring for your young, you also are asked to care for my children, the children of the wide plains. The land here is ready; it has been fallow sixteen years. The burning chemicals are not going to harm our innards; they've nearly washed away. Bring my children—and some of my burrowing brother's children as well—and the land will nourish them all."

Randall Goes to Gunner's

Amy

"No, I'm doing great, Mom," Amy lied into the telephone. Caroline had gone through rehab again recently, and now she worried about Amy more than Amy worried about herself. For a girl as wrapped up in herself as she was, that wasn't healthy. "Look, Mom, you've gotta stop worrying about me. Didn't you always say you wanted me out on my own as soon as I was eighteen?"

"Oh, that's just what mothers say," her mom explained. "How's Jimmy doing?"

"I gotta go, OK?" She hung up quickly. Amy was late for work. At first it had been glamorous having guys throw money at her, but now it was just tiring. Jimmy was gone, and his friends had been easily discouraged from hanging around her apartment when she locked the door and parked behind the bushes at the far end of the lot for a few days. She missed Jimmy a little, because he was actually kind of funny when they were alone together, and even sweet, but she didn't miss his friends at all. Except maybe Fish.

She dragged herself through the back door at Gunner's and found the owner. "What's up, Francis?" she asked, calling him by his real name just to annoy him.

"Call me Gunner if you want to keep your job," he corrected irritably. "You're late, and there's a guy who wants to see you."

"I'll bet he does," she said. The guys who came all the time had their favorite dancers. Sometimes truckers with a dedicated route would stop in regularly, and if she wasn't working, they'd leave without spending any money. Those were the creepiest guys. But because they were her biggest fans, she had to be especially nice to them.

"No, he didn't ask for you by your stage name, 'Misty Golden'; he said, 'Amy Martin,'" Gunner informed her. "And he won't come in. He's waiting in the lobby."

"Must be Jimmy," she told Gunner, and he shrugged.

"If he's not here to spend money and watch girls dancing," Gunner grumbled, "tell him to get the hell out. I don't give a shit who he is." Amy laughed and headed for the lobby.

"Randall? What are *you* doing here? Shouldn't you be … farming … or something?" He was looking at his toes, his hands in the back pockets of his jeans. *He's trying not to notice the posters on the wall, girls wearing next to nothing and carrying pints of beer,* she thought. She decided not to tease him. He was too nice a guy to be hanging around here, even Amy had to admit. One of the good kids, as Ben would have said in one of his philosophical moods. She knew what that made her—without anyone telling her.

"I was going to call you a couple weeks ago," she said.

"What for?" He looked startled.

"Oh, about some shit I was dealing with at the time … So why are you here?"

"Melissa sent me," he mumbled.

"What on earth would she do that for?"

"She couldn't get you on the phone. Can we go outside?" Amy followed him out where he breathed easier. He walked across the parking lot and leaned against the fender of his pickup.

"What's so … urgent? Why would she ever decide to send you on an errand to Gunner's?"

"He's back … er, Arnie's back in town," Randall began. "Melissa thinks you ought to meet him. 'The sooner the better,' she said."

For a long minute, Amy stood, speechless for a change. Finally she spoke. "So? What if I don't want to see *him*?"

"He's got a lot to tell you. He sat down with Gerald, Margie, me, and Melissa the other night. It's quite a story, what he's been through. He told us everything—all about this ghost buffalo he saw and ran away from, everything that happened in Alaska, and another ghost, a fish this time, and how he came back and *talked* to the buffalo ghost this time, so now he's ready to be a spiritual leader and take care—"

"A spiritual leader, huh? Well, whoopdee-do. What does he want, a medal? I have nothing to say to that man." She frowned. "I gotta get back to work. They don't pay me to wear this T-shirt; they pay me to take it off."

Randall felt his neck get warm. "Well," he fumbled, "does the, um, manager like you? I mean, are you good at what you do?"

Amy laughed and patted his hand. "Oh Randall. How hard is it to take *your* shirt off?"

"Right. So are you coming with me?"

"Look," she finally said, "this is how I make money. Randall, you're a nice boy; you shouldn't be here. If someone sees your pickup truck over here, it could start rumors back in Harmony that you and Melissa would have to deal with for months. Thanks for thinking of me, but I'm not going anywhere. Oh, and Randall? Tell Melissa I said hi. Wedding plans coming together?" He nodded morosely. "Good," she said as he got into his truck.

Amy walked back into the lobby, looked up, and saw one of the posters on the wall that had embarrassed Randall so much. She patted the woman in the poster on the posterior for good luck, then went back to work. But she was nervous. Her father was back. She couldn't remember what he looked like. All she could remember was her mother standing by the tractor in the field, pressing her back against the huge tire, a note dangling from her fingers.

A few hours later, Gunner asked her what the problem was.

"I'm fine," Amy said. Clearly she wasn't fooling him.

"Is one of these bums threatening you?" Gunner peered around the smoky bar.

"No," she said. Then she saw a guy at the bar who had been waiting for her in the parking lot when she got off work one day a week earlier. He had tried to feel her up, asking her to do explicit, dirty things with him for money and told her his name was Alberto, even though he wasn't a Mexican or anything. The sight of him made her sick. Amy decided it was easier to agree with Gunner than explain the truth. "Yeah, actually, *that* guy," and she pointed.

So Gunner rolled up his sleeves, pulled the man out back, punched him in the face and stomach, then pounded him with an uppercut to the jaw, which knocked his head back against the brick wall. "Alberto" slumped down in the weeds where he bled for a while with Gunner's words ringing in his mostly drunk, semiconscious ears. "Don't mess with my girls again! Next time I will kill you, man. I shit you not."

Miss America's Problems

Emily

Alice sat at the table in the break room drinking coffee and wishing she were anywhere else in the world when Kate came in. Jennifer, the new aide, was sitting there watching everything carefully. She had heard a lot about someone named Paul and realized she had big shoes to fill. The women poured themselves some coffee, and promptly at six o'clock Alice began her report. "Where's Emily?"

"She'll be here." Kate wasn't worried.

"She's late again," Alice grumbled.

"She's two minutes late every day like clockwork. She does good work. I'm not worried about it," Kate insisted.

"Well, it holds me up. I'm writing her up tonight."

"Not a good idea, Alice," and Kate counted to ten silently.

"I need to give report and go home."

"So give report. Emily knows what to do anyway."

Emily's slender figure slipped through the door frame; the clock said 6:02. "Good morning!"

Alice, more irritated than usual with Emily's chipper attitude, barked at her. "I'm sick and tired of you being late every day."

"It's two minutes. So what's the big deal?" Emily knew better than to be worried about Alice by now.

"Well, it's always two minutes. You think you're perfect, don't you, Miss Sunshine?"

This was a new attack, and it gave Emily pause. "No—"

But Alice wasn't done. "You come in here with your perfect hair, your bangs all up to the sky, your makeup just right, your whites perfectly clean, wrinkle-free, and all that, and you never had any problems in life, and you think you're just spit-and-polish perfect."

"That's not true!" Emily turned to the others for support.

"Of course it's true," said Alice before anyone else could answer. "You're tardy! Always!"

"I mean it isn't true that I never had any problems in life." Emily sat down.

"Really?" Kate sat forward curiously.

"What, you too?" Emily looked at Kate and saw Brutus.

"Emily, take a serious look at yourself," continued Kate. "What's the worst thing that ever happened to you? Everybody else has problems. You don't."

"It's true, you know," Jennifer added, trying to ingratiate herself with her bosses. "That's how most people see you."

Jennifer has been an aide for only a few days! How would she know how people see me? Emily thought. Emily looked at Alice, her eyes bloodshot, her shoulders slumping over her coffee. She looked at Kate, fat and stoic, and Jennifer, twenty-six and pushing forty-five. She felt her blood pressure rising.

"I don't have any problems? Here's a problem for you: I'm the idiot who's still trying to figure out where the darn gold went. I haven't been satisfied with the answers since sixth grade. I don't spend my days off with a handsome boyfriend; I go down to the historical museum, but I've already read everything about the gold. I know it all by heart, and there are no clues! You want more problems? I have this friend, Amy. She jiggles for the truckers, but like my dad says: You can't give a girl like that any advice; she thinks she's a big girl, that she can take care of herself. Then my other best friend Melissa gets engaged to Randall, and Ben leaves to go have a great time living in New York City, and all of a sudden … all of a sudden everyone is grown up, except me! I don't even know what I want to do with my life. I have a million ideas, but no direction," Now she was really getting worked up, but she couldn't stop herself. This job—and the people at the job—were starting to make her crazy.

"I still feel like a little girl! I liked high school. I didn't want it to end! Now they've bulldozed the place." Everyone was listening, so she plunged ahead like a mama bison looking for her calf in a snowstorm.

"No problems? How about this for a problem? I care about my work, and no matter what you do for them, people die. I have to sit and watch people die, and I'm thinking, 'Well, whatever they could have done in their lives, it's over now, their chances are gone, they left whatever legacy they could, and it is what it is.' It's so final, and life is so short, and I can hardly stand to think that I don't know … what legacy I want to leave.

"Could you even conceive of the idea that when everything has pretty much always gone well, and you have all the looks and grades and everything, and then you get out of high school just … stuck? And that could be a problem? Everyone tells me, 'You can do whatever you set your mind to,' and maybe they're right, but I don't know what my mind wants—or my heart. And I feel like I should just, you know, I should just know what it is, but I'm almost nineteen, and I just don't! I don't know! I know this, though: I don't like people treating me like I'm untouchably perfect, then hating me for it. I'm not perfect, and I get sick of being put in that box …" Kate sat with her arms crossed, listening carefully. A housekeeper came in to mop, sensed the mood among the nursing staff, and retreated. Alice poured herself coffee. Jennifer just sat there, not sure what to think.

Emily began sobbing at this point, and it was a few moments before she was able to finish. "I can't figure this out, and I'm afraid … I just can't stand not knowing what my life is about …" There was a sterile and only slightly sympathetic silence in the break room.

"I know what *my* life's about," Alice muttered. "Working in this hellhole."

Emily wiped at her tears. "There's got to be more than that." She looked Alice in the eye.

"Yeah, well, that's your perspective, Miss America," Alice said.

Emily kept trying. "Look at somebody like old Professor Owen. Still tells his stories. His life wasn't perfect, and you can tell he made mistakes, but he never gives up on the possibility that his stories might have some use. We all have our stories—even you, Alice," Emily finished.

"Well, that's true enough," Kate chuckled.

"I sure ain't tellin' any of 'em now." Alice turned away.

"I have people who need me," Jennifer ventured, trying to find a silver lining in her life.

"Well, I *need* to get the hell out of here," said Alice, getting up to leave.

"Wait a minute." Kate shook her head. "Aren't you going to give report?"

"Everyone's fine. There's nothing to report," Alice shrugged. "Oh—except old Owen. He checked out sometime between 1 and 2:30 this morning. My girls cleaned things up. Kate, you'll need to tell Bruce Miller when he gets in this morning down at the law office so he can notify next of kin. If there is any."

Family Reunion

Arnold and Amy

The morning after Randall's visit to Gunner's, Arnold knocked on Amy's door at her Kearney apartment. It was hard to believe his daughter, this little girl with a messy diaper who haunted his dreams, was eighteen now and living on her own. It would've been impossible to believe if AJ hadn't shown up in Anchorage three years before and proved that children who are left behind do grow up, no matter how their destinies appear to you in your dreams.

Amy peeked through the curtains before she opened the door. "What do you want?" she asked. "Should I know you from somewhere?" She hoped it wasn't some creep. She hoped even more that this wasn't Arnold, but somehow she already knew it was.

"Amy?"

"That's me." She opened the door, crossed her arms, and leaned against the doorpost, squinting at him in the sunlight.

"Amy, I'm Arnold. They mostly call me 'Arnie' around here."

"It's really you, huh? I heard you were back." *What business could he possibly have with me now?*

"Yeah, it's really me. I'm your dad." Arnold took a deep breath.

"Bull*shit*. All you ever gave me was chromosomes."

Arnold nodded. "You got a point there. I don't expect you to ask me in," Arnold went on, "and I know there's no apology that could ever make up for what I did to you and AJ."

"You're right so far. So what are you doing here?"

"I heard you were in a tough spot. Do you need money?"

"Who doesn't need money? No, don't give me anything. Like the Beatles say: Can't buy me love." His hand stopped halfway to his wallet.

"Is there anything I can do for you?" Arnold didn't want to end the conversation.

"You missed your chance," she said.

Arnold started to turn away.

"Oh shit," she said, grabbing a fistful of hair at the top of her head and tugging on it. "What the hell. Come on in, I guess. Just … don't pretend like you know me. Because you don't."

"Right," he agreed. That was the last thing he would think of doing.

Amy brought her father a Coke and pointed to a spot on the ratty sofa Jimmy had left in her apartment; Arnold sat, but she didn't. "Why come back now?" she asked. "I'm guessing you didn't drive all the way from Alaska to give me a hundred bucks."

"Well, I'm not sure how to say this … but I've had dreams. Or visions. Same as some others in our family have."

"So I've heard," said Amy. "Randall mentioned something about that last night."

"I've been talking with the spirit of a white buffalo. I saw things. I heard things. There's a lot I'd like to tell you."

"Like I said, Randall warned me. Missed Grandpa's funeral," she said, changing the subject.

"Yeah, I know I did, by just a few weeks. We were camping, and nobody could get a hold of us."

"No, I mean *I* missed it," Amy told him.

"Oh." He thought about this. "Why?"

"Grandpa Doc was a bum," she said with a shrug. "Why would anybody go to see more dirt piled on a guy as dirty as he already was?"

Arnold was tempted to reprimand her but realized he didn't have a leg to stand on. He thought for a moment. "I guess if that's how you see it …"

"It is. Besides, he reminded me of you too much." It felt good to say that. It felt true—satisfying and mean too.

Arnold flinched but didn't respond in anger. He just sat on the sofa and looked at the ceiling for a while. "Just so you know ... we've moved back here for good," Arnold said.

"That's weird; hardly anybody who leaves ever comes back. But so what?"

"Like I said, I thought you should know."

"OK, now I know. What am I supposed to do about it? You don't expect me to come to your girls' birthday parties, do you? Pop out of a cake and dance for everybody?"

"No, no," said Arnold, and lapsed into silence.

For a while, they didn't talk. Arnold sipped his drink. Amy pulled the drapes, folded some laundry, fidgeted. "We *could* get together now and then if you'd like," Arnold offered.

"I don't know," Amy said. "I'm pretty busy."

"Or not," Arnold added sadly.

"Look," Amy finally said, "over time, I sort of made you into something in my mind. Two things. Mr. Hyde and Dr. Jekyll. When I was angry about not having a daddy, you were this monster who had always hated me and never loved me. In my worst dreams, you were a headhunter in the jungle; you lopped off my mom's head and left her looking like a turtle. I was lucky to have escaped you.

"Other times, when I saw other girls with their dads having a good time, I pretended you were lost, or on a business trip, or that you died. You were perfect, but you were gone. Either way you could be who I needed you to be. Now that you're back, I'm really not interested in who you are, especially with your other family. AJ told me about your girls. He said your older one—Amanda?—wasn't that happy to meet him. Do us both a favor and stay out of my life. Maybe you can have one good family instead of making everyone miserable."

Arnold wanted to cry, but all he said was "OK," put his Coke can down, and headed for the door. How could he explain to Amy that Judy and the girls genuinely wanted to meet her? "I know you won't believe this, Amy, but I never stopped thinking about you. But the longer I was away, the harder it got to do the right thing."

Amy laughed a hard laugh. "Tell me about it," she said. "I don't even know what the right thing is in the *first* place." She opened the door for him. As he said a sorrowful "Good-bye" and went down the steps, Arnold noticed that his daughter watched him as he walked away.

Owen's Secret

Emily and Jean

Emily drove to the home late one morning on her day off. It felt strange to show up not wearing nursing whites. Instead, she was wearing a business suit out of her mother's closet that was appropriately somber. She walked down to 143 and knocked gently. Pete, Owen's latest roommate, was dozing on his bed wearing nothing but a hospital gown. He did not answer her knock, so she ignored him and walked in.

Many of Owen's personal effects were scattered about in piles on his bed, as though the graveyard-shift aides had been working on it for a while, then had been called away to more urgent issues in the night. As she went into the room, she saw a pitcher of water next to Pete, just out of his reach. She poured a new cup and set it where he would be able to reach it. Finally, she moved across to Owen's bed and sat down.

Owen's old helmet, the one with the hole in the top, lay on the bed. She picked it up. "Well, you did come here to die, after all," she murmured. "Nothing left but your brains in your helmet—no different from your best friend. You always tortured yourself about it. After all, it was a war, wasn't it? People go there to die. Not so different from this place."

Emily stood up and headed back to the door, ready to go. Just then something under the bed caught her eye. She stopped and bent down. It was Owen's favorite stone. Emily picked it up and felt its cool, smooth weight in her hand. "'Oh!'" she quoted softly. "'Jean brought me this rock from Nova Scotia. It pleases me more than the Rock of Gibraltar.' I must have heard him say that a hundred times." *Who* is *Jean?* she wondered. "'In Florida, the frogs—I don't know how they do it.'" She shook her head and turned to leave again. On her way out, she nearly ran into a woman carrying some cardboard boxes.

"Excuse me," the lady said.

Emily realized she had never seen this woman before, yet she looked familiar somehow. "Oh, hello! May I help you?"

"My name is Jean Michaels; I'm here to pick up a few of Owen Thibodeaux's things. Is this his room?"

"Yes—it was." Something was strange about this. The woman was looking around—and appeared startled when she saw Pete snoring on what had been Doc's, and later, Emery's, bed.

"Who is this?" the woman named Jean asked.

"It's just Pete," Emily explained. Then something occurred to her. "Did you say your name was Jean?"

"That's right. You know who I am?"

"Well, not really, but … this stone"—Emily dug in her pocket—"did you possibly bring it from Nova Scotia?"

"Oh yes I did!" Jean nearly dropped her boxes in astonishment. "I had almost forgotten about that!"

Emily felt a wave of excitement. "Owen used to say, 'Jean brought me this rock from Nova Scotia. It pleases me more than the Rock of Gibraltar.'"

Jean sat down on the bed. "So he *did* remember," she whispered to herself. For a long time she couldn't say anything. She wasn't the type to show emotion in front of others.

"Where are you from?"

"I live in Denver. Who are you? Are you a social worker? The administrator?"

Emily suppressed a laugh. Those both seemed like such grown-up job titles. "No, I'm one of the aides," she smiled. "It's my day off. Let me help you." They boxed up the things on Owen's bed, none of which Jean appeared to have any connection with, which seemed strange to Emily.

Jean picked up one of the boxes and stood looking at its contents. There were mementos from all over the world, not the types of souvenirs you purchase at a tourist market, but the sorts of things people in the backwoods give you. If you had the story that went with them, they'd be fascinating, but on their own, they'd be worthless. Turning to Emily, Jean asked, "What kind of aide comes in on her day off?" She raised the question more in wonder than judgment.

"Well, Owen ..." Now it was Emily who felt like crying. "He was my favorite resident. You're not supposed to have favorites, but it happens. I was just here for a few minutes to say good-bye." She wiped a tear from her cheek. "My name is Emily. But Owen always called me Edith."

Again, Jean nearly dropped the box she was holding, quickly setting it on the floor. "He thought you were *Edith*?"

"Yes, ma'am, he usually thought I was a nurse he once knew named Edith."

Jean looked confused. "He knew a *nurse* named Edith?"

"Yes, in World War I," Emily explained. "It seemed like there were two women named Edith. Sometimes he confused me with the other Edith, but mostly he thought I was the nurse."

Jean sat down in a chair and touched her fingers to her forehead. "What did he say about the other Edith?"

"Well," Emily thought carefully. "What did he say about her? Let's see ... She was a beautiful, intelligent student of his ... and I gathered that there may have been an affair. Um, do you know her?"

"Edith was my birth mother." Jean's face was ashen.

Emily was silent for a moment. Finally, with some hesitation in her voice, she said, "And Owen ...?"

"He was my birth father." Jean barely got the words out.

Emily sat down next to Jean and put her hand on Jean's arm. "But I thought you ... I thought Edith went to Denver for ..."

"There was supposed to be an abortion, but Edith loved that man so much. She couldn't go through with it. She gave me up for adoption instead." At the mention of her adoption, Jean seemed to become herself again, and Emily, who was about to give up on the conversation for fear she might offend the lady by asking too many questions, decided to continue. *Who knows,* she thought, *maybe Jean needs someone to talk about it with.*

"Wasn't Edith angry with Owen for even suggesting it?"

Jean shook her head. "Yes and no. Apparently it was originally her idea. She was going to do it and go back to school in the fall as if nothing had happened between them. When I finally found her, in my early thirties, she said that was the hardest part of the story to tell me. But, she said, she was very upset when he gave her the money. She was hoping he'd say, 'No, I'll leave my wife, and we'll go to Europe or Egypt and dig together,' or something like that. She took it that he didn't love her. Edith took the money, went to Denver, but she couldn't bring herself to do it. So, here I am." And Jean smiled. In that smile Emily saw Owen and realized what had seemed so familiar about the woman when they first met. Then Emily thought to ask Jean if Owen had known about her at all.

"No," Jean sighed. "Not until his wife died in '85. Somehow Edith found out about her passing through a mutual acquaintance. That's when she told me where I could find him."

"You didn't know until ..."

"No. When I first found my birth mother she wouldn't tell me who Owen was. I didn't understand, and I pressed her pretty hard on it. Finally, she said that my birth father's wife was too fragile mentally. Said she was barren, and she would've had a nervous breakdown if she had known about me. So Edith wouldn't tell me who my birth father was."

"She didn't want to make things worse for Owen." It was starting to make sense to Emily. "What did you do when you found out?"

"I was on vacation in Canada," Jean explained. "Edith called and said that my birth father's wife had just died. She then told me everything. I went for a *very* long walk on the beach. I tried to pray, but I didn't know what to say. That's when I found that smooth, little stone. Something struck me about it. I can't say what for sure. Edith had mentioned that Owen was a geologist, so I brought it as a gift when I came to see him. But I'm amazed that he remembered me; he was already becoming forgetful when I first met him, and the nurse said I shouldn't expect him to remember me."

"He loved to tell that story. I bet I heard him mention you and Nova Scotia and the Rock of Gibraltar a hundred times. Owen told stories all the time."

"Goodness," said Jean. She sat down on Owen's now-empty bed and looked out the window across the landscape Owen could have only hoped to see. Beyond the nursing home's grounds, the land was baked and dry, but in the distance, down by the river, a row of trees stood tall and green. Jean realized that without his sight, this small stone was likely the last tangible connection Owen had with the natural wonders of the world.

Emily sat quietly beside her, aware that this had become a sacred space for Jean.

Presently Jean continued: "Edith had said that was how he was—telling stories to all the students. I visited him here just the one time. I forced myself to do it when I found out because, as Edith told me: 'He's in his late eighties; go see him right away. You'll regret it if he dies before you get there.' So I came with this little rock and introduced myself to that strange man, feeling like I was looking in a mirror, seeing something of myself I'd never known. And yet, I'm sure you knew him better than I did."

"I suppose so," Emily conceded. "But I've only been here a couple of months."

"Yes, but every day. I only spent two hours with him." Jean stacked the boxes, one on top of the other. "So what about you?" she said.

"What do you mean?" Emily asked.

"What was it about Owen that he became … your favorite?" Jean said kindly, as though Emily were the one who had lost a relative.

"Well, like you said, he told such interesting stories. And he usually couldn't remember the end of the most important ones. So just about everything was a mystery. And he seemed so sophisticated, and had traveled so much. I've never been anywhere. I'm still trying to figure out what I want to do. He had all these places he thought I should go. 'Florida! Hawaii! Maine! The Black Hills! *La France* and *Italia*!' Even 'the Rock of Gibraltar!' It seemed like he did so much. We talked about regrets one day. I would regret staying here forever. I might come back, but Doc—he used to be Owen's roommate—he never went anywhere, and he'd have these awful nightmares. He dreaded death. Owen saw it as an adventure." Emily sighed.

Jean was surprised at this outburst. "You're so young to think about death this way ..."

"Oh?" Emily felt pleased to hear this. "Yes ... I suppose so. I watched Reverend Miller die of a heart attack. And Doc, Owen, and old Mrs. Murphy also passed on while I've been here. None of my friends have ever seen anything like that. Four people I knew died in two months! But I guess having a different perspective on death means a different perspective on life too."

"You're mature beyond your years," Jean said thoughtfully.

Now it was Emily's turn to be surprised. "Really? I mean ... thank you, I guess."

Together, they gathered up Owen's final things and carried them to Jean's car and put the boxes in the trunk. Jean thanked Emily for her help, then said, "Listen, Emily, I have one more item of business in Harmony. I have to go downtown and visit Bruce Miller, the attorney, at his office. Do you know where it is?"

"Sure," Emily said.

"Why don't you come along and show me? He was Owen's attorney-in-fact. I've been informed that Owen left an envelope with Mr. Miller to be opened after Owen passed. I don't know what it is, but since you obviously cared about my father, I'd be glad if you'd join me at the appointment."

"Why, yes," said Emily. "I'd be honored. My car is over here. I'll drive, and you can follow me."

Jean had set an appointment, so Bruce was waiting for them.

"Hello, ma'am. Good to finally meet you," he said, shaking her hand warmly. The lawyer looked at Emily. "Your daughter?"

"No, this is a local girl," Jean said. "Emily ..."

"... Zimmerman," Emily finished.

The lawyer nodded. "Of course. You take after your mother. Your father made this desk." He rapped his knuckles appreciatively on the top of the desk, then turned back to Jean. "You know, your father—"

"Yes, let's call him Owen, or Mr. Thibodeaux, please," Jean interrupted. "I wasn't raised by him, and it's really an adjustment for me to think of him as my father."

"Sure. Owen ... Now, as you probably know, he was a strange old bird in many ways. For starters, when he retired from teaching in Lincoln and he and his wife moved to Harmony, nobody could quite understand why. Why not Hawaii or Florida or any number of the other places he had traveled to and loved to talk about?

"Not long after I began my practice in this town, Owen came to me and said, 'Young man, I've heard you are an honest fellow, and you should be here well after I'm gone.' He then proceeded to give me this envelope. We attached a codicil to his will that the envelope was not to be opened until both your father—er, Mr. Thibodeaux—and another man, a Mr. Theodore Martin, were both deceased. Mr. Martin, whom we locals knew as 'Doc,' passed a few weeks ago, so I guess the time has come.

"I have to say, Jean, this is one of the biggest puzzles in my career. I've occasionally looked at this envelope sitting in Owen's file and wondered what on earth might have caused him to request such an addendum. Would you do the honors?" Bruce gave her the envelope. Jean held it and looked at it for a moment, then handed it to Emily.

Emily cocked her head to one side quizzically, but Jean nodded her insistence. So, after taking a deep breath, Emily tore open the envelope. In it was a smaller, manila envelope, which contained a key for a safety deposit box at the Bank of Omaha. Along with the key came a letter. Emily read it aloud.

April 15, 1981

To whom it may concern:

I bequeath upon the descendants of Mr. Theodore Martin, of rural Harmony, the contents of this safety deposit box. When I first came to Harmony in 1948, to see if there was any gold, I was highly skeptical, but upon breaking the code in "Papa" Martin's journal, I discovered that there indeed was gold to be found here, only not in the river. I intentionally made an incomplete report to my colleagues. The last coded entry in his journal included very precise coordinates indicating the location of the last of the gold his brother, Philippe, brought to "Harmonie" in 1876. It seems they were proud to have buried it instead of depositing the monies in the bank just before the Great Depression. Whatever remained in the box after his passing would be left for the person "intelligent enough to find it," as he said.

The problem was that at the time I found it, the land belonged to Mr. Theodore Martin, a sad, drunken excuse for a man. I was greatly concerned that should he discover that I had taken the gold from him he would call me out as a thief, which perhaps I was. However, I could not bear to see a small fortune wasted on one who would undoubtedly drink it away. Having taken counsel with the Mennonite minister, one Reverend Emery Miller, I decided that the findings should justly go to the treasure hunter, namely myself, to offset costs of my research into Harmony's dubious past as a gold mine, since this research was funded completely out of my pocket, not being a project large enough even to apply for an educational grant. Indeed, what gold there was easily covered what I spent over the previous four summers in exploring the South Loup for evidence of a vein, decoding the St. Martin journals, and finding the cache. I intentionally did not profit, but as my accounts are meticulously kept, I was able to take just what I needed to reimburse myself for my trouble.

And so I would stipulate that the gold that remains, which was almost certainly mined by Philippe St. Martin in California sometime in the late 1860s or early 1870s, be bequeathed to his nearest surviving kin.

It seems to me that since this entire town was founded upon a hoax of the highest order, perhaps it ought never to have come into existence. Therefore, my personal suggestion is that the gold be used to revitalize the prairies for the preservation and restoration of endangered prairie grasses and wildflowers, and if they are willing, members of the Martin family would use it in the acquisition of as large a herd of bison as they could purchase. I think this would be the best way to honor the memory of Harmony's matriarch, Ptaysan-Wee.

Owen Thibodeaux
Professor Emeritus of Geology
University of Nebraska
Lincoln

"Wow," said Emily softly.

Jean was a little more business-like. "So who is Theodore's next of kin?" she wondered aloud.

"That would be his son, a fellow named Arnold," said Bruce. "I hear he just returned from Alaska with his new family." The lawyer scratched his head. "I'll call Arnold's cousin Gerald and see if he can be located. I'm not sure they've got a place yet, since Doc Martin's old farmstead burned down a while back."

Bruce stepped into an adjoining office, with the door ajar, picked up a phone, dialed a number, asked a question, listened carefully, thanked the speaker, and hung up. He returned and smiled at the women as if to say, *That was easier than I thought.*

"Arnold's at Gerald and Margie's place right now, as a matter of fact. Without saying what this is about, I asked him to meet us at the bank in an hour; he said he'll be there. Have you eaten, by the way?"

They ate lunch at the Pizza Hut, which was just a block from Bruce's office. The bank was another block beyond. Bruce speculated about how much gold there might be. Jean shrugged. "What a remarkable man this Owen must have been," she mused aloud.

"Oh yes," Bruce agreed. "In the early eighties, after they retired—she had given private elocution lessons on a part-time basis—Owen and his wife were our neighbors. They lived just down the block. He used to drop by our place in the evening and discuss all sorts of things. He could talk about art and literature, geology, biology, zoology, political science, economics. He was particularly interested in the philosophical discussion of what makes us different from the apes. He became quite a good friend in the last few years before they began to decline enough that they couldn't care for themselves anymore."

"His wife, what was she like?"

"Didn't talk much," Bruce shrugged. "Never heard someone with such clear enunciation with so little to say."

"What's up?" Arnold said when they met him in the lobby of the Harmony branch of the Bank of Omaha. Judy and the girls had stayed back on the farm with Margie.

Bruce welcomed Arnold back to Harmony, introduced Jean and Emily, then invited everyone to have a seat in the overstuffed chairs in the bank's foyer. The attorney showed Arnold the key and handed him the letter. Arnold read it with growing interest, then let out a low whistle.

He looked up and glanced at the lawyer. Then his eyes rested on Jean. "And you are ...?"

"Owen's next of kin," Jean said. As Arnold's face clouded over, she quickly added, "We have no dispute; whatever is in the box is yours."

"Are you sure? What if it's ... a lot?"

"I like Owen's idea," said Jean. "How would you like to be a bison rancher—and restore the prairie grasses?"

Arnold laughed. He laughed harder and harder until everyone in the bank was staring at him. He had to sit down on a bench. He doubled over, his hands on his knees, his howling shaking his bushy, red beard. Bruce, Jean, and Emily looked at each other and chuckled.

"I'm sorry," Arnold said when his mirth subsided, "I can't really explain why this is so funny to me. But yes, I'd love to populate our fallow land with a herd of buffalo. I about broke even after selling my house and fishing boat in Anchorage. Believe it or not, I've already been to a couple ranches to check out some bison cows and a stud. I actually have an appointment with Bob for later today to talk about a loan—"

"Could we see what's in the box?" asked Emily, her teenage energy getting the best of her.

"Shall we?" asked Bruce.

Arnold nodded his assent.

"Could we see the manager? Is Bob here?" Bruce asked the teller. Bob was indeed there and, after expressing surprise to see Arnold so soon, he ushered them into a small room where they all sat around a table. Bob laid the box on the table, and Arnold unlocked it. From the box he withdrew a gun. Next, he pulled out a black leather satchel. It looked heavy. The group heard metal shifting inside as the bag moved.

"Bob, do you have a good scale here?" Bruce wondered.

Bob shook his head.

"I saw one in the glass case up front," Jean commented, "with the old cash register and some other antique banking items."

"You know, I think you're right," said Bob. "Wait here." Bob found another key and unlocked the old, glass display case in the foyer. He removed the scale, ignoring a couple of gaping employees as if needing a scale was an everyday occurrence. He quickly brought it back into the room and set it on the table.

The vintage scale could weigh items up to five pounds. They had to load it six times to determine that there were four hundred nineteen ounces of gold—more than twenty-six pounds. Bob looked up the latest exchange rate. "Gold is trading around three hundred fifty-eight dollars right now," he said. "That means there's roughly a hundred fifty thousand bucks sitting in front of you."

Arnold sat down again and looked at Jean. This time he wasn't laughing. "This changes everything." Arnold said. "With it I can purchase some cows and a stud bull bison, a real herd.. And I bet I'd have some left over for prairie-grass seeds ... get the flowers started. Gosh, not even sure what I'll do first. I owe Caroline, but I don't think money could ever—I'll have to talk to Judy. And not sure I can ever repay Gerald and Margie ..." Arnold realized he had been caught up in the moment, thinking out loud. He stopped and looked down. There was a weapon in his hand. "We'll give this gun to the historical society for the Gold Rush Museum. Plus, I think I'll give them a decent-sized nugget. That's what they really need—some actual gold. It'll complete their collection!"

He got no argument from anyone around the table.

Emily, Jean, Bruce, and Arnold stepped out onto Main Street. The sun was scorching the dry earth everywhere. The asphalt looked like it wanted to melt so it could run downhill to look for shade by the river.

Bruce shook Jean's hand once more, Arnold wished her safe travels, and the men went their separate ways. Jean and Emily walked the two blocks back to their cars at the attorney's office. When they got there, Emily stood for a moment looking up at the sun, tears glistening in her eyes. Jean noticed.

"Are you crying because you're ...?" Jean trailed off.

"I'm not sure what I am crying for," Emily said. "For years now I've been trying to figure out what really happened here. Now that I know, I'm ready to leave. I'll drive west!"

"I like that! Why don't you start by coming to visit me in Denver? Here's my card." Jean dug into her purse and handed Emily a business card, which said: *Jean Michaels, Independent Investment Advisor. Michaels Capital Management, Inc.*

"Really? Are you sure? You don't have to—" But Jean was digging in her purse again while Emily tried to protest.

Jean held out her hand to Emily. There was a roll of bills in it. "Here. This should help you get started. Let me know when you'll be coming through."

"But … this is two hundred dollars!" Emily was astonished.

"It's nothing. I'll put you up for a week or two if you'll tell me all the stories you can remember about Owen. He's a mystery to me. And I guess that means I'm a mystery too. I'm sure I'll learn something about myself from you. It would be more than worthwhile."

I've been putting this off far too long; it's time to get out of town, Emily thought. "All right. I'll do it!"

Jean smiled and turned to her car.

"Wait, I almost forgot!" Emily was putting the cash in her pocket when she realized it. "This stone … It's yours."

Jean returned, took the rock, and looked at it thoughtfully for a moment. "No," she finally said. "I don't think it ever was mine. You keep it. It meant something to Owen, and he meant something to you. I'll just be glad to know that you remember …"

With that, Jean handed the smooth stone back to Emily and drove away from Harmony for the second and final time.

An Artist's Rendering

Ben

When Emily got home from her spontaneous afternoon as Jean's tour guide, she found a letter from New York City in the mailbox. It was postmarked the twenty-third of July. She placed it on her bed. She removed her mother's suit, carefully hung it in the closet, and changed into a bikini covered by a T-shirt and cutoff jeans. She dusted and vacuumed her bedroom, moving furniture and doing a thorough job; she even took down the glass covering the light bulbs in the center of the room and washed the glass clean. Several times she paused in her cleaning, picked up the letter, and put it down again. She wasn't sure why, but she didn't think she could read it. Eventually, her work was done, and she had nothing left to do. She went to the kitchen and poured herself half a glass of lemonade and fumbled with some ice cubes. She moved to the back patio with the envelope and the glass. She removed her shirt and shorts, exposing her bikini-clad skin for sunbathing, turned the *chaise* lounge just so, and tried to get comfortable.

She got up and went back inside, leaving the letter and lemonade. Having found suntan lotion and a pair of sunglasses, she returned and seated herself again. A few clouds scudded along high in the sky in a fast jet stream, but there was little breeze. The grass was drying out; it hadn't rained for two weeks.

Emily got up once more and turned on the sprinklers, which began swishing and clicking just out of range of her place on the patio, using precious summertime liquid on her father's extravagance, Kentucky bluegrass, filling the dry air with mist and rainbows and the parched soil beneath with much-needed moisture.

Finally, there was nothing left to do but open the envelope. Biting her lip, she did so. Her fingers trembled as she withdrew the two pages and unfolded them.

Dear Emily,

I meant to send you a postcard a while ago, but I lost it. Sorry I haven't called either. I've been pretty busy working as an assistant for a well-known photographer named Tony Milano, who, oddly enough, grew up in Harmony. He has an older brother named Paul. Do you know the Milano brothers? They're both quite a bit older than we are. Anyway, it's a small world. I've come to love him, Emily, but he's dying of AIDS. While, yes, I now know I'm definitely gay, we aren't lovers in a sexual sense. I guess it's more mentor and student.

We're thinking about coming back to Harmony for just a few days to do a photo shoot early this fall, when the wheat is golden. We're tired of skinny, bored models lacking in imagination, unable to be playful, models without vision. Mannequins, we call them.

Tony wants to shoot something less angular, less pretentious, and less aristocratically cold. As much as he loves black and white, he wants to do a show in earthy golds and brick reds. He wants to shoot plump, aging farm women with auburn hair, bad sunburns, freckles, and moles in the muddy South Loup at sunset. He wants to shoot bony old women in their wheelchairs sitting on the deck outside the nursing home while they smoke. And he wants to shoot the most beautiful young women we can find, posing any way they want to pose, tapping their imagination. I've told him I thought you'd model for us; you would, wouldn't you? He wants to show New York a piece of his own, truest self. One last chance to say, "Here I am."

Tony wrote an artist's statement in connection with one of his shows a couple of years ago. I asked him for a copy of it.

"A masterpiece comes from the essence of what you've always known, the truth of beauty you internalized in your first decade on Planet Earth. It's necessary to have a broader perspective to interpret this for the outsider in a way that can be understood, but it isn't built on that broader perspective. It is built on the details you carry as an insider. Mundane details, to be sure, but never cheap. Because the beauty of your very first awareness of the world is not a beauty based on speculative generalization, it is a beauty of a certain recollection: your fingers finding a brittle, old arrowhead from the river; the smell of oily asphalt; and the flavor of orange pop at the gas station. It's the way your mom looked when she dressed up for her mother's funeral. It's the lazy sound of a baseball game on the radio in August when the team is in the cellar, how the resignation in the announcer's voice awakens your mind to the inevitability of failure for the masses and success for the few. Any of these things enhance your awareness of reality—and extinguish fantasies that were never meant to be as you move from child to adult. It's the sadness of fleeting beauty, the day your pet bunny died in the backyard, blissfully eating clover until the neighbor's German shepherd comes along and fulfills his evolutionary duty to destroy, to taste blood

in his mouth, to exercise his God-given instinct to be the survivor.

"So we too survive, but it's by treasuring these beautiful and fragile things—maintaining them like a carefully manicured lawn or a bonsai tree in the way your mind boils down that experience of them into a single moment you can grasp, cling to, even if you live to be a hundred. Not so much the things themselves, which you can sometimes hoard as keepsakes, but what strikes you in that moment, those things that are instantly gone, moments you can't re-create except in your mind. Then you try with your art to share what's in your mind and heart, and you always fail to some degree to translate it for the world, no matter how much perspective you add later. That is one reason artists are so often misunderstood."

Anyway, if Tony is strong enough, we're going to come in September and shoot what we know best. Frankly, I fear he isn't going to make it till then; he has gone downhill rapidly, so don't count on seeing me. I'm not coming unless Tony does. Emily, it isn't fun to find that you love a dying man, but I plan to stay with him and sit by his side as he breathes his last. I'm afraid, Emily. He is wise beyond his years. I only hope I don't run away at the last moment. I told him this, and he said, "Well, Ben, I can appreciate that, but I'll understand if you do run. Even Christ's disciples did that, and I'm not exactly God Incarnate. But I'd love it if you'd stay and take pictures in the last moments."

Even if I'm there, I don't know if I could do that. He didn't say it was his dying wish, but it is. I hope I'm up to the task. I'm no saint either!

I wish you could meet him. He's a dreamer, a visionary. And it rubs off on people.

If you ever make it to New York, look me up. I've decided not to become a lawyer, at least for now. So I should have time to show you around. The city is insane and intoxicating.

Love,

Ben

Emily laid the letter down and began to weep, without really knowing why.

Hot Night at Gunner's

Amy

Amy smiled to herself. She was getting a pretty good nest egg saved up. Her mom had never trusted banks, so Amy naturally kept her cash in a safe place under the corner of the carpet in her bedroom. She was certain that she'd made more money than any of her former classmates in the two short months since they graduated, and this gave her a certain smug satisfaction.

Things were busy at Gunner's on Friday night, and she noticed three younger guys she'd never seen before. They looked grungy—certainly fans of the new music coming out of Seattle. It wasn't as good as country, as far as she was concerned. These kids tried to look city-street tough, but they were probably suburban college boys. They were hanging out in the back corner, but they were watching Amy dance a lot more intently than most of the truckers. She could tell when they came in that the boys were probably there for their first experience with live dancing girls. Excited but frightened. *They might be musicians themselves,* she thought. *They all look like Scooby-Doo characters without the bell-bottoms. Maybe they're a band on tour with a day to kill between gigs.* A small wave of nostalgia washed over her when she realized how much she missed Jimmy. These guys were probably missing their girls at home too. She decided to go talk to them when there was a break. The conversation wasn't likely to be lucrative, but she anticipated that she'd actually be able to relate. She hadn't spent much time with people her own age lately, and as long as she didn't talk too long between lap dances, Gunner wouldn't mind.

Confidently, she sauntered topless back to the table where the boys began to elbow each other sharply and grin like idiots.

"Where you guys from?"

"We're headin' east. How'd you know we ain't from around here?" The shortest one did the talking. He had a funny accent. Instead of "here" he said "he-yah." He was looking Amy straight in the eye, which was disconcerting.

"Hey, big boy, you sound like Jerry Seinfeld," Amy said, perching on his lap. "Isn't it kinda obvious you're not from around here?" she teased.

"We've been in Seattle taking in the club scene," Shorty said. "There are some awesome bands out there. We had a few shows ourselves. I'm the drummer."

"We're in a grunge band from Ridgewood. I'm Buddy. I play bass," a chubby boy said, as though everyone knew where Ridgewood was. He stared at Amy's chest as though he had never seen a nipple before. *He was probably bottle-fed as a baby,* she thought.

Shorty jumped in: "Ridgewood, that's in New Jersey. Practically New York City."

"Oh, that's nice," she nodded. *New Jersey,* she thought. *No wonder they talk funny.*

"But we'd like to think we're from Vermont," said the third boy, a tall, skinny, blond kid with glasses who avoided looking directly at her. He seemed annoyed that the other guys had told her where they were from. She looked him over. His Adam's apple bobbed up and down as he swallowed nervously. This would be the one who could actually play an instrument, she decided. He could probably play a lot of instruments. She figured he could play drums, piano, guitar, bass, and a mean harmonica, as well as a horn or wind instrument—either the trombone or saxophone. He's the idealist, the worker, the real talent. He could rock, but he could also play jazz. He didn't want to be here looking at girls he didn't know. He wanted to play music. Maybe she could change his mind.

"What's your name?" Amy asked, winking at him.

"Gino," the boy replied.

Suddenly there was a commotion at the door. Amy stood up to see what was going on. Shorty said, "Hey, baby, sit back down here—" But a bright light and a loud *WHUMP* interrupted him. A moment later she could see flames, and there was a bang. Shorty jerked backwards, then pitched forward, clutching at Amy. For one surreal moment she thought he was making a pass at her, but then she realized that someone was shooting, because there was another burst of noise, and the chubby one, Buddy, screamed and flopped to the floor like a wounded whale, a splash of his blood hitting her in the face. Amy dropped to the floor between Shorty and Buddy. Now she was thinking clearly. Shorty was screaming, but his wound wasn't critical; it looked like the gunshot had broken his arm. But she saw that Buddy was bleeding profusely, a gaping wound in his chest. His eyes glazed over, and he said, "Tell Mom to give my gear to Gino," and then, shuddering as though he were very cold, he died. She reached out to comfort him but saw it was too late. Gunshot after gunshot rang out—and the fire seemed to be spreading. With unusual strength, Amy pulled Buddy's limp body on top of her as a shield, and then, terrified, she blacked out.

Amy didn't remember anything else after that. They told her later she had hauled Gino out of the burning building; a bullet had ricocheted off the floor and through his knee, and he couldn't walk. Shorty helped her get Gino out because somehow she had managed to keep Shorty from panicking. Together, according to what police told her later, they had pulled out three dancers who were trapped under a fallen beam, as well as the unconscious bartender, before the heat from the inferno became unbearable. There were several cuts on Amy's right forearm, and she had no memory of how she got them, but they weren't serious. Otherwise she was uninjured.

Gunner's Live Girls was gone. Gunner was dead, somewhere in the rubble, and so was the man who had called himself Alberto. He left a note in his car to the effect that he was glad to die if he could take that bastard Gunner with him; there was no question that he intended to turn the gun on himself at the last. Five others—including two dancers, Buddy, and two other patrons—also expired in the shooting and fire: a total of seven souls erased at the edge of Kearney, Nebraska. The firelight glinted off the fields of ripening wheat beyond the parking lot.

For the first few minutes Amy and the two boys from New Jersey sat outside shivering like cats trapped in a deep freezer for what seemed longer than nine lives. She wondered why the sun didn't come up. Paramedics found them eventually. They gave her a blanket to make herself decent and made her lie down with her feet propped up on a firefighter's toolbox. They also tended to the wounded boys from New Jersey, taking them to an ambulance; that's the last she saw of them. A paramedic checked Amy's pupils every few minutes. After a while the police began to ask her a lot of questions she couldn't answer about Alberto, along with a few she could have answered. But she had recovered her wits enough that she chose not to say too much to the cops. What the hell did it matter anyway?

Eventually they let her go. Paramedics were still concerned that she might be suffering from shock and made her sign a waiver when she refused to get into the ambulance after they bandaged her arm. Finally, a policewoman offered to drive her to her apartment, and she accepted the offer. By the time Amy opened her front door, the sun was coming up, and the officer made a pot of coffee, much of which she drank herself while Amy showered. She washed her hair twice, to get rid of all the blood from the dead Jersey kid that was caked in her hair. She got out of the shower, threw up in the toilet, and suddenly started sobbing in terror.

The policewoman found the bathroom door ajar. She wrapped a towel around the stricken, retching girl, then sat beside Amy and put an arm around her, patting and rubbing her back until Amy's fright dissipated and her tears slowed to a weeping of such penetrating sadness that the officer cried with her. Finally, Amy dried her tears with her damp towel, stood on shaky legs, and brushed her teeth.

Amy was just saying good-bye to the officer, assuring her she'd be OK and thanking her for the ride and everything, when her phone rang.

It was Emily. "Hey, Amy, it's time to go. Are you ready?"

"Ready for *what*?"

Emily sighed. Amy could be so wrapped up in herself. "Melissa's wedding."

"Oh shit," Amy said.

"What's the matter?" Emily sounded concerned.

"I forgot all about the wedding."

Emily started in. "Amy, how can you be so—"

But Amy screamed into the phone, stopping Emily in her tracks. ***"There was a shooting and a fire last night at Gunner's. All kinds of people got killed or burned! I'm lucky I wasn't one of them."***

Now it was Emily's turn to apologize. "Amy, Amy, I had no idea. I just got up and hadn't heard the news this morning. That sounds just plain awful. Good Lord ..."

"Well," said Amy, "This guy came in with a Molotov cocktail and shot the place up. It was pretty crazy. He killed himself too. And Gunner. I don't even know how many people died. I guess I blacked out for a while. I still don't know how I got out of there alive."

"Are you *OK*?!"

"Yeah. I'm all right. I have a bandage on my arm, but it's nothing."

"Are you sure?"

"Yeah, I'm sure. I just took a shower. Let me drink my coffee and get dressed."

"Well, all right then," Emily said. "I can pick you up at your place in less than an hour, and we can still get to the church on time. The wedding starts at ten."

"OK," Amy agreed, and hung up.

She called her mother, who wasn't working this Saturday, and told her she was fine. "What do you mean you're fine?" her mom asked, and Amy told her, "There was a little incident at work last night, but I'm OK." She was surprised her mother hadn't seen it on the news.

Amy hung up again; but suddenly she felt entirely unsafe alone in her apartment. *What if someone else who used to hang out at Gunner's went off the deep end? What if that someone somehow had followed her home and knew where she lived? Even one of Jimmy's old friends could come back and break in and do something horrible.* Amy didn't want to stay there any longer. She scrambled to her bedroom, packed a few of her better clothes in a gym bag, filled a shoebox with money from under the carpet, threw the essentials from the bathroom into her second-favorite purse, grabbed some cardboard boxes with important stuff in them, which had never been unpacked when she moved in, and gulped the remaining coffee until Emily arrived and honked her horn.

"I was just listening to the news on the radio. What a horrible thing to happen. Are you *sure* you're OK?" Emily eyed Amy as if she might suddenly erupt. Amy looked back at her. Emily's eyes moved to the pile Amy had stacked outside her front door.

"You're bringing all that stuff for the wedding?"

"Sure. Why not? Can you open the hatchback?" Amy gestured with her chin, her hands and arms occupied.

"A whole gym bag? Three purses? And five cardboard boxes?"

"I'm not coming back to this place. My landlord can go screw himself. He's a pervert anyway. Let's go! I'll figure out where I'm going next once the wedding's over."

After helping Amy pile everything in, Emily shifted the Chevette into first and stepped on the gas. There was precious little time now if they were going to be dressed on time. If they were late, Melissa would be calm enough, but Mrs. Stoltzfus would have a fit.

"I haven't seen you since graduation. How's your summer been?" Amy asked as Emily sped north along dusty back roads. She hoped small talk would replace any further obligation to discuss last night.

"Hard work. Met some interesting people," Emily shrugged. *Owen's secret might as well stay a secret.* "How about you?"

"Easy work. Met uninteresting people," Amy said.

Emily laughed. "We've always been kind of opposites, haven't we?"

"We're not so different," Amy said.

"What do you mean?"

"We're girls who have to pretend to be women—women who wish we could go back to being girls."

"You've been pretending to be a woman for a couple years," Emily pointed out, thinking of Amy's promiscuity. There was more she could say, but Emily bit her tongue. She had said it before and it hadn't helped their friendship any, nor had it changed Amy's behavior in the least.

"So have you," Amy shot back.

"How?" Emily asked again.

"Oh sweetie," Amy laughed. "You always act like you've got it together. Like you know where you're headed, like you're some kind of important … person. But it's fake. Admit it. Just like me. Pretending that I knew what I wanted. I always thought I wanted a man. I wanted men who could be like what I thought my dad was. Mysterious. And—and then he came back, and he seemed so normal. Really, I mean, he screwed things up, but isn't that normal?"

Emily gave her a look. Amy was serious.

"You're right," Emily said. "I don't know what I want or where I want to go, but I know I have to get out of here."

"What should *I* do?" Amy wondered.

"You're asking me?" Emily replied in surprise.

"You can go anywhere and be anything, but me? I'm just a slutty chick who doesn't know how to do anything but …" Amy broke off and looked out the passenger-side window. Emily couldn't tell what she was thinking, or even if she was crying.

"You think I can go be anything I want just because I got good grades? You're smart too, Amy. You're way more street-smart than I am. I can barely tell when a boy likes me. You know … you know *before* a boy likes you that he's *going* to like you. You read people; I read books. I've been trying all summer to learn what you do. Listening for what's most important in what somebody is saying. But I'm still not very good at it."

"What you're saying is that in some ways you're just as insecure as I am." Amy turned to look at Emily.

"Sure, I'm insecure. I don't know what I want. People expect me to, but I don't. There are a lot of places I could go and see, but the first step is to get across the state line and keep going. Maybe end up in another country for a while."

"Yeah," Amy nodded. "I can't stay here anymore either. I've never really been anywhere," she added. "For a long time I thought there was nothing for me here. Arnold came back, and I decided I couldn't really stand the idea of living in the same town with him. A long time ago I made my peace with the fact that I was never going to have a daddy, and then he shows up. When we talked, it wasn't like he expected anything of me. But he hoped he could make things right. I hoped he could make things right when I was eight. I think it's too late now."

"Yeah, I guess. I don't really know what to say; my dad—" Emily stopped herself.

Amy didn't answer. Instead she dug into one of her purses and applied some makeup—eyeliner and mascara. Soon you couldn't tell she'd been up all night and crying her eyes out at sunrise.

"Maybe at some point I could kind of start visiting Arnold and get to know him, but I'd have to leave town for a while first. There's nothing left for me around here right now. Guess it just goes to prove you can't go home until you leave first."

"For starters," said Emily, "I'm headed to Denver pretty soon." Impulsively, she added. "You wanta come along?"

"Why Denver?"

"Someone I know there."

Amy frowned. "I don't know."

"Look, no obligation to stick together; it's not a club. We've known for a while now that it was mainly Melissa who was the glue that held the three of us together. I'm talking about a ride west for a day or two. Then we can split up from there, maybe never see each other again. Maybe we find jobs and an apartment, maybe we keep moving." Emily shrugged her shoulders. "It doesn't matter to me."

"Cool," said Amy, warming to the idea. "That's cool. Sure, we can give each other a little boost to get over the hump, and once we're gone …"

"Right," Emily nodded. "Once we're gone, we have the momentum we need to keep going."

"OK then," Amy smiled. "Let's do it!"

Everybody Loves a Wedding

Randall and Melissa

August 8, 1992

After Melissa's mom realized that the wedding was going to happen whether everything was in its proper place or not, and Amy and Emily made it on time for the photographs, the wedding began as planned at Broken Bow Mennonite Church, a white frame building tucked into a cornfield.

Things soon settled into a very humid and otherwise forgettable ceremony. The officiating pastor mercifully kept his uninspired homily short and to the point. Marriage, he said to the crowd of parishioners, many of whom were nodding lethargically in the heat, is the backbone of a community, and faithfulness the backbone of a family. A cord of three strands is not easily broken, he reminded everyone, and as long as Melissa and Randall wove their marriage tapestry with God at the center, theirs would be a fruitful, long, and happy union. If you attended fifty Mennonite weddings in Nebraska in the summer of 1992, forty-seven times you would hear virtually the same sermon based on the same four or five passages of scripture.

Even though the preacher was to speak for less than ten minutes, Randall's grandmother, Nana, was soon asleep. In a vision she saw a tree and recognized herself as the root, six feet deep in the rich soil. Ever out of sight, she anchored that tree for another hundred years. It was a good dream. She awakened with a smile as her Randall placed a wedding band on Melissa's finger and bent to kiss her tenderly.

Margie and Gerald sat across the aisle from the Stoltzfus family. There were some Martins at the tiny Broken Bow church, and they were sure to ask Margie and Gerald whom they were related to sometime during the reception. Gerald decided to tell them that his great-grandmother's sister was connected to Black Elk's family and that they were all Native American shamans, including the groom, and watch their reactions. He didn't often mess with people, which made the game all the more amusing as far as Gerald was concerned. He was in high spirits. There would be another generation of Martins, he felt sure. Margie wouldn't admit it, but she was eager to be a grandmother.

Beth and Amanda sat with Arnold and Judy between them. There had been some hair pulling that morning, and the girls' parents were determined not to have the ceremony interrupted by howling. Beth had never been to a wedding before, and she decided that she would marry somebody exactly like her daddy or, better yet, her brother, AJ, because *he* had a motorcycle. Beth wished she could ride a motorcycle right now instead of sitting in this stuffy church with no air conditioning. The only things moving the air were one large ceiling fan and several cardboard fans stuck to a stick that folks could find tucked under the next pew with the hymnal.

Amanda was less impressed. Dismissing the wedding, she placed most of her focus on Amy, who was standing up front in the wedding party. She was very pretty, and Amanda hoped that she would grow up to look just like her half-sister. She decided to talk to Amy at the reception and ask her how to do her hair like that. If she could get her hair to go *poof!* exactly like Amy's, the all-important first day at her new school would be a good one; surely the boys in sixth grade would notice her. She wondered if Amy had any idea how petrified she was of being the new girl in sixth grade. There were some rumors already buzzing as people came into the church that Amy was some sort of superhero woman and had saved people's lives. It was probably mostly true, because if you looked closely, you could see that Amy had some bandages on her arm. Amanda couldn't imagine Amy being afraid of anything.

Arnold found himself thinking about his wedding day—the first one, when he and Caroline married under the big oak out at the farm. He was standing on top of that gold and didn't even know it. Caroline was four months pregnant with AJ, and, looking back on it, Arnold wondered why he hadn't run off right away. He detested, even despised, the girl he was marrying, but figured he'd make the best of things and do his duty. He reckoned that no husband likes his wife all the time. He was wrong about that. He liked Judy—all the time. They disagreed on occasion, but he genuinely liked her. Besides, marrying Caroline and staying with her as long as he did ... it was the responsible thing to do. If he hadn't stayed with her, he wouldn't have Amy. Not that she was really his daughter in any sense other than he gave her some chromosomes, as she had so aptly put it. But there she stood, next to her friend Melissa, and he was proud of her somehow. When his sense of responsibility lapsed, he lost her, and that hurt like hell. Arnold looked over at Beth, then Amanda. *Sometimes you lose, sometimes you win, and sometimes you win and lose in the same moment,* he thought.

While the pastor spoke, Emily found herself thinking again about what it might be like to marry. She wasn't ready, by any stretch. She wouldn't be trying to catch any bouquets. She thought of Ben and Paul. *Ben ought to be here.* She missed him as though he were a brother gone off to Kuwait or Iraq, not New York. An image of Ben's corpse, riddled with bullet holes, coming home in a body bag, came to her mind's eye, and tears began to roll slowly down her cheek. In fact, the odds that this would happen to Ben in New York City might have been higher than the odds of it happening to Amy's brother, AJ, in Iraq. That would have been horrible too. To keep herself from sobbing, which she was more inclined to do since her existential outburst at the home regarding her flaws and her future, she made herself think of Paul. *He also ought to be here.* He would've shared a lot of thoughts in common with her and might have been the only one she'd want to talk to during the reception. She made up her mind to write him and began composing that letter in her mind, and so she dried her tears.

To preserve her own sanity, Amy viewed Randall and Melissa with a sort of voyeuristic fascination as if they were in a soap opera in reverse. Nothing rattled them. They didn't have petty jealousies. They weren't all that great looking, nor were they ugly. They didn't lie or cheat on each other, and they didn't fornicate even when the engagement ring was already on Melissa's finger. Amy had trouble believing that they had saved sex for marriage, but Melissa assured her in whispers, while the photographer was shooting the men, that it was true, and Amy spent the ceremony wondering about these relatively banal realities. Her own composure, even when she noticed that Emily was weeping, at once amazed and pleased her. *I'm tough,* Amy told herself. *Last night proved it. I don't need anyone. I don't need Jimmy or Gunner or the cute, skinny blond kid from Ridgewood, wherever the hell that is, and I certainly don't need any more truckers trying to grope me.* She found that she was relieved not to have to project defiance. Nobody was staring at her. For all they knew, her bandages could be covering blisters from pulling poison ivy behind the barn on her Grandpa Doc's farm. Some of them certainly didn't know yet about the shooting and fire. Most of the good church folks of Broken Bow were so removed from the seamy side of Kearney that they didn't know who she was and what her occupation had been. Probably the majority of the parishioners assumed she was just one of Melissa's out-of-state cousins.

Melissa felt a sense of victory. *Certainly I am at my most beautiful.* Her eyes locked on her beloved. *I have wanted very little in life, and most of it has to do with Randall. I am contented.* She glanced back and to her right. *I know I have little of Emily's angst, nor did I ever desire Amy's recklessness.* They stood behind her as bridesmaids, yes, but also as examples of what she would never again be: unmarried. The prospect of the life ahead consumed her thoughts. She thought of the excitement and challenge of balancing the books for the farm as they grew their business, not to mention being queen of the house. She thought about babies—lots of babies. *But nobody should think of me simply as a baby-making machine, because I certainly wouldn't think of myself that way. I'm going to learn everything I can about everything. It won't be easy, but so worth it—keeping a family farm afloat. Afloat*—she smiled to herself—*as if it were a fishing boat, and it will be a miracle that couldn't happen without Jesus calming the storms*. Her thoughts might have made a better meditation than the preacher was presenting, whereas Randall's thoughts might have made most folks in the congregation downright uncomfortable had they been voiced!

Randall kept his eyes on Melissa, and his mind whirled. *There are a bunch of times when I'm a lot more nervous about things than I let on, but Melissa is my rock. I'm not afraid to go ahead with this. I want a lot out of life, and I know that Melissa will help me squeeze every last drop out of the lemons that will inevitably come our way. She looks amazing, this companion I will always cherish. I want to put her on my tractor and plow the fields with her all night long. I want to do her proud all my life. Or is it "do her proudly"? English was never my strong suit. I want to* do *her … Why on earth am I thinking about this? She's smiling at me; I better smile back.*

Leaving Harmony

Emily

Emily sat on her parents' back porch, waiting for Amy and writing.

> *Dear Paul,*
>
> *I quit working at the home; I'm going somewhere. Kate seemed excited for me. She said she wished she could come along, but her husband, who isn't well, needs her. And so do the residents. Kate needs to be needed, that's for sure.*
>
> *Melissa and Randall are married now. Randall looked funny in a tux. Melissa looked as pretty as any bride I ever saw; her dress was a creamy white trimmed with cherry red. Do you know how a quail hen looks in a fencerow when she's about to lay the perfect egg? I don't really either, but that's what I imagined. Quite pleased with herself, you know, and turning about this way and that for the photographer. If I had to guess, she'll be pregnant by Christmas. If you were a girl, I suppose you'd want details. Since you're a guy, I'll try to be brief! Amy and I wore cherry-red dresses with lots of cream-white ruffles; it was a little frilly for my taste, but you wear what the bride asks you to wear. Melissa's mother was in pink chiffon; she looked like a round ball*

of cotton candy. Randall's grandmother, Nana, wore an amazing hat to match her dress, with the most remarkably huge brim and all sorts of flowers and feathers on it. She presented Melissa a teacup to drink out of at the reception, and when I pointed out that the teacup matched Melissa's dress perfectly, the bride said that actually the dress matched the teacup.

That's about it, really. I've been to enough weddings, and honestly, besides matching the clothes to a teacup, Melissa did everything else about as traditionally as you could imagine, right down to the potato salad, so there's not that much to say about it. I can see the beauty inherent in the plainness of their ceremony; it's representative of what the simple life in this community is all about. If weddings are a metaphor, it's good.

As far as obituaries, I promised I'd send you the best ones, and as I haven't written yet, you'll want to know that Owen died July 26th. You were right, we all have our favorites.

Oh, and one more obituary I thought you might want to add to your journal:

August 8, 1992. Arthur Lang, 115. Boxer/Businessman. [Age unauthenticated.] Family claims he was born May 4th, 1877, on a farm near Van Wert, Ohio. His parents escaped slavery just before the Civil War broke out, and his father worked as a hired hand on various farms in northwest Ohio. In 1910 Mr. Lang moved to the south side of Chicago where he ran Lang's Bar-B-Q for more than 65 years, until he was nearly 100.

Arthur may have been one of the oldest two or three people in the world at his death.

As for me, I think I've basically patched things up with Amy. We have more in common than I ever realized. I admitted I wasn't kind about her various boyfriends, and she admitted she was a little foolish. She was a lot foolish, but I didn't press the issue; after all, I was a lot self-righteous. We both admitted some insecurities to each other. We're off together for Colorado today to see what life brings us in the Rockies or beyond. We're going to visit Owen's daughter, Jean. Yes, the Jean who brought him that rock from Nova Scotia …

I realize this is a rather short letter, but that's because it's not a love letter, Paul. And, since it isn't, I'm not going to feel any sense of obligation to write you again; maybe this letter won't ever catch up with your caravan anyway. It doesn't matter. Somehow I have a feeling you'll marry and stay in Morocco … or perhaps Mauritania. You'll lift a veil after a week of wedding feasting and find that the face attached to the eyes of your beloved is beautiful—and that her bosom is warm and soft to the touch until the day you die. Certain things in life are inevitable, as my father says: death and taxes. To which I would add: a man giving his daughter to another man to wed, then making babies. So there will be someone new to die. But not to die today—because no matter where we are, we should each say: "I came here to live!" Live well, Paul.

With my respect and enduring friendship,

Emily

Emily sat back and closed her eyes for a while, the warm August sun probing her pores. Everything she'd ever known was in Harmony, but it was time to go find her own melody. The worst two things that could happen: failure, followed by a return to Harmony, and death. Neither of them was as bad as the worst that could happen if she stayed. She wouldn't allow herself to become like Alice, or even Kate, despondently bitter or dependent upon others for meaning in life.

Emily dozed off and, in a lazy afternoon dream, she wandered among palm trees and rocks along an ocean shore. Across the water, she could see the tallest skyscrapers of a distant city. She stooped and found a smooth, round stone. She picked it up, meaning to skip it away into the ocean, but when she threw it, it returned to her like a boomerang, and slipped back into her hand, like a child's hand reaching for her father's reassuring fingers.

Emily awoke when Amy slid the screen door open and her flip-flops slapped on the patio flagstones. It was time to go. "What's that?" Amy asked, pointing at Emily's hand.

"It's my lucky stone," Emily said, slipping it into the pocket of her cutoff jeans.

"I have one of those too," Amy said. She reached into her pocket. "It used to have gold spray paint on it, remember? We found it in the river in sixth grade. But I've rubbed it for so long the paint is gone. It's the last of the Harmony gold."

Emily smiled. "Yeah," she said, "there used to be an awful lot of it. I wonder where it went."

Amy shrugged. "I don't know," she said, "and I don't really care anymore. Maybe someday somebody will find it, but I don't need any of it."

"Neither do I," said Emily.

"What changed?" Amy asked. "You used to be all about finding that gold."

"Oh, I guess I just realized there are plenty of other ways to be rich," Emily replied.

"Why don't we take my new car?" Amy offered. "I just bought it—a bright-red Mustang. It's out front." Emily decided not to object to this sudden change of plans.

Instead, she asked, "Do you have any money left?" For her part, Emily had saved nearly all her income from Harmony Halcyon Home, and with the money Jean had given her, she had about twenty-two hundred dollars.

"I paid cash for the car. It cost about half of what I made this summer," Amy smiled, "but I blew most of the other half." She shook her head and laughed without regret. "I have seventy-five dollars left. Should be enough for gas to get us to Denver with a little left over; if you pitch in some, we can get some sandwiches too."

"That Chevy is my dad's car anyway," Emily said, not at all disappointed to be traveling in something a bit more stylish than a rusted '84 Chevette. "We ought to have a DeLorean to ride into the future," she said with a grin, "but your Mustang should do just fine."

Wedding Gifts

Melissa and Randall

Melissa and Randall returned from Lake Superior's chilly shores after a honeymoon week of camping, fishing, lovemaking, and eating huge breakfasts. They consumed fresh lake perch, beer-battered walleye, pancakes soaked in Fred's Genuine Minnesota Maple Syrup, and scrambled eggs, washed down with Folger's instant coffee. There was a lot to do before the harvest season began. In their rented Broken Bow farmhouse, they set to the task of opening their wedding gifts, Randall meticulously recording on a ledger the givers along with the gifts they had given, and Melissa eventually writing thank-you cards. There were a lot of very practical gifts, as well as several cards with ten or twenty dollars in them. The three hundred seventy-five dollars in cash was just about enough to cover the honeymoon they had enjoyed.

Emily had given them a couple of picture frames, one of which already contained a photograph. It was a blown-up version of a snapshot someone on the yearbook staff at Harmony High had taken a short year prior, of five senior kids being silly around Halloween. There was Amy in a dramatic Marilyn Monroe-like pose; Ben in a leather jacket doing his best James Dean; Randall as fat, old Elvis; Emily as Elvira; and Melissa right in the middle of them all looking exactly like Pippi Longstocking. Or was it Anne of Green Gables? The Wendy's girl? It seemed so long ago—nearly a year. Melissa couldn't even remember the inspiration for her costume.

In the middle of the pile of wedding gifts, sitting on the table Jim Zimmerman had made for them, was a plain shoebox with no wrapping paper and no card. After opening it, Melissa said with a frown, "Look, Randall, what is this?" She held up something that stumped him for a moment, and then he began to laugh. Her face was puzzled, and this made him laugh even harder. Soon he was rolling on the floor.

"I think it's a sex toy, honey," he told her when he finally caught his breath. "Here, let me show you—"

"Not now!" she giggled, swatting at him. A moment later, Melissa gasped as she looked in the box again. "Look what else is in here," she said soberly. There was a roll of cash held together by a rubber band. Ones, fives, tens, twenties, and even a few fifties—and every last bill was dog-eared. The roll totaled the enormous sum of five thousand, one hundred twenty-two dollars. As they counted it, a little piece of paper fluttered out of the stack. It read:

For the down payment on your own farm. "Good luck!"

You're Cousin Amy

Epilogue: The White Buffalo

Omaha Newspaper

December 15, 1994

WHITE BUFFALO BORN IN BLIZZARD CAUSES FLURRY OF EXCITEMENT

HARMONY, NEB. Native American tribal leaders from around the Plains states have begun to arrive in Harmony, bringing gifts not of gold, frankincense, and myrrh but those appropriate for the rare birth of an albino female buffalo calf.

After central Nebraska was ravaged by three days of harsh winter weather, the storm abated, revealing what some Native Americans and other residents are considering a miracle. As soon as the weather lifted, Arnold Martin of rural Harmony checked on a cow in his fledgling herd of American bison. "She was about to drop her calf before the snowstorm hit," said Martin, "and I almost brought her into the barn, but bison aren't like cattle. Sometimes they can be headstrong." Martin explained that at first he thought the cow had lost her calf. "I didn't see the little one right off; she blended in with the snow," he said, laughing.

Martin, a descendant of the Sioux woman who founded Harmony with her French-Canadian husband, stated that many native tribal myths predict the return of a goddess in the form of an albino female buffalo calf, heralding a time of racial unity and harmony among diverse peoples and cultures.

Martin, a *heyoka,* or shaman, described what he saw in a vision, when his totem appeared and told him to open a buffalo ranch on land that has been in his family for as long as anyone can remember: "The Spirit of the White Buffalo Calf Woman, or Ptaysan-Wee, said I should 'pray and wait for the day when she would come, bringing peace and harmony to the world. When I return, you will see my coat change colors—four colors to represent the races united: white, red, yellow, and black.'"

Martin said he anticipates that his white buffalo heifer's pelt, which "now looks like a little lamb's," should begin to turn red by the end of the summer.

Dear Reader,

Through researching this book, I've had the pleasure of meeting rancher Peter Cook and his team at Cook's Bison Ranch in Wolcottville, Indiana.

I've discovered that bison meat is not only leaner than chicken(!) and by United States law must always be naturally hormone-free; but it's also really delicious. When I grilled up some of Cook's rib-eyes, my oldest son said, "Dad, what did you put on these? This is the best steak I've ever tasted!" I hadn't put anything on the steak at all; I just grilled it over charcoal, straight up, and let the quality do the talking.

Cook's sponsored the production of this novel; it was a natural fit for both parties. In a time when publishing is changing, agents are looking for fluff and junk. Quality is important to me, and I won't stoop to writing whatever is popular at the moment. There's no shame in self-publishing when you have something unique to say outside the traditional publisher's reach—more work to market and more expense up front. I'm very grateful to Cook's for their financial assistance so I could get this novel professionally edited and proofread. I know you know the difference.

Quality, healthy meat is important to me too. I know the difference, so I stock my freezer with meat from Cook's. Here's what I'm asking you do:

If you're anywhere within a couple hours of Cook's (LaGrange County in northeast Indiana) I invite you to come to their Calf Day celebration, which is always the Saturday on Father's Day weekend. Mark it on your calendar. Bring a cooler to take meat home with you. The kids and I had a lot of fun at this event in 2012. We ate bison burgers and ice cream, heard great live music, enjoyed the petting zoo, took pony rides, and went inside a tipi. The kids can try their hand at archery and, best of all, you can take a hayride into the pasture and feed the bison yourself! I plan to be on hand in the following years, signing books there. But even if you're not close by, no problem.

Cook's tasty products are available online, and I encourage you to check them out. Make sure to thank them for sponsoring ***White Buffalo Gold*** when you order. They'll give you a **10% discount** when you do!

Visit: **www.cooksbisonranch.com/bison-meat-sales.html**

Sincerely,

Adam G. Fleming

Acknowledgments

The Barn Swallow Theater, in Edwardsburg, Michigan. Thanks for accepting my play, *A Pebble Among the Rocks,* for your 2012 season. Without that event in October 2012, I might not have chosen to push this project along to completion. I hope all who enjoy the show will enjoy this book even more!

Jason Moore, Peter and Erica Cook, and the rest of the fine people at CBR Natural Meats and Cook's Bison Ranch in Wolcottville, Indiana.

Albert LaFleur, R.I.P. You inspired me "more than the Rock of Gibraltar."

Melissa Yeggy. Thanks for providing a sounding board for post-high school recollections in January 2009 during the early stages of writing this manuscript.

All those who read *White Buffalo Gold* in its infancy stages under the (horribly unmarketable) working title *Consolidating the Buffalo* and gave me critique and feedback: Raymond Balogh, Tim Stair, Scott Franko, Kevin Swartzendruber, Anna Pasquarello, Thomas Bona, Brandon Persinger, Rich Foss, and Lindsey Keesling. If I've forgotten any others, please forgive me; it has been a long four years!

Amber Butler, my content editor, project manager and fact-checker. "What? You mean to tell me that some sources on the Internet aren't reliable?" Without you I would've struggled to come up with a publication timeline. Your organizational skills were nearly as important as your input on the content edit. Many thanks.

Dan Shenk, my senior editor and proofreader. (Not Shank. He's a golfer for whom that spelling would be anathema. But Dan would've caught it, believe me, if it were wrong.) Let's get together for some *pad Thai.*

Danny Dean, my assistant editor and proofer. A true yeoman, as Mr. Shenk has said. Here's my chance to tell you that all your details made me dizzy, so my private nickname for you all along has been Dizzy Dean.

Jordan Kauffman, my graphic designer. Thanks for your assistance in building buzz on the Internet as we neared completion: You went above and beyond your contractual duty. I would gladly recommend you to anyone. I'm glad you're on the team!

Megan Fleming. Thanks again for believing in this project, for tolerating my all-night writing binges—and for all fourteen years of a truly awesome marriage. I love you!

Our four children—Timothy, Jonathan, Benjamin, and Acadia—to whom I hope to give far more than just my chromosomes. Keep learning to live in harmony with one another. I love you!

Almighty Creator God, of whom I often have no specific words to utter, only stories to tell.

About the Author

Adam Fleming was raised in the tiny towns of Tiskilwa, Ill.; Wembo Nyama, Zaire; and Wellman, Iowa. Fleming earned his first college degree in nursing and he worked as a C.N.A. and L.P.N. for five years, from 1992 to 1996, in nursing homes in Iowa and Indiana. Fleming is a longtime resident of Goshen, Indiana, together with his wife and four children.

In April 2009, the author completed a one-year professional leadership coach training course. Over the past several years Fleming has amassed hundreds of hours of coaching experience and he now coaches other leaders in the arts, business, and religious communities toward greater life balance and awareness of purpose, as well as attaining their growth goals. Writers interested in working with a professional writing coach may contact Fleming regarding availability and rates (both are subject to change). Serious inquiries only, please. Mention *White Buffalo Gold Coaching Inquiry* in the subject line when you email:

adam.fleming.lifecoach@gmail.com

The author's other artistic ventures include working as a sculptor and playwright. His first full-length theater production, *A Pebble Among the Rocks* (2010), opens for its world premiere run at the end of October 2012 in Edwardsburg, Michigan. *A Pebble Among the Rocks* is an early version of the story that the author gradually expanded into his debut novel, *White Buffalo Gold.* Readers interested in purchasing or commissioning a sculpture or considering attaining the rights to perform *A Pebble Among the Rocks* should contact Fleming. Mention *WBG-Sculpture* or *WBG-Pebble* in the subject line accordingly when you email:

adam.fleming.wrcc@gmail.com